THE
NOLAN

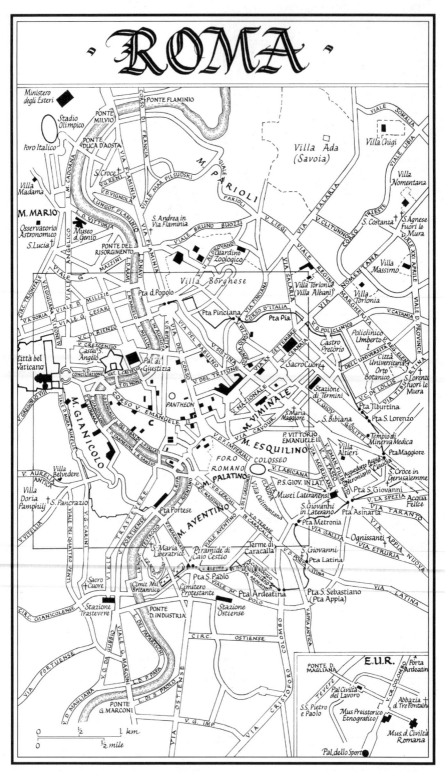

THE NOLAN

PRISONER OF THE INQUISITION

– A NOVEL –

Morton Leonard Yanow

A Crossroad Book
The Crossroad Publishing Company
New York

1998

The Crossroad Publishing Company
370 Lexington Avenue, New York, NY 10017

Library of Congress Cataloging-in-Publication Data
Yanow, Morton Leonard.
   The Nolan : prisoner of the Inquisition : a novel / Morton Leonard
Yanow.
      p.   cm.
   ISBN 0-8245-1747-4 (hc). – ISBN 0-8245-1728-8 (pb)
   1. Bruno, Giordano, 1548-1600 – Fiction.   I. Title.
PS3575.A58N65   1998
813'.54–dc21   97-39729
                                                         CIP

To Alexandra,
who never stops believing

Being an account of the nine-year trial
by the Roman Inquisition of
the Dominican Giordano Bruno,
also known as the Nolan,
as told by Pietro Guidotti,
Maestro di Casa of the Late Beloved
Robert Cardinal Bellarmine, S.J.

FOR THE WIND PASSETH OVER IT, AND IT IS GONE;
AND THE PLACE THEREOF SHALL KNOW IT NO MORE.

—Psalm 103:16

BOOK ONE

THE JOURNEY

*C*hapter 1

18 settembre 1621
Sant' Andrea
Roma

WHEN I DIE, just put me in a box and stick it in the ground. Don't waste a lot of time. I have as much faith as the next man, but dead is dead. I don't know what happens after that and I don't care. But I would as soon not be insulted with a funeral attended by my friends.

It was my master's wish to have a simple private ceremony. Instead, it was a carnival. A disgusting spectacle attended by a Curia of hypocrites. Do you think they came to pray for his soul? They came to touch his body for luck, press their beads to his face for some sort of belated blessing! They came to steal pieces of his clothing! Would you believe it, Finali and I had to dress him *three* times since yesterday.

At the Infirmary of the Gesù last night, while the pope's physicians performed the embalming, these so-called prelates hovered around his emaciated body like a flock of vultures waiting to snatch up a drop of his blood or his waters, a piece of tissue, anything they might take away for a holy relic. It made me sick to my stomach!

Today in church, even with his body high on the bier and surrounded by the Swiss Guard, still did they contrive with their knives and scissors to steal away with half his funeral vestments. I saw a cardinal — a *cardinal,* mind you — pull a stave from beneath his robes and use it to flip my Lord's biretta from the bier into the hands of his waiting servant! I can only pray that wherever the good man is now, he was spared the embarrassment of having to witness such unspeakable acts.

Well, he is dead and in a box and his problems are over. He has "gone home," as he used to say.

He told the physicians toward the end that he was on his way home and the best favor they could do him would be to allow him to go where his Lord called him. *Bella forza!* Their response was to apply more blisters to his swollen legs and more leeches to his poor head. Torturers! If he had not died, they would have killed him.

Yet, he knew better than they did. His information came from a higher source. He called the time on three popes, and he called his own. I heard him say to Brother Finali that he would live four more days and then go home. Which is exactly what happened... to the day. Leaving me with no job, no money, and no home.

The *maestro di casa* of a dead cardinal is like a carpenter without wood; and after thirty-three years with this particular cardinal this *maestro di casa* is like a carpenter without wood who has the wrong set of tools as well. Where would I find another employer who would be interested in hiring me to give away all his money to the poor? Which cardinal, which bishop, would have use for my intimate understanding of the ways of the Monte di Pietà and all the smaller pawnshops of Rome? Or for my skill at doctoring books so that *asini* like Vignanesi might have a few *scudi* to feed their household when the budget ran out the third week of the month? *Maestro di casa* for a prince of the church, and I had to pinch *giullii* like a common peasant.

We could have been rich. Why not? People expect it, it goes with the job, everybody knows that. I told him, I said name me one other cardinal in the college who lives as we do. Name me one who hasn't a palace in Rome, a villa in the *campagna*, and a fat bank account in Banco Vecchi or Banco Massimi. He could have written his own ticket. The tiara itself if he had wanted it, he came that close.

Not my cardinal. They sent him money? He sent it back. Cardinal Sfondroti once tried to give us four thousand ducats, simply for a little private consultation now and then. Did we accept? Oh no, my cardinal gave advice for nothing. When Philip III's ambassador offered us a pension of a thousand a month in gold, no strings attached, did we say yes? We said no. Thank you very much, God bless your king, but no thank you.

The more he refused, the more they tried to give. It could have been so easy. Where was the harm? Not my cardinal. To the rich he said no. To the poor he said yes. To me he said Give, my Peter of little faith, and the poor will get us to heaven. How will I get there now?

Of all the stars in the firmament of Holy Mother Church, I had to hitch my cart to a religious under vows, a stubborn Jesuit with no silks. Never mind that when he was promoted to cardinal — and even *that* he tried to refuse! — Father General Aquaviva released him from his vows, still he managed for twenty-two years to be the poorest cardinal in the entire college, unable even to pay for his own funeral.

I loved my cardinal like a brother. Like a father. Like a son. And I have no regrets for the years I spent with him. But I have no money either.

The *famiglia* is gone. Took off like the wind the minute we arrived here in late August. That's the way of it, I don't know why I am so surprised. Loyalty stops with the pay. The ten "gentlemen" have gone to wherever gentlemen go to become gentlemen again, together with their twenty servants. Our own remaining servants — we were down to eight or nine at the time he took sick and retired from active service — have joined other households by now, though if that miserable cook found work at all, he has either poisoned someone by now or he is butchering on a bench at the Scortecchiara in the Arenula where I always suspected Vignanesi found him in the first place. Not that our meager menu would have been the test of any cook worth his salt.

I hear Vignanesi has lined himself up a soft job at the Summer Palace. Trust that one to land on his feet with his hand in someone else's pocket. And I understand that Father Marcello Cervini has found work at St. Peter's. With my cardinal for a cousin and a dead pope for a grandfather, I don't worry about him either. He will go far with the church.

Which leaves me as the only one with nowhere to go. It would make no sense to go to Montepulciano. No love is lost between me and his family. Brother Tommaso with his fourteen bambinos, all with their hands out like a nest of chicks waiting to be fed. And Sister Camilla and that *cattivo arnese* of a husband of hers, Burratti — always one step ahead of the police, that one, forever whining that his brother-in-law the cardinal should pay his debts. All that family ever gave my Lord was grief. They never forgave him for not handing them plums the way the other cardinals do their families, nor for giving them so little of his money when he gave so much of it to the poor.

No, I would not be welcome there. Nor would I want to be. What would a Roman from Campo Marzio do in Tuscany? I would rather stay here with a thousand wicked smells to tempt my nostrils and the street noises at night to sing me to sleep. The abbot has offered me a room here at the novitiate. I have accepted.

✶

My name is Pietro Guidotti. I was until two days ago *maestro di casa* of Robert Cardinal Bellarmine, Society of Jesus, rest in peace. I am sixty-two years old. My teeth are gone, my hearing is poor, and I have a bad liver. But my eyes are still good and my hand is still steady, and I have a tale to tell that should be told, no matter how dangerous the telling. I will take my chances.

At the funeral today I saw my Lord's friend, Giacomo Fuligatti.

"Ah, Guidotti, we shall miss him. Our dear cardinal was a *santo*, was he not?" he said with a tear in his eye, his plump hands clasped prayerfully at his chest. He had dribbled wine on his shirt at lunch today. Or perhaps it was yesterday.

"A *santo*," I murmured, looking around for an escape.

Three days without sleep. My cardinal lies up there on a black velvet bier, his fellow clergy doing their best to send him to his grave stark naked, and him wearing the last of the four purple robes Clement VIII gave him twenty-two years ago, faded and frayed, but if they get that there's nothing left. The damn *castrati* are ruining the Requiem. And there are fifteen or twenty thousand Romans outside who have to see their *Padre de' Poveri* before we can get him into the ground. All I can think of is if that doesn't happen soon, they're going to have to put me in there with him. What I don't need right now is small talk with this puffed-up *pieno di vento* Fuligatti.

But a windbag has no control over his wind, am I right?

"You know, Guidotti," he went on in a very confidential tone, "they are already talking about convening a *Processo*. I have it personally from Cardinal Ludovisi. Naturally, I have begun to review my voluminous notes and journals in preparation for making my testimony as his official biographer. You knew I was doing a book? Ah, but of course, you would have guessed that, eh? Yes, of course. Who else but me? But look here, Guidotti, you knew him pretty well too..."

Knew him pretty well? I knew him better than you, you fat lump of pig lard! "...and it would not be too soon for you to think about making notes of your own for that purpose. I would advise it in fact, Guidotti. After all, Cardinal Ludovisi..."

"*Scusami*, there is something I have to do," I mumbled and moved away, which is what it was I had to do. I never could stomach that phony.

Fuligatti was probably right about a *Processo*, but I will need no notes for that. I know what stories they will want to hear about my Lord in order to beatify him and declare him a saint. He *was* a saint, even while he lived, and I will tell them so. Though I knew the other side of him too. No one is perfect.

But the notes I will write here in this room will tell a story they would not want to hear, for it does my master no credit, nor the Curia, nor the church. If they even get wind of what I am writing, it will be Indexed and I will finish my days at Sant'Angelo, or worse.

My master lived a long life. He served eight popes and outlived seven of them. He would have been seventy-nine in a couple of weeks, God protect him, and he worked almost to the end. He wrote many books. They'll best remember the *Controversies,* I imagine. They were his most famous. The way he turned the Reformists' arguments back on themselves was a thing of beauty. Then there was his help to Cardinal Cajetan during the siege of Paris (we nearly starved to death that time!), the episode with King James of England, the Galileo affair — though in spite of what people may say, he had great respect for Signore Galilei's theories. He told me that he was Galileo's friend, not his enemy.

I think above all he will be remembered for his love. For the people, for the church, and for God. There is not the slightest doubt in my mind that he will soon be St. Robert. Nobody ever deserved it more.

But they will not say much in the future about his role in the Inquisition, that is my guess, because that is all very hush-hush. They have a code: nobody talks. The records of the trials are never made public either. They never will be, I guarantee it. I know those people. They deal in fear. The master never understood that, because he was not like them. Yet, he was one of them.

I tried explaining it to him once, what terror even the name *Sant' Offizio* holds for most people, and what they will do to their own parents or children to avoid the rack or *la corda* themselves. But his was a different reality. He answered me with psalms, the Council of Trent, the wisdom of the church fathers, salvation.

He was a theologian. I was a man of the streets. He worried about souls. I worried about sleeping nights, about eating a meal or two a day and having a roof over my head. I believe I was closer to the people than he ever was, because I *was* the people.

Unlike my master, I have no importance. I will not be remembered. I know my place. I am like a tiny crawling ant in a long line of ants that stretches between the horizons of time, soldiers dying in battles we are not even aware are being waged. And yet, for one vicarious moment I was plucked from that line, given eyes to see what still, more than twenty years later, haunts me day and night.

They are each dead now, my master the cardinal and that crazy little Neapolitan. I am the only one left with both sides of the story.

✳

I have been out walking. There is such a thing as having too many thoughts at once and no way to begin. I had a need to get the noise out of my head. Walking does that for me.

Not riding. I hate horses. They may be essential for traveling long distances, but never, never for pleasure. As for carriages, we already have too many in Rome. Thanks to Sixtus V's obsession with wide streets and flat paving, the *maestri di strada* have been lining their pockets with graft for the last thirty-five years and Rome is never going to be the same. Carriages dull the senses of those who use them and threaten the lives of those who don't.

Only on foot does Rome come alive for you, can you feel her pulse and touch her roots. When I walk I am a Roman. This is *my* city.

I am not strong or fast anymore. Returning to the novitiate just now, I had to stop a number of times to rest and catch my breath while climbing the Quirinal. I can remember when I could race up and down all seven hills — Capitaline, Palatine, Aventine, Coelian, Esquiline, Viminal, and Quirinal — all seven in the same day and not even be winded. In less than two hours I could cover the distance from Monte Testaccio, where Caius Caetius built his pyramid outside the Porta San Paolo, to the Porta Salaria, where Alaric the Goth entered Rome in 410 A.D. and sacked it. Then I would circle the entire Aurelian Wall at a trot and not even get tired.

I love this city. Built on the ruins of gods with the sweat of fools. Inexhaustible! She is like an old woman, you know, who each day adds new makeup right on top of the old. Layer upon layer of rouge since Romulus and Remus.

You can't walk a single place anywhere in Rome without hearing echoes of the Caesars. All Rome is a stage full of props. My favorite as a boy was the Palatine. I would climb over what was left of once elegant and sumptuous homes and pretend I was Tiberius, Augustus, Caligula. In the Campodoglio I was Cicero making speeches in the Forum. I was Septimius Severus strutting victoriously through the arch they erected in my honor, Titus in the Colosseum turning my thumb up . . . or down . . . as it pleased me, to the roar of approval from forty-five thousand of my loyal subjects.

The Palatine is covered now with crumbling Stones and Circus Maximus is a dung-strewn swamp. But not Ancient Rome. Ten times the number who live here now lived here then. And I was one of them.

Yet, I am a modern Roman too, living in a city of churches and bell towers, monasteries and convents, of Botticellis and Bellinis and Raphaels and Titians and Correggios and Caravaggios and Michelangelos. Church built. Church bought. Church worshiped.

The pope is Caesar here now. Christians are no longer eaten by lions but by each other. With blessings on their eternal souls. Incense and holy water. Betrayal and crucifixion.

I went again to Campo di Fiori today. Always I am drawn back to that place. Always to relive that day. And always with the same feelings of guilt and frustration.

Rome has heart, but there are some within it who have had none.

These men of God in reds and purples and blacks, intrigue behind their religion. Whites also, there, I've said it. I will hold nothing back. *Che pecora si fa lupo la mangia* — He who behaves like a sheep gets eaten by a wolf.

Add also that little wolves get eaten by bigger ones.

✠

Rome is Catholic. The pope lives here. Seven thousand priests and nuns live here. The Sant'Offizio lives here. Rome is Catholic because it can be unhealthy not to be. There are a few exceptions, but the Protestants keep their mouths shut, the Jews stick to themselves, and Buddhists, Hindus, and Moslems are smart enough to be just passing through and do their praying after they leave.

It is very convenient to be Catholic in Rome. There are 350 Catholic churches in this town. Also very profitable. Half of us earn our money from the church, the other half from the religious pilgrims who arrive with their hearts heavy with sins and their pockets heavy with gold and silver. Less what the *banditti* manage to steal from them in the *campagna* before they get here. (Even *they* are Catholic!) This is a one-industry town.

It is easy to be Catholic in Rome because everyone else is too. It's more like a nationality here than a religion. We have allies and enemies, we have a king, princes, palaces, we have pomp and pageantry. True, we also have catechisms, but these are simply rules of the realm, not easily enforced, and aren't people happier knowing what is expected of them even though they do not always do it?

A Roman could choose not to be Catholic, I suppose, but the penalty for doubt is perdition. It's not worth the risk. Better to attend Mass on Sundays and be bored, confess to a few minor sins now and then. That is the way most Romans figure it. I was no different. A Sunday Catholic. Six days for me and one for Christ.

The master tried his best, but he never did succeed in reforming me, not in all the years we were together. You might wonder did I not spend a whole lot more than just Sundays in and around churches, working for Bellarmine, but for me it was a job, not a religion. I doubt it brought me any closer to Christ. The opposite perhaps, once I saw the church from backstage and began to understand the performance.

I was a sore trial for my boss. It surprises even me that we got along so well. Guidotti and Bellarmine were cut from different cloths. When we met, he was teaching Controversial Theology at the Roman College, while I was working on the docks in Ripa and pimping for five prostitutes who rented rooms on the ground floor of Cardinal Cardelli's *palazzo*. (Roman prostitutes are Sunday Catholics too.)

He was forty-six. I was twenty-nine. He said that God must have sent me to him that day. I personally think it was pure accident. I was drumming up business for my ladies near the Via Vecchio when there was a huge thundershower and I ducked into the nearest building I could find to get out of the rain. I looked for somewhere to sit down and wait out the storm. It happened to be his classroom.

He was an interesting looking little priest with a red beard and big wide eyes that caressed you even as they peered into your soul. I liked him immediately. But there are times when I cannot keep my big mouth shut. I made some loud wisecrack, right in the middle of his lecture, and he asked me to remain after class. I apologized, he served me some chicory and discussed saving my soul, and that's how we met.

I knew how to read and write, and I knew my way around Rome, so to speak, so I did him some favors now and then. Pretty soon I ended up working for him full time. It was this way...

I knocked around Rome all my life, odd-jobbing, one thing or another, living from hand to mouth. My mother died birthing me, my father was a barber and a bone setter in the Piazza de' Cenci. I was his apprentice until he died. Then I paged for Cardinal Ridolfi for a year, but I quit. He made me pray too often. After that I worked for a Jew physician for a number of years. It was he who taught me to read and write, but he died too.

I delivered mail to Florence and Naples for a time, but I did not enjoy the traveling. For one thing I couldn't stand the stink of the mules, and for another it was worth your life to tempt those Corsican *banditti* in the hills. A few other jobs here and there, and eventually I went to work in Ripa. That went fine until I tangled with a Corsican over a woman. The Corsicans run the docks as well as the hills. I was big but he was bigger. Which made leaving both the woman and Ripa an easier decision.

The summer tourist season was approaching, and my ladies would not be needing my help. They could get all the work they wanted without me. I was out of a job again. So when this little priest said he could use someone full time, it seemed like a good way to get off the streets for a while. The pay was not much, but it was room and board, after all. And the Roman College is as safe from the Corsicans of Ripa as one could be in Rome, short of the Vatican; and judging from the way everybody at the college talked about my new master, it might not be too long before he got me to that place as well.

Working for Father Robert Bellarmine seemed a good short-term solution to my problems. As it turned out, the job lasted thirty-three years and ended up creating a much bigger problem for me.

*C*hapter 2

gennaio 1597
Casa Penitenzieria
Roma

"Boss, we don't have this kind of money. I can't...oh! Sorry, your Reverence, I didn't know you had somebody with you. Good morning, Padre."

My mouth always precedes me. It is a bad habit. I had expected my master to be alone. He was not, and he greeted me with a frown. He did not enjoy my calling him "Boss" in front of people. Proper respect, Guidotti, he used to say, show a little respect for God when other people are around. How was I to know Cervini was with him?

Bellarmine never deviated from his schedule. Up at four — he had that little round alarm clock from Cardinal Baronius — to say Matins and Lauds on his knees, then an hour of meditation, then Prime, then he dressed. Then Terce, then Mass. And that was just the beginning. He put in a heavy day of prayer, let me tell you. Then Sext. Then correspondence for one hour, which is what I expected he would be doing when I came in waving his latest alms requests in the air. I was not expecting to find Cervini there.

"Good morning, Pietro. God bless you."

The frown was gone as suddenly as it came. Smiling, the master stood up and offered me his chair. There were only two chairs in the room and Father Cervini had the other one. We were not living in the lap of luxury, you understand. Penitenzieria House was a far cry from our last two years as provincial in Naples.

He looked terrible.

"Would it be convenient for you to wait?" he asked. "Father Cervini is helping with my letters this morning. As you can see..." (the physicians had swathed his right arm in bandages and put it in a sling) "...my arm is not yet operative, and I am unable to write for myself. We should not be long."

"Sure, I'll wait. You go ahead and sit, your Reverence. Can I get you something from the kitchen?"

He smiled wanly. "No thank you, Peter."

He was fasting again.

"Would you be so kind as to read back what we have written thus far, Father? I fear the interruption has caused me to lose my place." Cervini read:

"'Your letter of November last has been forwarded from Naples and only recently arrived. Though I hope not to distress you with the news that another disease of the nerves has attacked my head and right arm, rendering both equally useless, I fear — the physicians in their usual zeal have removed much blood, covered me with fomentations and ointments, and instructed me to rest . . . as though I could! — I am certain that you will not be displeased to discover that our dear cousin Marcello is assisting me in the drafting of this letter and that you are thus being spared the agony of having to read my usual *zampe di gallina,* chicken scratch, of which you so rightly complain . . .'

"'I was distressed to learn of the death of your eldest, my dear nephew and godson. Five years was indeed a tender age. He goes with God, Tommaso. If you are correct in attributing this sadness to the malignant act of local witches, then when you have discovered their identity and are able to prove that they are such, you will render God a service by denouncing them to the Holy Office, which will not fail to do its duty. However, you must take great care lest your sorrow should lead you to make unfounded accusations.

"'I do not know what else I can say to you about the matter. I have not spoken to Father Clavius, as he left Germany when quite young and knows nothing about charms and spells. I myself have studied the *Malleus Maleficarum* and the book of Sylvester Mazalino, *De Stringibus,* and I lectured on these questions when I was a professor of theology. The remedies both preventive and restorative are briefly, first and foremost, firm faith in God and the most holy sign of the Cross. Many examples might be given in proof of the efficacy of these remedies. Second, Confession and Communion on the part of the father and mother. Third, objects blessed by the church such as Agnus Dei, holy water, palms, et cetera. I once possessed a little piece of wood of the true Cross and several other fine relics, but I gave them all to one of our fathers who was going to the Indies. I will see whether I can find something for you and send it on, but I would like very much to know when the new baby is expected so that the relic may arrive in time . . .'"

Another baby? Good Christ, Tommaso was setting out to double the population of Tuscany with his seed! He had married only five years before, at the age of fifty-two, and already had sired five offspring. A good thing he had picked a young wife, else she would surely wear out before Tommaso.

"Pietro," my master said to me, "perhaps one of the keepsakes dear Father Realini gave us in Lecci? I seem to recall that they are all in one of the crates still unpacked in the storage room downstairs."

"Sure, your Reverence. I'll see to it this afternoon."

"If you wouldn't mind, Pietro." He turned back to Cervini. "Please continue, Father."

Cervini read in a dull monotone from the pages the boss had dictated. I had little use for Cervini, but when it came to writing I have to admit he did have a beautiful hand.

" '...As you can see, I am returned to Rome. I was summoned in December by the most reverend father general at the express wish of His Holiness. As you know, Cardinal Toledo, that most blessed of God's servants, recently rejoined our Lord Jesus Christ from this land of our own exile, and though I am certain I shall never achieve his level of scholarliness, I have the honor of replacing him as principal theological adviser to Pope Clement VIII. It was also the wish of His Holiness that I take apartments in the Vatican, but I successfully appealed to his nephew, Cardinal Aldobrandini, to honor our desire to be close to our brothers. Hence, our residence here at the Penitenzieria House of the Society, which is of course quite close to the basilica.

" 'Lest you leap to your usual conclusions, I hasten to add that this is in no way indicative of a step toward the purple. I am aware of the rumors to which you refer, but I continue to resist such a move to all who will listen, Valiero and Baronius particularly...' "

He could resist all he wanted. The pope was going to have him in the college of cardinals one way or the other; it was only a question of time. They knew it and he knew it. I didn't understand why he fought it. Twelve thousand ducats a year. A house. Maybe a palace if he wanted. Servants. What priest in his right mind would refuse a cardinalate? That was how much I knew in those days! Oh, he wanted the power, all right. But his way, not theirs. As for the money, how was I to know he would one day have me give it away for him like a drunken sailor? He was very complicated for the likes of someone like me, and I still did not fully understand his Jesuit vows.

"'As I grow older, my bodily health, which has always been poor, grows worse. My hearing is nearly gone, the headaches never leave me. I wear glasses now and my hair has turned white, while you, two years *older* than I, are having babies! You, at least, are upholding the tradition of our father's family, propagating as God wishes you to. My pleasure, on the other hand, is in study and quietude. Marcello assists me in the paperwork, and Pietro Guidotti manages the rest of my worldly affairs. What more do I need? I am a religious, after all, not good at temporal business. As for gaining the purple so as to be of greater assistance to my family, you must surely know by now my...'"

"That is where you left off, Reverence," Cervini said, looking up.

"Ummm. Write, please: You must surely know by now my opinions regarding dispensations to relatives. On this point the Council of Trent was clear: 'The goods of the church are on no account to be used for the enrichment of relatives, but only for the relief of their poverty, should they happen to be poor.' This was St. Augustine's policy and it would be mine. I hope that does not displease you. In any event, this matter is in the hands of God and of His Holiness, and there it shall rest, as far as I am concerned. Each of us must pursue life as our conscience directs. Meanwhile, you have my devoted love, your brother in Christ, and so forth.

"Thank you, Father. You have been most helpful. We will continue tomorrow at the same time. God bless you for your help."

He looked at me and smiled.

"My *molto magnifico fratello* will not be satisfied until he has made me a cardinal. You also wish it, I suppose?"

It was a poor joke, all his relatives wanting him to become a cardinal just so they could cash in. But the joke was on them. All he cared about was his work. *Che tipo*, what a character! He had about as much interest in money as he had in food. Garlic and chicory, garlic and chicory. Fast, fast, fast. Three days a week he ate nothing, the other days he ate garlic and chicory like a peasant. And every day he worked and prayed, twenty hours out of twenty-four. And Tommaso, the stud, only wanted him to get rich and spread the wealth. Some joke, all right. The boss and his brother were *due pali opposto*, total opposites

When Cervini was out of the room, I said, "Holy Mother Mary,

Boss, you look terrible! Uh...*scusi*, that just slipped out. Did you get any sleep last night? I bet not. Look, why don't you let me get you something to eat, take a nice nap afterward, get a little rest? My business can wait."

"Don't be a mother hen, Guidotti. Sit down. We have work to do. Tell me first what you have on your mind, Pietro. Then I have something important to discuss with you."

"What is on my mind, Boss, as always, is that you want to give away more than we've got. Take this little item here: 'Please give five *scudi* to Madame Rosalio.' Now, that's the old whore...*scusi*...old lady from Campo Marzio who we just gave five to last month on one of your 'walks to the poor.' I know that one. She will hit you up every month if you let her. She's got a room off Via di Ripetta and she just waits for people like you. Let her put the touch on the Dominicans this month. They have more than we do."

"Give her the five *scudi*, Peter. The Dominicans may have more than we do, but we have more than she does. The money will buy her wood. It is only January. Would you have her freeze?"

"It doesn't have to do with what I want, it has to do with what I've got, which is just about nothing. We are almost broke and payday is not for two weeks yet."

"What about the silver jug? Is it back from the pawnshop?"

I nodded.

"Pawn it again."

"So all right, that takes care of the little old lady's wood. The rector requests to know, with respect, what is he to do about the growing number of freeloaders at the back door every morning who claim you invited them for breakfast?"

"Feed them."

"I think you had better be the one to tell him that, Boss. He complains the house is using twice as much food since we moved in and he is going way over his budget."

"I will speak with Cardinal Aldobrandini about increasing our food allowance. Tell the rector to give my share to the poor. And tell him that I will speak to father general about an increase in the rector's budget. Next?"

"Camilla."

"What about Camilla?"

"The bailiffs are going to seize her furniture unless Burratti comes up with the taxes, and he is out of work again. Camilla picked a real loser when she married that one, if you ask me."

"My sister sometimes exasperates me. Why does she write to you about such things and not to me?"

"Because she is frightened of you. She knows how you feel about Burratti."

"How much?"

"Twenty-six *giullii*. She's a good kid, Boss. If the old lady in Campo Marzio is worth five *scudi*, then even Burratti is worth one. For Camilla."

"Have we anything else to pawn?"

"Only your good crucifix."

"Pawn it. I will use the spare."

"Right. Another thing: I took your gaiters to the Jew Simon in the Borgo. He says they are too far gone to repair. He will make you a new pair for only five *giullii*. I said I would have to let him know."

"Forget it. I will wear them as they are. Did you know that St. Thomas had no gaiters at all?"

"You know, I think you really enjoy being poor. You won't be happy until we are bankrupt."

"My son, I am rich in my Father's glory, and that is all the riches to which I aspire. As for bankruptcy, so long as we give freely and generously, God will see to it that we do not become bankrupt. God and the pawnbrokers, right, Pietro?"

He winked at me. A little joke between us.

"One final item: Father Cervini has not been paid in three months. Even *he* has expenses."

His eyes flashed. Danger signal.

"Enough about money, Guidotti! Father Cervini will have to wait. He is a Jesuit. He knows how to wait."

"Don't blame him. He did not ask me to talk to you, honest. I took it on myself to mention it."

"Take it on yourself to forget it then. We have more important matters to discuss now."

I did not only spend his money and run his errands; our relationship was not so simple as that. He used to call me his *altro l'io*, his "other self." He had been married to the church all his life; since sixteen, a Jesuit. He never drank stronger than watered-down wine, never smoked, never cursed. He never had a woman, nor, as far as I knew, a man or boy. Bellarmine was a theological scholar. What he said to Tommaso about being no good at temporal affairs was accurate. When it came to church affairs he was a tiger, but in worldly matters he was like a child.

Now me, I was different. I never had formal schooling. I spent all my life in the streets. I drank, I cursed — never in front of him, there is a time and a place and I pride myself in knowing what to say when and to whom — and I knew women. I am not suggesting that he missed having all of that or that he might have wished to have lived his life differently. So far as I know — and he held nothing back from me, I knew all his secrets — he loved his church, and he was content with his life in it. *A contento.*

He used me the way he used his Latin or his Hebrew books, as a reference. And for perspective. I never knew anyone so acutely aware of his limitations nor so tenacious about overcoming them. In this case, through me. I knew about people and he did not, so he used me to know them. It was as simple as that.

I had something he didn't, and he needed it. People talked to me. Not to ask for money or benefices or dispensations or intercessions, the way they did with him, because he was who he was. They talked to me because I was one of them . . . nobody.

All my life, people have told me their secrets. I did not ask them to. I could be standing on the side of the road waiting for a wagon to pass, and somebody would tell me his life history before I crossed the road. You would think someone as big as I am would be threatening to people. Instead, they looked upon me as their protector.

I was a very good listener. After years of people telling me their troubles, I could even hear what was on their minds half the time without their telling me. All I had to do was smile and nod my head and people would spill their guts to me. Plenty of times they told me things they shouldn't have. I never used it against them. I'm proud of that. My *babbo* would have been proud too. He was a good man. "Tell the truth, do what you say you are going to do, don't ever hurt anybody unless they hurt you first." These were the only words of advice my father ever gave me. About twenty times a day. But it was good advice and I took it.

The boss reminded me of my *babbo*. There were many levels to our relationship. I was big, he was small. Little men like big friends. I was healthy as a horse, he was frail and sickly. I was all the time joking with him and teasing him, calling him "Boss" when everybody else called him "Reverence," and later, "Eminence." I was the only one who had the nerve to argue with him. If he was wrong, I wouldn't let him get away with it. There was no pretense between us. Not ever. He knew he could trust me.

It worked both ways. I used him too. At first it was just a job.

Room, board, and a chance to stay out of the way of the Corsican from Ripa. But as time went on, I grew to admire the way his mind worked. He did not waste time on process; it was always the concept he was looking for. He would dig until he found it. If it belonged to someone else, he would absorb it as though it were his own, then turn it inside out. He had unbelievable patience. He could study someone's arguments for days, weeks, even months if he had to. But once he discovered that underlying concept, he would slice it up as deftly as sectioning a ripe pear. Even the great Doctor William Whitaker of Cambridge, his most learned foe, publicly expressed respect for the boss's genius. My master was Rome's champion.

I learned much from him. His mind was far more subtle than mine. He wanted power and he knew how to get it. Power, to him, was the glory of God, which he believed to be the sword of the church. No one ever handled that sword as he did. If I knew the people, he knew his churchmen. They were crafty, he was craftier.

His spider's web was humility, and he snared them all in it... bishops, cardinals, even popes...this tender, loving, humble little priest who asked nothing for himself but the honor of defending the Word and protecting the church from the attacks of heresiarchs. His pen was irrefutable. Everything he ever wanted, he obtained with the honey of God's love.

Oh, he was good. He was the best.

We made a fine team. "What do you think of this?" he would ask, sometimes in the middle of the night, and then he would read me a new chapter or discuss a new idea he was planning to present to the pope or perhaps to one of the congregations on which he served. Many times I did not fully understand what he was talking about, but always I told him what I thought, and always he would say: "Thank you, Peter, I knew I could count on you." Occasionally, I offered suggestions for improvements. He appreciated that. And whenever he needed something special, some background research for one of his ideas, talk to this cardinal's people or feel out that one's banker, I was the one to do it.

I was his friend and partner. No one on the outside knew. When he became cardinal, he appointed me *maestro di casa*. It was necessary to maintain our roles in public and before the *famiglia*, but in private things were different. We never defined it. We never discussed it. But we were a team.

That's the way it was between us.

✠

Bellarmine removed his glasses and placed them carefully on the writing table. He closed his eyes and massaged them gently with his left hand. Another headache. He must have been up all night.

"Peter, how long have you been with me now?"

"Nine years. Why?"

"Are you happy here?"

"Do you mean in this house, in Rome, or with you? Because if you mean am I happy in this house, then I don't mind telling you..."

He dismissed the question with a wave of his hand and started over.

"St. Thomas writes in the *Summa* that it is better that all things be regulated by law than that they be left to the decision of judges. It is his feeling that lawmakers judge universally and about future events, whereas those who sit in judgment judge of things in the present, toward which they may be affected by love, hatred, or cupidity, and thus their judgment becomes perverted. What do you think, Peter?"

He was thinking out loud, using me as a sounding board. Whatever ghosts he had been wrestling with all night were still in the room.

"It makes sense, but is it practical?" I asked. "As far as I can see, we already have too many laws."

"An excellent point! St. Thomas must have wondered about that himself, for a little later he adds: 'Certain individual facts which cannot be covered by the law have necessarily to be committed to judges.' Now what do you think?"

"I think St. Thomas was nobody's fool. He leaves the back door open in case he can't get out the front. Listen, Boss, maybe if you told me what this is all about, I could help. That is what I am here for, right?"

But he seemed not to be listening.

"'In the middle of the journey of our life, I came to myself in a dark wood where the straight way was lost.' At that point, Dante could have used a man of action like you. I am indeed fortunate God sent you to me, for I am in greater need of your assistance now than I have ever been. Put away your notebook, Pietro. This is for your ears only. You must put none of this in writing, for should any record of this conversation fall into the wrong hands, I would surely have fear for your safety and perhaps even for my own."

Now, my master was a cautious man, but he was no alarmist. If he said there was danger, then this was serious business.

He put his glasses on and picked up a single sheet of paper. He studied it in silence for several minutes before continuing. Though the seal had been broken when the letter was opened, I recognized it immediately. It was the most ominous seal in all of Rome. Santa Severina, grand inquisitor of the Sant'Offizio. Trouble.

"Yesterday morning, I received this communication from His Eminence Cardinal Santa Severina, in which the cardinal requests a personal favor of me."

"A favor?"

"A favor," he repeated, ignoring my sarcasm. "And during my regular afternoon audience at the Vatican, the Holy Father made a similar request. Both of these requests were made informally, though I do not think they were such. Nor do I ascribe to coincidence that they both made essentially the same request."

"Which was . . . ?"

"In a moment. Bear with me, this is a most delicate matter. I am not accustomed to such intrigue. I want you first to understand the nuances of this situation into which I appear to have been drawn."

He reviewed his relationship with the grand inquisitor. When Bellarmine published the first volume of *Controversies,* there was a passage in the book that suggested that the pope did not have direct temporal power. The pope was not the immediate and sovereign master of the whole world was, I believe, the way the boss put it. We were in Paris under siege at the time the book came out. Sixtus V was furious. He declared the idea heterodox and put *Controversies* on the Index of Forbidden Books. This was in '90.

Aquaviva took the pope's action as an affront to the Society, which was having trouble enough, what with all the backbiting cliques in Rome, without this for more. He contacted everyone he could think of who might come to Bellarmine's defense, but the pontiff was determined and the listing was published.

Right after that, Sixtus died, and then came Urban VII. We were on our way home by this time — I had my hands full nursing the boss, who had come down with the dysentery and was sick almost to death — so we did not hear the rest of the story until we arrived in Rome almost three months later.

Santa Severina, it turned out, was a great fan of Bellarmine. On Urban's second day as pope — the poor guy only made it for twelve days and then dropped over himself, I guess the job was too much for him — Santa Severina convinced him to remove the book from the Index.

So now my master was sort of in Santa Severina's debt. Anyway, you do not exactly refuse a request from the grand inquisitor, not in the real world you don't. (Of course, it cannot be said that the level on which the boss operated was always the real world.) Plus, one hardly refuses a direct request from the pope, informal or not.

But all of this I pretty much knew already.

"Come on, Boss, I know the history. What did Clement have to say?"

"His Holiness and I have touched on the subject of a cardinalate before, as you know, and I have made known my desire to remain a simple religious. I doubt my wish will prevail. My best guess is that it will happen sometime early in the New Year. This is between us, Pietro…"

I crossed my heart and looked up at the ceiling. He appreciated such gestures.

"…Based on this note from his eminence, I have little doubt that when I am named to the purple, I will be assigned to serve on the Inquisition. Cardinal Santa Severina makes it very clear that it is his desire that I work at his side on this particular matter. The problem is that with Cardinal Toledo gone, I would be the only Jesuit inquisitor general. All the rest are Dominicans, as they have largely been since Pope Paul III's bull *Lecit ab initio*. I am made more uncomfortable by this prospect, because His Holiness has also asked me to consider as a high priority the controversy, on which I have already been working, between Bañez and Molina on the subject of divine grace, a controversy which may well eventuate in discord between the Society and the Dominican fathers. Thus, I am already made aware of the pressure to be brought upon the Society through me when I become a cardinal. There are also…"

"The favor," I prodded, "what is the favor they ask?"

"…a number of politically sensitive international situations of which I think you ought to be made aware. The Holy Father enjoys a rather shaky relationship with Philip II that dates to the misfortunes of the Spanish Armada — debacle is perhaps a more apt description — at the hands of the English navy; that, and of course choosing to ignore Philip's objections over the absolution of Navarre. The kingdom of Naples is yet another area of sensitivity between Rome and Madrid, since Naples remains under Spanish control. This complicates the issue, where you are concerned, in that the prisoner in question is a Neapolitan."

"What prisoner? What Neapolitan? Are you trying to kill me with suspense?"

"In France, meanwhile, Navarre — King Henri IV — is no great friend of the Society. The truth is we were not among his supporters in the early days. Father general fears our brothers in France may be expelled at any moment. The climate may be dangerous for you there as well. Now, in England..."

"What are you talking about anyhow? Naples? France? England? What...?"

"...in England, Elizabeth is growing old. There are many problems in the empire, and she may lack the money and the power to solve them. There are powerful figures in the Church of England who have gradually undermined the more liberal attitude toward Catholics that marked her early reign. Life for our brothers and sisters in England threatens to become increasingly harsh. If Elizabeth should die or be deposed, then, God forbid, there could be a bloodbath. Much depends on who will succeed her to the throne. England, potentially, is the most dangerous place for you of all."

"That does it!" I said, standing. "You tell me what this is all about, now, or I quit!"

When we were both standing, my master barely reached to my chest. But with him sitting and me standing, as we were now, I towered over him like Colossus. I assumed my most threatening glare, which was not altogether an act because I had the distinct feeling I was being toyed with, and nothing gets my hackles raised more!

He chuckled.

He *had* been toying with me!

"All right, Pietro, forgive me. Sit down and I will fill you in on as much as I know myself."

And this is what the boss told me:

The Sant'Offizio was holding in Castel Sant'Angelo a Dominican friar from Nola by the name of Giordano Bruno. Friar Bruno was being charged with thirty-four articles of heresy. The Holy Office considered him a troublemaker. He was apparently quite a character, hired and fired from half the royal courts and universities of Europe. But no dumbbell. Bruno had written more than a dozen books on memory, philosophy, and cosmology, plus a couple hundred articles, poems, and plays, in Latin and also some of them in Italian. And he was giving the Sant'Offizio a very big headache.

Philip II was putting pressure on the pope about this friar, Clement was putting pressure on Santa Severina, and now they were both starting to put pressure on Bellarmine. They were all out to nail Bruno, yet none of them was proving an equal match for this philosopher. So Santa Severina was proposing that my master study Bruno's work for a while, take as much time as he needed, and then join the Sant'Offizio as a consultant. That was the "favor" he was asking, the same favor that the pope was asking except that the pope was putting a sort of time limit on it by tying it to the cardinalate. What they both understood was that there was nobody in Christendom who was better than Bellarmine at punching theological holes in philosophical arguments.

No one was in any great hurry. The one thing the Sant'Offizio has in its favor is time. They claim it is the soul they want to save, not the body, so they will let somebody rot in prison for a lifetime and could care less. This poor friar had already been in a cell for four years, plus another year or so on trial up in Venice before that. The wheel of justice, turns slowly where the Sant'Offizio is concerned.

"Rot" is the word of choice. The way the Sant'Offizio operates, a prisoner has as much chance as snow in hell. You are not told what you are accused of, or who your accusers are, you may not have an advocate, you may not hear the testimony against you, or examine evidence, or call witnesses of your own, and it is not enough to say you repent; you must name the names of other heretics and then trust in the mercy of your judges.

Clement was not a merciful pope. It was his court, and he ran it with a tight fist. He was not soft on heretics. Considering his problems with the English Protestants, the Calvinists, the Lutherans, and the rest, he could not afford to be soft. Eight heretics went to the stake in Rome in '95, seven more in '96. No telling how many would go this year. I would not want to be in Bruno's place. But I did not work for Bruno, I worked for Bellarmine. And my poor master had his own problems, I could see that.

"That is as much as I can tell you at this point. Now you know as much as I do," he concluded, after giving me the details. "The Holy Father has hinted that he may find it necessary to make an example of this Dominican father who has championed Copernicus and attacked Aristotle. There have been an increasing number of philosophers, mathematicians, and astronomers writing in direct contradiction of Scripture and the church fathers on such subjects as the epicycles, divine power, the soul, infinity, and metaphysics.

"These are important themes. I do not doubt that we are being confronted with them during what may prove to be a transitional period in the life of our church, and that one day we may reconcile what now seem contradicting views. But the church must have time to study these issues. Church doctrine should never be static; it should evolve as the result of a dynamic process in which interpretations are allowed a certain latitude; but the church must not be forced into making sudden, impulsive, and ill-considered decisions, merely because of the teachings of a few heretics.

"If only these people would confine themselves to stating their findings in the form of theory rather than promulgating them as 'fact.' I have discussed this very point with Father Clavius on many occasions, and he agrees. Yet if people like this friar persist, what are we to do? The issue is a critical one. How we deal with it will have profound impact on the future of the church. In that context, this trial provides an interesting challenge.

"On the other hand, there are political undertones which cause me great concern. Why, for example, have they chosen me for this job? Is it because I am the best available, or is it because I am a Jesuit? There are any number of qualified theologians in Rome capable of dealing with the Bruno case. However, the accused is a Dominican and so are the members of the tribunal. If this case backfires, they would no doubt prefer to fix the blame on a Jesuit.

"There are those in Rome, Pietro, who are jealous of the Society. Since the time of Pope Sixtus V, they have attempted to undermine our influence in the church. We must always be wary of traps. Though I seem this time to have little choice, since both the cardinal and the pope seem to have drafted me for this assignment, I want to be certain that I am absolutely prepared.

"I am going to request that I have until the end of the year, so that I may study these works of Bruno thoroughly..." (he gestured toward a stack of books and manuscripts) "...as well as all of the testimony thus far, both from Rome and from Venice. Then, there are a number of other relevant works that I will need time to gather and study. And, of course, I have all of my other projects to consider. I have been assured that I may take all the time I require.

"Meanwhile, to understand this man's work, I must also understand the man. This is where I will need your help, Pietro... (at last!)...You must go and find out about him. Talk to the people who knew him, who worked with him, who were his friends and his enemies. Find out about his private life. Find out everything you can about him and then report back to me. You are the only one I can trust to do this.

"For your safety, Pietro, only you and I will ever know about this mission. If anything ever goes wrong, you understand? You must be discreet. No one must discover your true purpose. Not even that you are associated with me. Should you get into trouble, it is unlikely I would be able to help you. Here is a list of places and the names of those who may have been connected with Bruno in each place. It is unfortunately incomplete and may already be outdated, but it will be a start at least. Here also is a list of our agents in these places. They may be used for limited assistance, funds, a place to stay, information and so forth, but they must not know your mission. Nor will they ask. I will give you a password by which they will know you are to be served, no questions asked. If you get into trouble, don't ask them for help; they cannot give it. Nor should you appeal to papal nuncios for help, not even as a Roman citizen. There are reasons. Commit these lists to memory and then destroy them.

"Now then, Peter, I have discussed with you in absolute confidence, matters which I have never discussed with anyone other than my father general. I have done so because if you decide to take this mission, you have a right to know. Please believe that I do not desire you to take this risk against your wishes, and that I will understand if you do not. Would you like to take some time to think it over?"

"I just did. When do I leave, Boss?"

✠

There were times during the next eleven months when I would gladly have given my last *giullii* to be back in Rome safe and sound, times even when I began to doubt my own sanity, but I never regretted that decision, not even when I failed.

Chapter 3

I WILL POSE TO YOU a gift in the form of a mission, a mission in the form of an adventure: You will travel the world on your own, with gold in your purse and no one to tell you how to spend it. You will be free to go where you please, when you please, how you please. You will be your own boss, responsible to no one but yourself for the better part of a year. And you will get paid for it.

Could you refuse such a gift? Only a coward or a fool would. I was neither.

Nine years with Bellarmine was the longest I had ever lasted at one job. The problem was that I had an itch in me to be doing something new, something different. Whenever a job got so I could do it with one hand, the other hand would grow restless to scratch that itch. What made working for Bellarmine so different was that I always needed both hands.

As Bellarmine moved up the ladder of the church, gaining in stature and importance, my responsibilities increased accordingly. With every job I ever had, one lesson repeated: there is no mystery, only information.

The church was no different than the Ripa. The more experience I gained, the better I was at the job; the better I was, the more I was trusted to do. But instead of moving from job to job the way I had most of my life, with Bellarmine I was able to let the jobs do the moving. Rome to Paris to Naples to Rome. And now to Naples again.

My work at this job had until now revolved around my master's needs and schedule. That meant having to worry about his health, which was generally poor, and nursing him whenever it got worse. It meant looking after his belongings, arranging for his food and lodging when traveling, keeping his accounts, paying his bills, caring for his animals, oiling his lute and violin, seeing that he was free to study and to write with a minimum of distraction, since if it were left to him to decide, he would see all who called upon him, down to the lowliest beggar looking for an easy touch.

It also meant having to observe church protocol. When others were present, though he gave me great latitude otherwise, I had to curb my tongue and remember my place. I preferred to think of my job as working *with* Bellarmine, but this public pose of subservience was a constant reminder of the truth: I worked *for* Bellarmine.

Until now.

I left Rome with the thrill of a falcon loosed on the wind from his master's glove.

This was to be my great adventure! Nothing negative could dampen my excitement. Not the dreary rain and fog that accompanied my dawn departure. Nor passing the Catacombs, which other times never failed to depress me. Not even the thought that Giuseppe Vignanesi was to be at the boss's side during my absence.

I had known Vignanesi from Campo Marzio and from my dealings with the late Cardinal Toledo's household, in which he had been employed. He was a skinny, weasel-faced Sicilian with small, beady eyes, always looking for the shortcut and a few quick *scudi*. I did not approve of the boss's choice, and I told him so.

"You don't know this guy the way I do," I warned him. He has *la lingua sciolto*, a loose tongue. He's lazy and shiftless, and I would not trust him further that I could toss him."

"You do the man an injustice, Pietro. I assure you he speaks highly of you and with respect. He is aware that the job is temporary and has promised to do his best, though he freely admits he could not perform the duties as well as you."

"Ha!"

"If Cardinal Toledo trusted him in his house, than we shall have no reservations about him in ours. I have told him that when you return, we will find something else for him to do. If my promotion goes through next year, we shall need more help anyway. Meanwhile, he is without a job and I am without you. God's will be done."

"But Boss...!"

"Enough, Guidotti."

And that ended the conversation.

But as I set out that morning in the company of the Rome-to-Naples "Mule Express" and passed through the San Sebastiano Gate onto Via Apia, I left all that behind me. Vignanesi was small cheese. Let him wrestle with the laundry and the bills and the fomentations, let him run all over town doing silly little errands. I would be busy with more important matters.

I had not the vaguest idea what to expect, of course, yet I had no doubt I could handle it. In those days I still believed there was nothing I could not do.

✠

The first name on the Bruno list I had memorized was that of a Father Anselmi, the Dominican friar who had been Bruno's mentor when he entered San Dominico Maggiore in Naples. That was thirty-two years ago. I had no way of knowing whether this friar was still at the monastery or even that he was still alive. All I had was the name and the place. I had to start somewhere.

At least I knew Naples, having just spent two years there with Bellarmine. I would have preferred to set out immediately for distant and exotic shores. Just the thought of journeying to England set my heart racing with excitement. But it seemed prudent to get my feet wet in familiar waters first. Besides, Bruno was Neapolitan. Naples was where he had his beginning. If I was to get to know this man for my master, then I should begin in Naples.

First I would nose around Nola, the town where he was born. It is an ancient town east of Naples, where the slopes of Mount Cicala meet the River Agno. I did not so much want to talk to anyone there as to see what Bruno might have seen as a boy. I had the feeling that to understand Bruno, I was going to have to get inside of him. To see the world as he saw it, I was going to have to look at it through his eyes and not my own.

Right now, I could see very little. We were surrounded by a flat, monotonous gray. Normally, Via Apia affords travelers a colorful and picturesque view of the countryside. It is one of the few famous old Roman roads that is still maintained in modern times, lined with stately trees that give way to the broad plains and rolling hills of the *campagna*. But today it was instead shrouded in a chill wet fog that gave the impression of passing through a long dreary tunnel without beginning or end. I was soaked through to my skin.

Adding further to my general discomfort was the beast under me that passed for a horse. He had been cheap and available on short notice. As I was now learning, that counted for very little in the selection of a horse. I called him "Cammello" because with his withers and rump forming two mountains and his swayback the valley between, he more resembled a camel than a horse. He had the gait of one as well, and I was already queasy in the stomach. This promised to be a tiresome journey.

There are two routes from Naples to Rome. One winds through the hills by way of Frosinone, then cuts straight across the plains through Cassino and Capua. The other heads directly south on the Apian Way to Terracina, then along the coast to Naples. This time of year the coast road can be unpleasant. Either the southwesterly *Libecchio* blows its pestilence across the sea from Africa, or else the bitter blustering northeasters of the *Tramontana* whip down from the snow-covered mountains. There are even days when you can have both, first one, and then with a change of wind, the other, as though they compete in a tug of war with you as the rope. On the other hand, *banditti* operating north of Frosinone had been lately active, making the first route too perilous for the slow-moving mail train, despite our escort of six papal musketeers. The coast route was the safer choice.

The mules were slow, making barely twenty miles a day. With mules a three-day trip stretched to a week. Any other time I would have welcomed the chance to dally, but the weather was raw and I was anxious to try my hand at this new job. I rode with the train as far as Terracina, then proceeded ahead alone.

When I reached Naples, I skirted the city and proceeded directly toward Nola. I climbed the hill just west of the town walls, where I sat and gazed at Vesuvius rising majestically from the plain to the southwest. I tried to imagine myself as Bruno the boy at ten or twelve years of age. Perhaps he sat on this very hill and daydreamed about his future. I tried hard, but I did not succeed.

It was then I realized that I knew absolutely nothing about Giordano Bruno. Nothing but a list of names. How could I presume to imagine what went on in this man's mind as a boy? How could I hope to see Vesuvius through the eyes of a total stranger? I was beginning to understand the measure of this job. It would be like no other I had ever performed. Bellarmine had handed me a blank scroll of parchment and told me to reconstruct a man's life upon it, and all I had to work with was his name and a list of less than a dozen people who might or might not have known him, who might or might not still be living, who might or might not be willing to talk to me about him. To accomplish this, I would have to travel ten thousand miles in eleven months, run the risk of wars, bandits, and plagues, and possibly wind up in a foreign prison if my mission was discovered by the wrong people.

If this was a gift, there were strings attached. I had been cast loose in a boat with no oars!

The storm clouds passed and the sky improved to a pale winter blue. The wind had all but died. Vesuvius, backlit by the late afternoon sun, sent a trail of smoke drifting lazily upward from the crater between its twin peaks and spreading out like a mushroom cap high above it. "The old man is smoking his pipe" is the way Neapolitans refer to the volcano on days like this. So beautiful, yet so dangerous.

For the two years that I had lived in Naples with Bellarmine, I prayed to God like the sole survivor of Pompeii that He keep the lid on that volcano. I fear no man, but I never got used to living so close to Hell.

I mounted Cammello and headed toward Naples. If I was to begin the portrait of Bruno, it would be there, not daydreaming about Vesuvius from a hill near Nola. The sun would be down in a few hours, and there was one who lived just inside the towers of Porta Nolano who would be happy to see me once again in her bed. Morning would be soon enough to seek out the old Dominican friar at the monastery. By that time I would have a cover story worked out as to what I was doing back in Naples, for I was not unknown there and there would be questions. Though none, I wagered to myself with a grin, would be forthcoming from my friend in the house near Porta Nolano; she would be too overcome with joy to ask questions. And too busy.

✠

I hate Naples. It is half the size of Rome with twice the population, has four times the number of beggars and none of its beauty. The bay is nice, but the city is squalid. With narrow, crowded streets, loud and boisterous, its houses are built upon houses so that you feel so hemmed in that you can hardly draw breath. And when you do, it is only to choke on the dust. The noise in the *Mercato* from the shrill bargaining of Maltese, Arab, Levantine and Jewish traders in all their coarse languages is an assault on the ears. The fish stalls of the Santa Lucia are even worse, and the overpowering stink of rotting fish guts is enough to ruin any man's appetite forever.

Naples has belonged to the Greeks, to the Romans, to the Normans, the Saracens, and the French, and now it belongs to the Spanish. I cannot for the life of me understand why anyone would want it.

What was causing me to hate Naples even more than usual this morning was the discovery the night before that someone else was warming my lady friend's bed now; that, and having spent the night alone at a nearby *osteria,* where I drowned my disillusionment in too much red wine and had barely managed three hours' sleep before the awful clamor in the streets startled me awake with a head ready to explode.

The backs of my eyes were throbbing like the anvil of Satan. My tongue was too large for my mouth. To suffer such agonies for an unappreciative woman! A glance in the looking glass confirmed the worst. There was red where the whites of my eyes should have been.

When I freed my mouth of its oversized tongue by sticking it out, I saw in the glass a fat field of cotton protruding from my dark beard.

I was struck with remorse. My master had entrusted me with the most important mission of my life, and look what I had done. The very first time on my own in nine years and all I had on my mind was carnal pleasure and drink? I had betrayed my master's trust!

These self-recriminations only served to heighten the feelings of inadequacy that had begun to stir within me since the hill outside Nola. What if I could not locate Anselmi? Suppose he was dead? If I did find him, what would I say to him? Suppose he refused to talk to me about Bruno? Doubts eroded my confidence like waves on a beach of sand. I had not yet conducted my first interview and I was already conceding defeat.

What finally motivated me out of that room — aside from the bucket of cold water into which I first plunged my head — was the certainty that, no matter what transpired in the next few hours, I would at least be able to leave Naples when it was over, leave it forever. Which could not be too soon for me.

As I fought my way to Via Biagia, pushing and shoving through a sea of horses, carts, and donkeys that filled the width of the narrow, garbage-strewn streets, I conceived a story that would cover my presence in Naples and my interest in Bruno.

Many times I had heard my master mention the "Molinist Affair." Something to do with a controversy between the Dominicans and the Jesuits concerning grace and free will. A family squabble between the two sects. They were always arguing about something. The Jesuits accused the Dominicans of being too conservative, of dragging their heels in history; while the Dominicans on their part viewed the Jesuits as radical upstarts, out to change the church and do away with tradition altogether.

This particular clash began between a Dominican named Bañez and a Jesuit professor named Molina. Caused a great ruckus in Spain. Molina was denounced by the Spanish Inquisition, and Pope Clement had intervened, at the request of both my master and Aquaviva. The last I had heard, my master was on some congregation or other that was investigating the whole affair. That had been dragging on for years.

Since Bellarmine had been provincial in Naples, and Naples was Spanish territory, and the monastery was Dominican, I would tell people I was gathering information for my master on the Molinist Affair. As for Bruno, he was a Dominican writer. Probably no one here knew any more about his work than I did. I could vaguely include him in the investigation if anyone asked.

Probably this story would not have held up to close scrutiny, but it was the best I could think of on the spur of the moment. I could not say I was on vacation, after all. In my condition, I was lucky to come up with any story at all. Besides, I had almost reached the top of the hill where the church was located. There was no time to concoct anything better.

I stopped for a moment to straighten my tunic, spat on my hands and ran them through my tangled mass of hair. An elderly beggar approached me for alms. I was in no mood. I growled her away. Looking the way I did, red-eyed and wild, she took fright.

She stuck a bony fist in my face, her first and fourth fingers pointing at me to cancel out the Evil Eye, and spat three times on the ground in front of me *ptui! ptui! ptui!* Then she turned away with a cackle of satisfaction. Neapolitans are a strange and superstitious lot. I was left with heartburn to add to my miseries.

✠

The church and monastery of S. Dominico Maggiore lie in the shadow of St. Elmo, in one of the more fashionable quarters of Naples, surrounded by a number of splendid palaces, remnants of the decaying nobility of the kingdom. Since the days when Don Pedro de Toledo had been Spanish viceroy, the barons of Naples had been on their way out. But nobility dies hard, and they still lived well though their power was gone. The church itself is a great Gothic affair, rebuilt by Charles II. It had originally been a church of Basilian monks, and later of the Benedictines. It stood on rising ground, on the western side of Neapolis, the ancient Greek city that had long since crumbled into rock and stone to the east of modern Naples. It held an excellent view of the bay, and on a day as clear as this one, one could see Capri rising up from the sea in the azure distance.

The main entrance to the church was through a courtyard that led from the street, but I did not want to be seen by anyone who might recognize me, so I chose instead to enter through the Largo at the east end. I hurried through the chapel in the apse and followed the winding staircase of the south transept.

It was still early. Mass would not be for another hour, and the chapels were all empty. In the Chapel of the Crucifix, the seventh I counted on the south side, I found a young novice polishing a railing on the other side of which was featured a relic belonging to St. Thomas.

"He studied here, you know," he observed in an assured voice, as though he had known Aquinas personally. He affected that phony beatific smile that all novices seem to adopt with lay people as soon as they don their robes. It comes with the tonsure, I suppose.

"You are permitted to speak, then?" I asked.

"Oh, yes," he replied enthusiastically, the smile momentarily forgotten in his eagerness to converse. "We are permitted to suspend our vow of silence in the public area."

"Perhaps you can help me," I began. I blurted out the story that had come to me while nursing my hangover on Via Biagia. The look of confusion on his face told me what I should have realized from the start, that nobody ever explains anything to a lowly novice; it is quite beyond their expectations. I mumbled through my embarrassment as he waited patiently for me to conclude. Then he told me that Father Anselmi was indeed still with the monastery.

The abbot was away on church business, and the prior was laid up with an unpleasant attack of the gout, but the novice was certain it would be permissible to visit with Father Anselmi in the garden. I would find him working on his "vegetables." This last he added with a most peculiar look on his face.

"You know Father Anselmi?" he asked politely.

"I've never met him," I admitted.

"You will be kind to him? He has been here for a very long time. There is nowhere else for him to go. We all love him dearly, but he is . . . uh . . . not exactly right in the head, you see."

He made a circular motion with his finger at the side of his head.

With directions to the monastery gardens, I left the chapel. I could hear the novice reciting a litany to himself as he resumed his work, rehearsing no doubt for duties more seemly than polishing a rail. I made my way toward the monastery to interview an old monk not exactly right in his head (working on his vegetables in January?) about an accused heretic I had never met and who he had probably not seen in twenty or thirty years. My headache was back.

Chapter 4

febbraio 1597
San Dominico Maggiore
Napoli

I STOOD IN THE SHADOWS of a stone archway and observed him working with a hoe on the other side of the garden. The area was marked off with a border of rocks. On the side nearest me, a wooden plaque was stuck in the ground, hand lettered: "Enter ye the kingdom."

Some kingdom. A patch of grubby weeds and hard clay. He attacked it as though with the wrath of God, shouting from time to time and shaking the hoe in the air. He seemed oblivious to the world outside his rock border.

He was tall though bent with age, taller than I had he been able to straighten up. And old. Flowing white hair down to his shoulders, a long white beard that hid the lower half of his face and continued to a point two-thirds of the way down his chest. His habit was faded and frayed at the hem. The cord around his middle — it was only a rough piece of hemp — kept coming undone, and periodically he did a little jig, hopping in a circle on one foot and continuing to work the spade with one hand while he attempted to tie the cord with the other. And not doing it very well, which is why it continued to come undone. All this with constant waves and flourishes of his arms and periodic shouts and dark looks toward the heavens.

His feet were bare even in this cold weather, and his toenails were long and curved and crusted with dirt. His tonsure glistened with sweat. He had a wild look about him. It made me nervous. Should I come back another time? Or possibly forget the whole idea?

He beckoned to me. He had never so much as glanced once in my direction, yet as he hacked away at the weeds he lifted the hoe and used it to motion me to him. How had he known I was there?

I took a deep breath and walked toward him. He continued to work steadily, without looking up. The Corsican from Ripa had not made me half so nervous. At least with that one I knew what to expect and was smart enough to know when to leave. I felt ill-prepared for this endeavor.

I had brought him a present. Something I came upon where the Volturno meets the sea along the coastal route to Naples and on a whim had picked up and taken with me. It was a stout tree branch, sanded smooth as satin by the river as it roared its way down from the mountains and then bleached white as snow by the sun as it lay waiting on the bank near Castel Volturno. For some reason I thought he might like it.

"I brought you this staff, Padre," I told him, thankful for a beginning.

He took it without a word, handing me the hoe in exchange. His hands were the most beautiful I had ever seen on a man, long and slender, with tapering fingers that might have belonged to an artist or a musician. But the palms were blemished with calluses and open sores from working in the hard clay.

He examined the wood carefully, almost lovingly, feeling its texture with the backs of his fingers, caressing his cheek with it. He was obviously pleased with my gift. He carried it over to the rock border, laid it carefully on the ground beneath his plaque, and returned.

"'The harvest truly is plenteous, but the laborers are few' – Matthew 9:37," he said. Then he frowned. "Are you new here, my son?"

"Yes," I answered. "My name is Pietro. I am from Rome."

"From Rome? That is a long way. No matter. I shall call you Judas until you prove to me otherwise." He noticed the hoe still in my hand. "Why are you standing idle!" he shouted. "Work! Work! 'Every man shall bear his own burden' – Galatians 6:5!"

He dropped to his knees and began pulling furiously at the weeds with both hands, throwing them wildly over his shoulders. It was the first time I had ever held a hoe. I was not very adept at using it. I tried to hack at the ground the way I had seen him doing, but I only succeeded in showering him with clumps of dirt, of which he seemed totally unaware. Special Investigator Guidotti from Rome on a secret mission of great importance, and here I was breaking my back with a hoe in the garden of a madman!

At last he stopped working and held up his hand for me to do likewise. He stood and produced a wineskin from beneath the folds of his habit.

"'Drink no longer water, but use a little wine for thy stomach's sake,'" he recited, winking broadly. He took a long swallow, missing his mouth with half the stream. "Uh...don't tell me...wait a moment...ha! First Timothy 5:23! Aha!"

I reached for my turn of the skin, but clutched only air as he pulled it away from me and tucked it quickly back into his robe.

"What can I tell you, Timothy?"

"Pietro."

"Judas!"

"Padre, I have come all the way from Rome just to see you. I wish to speak with you about someone you knew a very long time ago. I am...(what to say?)...uh...reviewing his books for the College of Rome, possibly to be used as texts next year...(not bad!)...perhaps you will remember him. Giordano Bruno?"

"Don't know him!"

"Would you please try to remember. It is important to me. I know that it was a long time ago, but..."

"May I interrupt you? I was in Rome once. They thought I was eccentric, or possibly out of my mind. They all think so. Christ Jesus knows differently. I don't care. Why should I care? Pius...what number? Oh, I forget! My memory, you know. Uh...what was I saying?"

I knew people like this in Campo Marzio. Everybody laughed at them or spat on them for good luck. Not me. They did no harm by being crazy. Their mind just raced in circles, like a dog chasing his tail. What you had to do was wait for them to slow down and go the other way. When they changed direction was when they made the most sense. But you had to listen carefully to connect the pieces.

"Giordano Bruno," I prompted.

"Filippo."

"No, I'm Pietro."

"Filippo was his given name. I chose Giordano for him when he arrived, named after the second general of our order. He came here from the Studium in '65. See, I remember. Jesus knows! I remember them all. Giovanni in '54. Giuseppe and Alberto, the twins, in...uh...'58, no, '57. And then there was...I will say no more about them...they were all my...goodness, I am using my hands to speak with and you must think...what was his number? I forget. But don't tell me. Wait! Aha! It was Pius V! Yes, yes, that was who it was...and then in Rome...and uh...ohhh!...he got into a lot of trouble!."

"Pope Pius?"

"Oh, dear, no! Giordano! That was his name. He had a woman. Oh, the sin of temptation! 'Abstain from fleshly lusts, which war against the soul' – First Peter 2:11."

"Did Bruno get into trouble with a woman in the monastery, or with Pius in Rome?"

"No, no, no, no, no!"

"Slow down, Padre. You know where you are, but I am lost."

The bells of the church began to peal. I looked up with a start.

"Don't go yet!" he pleaded, grabbing my sleeve. "It is only for Mass. I am excused! Please stay a while. I will remember for you, I promise. No one comes to see me. I am all alone. Please stay."

There were tears in his eyes.

"Sure, Padre, don't worry about it. I have plenty of time and I'm not going anywhere. So now, tell me about Bruno. He came here in '65, you say? Was he a novice?"

"First a probationer, then a novice. He was very bright. Very bright. But a little devil too. 'The tongue can no man tame; it is an unruly evil' –James 3:8. Well, then it became...that was where we were trying to get him, you see...he read the wrong books...the Trinity...oh, Lord!...and he doubted...'that which cometh out of the mouth defileth a man'...oh my, yes, serious trouble. I told him not to take it down from the walls. I...what was I saying?"

"Bruno was in *aqua calda?* With the abbot? Was he in hot water, too, with the abbot?"

"Prior Pasqua? Who?"

"Giordano Bruno."

"Don't know him!"

I sure could have used some of that wine.

"Yes, you do know him. Giordano Bruno. You said so. Now, you said he was in trouble for reading the wrong books? What books?"

His brows knit in deep concentration.

"Giordano Bruno, you say? Well, yes. Plato, Cicero, Virgil, Euclid, Ptolemy, Pythagoras, Anaxagoras. I was the librarian then. He read them all. Lucretius was a favorite. Cusa too. Not Aristotle, no. I warned him: you must not scoff at the Philosopher; that will cause trouble for you! Not even St. Thomas scoffed at the Philosopher."

"But these were not forbidden books, were they? Why should reading them get him into trouble?"

His eyes narrowed to slits.

"Ravena. Ficino. Lull. Erasmus."

This last name he pronounced with a hiss: E-raz-musss. Then he lowered his voice still further. "He defended Arius." Again he hissed the name like a serpent.

Now we were getting somewhere. Even I knew the name of Arius, the heresiarch. It was a name that set my master's pen flying.

"Was Bruno an Arian?" I asked the old man. Theology was not my strong card, but I wanted to stoke the fire to keep him going.

He brought his face close to mine and his eyes went as wide as two gray moons.

"Who are you, Judas? Have you come to betray me?"

His breath was so foul with garlic and sour wine, I had to turn my head away to breathe. He cackled gleefully, pulling a great sprig of parsley from somewhere beneath his robe and stuffed it into his mouth.

"We will work some more, my son. 'Where the Spirit of the Lord is, there is liberty' – Second Corinthians 3:17."

Anselmi handed me the hoe, producing for himself a hand trowel from beneath his robe — it seemed to house no end of supplies! — with which he began to dig a series of small holes. I never did discover what those holes were for. He filled them in again in the afternoon.

I tried several times to engage him in conversation about Bruno while we worked, but he continued to chew his parsley and to dig his holes without another word. Now and then he spat a long stream of green juice from his mouth. Soon it had stained his white beard and given him the appearance of having fat green lips. He seemed unaware of my presence.

I hacked at the weeds with the damned hoe, cursing at them beneath my breath. My master was getting his money's worth.

✠

It went that way all morning. Work spurts. Questions. Pieces of answers. His memory was full of holes. The serpent of his madness slithered in and out of those holes until you couldn't tell its head from its tail. It was dizzying trying to connect so many fragments!

This is what I was able to piece together:

Bruno came to the monastery when he was seventeen, after three years of studying at the Studium Generale. He wasn't anxious for the priesthood, but his father, Giovanni Bruno, was a soldier down on his luck. He couldn't afford to send the kid to school anymore. So it was the church or nothing if he wanted an education.

A good student, but a hothead with a big mouth. He was constantly breaking the rules. Anselmi took him under his wing. Anselmi was librarian of the monastery, so Bruno ended up reading a great deal. The next year when he took his vows, they made him a subdeacon, then a deacon, but he was having doubts and brought them to Anselmi, who tried to cool him down.

Anselmi was already an old hand at the place. A Norwegian, but he added an *i* to Anselm "for Italy." Bruno became his favorite. Anselmi let him get away with anything and did his best to protect him from the other priests.

Bruno had doubts about the Trinity. He had doubts about images and relics, and took everything off his walls but the crucifix. He read forbidden books. He even recommended them to other novices. Complaints about him piled up. Eventually, they complained about him to the Holy Office in Naples.

The business about Pius V and Rome was a strange one. It seems Bruno studied memory systems in his spare time. The Greeks, the Hermetics, Ramon Lull. He got so proficient at it, he constructed his own system. Anselmi wrote a bishop friend in Rome about Bruno's system, the bishop got word to Pius, Pius sent a carriage to Naples for them both to come to Rome to give a demonstration.

They say old Pius used to do things like that. Imagine sending a carriage all the way to Naples, just so some kid not even a priest yet could come to Rome to do a memory trick for the pope! Clement would never do something like that, too stingy. Bruno recited the entire *Fundamenta* in Hebrew. According to Anselmi, the kid didn't understand one word of the language. Now that was some trick! Pius was impressed. So were the abbot and the prior when they got back. So for a few years the heat was off.

Bruno earned his habit. Preached at St. Bartholomew for several years, nice and quiet. But in '75, he was in trouble again. Serious trouble this time. Anselmi got wind that the provincial was preparing new charges against Bruno for heresy. This time they had more than just a scare and a slap on the hand planned for him. Anselmi warned Bruno he'd better take off while he could.

That much of the story took the entire morning.

I gathered that Bruno was less of a troublemaker at the monastery than a trouble*finder*. He just could not seem to avoid it. As a result he made many enemies, just about everybody but Anselmi from the sound of it. He was a hothead, but a bright one. Anselmi described him as short, dark, skinny, and all mouth. Big eyes, big ears. "Who hath ears to hear, let him hear," was the way Anselmi put it. Matthew 13:9. There was no problem with the old friar's memory for quoting from the Bible.

In January 1576, Bruno took off for Rome. Anselmi never saw him again. But he did hear about him from his bishop friend in the Vatican. I pried the rest of story from him after the noon meal. It was like pulling teeth.

✠

At the noon meal I sat with Fra Anselmi in the rear of the dining hall, away from the rest of the community. The hard bench on which we sat and the old wooden table off which we ate were apparently the exclusive preserve of the old man. No one made a move to join us. A young probationer, barely sixteen, set before us wooden bowls of steaming hot potato soup, a hard piece of dark bread, and a small bit of goat cheese.

(*Ti sta bene*, Guidotti, it was you who picked the church to work for, remember.) Dominicans eat no better than the Jesuits. Some day I would like to find one Catholic order that appreciates good food.

I was an object of special attention. After Grace, Amens, Ave Marias, and the rest, there was silence, save for the slurping noises of sipping the soup and the scraping of wooden spoons on the bottoms of empty bowls, but there was many a furtive glance stolen against the rules. Visitors were a rarity at the convent. Especially one visiting with the old crackpot. Anselmi remained oblivious, lost in thought as he held the bowl to his lips with both hands and drank his soup.

Suddenly he flung the bowl down, beat his wooden spoon on the table for attention, and began reciting the "begats" of St. Matthew with a frenzy of emotion at the top of his lungs:

Abraham begat Isaac; and Isaac begat Jacob; and Jacob begat Judas and his brethren; and Judas begat Phares and Zara of Thamar; and Phares begat Eshrom; and Eshrom begat Aram; and Aram begat Aminadab; and Aminadab begat Naasson; and Naasson begat Salmon; and Salmon begat Booz of Rachab; and Booz begat Obed of Ruth; and Obed begat Jesse; and Jesse begat David the king; and David the king begat Solomon of her that had been the wife of Urias; and Solomon begat Roboam; and Roboam begat Abia; and Abia begat Asa; and Asa begat Josaphat; and Josaphat begat Joram; and Joram begat Ozias; and Ozias begat Joatham; and Joatham begat Achaz; and Achaz begat Ezekias; and Ezekias begat Monasses; and Monasses begat Amon; and Amon begat Josias; and Josias begat Jechonias and his brethren, about the time they were carried away to Babylon; and after they were brought to Babylon, Jechonias begat Salathiel; and Salathiel begat Zorobabel; and Zorobabel begat Abiud;

and Abiud begat Eliakim; and Eliakim begat Azor; and Azor begat Sadoc; and Sadoc begat Achim; and Achim begat Eliud; and Eliud begat Eleazar; and Eleazar begat Matthan; and Matthan begat Jacob; and Jacob begat Joseph the husband of Mary, of whom was born Jesus, who is called Christ.

Just as suddenly as he had stood up to recite, he sat down and tore into his bread.

I had never heard such a recitation before! Yet the whole time not one of them even looked up. Only the young novice who had earlier given me directions to the garden permitted himself a secretive smile, as if to say: see, I told you so. Either the old man did this sort of thing so often they were no longer impressed, in which case I thought he deserved at least their respect; or they dismissed his outbursts as no more than part of his madness, in which case they were mistaken. Just because he was crazy did not mean he wasn't smart. The old friar had plenty going on inside his head. And I for one was impressed.

Still, the sooner I could leave this place, the better. I had no taste for monastic life. The food was terrible. The work in the friar's "vegetable patch" had rubbed my hands raw with blisters. And I was all but worn out wrestling with his demons. Interviewing was harder work than I had imagined.

We returned to the weeds. It looked to me like new ones had grown up while we were gone. As we began our work, I realized there was no more order to his garden than there was to his mind. I wondered if the old friar ever actually grew any vegetables in that garden? I never returned to find out.

I knew the routine by now. I took the hoe and pretended to work, while he filled in the holes he had dug that morning. This lasted only several minutes. Then out came the wineskin. This time, after taking some himself, he passed it over to me. I have finally won his approval, I thought, and I gratefully took a long pull of the wine.

I almost choked. My mouth and throat were on fire! I went into a coughing fit that almost did me in. All the while the old fool slapped his thigh and howled with glee. I have had some heady stuff in my day, and I always thought I could drink with the best of them, even those Corsicans in the Ripa who drank the strongest rotgut from Greece, but never in my life did I suffer the likes of anything more vile than that old friar's homemade.

"More?" he asked with mirth still dancing in his eyes.

I would have given anything to be able to down that whole skin, just to wipe the smug look from his face, but I could not, not then, not ever. I shook my head in defeat, still gasping for breath.

"*Cucullus non facit monachum,*" he said with sarcasm. "'The cowl does not make a monk.'"

But he became distracted and his mind wandered away again.

"Padre!" I said in a loud voice, trying to pull him back from wherever he was. "You said this morning that your friend the bishop..."

"Don't know him!"

"...that your friend the bishop wrote you from Rome about Bruno..."

"Don't know him either!"

"...after he left the monastery with the Holy Office on his heels."

"Oh, say...heh, heh...we had some good times together... Marco and me...long time ago, that was. Then he made bishop. A regular big shot. They took away my library, did I tell you that? And that was when...uh...they said I needed a long rest! Well, nobody...where was I?"

"Bruno in Rome."

"Oh! You see, we lost our trend of thought, and uh...?"

"Bruno in Rome," I repeated.

"Oh sure! They arrested him for murder, you see. Then there is another story in that."

"Who was arrested for murder? What murder? Wait a minute, I thought you said the Holy Office..."

"Bruno! I told you! In Rome! Why are you asking me these questions?" He brought his face close to mine. I tried not to breath through my nose. "Judas, how many pieces of silver did you take for this?"

I sucked in air through the corner of my mouth. No backing away now.

"Who did Bruno murder in Rome, Father Anselmi?"

"No, no! He didn't murder anyone! There was a woman. What was her name? Wait! That was the story Marco wrote to me. Oh, that wicked boy! 'Owe no man anything, but to love one another; for he that loveth another hath fulfilled the law' – Romans 13:8. 'Put ye on the Lord Jesus Christ, and make not provision for the flesh, to fulfill the lusts thereof' – Romans 13:14. 'A city that is set on a hill cannot be hid' – Matthew 5:14..." (He was out of control now. Was it the murder or the woman that had set him off?) "'...He that glorieth...'"

He was trapped in his Bible and growing hoarse. I could not allow this to continue or I would lose him and never get him back. He was teetering on the edge.

"Padre! Come on, Padre, don't leave me now! Just a little more. Please try. Who was murdered? What was the woman's name? Try, Padre!"

"Silvia," he croaked. "And her *cognome* was...ohhh! I cannot remember her family name. But I will, I will, I will! He was with her, you know. Oh, very influential. His alibi, you know. It was one of the brothers here, the one who complained about my Giordano...my son...he was like a son to me...is he well?...of course he is, he must be!...they found the body in the Tiber...headquarters assumed...but she stood by him...Silvia...and uh...oh! they let him go, you know...but heresy...flee, Giordano!...heh, heh...her *cognome* was...I *will* remember!...but you see, I must get my garden ready for spring now...'Let him glory in the Lord'...I never finished that one...First Corinthians...but what number verse?...I will remember...let me see now..."

Anselmi had slipped over the edge, stuck somewhere in First Corinthians. His face was contorted in confusion as an avalanche of memories tumbled over each other inside his fevered brain. There was no way to bring him back. I would get no more from him on Bruno. I thanked him and said goodbye. I doubt he even heard me. I left him standing in the middle of his garden muttering about Corinthians and hacking mercilessly at the weeds with his hoe.

As I retraced my steps through the church, out the East Largo and down the hill, my mind reeled with the many pieces of Anselmi's fragmented and disconnected story. The Biagia was nearly empty. Everyone was at home preparing the evening meal.

Suddenly I heard a commotion behind me and the pad of bare feet running down the hill.

"Wait! Wait!"

It looked back to see Anselmi, the rope around his middle undone again and trailing behind as he raced to catch up, one hand holding the hem of his habit so as not to trip, looking even wilder than before.

I waited, the sight of this mad old priest racing hell-bent down the street just to tell me he remembered the chapter and verse from Corinthians was *la goccia che fa traboccare il vaso,* the final touch of irony in my trip to Naples.

But it was not Corinthians.

"Gandini!" he gasped. "Silvia Gandini!"

He stared intently at me for a moment, then raised his hand in blessing.

"'And the God of peace shall bruise Satan under your feet shortly' – Romans 16:20." He wheeled and strode rapidly up the hill, waving his arms toward the heavens.

The canvas my master had handed me was no longer blank. I had begun my portrait of the man who was held by Santa Severina in Castel Sant'Angelo.

Chapter 5

Tempo da cani. Weather fit for dogs! The mail train elected to use the coastal route again for its return to Rome, but this time I selected the more direct way. It meant traveling alone, but I was anxious to get back. Even on Cammello, it would be a day shorter at least, and hopefully drier as well.

The weather did clear. However, when I reached Frosinone I learned that on the preceding day a lone traveler had been robbed and killed by *banditti.* I decided I was not in that big a hurry and looked around for some company. I managed to attach myself to a lumber train making its way to the city from the slopes of Monte Lepini.

The *campagna* supplies Rome with many essentials, meat, grain, olive oil, firewood, and the fine Lepini hardwood used in the construction of churches, palaces, and the better homes of Rome. The *banditti* in the hills north of Frosinone helped themselves to a share of most of these goods — always leaving the traders enough to sell in Rome so they could help themselves to the profits when the traders returned — but hardwood was a commodity for which they had little use, living like nomads in the hills, so they rarely bothered the lumber trains.

It was slow but it was safe. Once past the Corsicans, I was able to proceed ahead on my own.

✠

I was happy to be in Rome again. The trip to Naples had been tiring. A whole week on the road for one day in Naples, and I wasn't even sure how much I had learned. Nor how much of that to believe. The old friar's craziness had pushed credibility to the limit. Still, I had brought back a new lead and I could hardly wait to share it with my master.

When I returned to Penitenziaria House, however, he was gone. I was informed he had left to accompany the pope to Ferrara to visit the ailing Duke Alfonso, thence to Villa Bel Riguardo, where His Holiness intended a week of rest. No word was left for me. Vignanesi had gone with him.

Alfonso was the last of the House of Este, discounting the illegitimates that were scattered around, like the duke of Modena. The master said that when the family died out, the duchy would come under the jurisdiction of the Holy See. Clement was getting itchy to pluck a ripe plum, was my guess, and that meant Bellarmine wouldn't be back for several weeks. By that time I would be gone.

I was disappointed. All the way back I had been looking forward to dropping Silvia Gandini in his lap. Even my master knew that name. She was probably the most unapproachable woman in all of Rome. I had been counting on him for an idea as to how to approach her. Now I was up a tree. By all accounts she had become a complete recluse since the death of Cardinal Farnese eight years before.

The Farnese, you may have heard, are an old, rich, and powerful Roman family. Not so old as the Colonna, Orsini, or Icobacci. Not so rich as the Mattei, Altoniti, or Massimi. And not so powerful as the Medici or Borgia, the Goldi or Strozzi. But Farnese is a name to be reckoned with in Rome. Alessandro Farnese in his time may have been the most powerful cardinal in all Italy.

It has been said that Rome is the capital of gossip. Considering the large number of servants serving in the many palaces and wealthy households of this city, and allowing that most of them have *la lingua sciolta* (loose tongues), it's a wonder there are any secrets at all in Rome. Everybody knows everybody else's business, especially when it is "monkey business."

Silvia Gandini was Cardinal Farnese's mistress and the whole town knew it.

She was not a whore. Rome has its share of whores, God love them all, wolf-whistling from their windows, circulating in the streets and in the *stufe*, the public baths, forever changing their first names and never telling you their last. Whores are a Roman institution that goes all the way back to the Caesars.

Every pope tries to get rid of them. The men of Rome will not allow it. Sanctimonious prudes, some of these popes. Paul IV, for instance. He even had Michelangelo's Sistine nudes clothed with draperies! If that was not insult enough, Pius V actually ordered all the whores out of Rome. It put the city in such a panic that he was forced to rescind the order the following day.

Roman men will put up with a great deal from the church. They will fight the church's wars, pay the church's taxes, even allow the church to tell them how to conduct their private lives, up to a point; but two things you do not want to try with Roman men: you do not want to go rationing their wine and you do not try to get rid of their whores. I think if Pius had not rescinded that order, the entire Roman

Catholic Church could have collapsed. It is often the little things that shape world events.

But Silvia Gandini was not a whore. She was instead a courtesan, in the best tradition of the *corteggiana honesta*. Strictly high class. There have been courtesans more famous than Silvia Gandini — Imperia, who numbered Raphael and Giulio de' Medici (Clement VII) among her admirers; Tullia D'Aragona; Matrema, the poetess; Mantuccia, who caused that great scandal in the Carafa family; Pantha, who became the queen of Roman society — but none was more influential.

They say she was so beautiful even at forty that she intoxicated half the young nobility of Rome with her charms before she finally settled on Farnese. Ambassadors, dukes, princes, cardinals, judges, bankers, famous artists, and rich merchants from around the world, they all flocked to her company. They say that if you were fortunate enough to be invited to the salon of Silvia Gandini, you were as good as made, she had that much influence back in the '70s and the early '80s.

No more though. She was an old woman now and never stirred from her house in the Borgo. The gossipers of Rome had long since forgotten Silvia Gandini.

What was the connection between Silvia Gandini and Bruno? A twenty-eight-year old runaway priest fresh out of a monastery, wanted for heresy and murder, and the most influential courtesan in Rome, old enough to be his mother? It didn't figure. On the other hand, Father Anselmi may have been crazy, but he sure seemed to know what he was talking about. He did not pick Silvia Gandini's name out of the air.

Ecco. There was one way to find out. I had to talk to her. But the how of it was not going to be easy. I couldn't let her know who I was, or who I worked for, or the real reason I wanted to see her. Whatever I told her was going to have to be awfully good. The story was that she saw no one these days.

It was late and I was tired from the road. I would sleep first and think about this problem in the morning. Perhaps something would come to me in the night.

✠

There was a knock on the door, gentle but insistent. It was Thomas, one of the young brothers in the house.

"The father rector asked that I deliver this letter. It came for you early this morning. I have brought you some chicory also. I fear you have already missed the morning meal. The kitchen will serve nothing now until midday."

I had overslept. I grunted my gratitude to Thomas and reached for the steaming brew. I would have preferred coffee but these people did not believe in it. Chicory would have to do. My disposition upon waking was well known in the house. I am not good for much, even with the sun already high, until I have had my first cup of the day. The letter from Bellarmine would have to wait.

But as I finished the chicory and took up the letter from the bed, I saw immediately that it did not bear the master's seal. It was instead an unusual design, the astrological sign of Scorpio in deep red. I broke the seal and opened the letter. The writing was clear and bold, elegant without flourish:

Signore Guidotti,
    I shall be pleased to receive you at my home today at two o'clock.
Via Sindoni, No. 12.
                            Silvia Gandini, with her own hand

I don't mind telling you, I was nervous. For all the gossip about her, Silvia Gandini was still a mystery. I knew nothing about her, save that she had entertained the richest and most powerful men of Rome. True, I knew my way around women — you get to know many different types, growing up in Campo Marzio — but this one was beyond my experience. Her kind and my kind did not socialize. Working for Bellarmine, I had come up in the world, but I was only part way up the hill and she had been all the way to the top. I was not even sure how one addressed a courtesan.

My head was spinning with questions. Amazing that an invitation of only one short sentence could raise so many issues! She knew who I was. She knew where to find me. She knew the very day I had returned from Naples. She must also have known that I worked for Bellarmine.

But how? How did she know so much, cooped up in her house in the Borgo? What else did she know? Did she know I was in Naples? Did she know what Anselmi had told me? Did she know about my mission? Why did she send me the note? What did she want from me?

By the time I reached No. 12 Via Sindoni, I was shaking. It was a modest little white house, almost in the shadow of the papal palace. I grasped the knocker, rapped gently, and waited.

The door opened. There was no one there. The entrance hall was dark and I strained to see into the shadows. The sound of an impatient cough at my feet drew my attention downward. Standing before me, reaching barely to the middle of my thighs, was an old dwarf. He was dressed in livery, his sleeves rolled to the elbows, an apron tied at his waist. He was frowning.

Bewildered, I handed him the note. He glanced at it briefly, snorted, and thrust it back at me. Without a word, he turned and led me through the darkened hall until we reached the doorway to a large drawing room. He pointed imperiously, indicating I should wait inside. Then he padded down the hall in the other direction.

It took me several minutes to adjust to the lack of light in the room, for it, too, was darkened like the hall. It occurred to me that all the drapes in the house were drawn to block out the sun. How curious. As my eyes became adjusted and the room came into focus, I realized it was truly an amazing room, the most richly appointed room I had ever been in. I had not seen its match for taste even in the Palazzo Venezia or the Villa d'Este.

The floor was a soothing gray terrazzo marble, covered with thick oriental carpeting. The furniture and draperies were in the finest plush velvet, in deep rich tones of reds and dark greens. There were paintings on the walls, and Flemish tapestries, and marble and stone statuary were scattered tastefully throughout.

I moved closer to study the paintings. Some of the smaller ones were portraits of recognizable princes and cardinals. The two larger paintings contained scenes of naked wood nymphs, bathing and frolicking in the woods. I spotted two Titians, a Raphael, and a Botticelli among the signatures on the paintings.

One entire wall was devoted to books, shelves and shelves of books, a vast library supplied with romances, history, poetry, theological and philosophical works. Ariosto, Aretino, Ovid, Petrarch, Boccaccio, Cicero, Montaigne, Dante. The classics and the moderns. More books than I had seen in most cardinals' homes. In Latin and the vulgar, in English and French and languages I did not know well enough to know where they were from. Did she read in all these languages? This was no ordinary woman!

There were two slim volumes lying together on the shelf before me. I picked them up. One was Giovanni Boccaccio's *De Claris Mulieribus* (Concerning Famous Women), the other was *The Book of the Courtier* by Baldassare Castiglione. Both were worn, with pieces of cloth sticking out to mark certain pages. I opened the second book to one of the marked pages and strained to read the passage in the dim light:

The Attributes of the Court Lady
and Character of Women in General

The Court Lady as described by the Magnifico is to possess the same virtues as the Courtier and undergo the same training in letters, music, painting, dancing and other graces; also she should avoid affectation and cultivate *sprezzatura*. She is to avoid manly exercises and manners and preserve a feminine sweetness and delicacy. For example, she should not play on drums or trumpets, or take part in tennis or hunting. Above all she should acquire a pleasant affability in entertaining men, being neither too bashful nor too bold in company.

Added in the margin at the end of the passage, in the same bold hand as was in the note I received that morning, was: *And she had better be damned good in bed!* By god, she was an *anima gemella,* a soulmate, this Silvia Gandini, she was one of us!

It really struck me funny, that comment in the margin, and I was chuckling to myself when I became aware of another presence in the room. She was standing just inside the doorway, a hand on the shoulder of the dwarf, observing me.

"I see you find Castiglione as amusing as I do, Signore Guidotti," she said. Her voice was low and husky.

She moved to a love seat and sat with her back to the windows.

"Poco," she said, addressing the dwarf, "please pull the drapes back enough so that our guest need not remain in the dark." Patting the love seat beside her, she added to me, "Come and sit down next to me. I am too old to bite."

The dwarf cracked the draperies, throwing light into the room. I had my first good look at Silvia Gandini. The stories of her beauty were no exaggeration. She had to have been a knockout when she was younger. She still was. Her face could have been chiseled in Carrara marble by Leonardo. She had almost perfect features, a high forehead and cheekbones, straight nose, full and sensuous lips. She had hardly a wrinkle. The line of her chin was one smooth continuous sweep of a painter's brush. Her hair was the color of delicate pink sand, dyed, I suppose, but so subtly as to seem natural, and she wore it pulled back from her face. Her neck was long and slender, her shoulders graceful, her breasts still firm and high, or so I imagined them beneath her gown. I thought she must have been the most strikingly beautiful woman in Rome.

She offered me her hand. I bent low to kiss it and was enveloped in roses.

She smiled, revealing a perfect set of pearl-white teeth (at her age!), and murmured softly, *"Très gallant."*

She was wearing glasses with dark lenses. I could not see her eyes, but I knew the meaning of that smile.

"I don't know what *très gallant* means," I said with a grin, "but if it has anything to do with your being too old to bite, I don't believe a word of it and I would love nothing better than a chance to find out for myself. Then I could die happy."

She threw back her head and laughed.

"Ah, Guidotti, they warned me you were a rogue! But they didn't tell me you were so good looking. It has been a long time since there was some real virility in this house. Too long." She sighed. "Alas, what you behold is simply an illusion, my dear. The results of a cosmetic art intended more to re-create the past than to highlight the present. But then, it is the past you have come to explore, is it not? Don't look so surprised. I still make it my business to be well informed. Will you take some sherry?"

Poco had returned with a tray containing a crystal decanter and two crystal glasses. He poured no more than a finger of the amber fluid into one glass and handed it to her. Mine he filled to the brim.

"Poco allows me a treat today. *'Tutti i nodi vengono al pettine.'* Are you familiar with that proverb? 'All knots come to the comb.' I am paying now for my youth, Pietro — I may call you Pietro? And you shall call me Silvia. But *cosi va il mondo,* eh? As Ovid said: *Casta est quam nemo rogavit.* 'A chaste woman is she whom none has tempted.' He was not speaking of Silvia Gandini, of course. Look around you. Not too bad for a little girl from Campo Marzio, eh? I surprise you again? We are two birds of a feather, my friend. It only takes a good head on your shoulders and a good teacher. Fortunately, I had both."

She sipped her wine.

I drained my glass and poured another. The dwarf had withdrawn. I settled down for a long afternoon. Eight years this lady had not talked to a man.

Chapter 6

febbraio 1597
Via Sindoni No. 12
Roma

I HAVE HAD MANY WOMEN in my lifetime. I say this not to brag, since I see it as a measure of my desire and not my skill. Theirs too, for I believe that women are no less subject to desire. But I do not think I ever really knew any of them, no more than they ever knew me. We satisfied each other's animal lusts, nothing more. There was no love. I never married. At first because I was too busy surviving. Then, as my friends all began to marry, it seemed to me that none of them was very happy in it. They fought with their wives, they complained about supporting so many bambinos. In spite of which they wanted to marry me off to their sisters. The harder they tried, the more I resisted the idea.

After I hooked up with Bellarmine, there was simply no room for a wife. He was married to the church, and I was married to him. Women I only saw in my free time, and there was not much of that working for my master, I can tell you. A couple bottles of vino and a quick roll in bed on a Saturday night was the extent of my intimacy with the opposite sex. More often than not, our conversation was confined to fixing the price.

So much for my great knowledge of women. Until that afternoon with Silvia Gandini, I never understood what I was missing. She drew things out of me I did not even know were there. She made me feel like a man, not just a stallion. As though my mind meant as much as my body. She made me feel...special. And with the most subtle of her courtesan's skills, she led me to think I had the power to make her feel special too.

We conversed about literature, politics, philosophy, subjects I had never discussed with anyone. She seemed actually to be interested in what I thought. No one ever talked to me the way she did, not even my master. It was as though at that particular moment, I was the most important person in her life. I was aware it had been her business to cause men to think that, and that she had been one of the best, and yet — how can I explain? — the measure of her skill was that my knowing altered nothing. In one afternoon that woman not only changed my opinion of myself, she changed my ideas about women forever.

Nor was this a purely mental experience. I was thirty-eight and she was well into her seventies, yet I am not ashamed to say that she aroused a throbbing in my loins beyond description. Without our ever touching. She was so sensual. Her mouth, her body, her smells, her very gestures caressed me in a way no woman ever had. When I told her as much, she seemed pleased to know that she still had such effect on a man.

"I really should have been a Medici," she mused. "My kind are out of fashion these days. My mother was a courtesan, and hers before her. Alas, motherhood was not one of the skills I acquired from them, or there would be another to take this house over when I am gone. I fear I have broken the chain.

> See Time, that flies, and spreads his hasty wings!
> See Life, how swift it runs the race of years,
> And on its weary shoulders death appears.

Do you like Petrarch, Pietro? He is one of my favorites."

She drained her glass, placed it back on the tray, and dabbed at her lips with a lace handkerchief which she tucked back into her sleeve. We had been talking for two hours, and the name of Bruno had yet to be mentioned. I worried that she would soon be tired and unable to continue, yet I was unsure how to broach the subject.

"I suppose now would be a good time to talk about Giordano Bruno," she said nonchalantly.

Taken by surprise, I began with an awkward explanation of my mission, but she smiled gently and told me that wasn't necessary.

"You may recall that it was I who sent for you," she said. "Remember, I am well informed. I know of the man in Sant'Angelo. There is nothing I can do for him myself. My cardinal is gone. I have little influence among this new breed. Pope Clement has decreed that it will go hard for heretics, and he seems anxious to make the point. He may need a scapegoat.

"I believe this man to be harmless. Nevertheless, he appears to have led an irresponsible life and is now suffering the consequences. No doubt he repents; they all do. Men always seem sorry after the fact, never during. Still, I would help him if I could. My understanding is that your master may be destined for a position of some importance within the church. My cardinal always thought highly of Monsignore Bellarmine. He said he was one of the few clerics with a head on his shoulders and a rare sense of perspective, though I myself never look for purity of motive and suspect that your master has his own needs for power.

"I sent for you because it may be of help to your master when he sits on the tribunal... (She *was* well informed!)... to understand something of Giordano Bruno in his younger days. If that is so, then I shall have been of some small service to them both in what I am about to relate.

"I am told this prisoner is *pieno di sè*, full of himself, and will listen to no one. When I knew him, which was only briefly in February of 1576, he was all ears, soaking up information like a sponge. He was young and charming and terribly naive. I will tell you what he was like then, before he went off to tell the rest of the world how it should be run. The two weeks we spent together in this house, we were lovers. He was as quick to learn with his body as he was with his mind. He was in all respects exceptional."

This, then, is the story Silvia Gandini told me, exactly as I remember it. We took all afternoon and well into the evening. She held nothing back in her answers to my questions. She was a bold and ambitious woman who had shaped a rich and fulfilling life by dint of her own strong will, and she did not mince words.

At times I found myself unreasonably jealous of Bruno for those two weeks he spent with her. I had no difficulty imagining what it must have been like. Even now, I find myself wishing I had been the one to know her that way, though I consider myself lucky to have known her even for that one afternoon in her house.

Before I left Rome for France and England, I sent her a note with one of the brothers, promising that I would call upon her on my return. But I never did see Silvia Gandini again. She died that August during an outbreak of typhoid.

She was a hell of a woman.

✠

Q: How did you get from Campo Marzio to Via Sindoni?
A: It was more a question of making it back. My grandmother came from Sardinia. She was the mistress of a Genoese banker stationed in Rome. I know little about her except that my mother was born from that union. When the banker was posted back to Genoa, he deserted them both. My mother, too, became the mistress of a Genoese banker. The women of my family were stuck in a rut, you might say, although this one proved more *simpatico* than my grandfather.

My mother's lover was a Gandini, cousin to the Altoniti family and a partner in their bank. In those days the Banco Altoniti handled much of the Vatican's business, and Gandini was in charge. Signore Gandini—my father—was good to my mother and me. He set us up in a house in the Ponte, provided me with tutors, and even sent me to school in Lyons for two years. Before he died, he acknowledged me as his own daughter and permitted me to take his name. Unfortunately, he left my mother nothing, and the Altoniti family turned their backs on us. We were forced to take up residence in Campo Marzio.

What money my mother had set aside for this eventuality—each of us learns from our mother before us, you see, so, unlike her mother, my mother at least put something aside — she used to complete my education and to groom me for independence. What I learned about history, languages, and the arts, I learned from tutors. But what I learned about men, I learned from my mother. She was an excellent teacher. *Rien ne réussit comme le succès,* as the French say, "Nothing succeeds like success."

My mother worked to keep up appearances and to maintain her contacts in important circles, especially among those from the Vatican who had frequented her soirées at the house in Ponte, prelates, ambassadors, bankers. She found me many lovers, but none completely suited her until Cardinal Farnese. Believe it or not, though I was already forty, it was my mother who negotiated the contract.

She drove a hard bargain. A wonder she did not frighten the poor cardinal away! But he was smitten with me and acceded to all her demands, including this house in my own name. Once established here, with a legally binding contract between the cardinal and me, my mother decided her work was done. She died one month after we moved in.

Q: When did you meet Giordano Bruno?

A: In early February 1576. My arrangement with Cardinal Farnese was a unique one. I had a great measure of independence. In part that was due to my mother's talent as a negotiator, but it was also due to Cardinal Farnese's concern about appearances. I was a courtesan. Alessandro was a prince of the church. There is no way to keep such an arrangement a secret, but there is at least a protocol for keeping it private. We never appeared together in public, for example, even though we attended many of the same social functions. Another thing, his thrice-weekly visits were according to an explicit schedule, from which he never deviated without notice. On these visits, he was lord of the house and only his closest friends were entertained. There were three weeks every August and one week every March during which we vacationed quietly at Villa Farnese near Tivoli. The rest of the time I was free to entertain whenever and whomever I pleased.

Q: But what had this arrangement to do with meeting Bruno?

A: Patience, my young friend, I am coming to that. I promised you the story of those two weeks and you shall have it. Alessandro was a dear friend and a marvelous companion for many years. We had much in common. We enjoyed each other's company; we understood each other's strengths and weaknesses. Our aesthetic appetites were similar, good food, fine wines, art and literature, we even shared similar interests in politics. His sexual appetite was more, shall we say, "quiescent" than mine, however. On the subject of that difference he was forbearing, allowing me unusual latitude. It was not uncommon for me, therefore, to have periodic lovers — "dalliances," he called them — an activity which I made certain neither intruded upon nor impeded our relationship. I believe Alessandro actually enjoyed feeling jealous on these occasions. It improved his performance in bed.

Q: Silvia, at this rate we will never get to Bruno!

A: Very well, it was during one of those dry spells when I was feeling the urge for a lover that I came upon young Bruno. He was, I believe, twenty-eight, and I would have been...let me see...fifty-four. I was on my way by carriage to a party at the Palazzo Venezia. That particular Venetian ambassador — was it Morosini? no, he went to France about then...De Guzmán? no, he was the Spaniard...well, it does not matter — that particular Venetian ambassador was a lavish entertainer. Some of them are, you know. He threw fabulous parties, and all of Rome came to them. On the way to the palace, we passed a priest sitting on the railing on the far side of Ponte Sant' Angelo. He looked so forlorn, so desperate, I feared he might be contemplating ending it all in the Tiber.

I instructed my driver to stop and entered into a conversation with this priest. He told me that his name was Giordano Bruno and that he was in great trouble that was none of his own making. I said: Hop in and come with me to a party. We'll cheer you up and I guarantee you will forget your troubles. I had more than a bit of sherry already, I suppose. In those days Poco would never — he is a mute, you understand, a gift from my cardinal, who believed in silent servants — in those days Poco would never have dreamed of rationing my sherry. And I was feeling quite naughty with this young priest. To bring him uninvited to the ambassador's party was certain to start half the tongues in Rome wagging. I could not wait to see Alessandro's reaction! Occasional "dalliances" in the privacy of my bed were one thing, but it would be quite another for the courtesan of the most powerful cardinal in Rome to attend one of the biggest parties of the social season with a wayward priest as her escort. Alessandro would have a fit! Oh, I was feeling naughty indeed!

Q: How did Bruno react to all of this?

A: He was shy at first. Never left my side. He had never been to a party before, much less one so sumptuous. The sight of so many important prelates frightened the poor dear half to death. Of course, I had no inkling yet of his problem or I might have thought twice before exposing him in this fashion, although there was no real risk since he was unknown. But he caught on very quickly to the game I was playing. He drank some wine, he lied through his teeth when questioned by anyone, and he really began to enjoy himself.

I took him home with me afterward. He stayed for two weeks. On the first night, I let him sleep alone. I did not want to frighten him out of his wits altogether. He had had too much wine and probably would not have been up to it anyway.

Q: What about the cardinal? Didn't Bruno's presence in the house "intrude and impede"?

A: It was the only time I ever lied to Alessandro about a lover. I kept Giordano out of sight during the cardinal's visits. I was having such a good time! It was like having a new toy. Oh! I've made a pun! Besides, Giordano really was in trouble, and he needed a place to hide until he could decide what to do. I could not very well turn him out, now could I?

Q: You have mentioned that you were lovers for two weeks, but not on the first night. When?

A: I am enjoying telling you this story after so many years. I have never told anyone the details. Poco knows, but of course that does not count. I am so happy you turned out not to be too stuffy to listen to an old woman tell her little sex stories, Pietro. Were I younger, I might even demonstrate. As it is, all nature permits me now is a swallow or two of sherry and the memory of greener pastures. *"Adieu les regards gracieux / Messangers des coeurs soucieux / Adieu les profondes pensées!"* I apologize for this darkness in my house, dear. What remains of my eyesight has become overly sensitive to the light of day. An irony of my "profession," do you suppose?

Are you familiar with the story of Nanna, the old prostitute in Aretino's *Dialoghi?* My mother introduced me to it when I was quite young. In the story, Nanna relates to young Pippa, a new prostitute, the things she must learn: that one man wants boiled meat and the other wants roast; that men have all discovered the aperture behind, the legs on the shoulders, the Giametta style, the crane, the tortoise, the church on the belfry, the stirrup, the grazing sheep, and other postures, as she says, more far-fetched and extravagant than a play-actor's prancings. Well, I learned, as Pippa did from Nanna, that was only the beginning.

I enjoy Aretino, do you? More than Ovid. Poor Ovid, his life was not nearly so lascivious as his pen! Did you know that Aretino wrote a manual for sex, and that Giulio Romano illustrated it? It is very naughty. I have a copy. Would you care to see it?

Q: Another time perhaps. We were talking about you and Bruno...?

A: You are tenacious, Pietro! Well, I used Nanna's descriptions to Pippa, and Aretino's sex manual, for Giordano's education. He was very inexperienced, but I found him a quick learner. On the second day, I asked him whether he had ever had a woman, and he lied to me. He said yes, many. When I pressed him to be truthful with me because I would know soon enough for myself, he admitted the truth. Twice. Once at sixteen with a farm girl in Nola, and once with a priest at the monastery. Some of these old priests are like the men in prison. They find it impossible to resist the innocence of young boys, and of course risk their very lives with the Holy Office if they are found out.

Was that all?, I asked him, just the two? That was all. Twice in twenty-eight years! Well, I said, you are about to be introduced to the wonderful world of frequency, and I shall be your guide. Then I led him to my bed. That was the second day.

He was nervous about everything, which was understandable, but mostly he was nervous about the size of his sword. He was small and slender, with a sword to match; and he was uncertain of its worthiness. I explained to him: it is not the size of a sword in a fight that counts, but the size of the fight in the sword. And the skill of the swordsman.

He was reassured. Though his sword had only twice before been unsheathed, he was over his reticence in no time. Within a day or so, he was a confident and gratifying lover. Before long, in fact, the impetus for our bedtime romps shifted, became more his then mine, several times a day at least. I confess I wore out before he did.

Q: So he had stamina in bed. In other ways too?

A: Oh, yes. He slept very little. He kept me going the whole time. Though he was very well read, there was much in my library that was not in that of the monastery, as you might imagine. The romances were of no interest to him. Perhaps because he had his own going at the time. He had already read whatever I had in the way of philosophy and theology; knew most of it verbatim and could easily quote long passages from memory. But he was interested in the poetry, as well as much of the history. I never met a man who could read so quickly and retain so much. He had a system for doing that. He tried to teach it to me, but I could never understand why anyone would want to go to such inordinate lengths to memorize something, when all one had to do was pick it off the shelf.

He discussed scientific and philosophical issues. Not so much discussed as preached. He was extremely opinionated. But when it came to politics, which was one of my loves, he had no interest whatsoever. Interrelationships between nations, dealings between the pope and the king of Spain, Henri of France, and the English queen, of these he wanted no part. I found him poorly informed on even the most basic issues; the subtleties escaped him completely.

Certain subjects rang instant alarms. Aristotle rang the biggest. Mention the name of Aristotle, and he would be off for hours. I confess I was quickly bored by these diatribes, which seemed only to cause him to agitate himself even more. But then he would suddenly break off in mid-sentence and drag me to bed for another "lesson." He never tired of new ways.

He was intense. I have never known a man that intense. Not that he disliked humor, just that he seemed not to have the time for it. A humorous remark would pass him right by. He would simply continue what he was saying as if you had never said a word. I could never tell if he was showing me all of his inner self, or none of it.

> Alas! this heart by me was little known
> In those first days when Love its depths explored.

Q: What did Bruno tell you about why the Sant'Offizio wanted him?

A: Nothing, only that he had learned at the Dominican headquarters in Rome that proceedings were being drawn against him for heresy. He said he was on some counts falsely accused and on others misunderstood. He had written an allegory while at the monastery — titled "Noah's Ark," I believe — in which he had unintentionally insulted several of the brothers. These had accused him of scorning devotion. That was all he told me. He rarely spoke of his own life.

Q: Did you not think that strange?

A: Not especially. I told him nothing about mine either. Lovers have no pasts, no futures. Only the present is for lovers.

Q: What about his dreams, his goals? Did he discuss them?

A: No. I think he was confused about them. He had never intended to be a priest in the first place. Now that he was, he was unsure how to be one. Nor was he certain he wanted to know. Yet, he did not seem to know what he would do if he were not a priest.

Q: What of this charge against him for murder, what do you know about that?

A: So you know about that too? You know more than I thought about my little Giordano. Do you know what my pet name for him was in bed? "La Cresta." The rooster's comb. He was a cocky one. Still, he was frightened of these charges, and who could blame him? The Holy Office wanted him for heresy, the secular authorities wanted him for murder, and his order wanted him for running away.

He had courage though. He went one morning to his headquarters, which I thought foolhardy. He wanted to check with someone he knew in order to find out the status of the proceedings against him at the Holy Office. He said he had to find out how much time he had left before he would have to flee Rome. No sooner was he inside the building when he was spotted and arrested. He thought they were agents of the Holy Office, but he discovered they were from the secular authorities. He was under arrest for murder. One of the brothers who had testified against him in the hearings had been found floating in the Tiber with his throat cut. Giordano was the prime suspect.

I learned all of this when I went to see him. He was being held in Nona Tower. Poor Giordano! No "La Cresta" now. Just a frightened little priest waiting to hang.

Q: What did you do?

A: What *could* I do? I appealed to my cardinal to intercede. Naturally, in order to prove that he could not have committed the crime, I had to admit that Giordano had been with me for the last two weeks, day and night. Alessandro was furious! But he could not afford to have that story leak out, or he would be the laughing stock of his friends. We struck a bargain: he would intercede as I requested, but for my part I must never see Giordano again. Moreover, I had to promise that henceforth my "dalliances" must never be for more than one night, and *never* when he was in the house.

Q: A stiff price.

A: (laughing) You know what Ovid says in *The Art of Love?* "A promise hurts you not; then promise much. It makes those that are not rich seem to be such." I promised my cardinal on my mother's grave that I would never do that again. I was certain she would understand. Between you and me, I doubt Alessandro believed it — he knew me too well, my cardinal — but he pretended to, because he was a practical man.

It was a delicate business for him, getting Giordano released when at the same time there were proceedings being prepared by the Holy Office. He could not afford for it to be known that he was in any way involved with Giordano's release. Even a powerful cardinal must be wary of the Holy Office. But he had his ways. Probably he had more on the magistrate who signed the release than the magistrate would have on him because of it. In politics, it is not so much power that shapes events as the balance of power. And that was a game at which Cardinal Farnese was exceptionally skilled.

Q: Is there anything else you can tell me about Bruno?

A: No. Those two weeks were a time in my life unconnected with any other. I no longer recall the minor details. He was a small man with a large ambition. Serious, somber even, but with a fire burning in him that could not be quenched. I think I came into his life at the beginning. You will discover more from others who knew him after he left Rome.

Q: Do you have any idea who these others were or where he went next?

A: None. We often discussed what he would do when he left Rome. Work his way north teaching, he supposed, if there would be any money in it, and writing. But it was only the vaguest of plans.

Q: And you did not see him again after that visit in prison?

A: No, never.

Q: So, what impressions were you left with, after those two weeks?

A: The same as with any other man. I hope that does not disillusion you. No doubt you still believe in such a thing as "love." To a woman, especially to a courtesan, love is a luxury she cannot afford. It is far more important to know what it takes to control a man. My mother used to say that a courtesan does not gain control of a man by being beautiful or amiable or sweet or intelligent or tender, though all of these are at times required. A woman controls a man by redeeming him. In those two weeks, I redeemed Giordano Bruno. I prepared him for the world.

Chapter 7

I FEAR MY LIMITATIONS. Bridging the past to the future carries with it a great responsibility. It troubles me that what I write, sitting alone in this room at the novitiate, will make me accomplice to your conclusions though we are strangers and shall never meet. Will we have sufficient in common to overlook our differences? Will you judge what I tell you, and not the telling? Such agonies plague me. I am shamed by my need to express them. But the way ahead is long and I must go on. As with Bruno himself, Fate rules me now.

I took a day or two to sort out what I had learned. Ripe fruit shrivels in storage; it dries with age and loses much of its juice. If you could judge a man's character by listening to his friends and his enemies, the rantings of a mad friar and the delightful though hazy recollections of a long-retired courtesan might still seem too far removed from the living Bruno to serve as reliable information. I needed fresher fruit.

Some traits did emerge. That he had a knack for getting into trouble, for getting out of it as well, each unintentionally, that is, less by his own doing than by that of others. That he was bold, or naive, or else a fool, possibly all three, but that he was not stupid. That he learned quickly. That at least one of his teachers was remarkable. (Silvia was attracted to Bruno. I was attracted to Silvia. Was there a common thread in this triangle, between Bruno and me?) And that he appeared to have a distinctly unconventional originality.

Something else gnawed at me. I drew a crude map using the list of places my master had prepared for me from Bruno's testimony in Venice:

Napoli, Roma, Siena, Lucca, Noli on the Mediterranean, Savona, Torino, Venezia, Padova, Brescia, Bergamo, Milano, Torino again, Chambery, Geneva, Lyon, Avignon, Montpellier, Toulouse, Paris, London, Oxford, London again, Paris again, Mainz, Wiesbaden, Marburg an der Lahn, Wittenberg, Prague, Frankfurt am Main, and Venezia again for the last time.

I was no cartographer and most of these cities were unknown to me. I had to look up their locations in the library of Penitenziaria House, but when I then connected them, the line spanned most of Europe. In the sixteen years between his flight from Rome and his arrest in Venice, Bruno had been almost constantly on the move.

No man travels like that for pleasure. It is more natural to remain in one place, to grow roots, make friends, raise a family, or at the very least to grow old and die and be buried in familiar ground. Gypsies travel like that. Soldiers, traders, pilgrims, diplomats, and emissaries also, when the occasion demands. A man might travel on holidays, visit somewhere different, and then return home. Or he might serve the church, as I did with Bellarmine, and travel on occasional missions like this one. But none of these explanations fit Bruno's wanderings.

No, something has to drive a man to do that much moving around between countries, always the stranger, always the foreigner, always alone. Something inside him. Some torturous yearning that gives him no peace.

Bruno was a driven man. If I could find out what it was that drove him, then I might know him.

✠

I needed another animal to carry the baggage for my journey. The rector's suggestion was that I purchase a mule. As he was knowledgeable regarding such, I asked if he would make the selection, hinting that my master would be grateful for any assistance he might give me. Such hints had gained new currency of late. It was no secret the master was one of the pope's favorites and would soon receive the purple. The rector was not above playing a little politics. Jesuits claim not to be political, though I notice their hands always seem to be in it.

The rector's selection was a sturdy young female mule of mild disposition. I named her "Cavallita," a joke intended on Cammello, to call him a camel and her a horse. I soon discovered the greater insult was to the mule. The mule was smarter, stronger, and more surefooted. Many a time, especially crossing the Alps, I rode her and let Cammello carry the baggage. If it was a question of losing the baggage or me in a fall, the baggage was less breakable. If Silvia Gandini had changed my opinions about women, Cavallita changed my feelings about mules. I recall both with equal fondness.

I departed Rome through the Porta del Popolo, passing the statue of St. John on Ponte Milvio. I would have to cross many another bridge before I would see this one again, so I was not above a silent prayer to the patron saint of bridges for his blessing. With feelings of great excitement, I set out along Via Flamina, whistling with such gusto that people laughed and waved to me as though I were a minstrel.

The bridge was the terminus for the mail coaches, and also the arrival point for travelers from the north. Thus, the road at this point was much congested and the resulting clamor and confusion added to my excitement as I passed. Traffic heading away from Rome, however, was light, and soon I had the road to myself. The animals and I settled down to a quiet, steady pace.

It was that way throughout much of the journey, congestion near the cities, solitude otherwise, interspersed with chance meetings with fellow travelers that became, once each assured himself that the other was not a *ladrone* bent upon relieving him of his purse and slitting his throat, an occasion for immediate celebration, during which there would be an exchange of news and a sharing of wine, cheese, and the latest jokes from along the road.

Most travelers journeyed with companions or servants; few traveled alone. Because of the danger and the loneliness. I was unconcerned about the first. If you can survive the Corsicans of the *campagna,* the highwaymen of Europe hold little fear. It was the second that took some getting used to, the loneliness. I had seldom been alone in my life. As a youth, I always sought out company, of which there was no shortage in crowded Campo Marzio. Later, the church offered me the same security of numbers, although there someone was always watching you and you sometimes wished you could be alone.

Eventually, I learned to enjoy my time alone on the road. I had my animals for company. We talked to each other, each in our own way. And I appreciated the quiet. Still, I was always happy to see another person.

I had many interesting experiences on the road, and I heard quite a few fascinating tales during those brief encounters with passing travelers. Strangers are so certain they will never meet again that they will often let down their guard completely, tell you things they would never tell to someone they know. Some of those stories you would not believe! But of course this is not the time for digression.

✛

My time was limited. I had to decide where to go and where not to go. The trip to Paris with my master and Cardinal Cajetan had taught me the relationship between distance and time, and how the unexpected can affect them both. It took us two and a half months to make the return trip to Rome in the fall of 1590. By subtracting the excessive delays along the way, plus that week the master was down with the dysentery, and then allowing for enough time to gather information while I was there, I was able to calculate that it would still take me the better part of three months just to make a round trip to Paris. There were also London and Venice to think about. These three cities contained most of the names on my list. Add another month to get to London and Venice, a month or two to locate the people I needed to talk to, allow maybe a month for delays of one kind or another, hold a month or two in reserve to be allocated when I knew more about what I was doing. That would take pretty close to the end of the year, all the time the master had allowed me.

I decided to skip the other Italian cities, saving only Padua and Venice on the way back. I could decide about Saxony and Bohemia later. Geneva first, through Siena, Lucca, and Torino, then cross the Alps at Monte Cenis. My plan was as crude as my map, but as both were flexible, I would fill in the blanks as I went along.

Chapter 8

marzo 1597
Rue du Puits-St. Pierre No. 6
Geneva

I HAD BEEN WATCHING this man for some time. He stood behind the counter, making entries in a thick ledger. I was almost certain he was the right one, but there were others near him. I wanted him to be alone when I gave him the password, just in case. If he was who I thought he was, he would be Nicco Baroniti, *locandiere* of the Albergo Milano in which I was now taking my dinner, and, according to my master's list, a Jesuit agent.

The building was old, several hundred years old at least, and no doubt it had seen prouder usage in its past. With any luck it might again in its future, but at the present time it was undoubtedly the most dilapidated inn in all Geneva. Still, need exceeding want, and want exceeding finances, I had little choice but to take a dinner here of coffee, bread, and cheese. The coffee was at least hot, the bread was fair, but the cheese was a disgrace to the goat that had lactated the milk from which it was made. Despite this unappetizing fare, I concentrated on attracting the man's attention with deliberate, and, I should have thought, obvious looks, doing my best thereby to draw him to my table.

I could see he was annoyed by this. He began to make mistakes in his ledger, scratching them out and starting anew, pretending to be unaware of my interest in him. Finally he threw the pen down in disgust, closed the ledger, and approached me.

He was a thin, balding man with round spectacles, pale and sickly looking, I thought, with rounded shoulders, a bowed head, and down-cast eyes that gave the impression he had lost so many battles in his life that he might never raise them again to look someone in the face. He certainly did not look like much of an agent to me.

"*Que voulez-vous?*" he asked hesitantly.

"Nicco Baroniti?"

"*Pourquoi?*"

"Are you Nicco Baroniti, *locandiere* of this excuse for an inn?"

"*Oui*... uh...*si*, *Signore*. How may I serve you?"

He responded now in Italian. He seemed exceedingly nervous.

"'My helmet is Salvation.'" I had repeated the first half of the password from Ephesians.

His eyes darted to mine for an instant.

"Dio!" he whispered, glancing furtively around the room. "Please, not so loud, Signore. Even the walls have ears." Then he lowered his voice still further, to a little croaking squeak, and recited the second half of the password from Ignatius of Loyola's favorite passage: "'My sword is the word of God.'"

"Good. I need your help, Baroniti," I said.

"Not now, please. Too many people here. Come back at closing. *A dix heures,* at ten o'clock."

"Okay. Don't be so damned nervous, Baroniti," I said with a grin, getting up from the table and ready to leave. "Believe me, nobody's paying any attention to us."

He followed me to the door.

"But Signore," he whined, wringing his hands, "you have not paid your bill!"

"Just charge it to expenses, eh Baroniti? I'm sure our mutual friends can afford it," I flung over my shoulder with a laugh and walked out.

Why should I pay his bill when he was going to be giving me money soon anyway? Besides, he should pay me for eating that miserable goat cheese! Next time, I would order meat, the best in the house. After all, I was the one taking all the risk, wasn't I?

I walked along the Grand Rue in a foul mood. Geneva was an unfriendly town, austere, unsmiling, too neat and orderly for my taste. All the houses were in straight lines, looking alike and colorless. Just like the people. It was as though the snow of the Alps had melted and seeped into their veins to replace their blood.

No one looked at me as I passed. They saw me all right, the people of Geneva miss nothing, yet not once did I catch them at it, not once did our eyes ever meet. In Rome you look somebody right in the eye; you don't glance sideways like a thief. And when you talk, you use everything you have, not just your mouth. That is why God gave you hands. I never trust anybody who keeps his hands in his pockets when he talks.

If this was what Calvinism was like, I was glad to be a Catholic. There was nothing to do in Geneva. No way to have fun. At least in Rome you could sin. In Geneva all you could do was pray!

I walked down to the lake and my mood changed. If Geneva was dead and gray, the lake and the mountains were alive with color, even in the wintertime. The lake was an immensity of aquamarine, a deep blue-green that complemented the light blue sky, with images of white puff clouds skimming across the rippled surface, rimmed by stately mountains. In the distance I could see Mont Blanc, cold and severe, rising majestically above the other snow-covered peaks of the Alps.

Lower down the slopes, patches of yellow-green alpine meadows were beginning to show in the pre-spring thaw. I could imagine those meadows in another few weeks, ablaze with fields of flowers. It seemed such a paradox that God should have created such natural color, and that Calvin could have converted it all to gray in His name.

I was thankful the weather had turned warm so unseasonably early. Crossing the Alps had been uneventful but terribly cold. In Siena, Lucca, and Savona, I had been unable to turn up a single trace of Bruno.

In Noli, however, about eight miles down the coast from Savona, I did succeed in locating an old fisherman who recalled a small, dark priest with a little beard and wearing a monastic habit. The reason he remembered the priest, he said, was because the priest had confided to the elders that he came from a village with a name similar to that of their town...Nola. This priest had remained in Noli for several months, earning his money teaching men of the village about the stars in the heavens by which they might navigate their boats at night. But their own priest had warned that this was magic, and so the stranger had moved on. That was all he could remember, not having spoken to the priest himself.

I continued to Torino, a small city on the Po where many people speak in the French tongue. I myself do not speak French, although there were a few phrases I remembered from that *spiacevole* stay in Paris during the siege, the most repeated phrase being *j'ai faim,* meaning I am hungry. I hope never to be that *faim* again as I was during the siege.

Where the words in French were similar to ours, I could sometimes understand what was being said. I could even make myself understood at simple things. But when the French spoke too rapidly, which was almost always except when they were drunk, or when they used expressions that only Frenchmen are meant to know, then I was lost. The master had been even more helpless with the language, which made me feel better, that what little I knew, he knew even less. What helped more than anything was that the French speak with their hands the way we do. When all else fails, the hands convey what the tongues cannot.

From Torino I headed for the Monte Cenis Pass. It was bitter cold, and there was much snow on the ground. Thankfully, the steep and narrow road was well packed and not dangerous. The worst spots were protected from avalanche by stout barricades. There was a steady stream of travelers on the Strada Romana, as it is called, between Susa and Lauslebourg in both directions. Many rode in the *chaise à porteur*, carried by four *maroni*, sturdy fellows, they were, and led by the guides of Lauslebourg who have earned their living guiding important personages across these mountains for generations. As for me, Cavallita did just fine, and at far less expense, while good old Cammello brought up the rear with my baggage.

It turned out to be a considerable saving to own my own animals. The *scuderi* at the posts along the way are infamous robbers, charging two and three times what you would expect to pay for the rental of horses from post to post. That was not the only gouging on this road. The keepers of the inns placed along the way are hard pressed for guests out of season, summer being the only time they are full-up with pilgrims and vacationers, and they are fiercely competitive with each other. So they send out their servants to drum up business on the road. These servants are empowered to grant many favors, from reducing rates to even more extravagant inducements. Carry your baggage to the inn, Sir! Free guide, Sir! Free meals, Sir! Free women, Sir! They would promise the moon if it would entice an unwary traveler.

Ah, but once you have registered in their inn and paid the advance, the tune changes. Extra for blankets. Extra for firewood. Extra for food and wine. (It was only the bread that was free!) And if you fell for that offer of free women, well, the woman is free, true enough, but if you desire her services, the charge will be five *giullii*. A woman or a horse, the price is the same: five *giullii*, post to post. Anywhere else, the price is two for either. On the other hand, if you buy the woman's services, you may save on blankets and firewood, as the women are usually fat enough to keep you warm without them.

The road over the Alps is neither difficult nor dangerous, only steep and slow going. The way it has been constructed, there are no precipices as one might imagine there would be, and the *banditti*, clever fellows, all head south for the winter, leaving the road safe for those who would brave the cold.

Once into Savoy, the food, the wine, the service, the weather, and the women, all improve. I spent a delightful two days with a young widow in Chambery — at no expense to the church, I hasten to add, as men were in extremely short supply in Chambery — and then proceeded north to Geneva, where the fun stops at the city gates. I did not see another woman's bed until Paris.

✠

I returned to Albergo Milano at the hour I had been instructed. The place was dark. I entered, closing the door behind me. I could not see a thing.

"Bolt the door."

It was a command, not a request. I did as I was told.

A match was struck. I was blinded momentarily by the light, as the hand holding the match reached to light a candle on the table where I had eaten dinner earlier. I could make out the figure of a man at the table, but could not see his face.

"Come here and sit down."

There was something familiar about the low, commanding voice, but I could not place it. As I crossed the room and sat down, the man leaned toward the light of the candle. It was the *locandiere*. But the spectacles were gone, the head was erect, and the eyes bore into mine like two hot pokers.

"Now you listen to me, you dumb Roman sonofabitch, and you listen good," he hissed. "The next time you walk out of my place without paying the bill and tell me for everyone to hear that I should put it down for expenses, I am going to personally slit your throat in your sleep. I have a year more to do in this pisshole before I get rotated back to Milan, and no stupid overgrown Roman turd is going to spoil my operation in the meantime, you get it?"

"Wait a minute, I don't..."

"Don't interrupt me when I'm talking! That was an asshole stunt you pulled in here today. I don't intend to get myself killed for an amateur, you hear me? I don't care who you are. This town has more spies than virgins. Savoy, Henri, the Consistory... what do you think an agent for the Consistory is going to suppose, for instance, when he hears somebody make a dumb crack like that to me? Good Christ, man, they're dumb but they're not stupid! Do you have any idea what it's been like living in this Calvinist hellhole without whores, without wine, without dancing, where the only singing is in church and the only gambling is whether you go to heaven with or without a rope around your neck? I've done my time! Another year and I'm home free, wine, women, and decent olive oil, and if you so much as look at me cross-eyed in public again, so help me, I don't care how big you are, I don't care if you are the pope himself, I will skin you alive and hang you out to dry! Now that we have that straight, tell me what you need."

It takes a lot to tie my tongue in knots the way Nicco Baroniti did that night. The transformation from a mild, nervous, bespectacled, skinny guy who was afraid of his own shadow, to this hissing viper, whose sting, I was certain, was as lethal as his speech, took me completely by surprise. I had much to learn about the spy business.

I attempted to apologize. He was unmoved. I needed him on my side, so I did my best to make friends. That was another mistake. Baroniti was a professional. Friendship was not part of his game. This man was as hard as iron and as cold as ice, but he had his orders and his orders were to help anyone whose helmet was Salvation. He did not have to like me, but he did have to help me. When I understood that was when we started to communicate. It wasn't easy.

"I have been sent by..."

"I don't want to know," he said in a bored tone.

"My mission is to..."

"I don't want to know," he said again.

"All right, my name is...," I tried a third time. He interrupted a third time.

"I don't want to know."

"What the hell *do* you want to know?" I asked, exasperated.

"As little as possible. Listen, you mother's son, the less I know about you, the better it will be for both of us. Understand? I already asked you what you need. I don't get paid to ask that question twice. Christ, why do they always send me amateurs!"

"Money. I need money."

"Why didn't you say so? Done. What else?"

"Information. There are two people I have to see. I have to talk to them about...someone. Someone they are supposed to have known back in '79. I cannot let them know who I am or the real reason I am inquiring about this man."

"The names of the two people?"

"The marchese di Vico is one. Professor Antoine de la Faye is the other."

"And the name of the person they are supposed to have known?"

"Giordano Bruno."

He showed no sign of recognition. I doubt he would have had I mentioned his mother's name. His eyes never left me, his expression never changed.

"Who is...?"

"A heretic priest who wrote books," I answered simply. I was learning.

He thought for a moment.

"Galeazzo Caracciolo, who was the marchese di Vico, died eleven years ago. The marchese's majordomo and secretary comes here often. He is a third cousin of mine, twice removed, but I don't trust the son-ofabitch, so we'll have to give you a cover story he can believe. Your name will be...Luigi. Luigi Massanni from...where is this Bruno from?"

"Nola, near Napoli."

"Luigi Massanni, a tax collector from Naples. Don't worry, my fat cousin has never been near Naples. You tell him this Bruno is one of a number of Neapolitans who are behind in their taxes. They headed this direction on their way to France, and you are hot on their trail. He'll believe you. He's not too smart, my cousin, very gullible; but he pays his taxes and he obeys the laws. With his fingers crossed and his hand out, naturally. If he knew your man, he will talk to you. He will figure there is something in it for him, so dangle something, a commission or something. I will get him here for lunch tomorrow and introduce you as a guest at the inn. You take it from there."

"What about the other man, the professor? Is he dead also?"

"Would that he were. No, he is alive, but meeting with him will be more difficult to arrange. He is a good friend of Theodore Beza, who is Calvin's successor and rector of the university. These people are poison. De la Faye is a very dangerous man. Probably you will get nothing from him but trouble, but if you must see him, there is a secretary at the university who owes me a few favors. I can get him to arrange an appointment for you. You will have to use a different story for de la Faye."

He thought for a moment.

"You represent a printer in Rome who wishes to reprint one of Bruno's books. Flatter de la Faye into thinking you might also convince your printer to print one of the professor's essays on Aristotle. He is something of an expert on the subject. It's worth a try, but you must be careful. He is a sly one. A slip could cost you your head, which would not bother me except that your head could somehow lead him to mine. Well, is that all...di Vico, de la Faye, and money?"

"Yes," I answered. He made it sound so easy.

"Good, because I am tired. Your room is at the top of the stairs, first door on the right. You will find the money in a sack under your pillow." He enjoyed my look of surprise and allowed himself a tight little smile, explaining that only those who were short of cash ordered his goat cheese. Then he turned serious again. "Tomorrow, you don't know me. We never met here tonight. We never had this conversation. You will sit at this table for lunch. I will send over my cousin. Got it?"

"I understand. This table at lunch tomorrow."

"One other thing."

"Yes?"

His eyes narrowed.

"Pay your bill."

Baroniti blew out the candle and left me sitting there in the dark, alone. I swear I never heard one footstep as he left the room.

✠

I was at my table the next day for lunch. I ordered their best, the lamb pie, and for dessert *frutti* with honey. Some of the fresh fruit was out of season, brought in from Provence or Languedoc probably, and expensive; but the sack under my pillow had been a heavy one; it would last until Paris. In Paris I would get more. Now that I knew how to do it, there would be no more goat cheese for me on this trip. With an expense account and no accounting, would you eat goat cheese?

I caught Baroniti's eye once and smiled. He looked right through me. What a cold fish. After all, he was the innkeeper and I was his guest. Would it not have been perfectly natural for him to return my smile? "Tomorrow you don't know me," he had said. Okay, Baroniti, I don't know you. I would play his silly game.

I ate my meal without looking up again until his cousin came over and sat down. He was a fat, paunchy man with heavy jowls and dirty fingernails, and he smelled like one. No wonder Baroniti did not trust his cousin. I didn't either. But I returned his insipid smile when he introduced himself.

"So you are Luigi Massanni from Naples? I am Diego Baggio from Vico. *Mio cugino, Nicco, il pezzo grosso locandiere*, he says maybe you and me can do some business, huh? Why not? We wops gotta help each other, I always say. It's us against them, Luigi, am I right? So Nicco tells me you're a tax collector. I got nothing against tax collectors. Everybody should pay, that's what I always tell Nicco. I still pay my taxes in Vico, send it to them every year, even after living here all this time, because I'm still a citizen of Vico. My master became a citizen here. Well, what could he do? He had to prove himself to these people after his uncle became pope back in Rome. But not me.

I'm a man of many countries, I know all the languages, but I am still loyal to my homeland, see, and I know my obligations. If I can help you catch these tax-evading *bastardi*, it will be a pleasure. But if you succeed, you give me a little "help" in return, right?"

He winked broadly, rubbing his thumb and forefinger together. The fat *cafone*, he not only looked like Fuligatti and smelled like Fuligatti, he sounded like Fuligatti!

"Certainly, Signore Baggio," I said, laying it on thick. "I am empowered by my people in Naples to pay handsomely for any help you may be able to give me, what we call a 'recovery fee.' Five percent of what we collect. If I succeed, you could be a rich man. You know, I admire your attitude, Signore Baggio..."

"Call me Diego."

"Diego, if every citizen were as honest and loyal and trustworthy as you, my job would be much easier."

He was beaming.

"Now, Diego," I continued, "one of the men I am tracking down goes by the name of Bruno, Giordano Bruno. He sometimes poses as a priest. My information is that he may have been friendly with your former employer, the marchese, about eighteen years ago when he passed this way last."

"This guy owes so much, how come you don't catch him in eighteen years?"

Baggio was suspicious.

"Because he is very clever," I lied with a straight face. "He has been back and forth many times. Every time we think we have him, he disappears again. This time I think he may be in France. I was hoping that your master might offer some insight into his character, something that might help me locate him. I was not aware until yesterday that your master had died. Bruno has fooled everybody, Diego. He is very rich. There could be a great deal of money involved. Your assistance could be very profitable to you. All very legal, of course."

This time it was I who winked and rubbed my fingers together. Baggio's greed got the better of his suspicion. He wasted no time getting down to business.

"So that Bruno was rich all the time, huh? He sure fooled us! Yeah, it was a long time ago, but I remember him," he began, wetting his lips with his tongue. "A nut if I ever saw one. He came to the house one day. All the Italian refugees came to the marchese when they got to Geneva, especially the converted Catholics. It was well known that he had influence here and could help them get settled. Now, this Bruno came to the house one day and my master...

✚

"Ecco, my young priest, you have had a nasty time of it, as anyone can see. But you have come to the right place now. You shall be among friends here. Geneva is a secure haven from the papists of Rome and Paris. Baggio here will tell you. We have been pleased to help many refugees like yourself. Now then, tell me, what are your needs? How may I be of assistance? Come, do not hesitate. I assure you, you shall not want on my account, I am your friend. You are in need of money? I can advance what you need until you have an income of your own. You will need employment. I am certain we can find something commensurate with a man of your abilities and talents. You will need a place to stay, a place of your own. Baggio will help you. What else?"

"Grazie, Signore le Marchese. This is most gracious of you. I do not know how to express my gratitude."

Giordano was in fact overwhelmed. He had sought only permission to remain in Geneva. He had not dared hope for more. Since leaving Rome, he had not been the recipient of a single act of Christian kindness in three years. To find a fellow countryman, especially one of such wealth and social position, willing to advance him money, help him find employment and a place to live, was the answer to his prayers. Tears welled up in his eyes and he looked away, embarrassed.

"You need not thank me, Padre," said the marchese gently. "I know exactly how you feel. Do you know why I am in Geneva these thirty years, and not with my first wife and nine children in Vico where I belong? It is no secret. Because I am an exile too! Because my dear uncle, who was then Cardinal Carafa, head of the Inquisition, became Pope Paul IV. I was an embarrassment to him politically, because I elected to follow the teachings of John Calvin, may his beloved soul rest in peace. And because I believed in Calvin — he was more Catholic in his love of Christ and his fellow man than my uncle the pope could ever be! — I was forced to give up everything. To relinquish my lands, my home, my family. So you see, we have much in common, you and I."

"But I no longer care about religion, Your Grace. Only about my work. There is too much politics in religion for me. To study, perhaps to teach, to write, that is all I care about now. Will I be permitted to do so here in Geneva?"

"Why, of course you will! We are not papists here. There is no Sant'Offizio here. We all work and worship together, as equals. But tell me, how is it, if I may ask, that you, a priest, can say that you do not care about religion?"

Giordano became suddenly tense and agitated. He was on his feet, pacing back and forth across the marchese's study, gesticulating wildly as he spoke.

"It was all a terrible mistake! I never should have become a priest. I was fed to the wolves, because the monastery was the only place a poor soldier's son like me could continue his studies. I was only seventeen. How was I to know what it would be like? That they would tell me what to think, what to believe, that I would be permitted no thoughts of my own! There is no freedom in the priesthood. I could not breathe! I was ruled by suspicious men who cling to their relics and their sacraments and mouth empty words about what is God's will. God's will! As if they could know! Those pedants never understood me. They force you to accept everything they teach, no matter how absurd, and if you do not agree, they accuse you of heresy!"

He sat down abruptly, on the edge of the seat, as though he feared to get too comfortable before the marchese threw him out. Once again he had said too much. He was always doing that, letting his emotions get the best of him, getting into trouble because of it, forgetting himself before the very people he wanted most to impress. Now he had perhaps antagonized the one man who had offered to help get him established in Geneva. God, but he was tired of all this! Was there no place he might speak his mind, where he might express the new ideas that were burning inside him, without forever having to worry about the consequences?

But then Giordano noticed that the marchese was smiling, sympathetically, as though his outburst had been perfectly reasonable and happened to everyone. Giordano relaxed a little and leaned back in the chair, relieved that he was not to be tossed out after all.

The marchese di Vico continued to interrogate this surprisingly intense young Dominican.

"It seems to me, Father Giordano, that the solution to your dilemma ought to be obvious. Give up your habit. Surely if what you say is so, then you entered your order with reservations that have since been confirmed. Your vows are therefore without substance, meaningless, and it would be hypocrisy to continue in them. If I might make a suggestion: Discard your habit, and with it your vows. Renounce the papist heresy in which you no longer believe, and join the true church of our Lord. You will find in it the warmth of fellowship, the generosity of acceptance, and the love of Christ which have been missing from your life. 'Prompte et sincere in opere Domini.' That was Calvin's motto and it can be yours. I will personally sponsor you at Sunday School. You will learn Calvin's catechisms. And you will discover that the sacraments do not confer grace — which is the papist fiction you rightly abhor — but rather, that through them Christ communicates Himself to us. Do this, Giordano, and you will find that the doors of Geneva will open to you and you will be welcomed into her bosom."

Di Vico's face was radiant with the light of fellowship. His eyes were bright with Christian love. Nothing made him feel closer to God than to lead another wayward Christian to Christ.

But Giordano was wary of this promise of salvation. He had no intention of converting to Calvinism. He had had enough of religion, anybody's religion, and all he wanted was to be left alone to pursue his own path. That was why he ran away from the monastery, that was why he fled Rome and had come this far, because he wanted to be left alone. Only, no one would leave him alone. Catechisms? They were the last things he wished to learn!

"I thank you for your excellent suggestion, Your Grace, and I am flattered by your offer of sponsorship," he began cautiously, "but would it not be possible for me to simply pursue my work in philosophy here in Geneva, without becoming active in the Calvinist Church? Because, I frankly do not think I . . . "

Di Vico's countenance clouded over like an approaching thunderstorm. He interrupted Giordano with a stern warning:

"Be not deceived by the placid nature of our town, young priest.

Our splendid lake, our surrounding mountains. They appear to offer you protection, but in reality all Europe is at war and we are besieged by enemies on all sides. By Savoy. By the Swiss who claim to be our friends. By Henri and the League in France, and by Philip in Spain, and by that heretic in the Vatican. We have a saying here: if you are not with us, you are against us. In these troubled times, no one is permitted to sit on the fence, Italians least of all. We Italians are a very small colony in this city, and we have already had to live down our share of traitors. Matteo Gribaldi for one, who was expelled for his heretical views on the Trinity; Giovanni Gentile for another, who thank God was at least in Bern and not here when his head was parted from his shoulders for heterodoxy. Even I, a citizen since '55 and a member of the Two Hundred, even I am not above suspicion. There are many papist spies in Geneva. The Consistory is suspicious of all Italians. Make no mistake, the judgment of the Consistory is harsh. Fair but harsh. Not something to be tempted. If you do as I suggest, you can count on my help as your patron. But you must attend Sunday School regularly, you must sing the Psalter, you must recite the catechisms, you must take Communion. You must, in short, be like the rest of us. If not, I wash my hands of you completely."

✠

"And did he?"

"Did he what?" Baggio sputtered, his mouth full of bread and cheese. It was the middle of the afternoon. Baggio had been stuffing his face ever since he sat down at my table. His stomach was a great bottomless pit. He was adding chins before my eyes! Did Baroniti intend to charge me for his cousin's food as well? If so, my sack of gold crowns was going to be considerably lighter by the end of this interview. This Baggio was a pig.

I ordered him some fruit and said nothing. It was Jesuit money, not mine. So what if Baroniti got some of it back? He was earning it, living in this place. Besides, I had to admit Baggio was giving me some great stuff on Bruno.

"Did Bruno turn Calvinist?" I asked.

"He did not. He took off his habit, that he did do. And I believe he may have attended Sunday School a few times. But as far as I know, he never took Communion. That didn't please the marchese, I can tell you. But in the end it was not religion that got him into difficulties, your little tax evader."

"A woman?" I asked.

"Nothing so simple." Baggio laughed. *"Un fiasco grosso!"*

He smacked his lips as though he were trying to decide what else to eat.

Then, almost apologetically, he said, "I am still a little hungry. Perhaps I will have some of that cake and a piece of pie."

I ordered the desserts.

"My master had arranged a position for him as proofreader for a printer of scholarly books. I myself found him rooms in a house on rue de Martin Luther. The marchese introduced him to members of the university faculty. You must understand, the marchese di Vico was one of Geneva's leading citizens. An elder in the Italian church, active in many charitable works, a member of the Two Hundred. Calvin himself dedicated one of his books to the marchese. If the marchese was your patron, you were accepted everywhere, no questions asked.

"This quarry of yours came to our house often, to the marchese's parties and suppers. He was becoming 'known,' as they say. Oh, he was an interesting enough fellow. But of course he talked too much. And the master found his ideas too eccentric, especially those on magic. The main problem, though, was that he had no social graces. He attacked the ideas of the other guests, without any regard for their station. This caused the marchese a good deal of embarrassment. Also, Bruno spent all his money on books. More than once the master had to advance him additional sums so that he might eat, wear decent clothes, contribute to the poor box on the Sabbath."

The cake disappeared into the dark cavern of Baggio's mouth. Then the pie in two bites. He glanced at me questioningly. I ordered more pie. He smiled weakly.

"The trouble came that summer," he continued. "Bruno was attending the lectures of Professor de la Faye on the subject of the philosopher Aristotle. Bruno disagreed with the professor. He talked his employer into printing a pamphlet written by himself, entitled *The Twenty Errors of Professor Pedant*. It was a dumb thing to do. The marchese first learned about this pamphlet when two members of the Little Council came calling on him and demanded to know whether the marchese supported this absurd attack on de la Faye by his protégé. Naturally he was appalled. He immediately disavowed this lunatic priest from Nola.

"Bruno was arrested. So was the printer, but he managed to get off with a small fine and a reprimand by claiming that the priest had duped him. Bruno, however, was forced to make a public apology to Professor de la Faye and to destroy every copy of the pamphlet before they would release him. The marchese wouldn't even admit him to the house after that..."

✠

"Sir, he's back again."

"Send him away."

"He says he wishes to apologize and to explain that he has been misunderstood."

"Send him away, I said! I must not see him. I *will* not see him. Kindly convey that he is no longer welcome in my house. He has all but ruined me with this latest insolence before the Consistory. Imagine accusing the Consistory of pedantry! That was the height of effrontery. It reflects on my good name in the community. I would no sooner traffic now with a man who has been denied participation in the Sacrament by Theodore Beza than I would traffic with the Devil. You tell him for me that I have no concern whatsoever about his future; however, for the sake of the good Italians in Geneva — not to mention if Bruno values his head and would prefer to keep it on his shoulders! — I would suggest that he very seriously consider departing Geneva immediately. Mon Dieu, cet un imbécile! Dépêche-toi, Baggio! Send him away before someone sees him at our door and reports it!"

✠

I should have listened to Baroniti when he warned me not to see Professor de la Faye. Especially having heard of Bruno's troubles when he tangled with the professor. But I was stubborn. I had two names on my list for Geneva. I was determined to see them both. Baroniti set up the appointment. But I knew it was a mistake from the minute I sat down in his office at the university.

"I am flattered, Monsieur..." (he glanced at a slip of paper on his desk) "...Massanni, that you have come all the way from Rome just to see me. But my secretary was a trifle vague regarding the exact purpose of your visit. You will clarify that point, please."

He had a polite if condescending smile behind his trim beard, but there was no smile in his eyes. They were cold and piercing, narrowing almost to slits as he took me in, the way a cat studies a mouse while deciding just when to eat it.

"My employer is a publisher of philosophical books in Rome," I began, using the cover story Baroniti had suggested. "He is considering the expansion of our line of titles to include a number of additions relating to the works of Aristotle, criticisms both favorable and opposed. He has charged me to conduct preliminary discussions with several professors of philosophy like yourself, so that he can make a final selection."

Not bad, I decided. I hoped he wouldn't ask me for the names of the other professors. His expressionless look was disconcerting.

"The name of your employer?" he asked, his pen poised.

"Why...(think fast, fool!)...uh...Marcantonio Spada," I blurted out. Spada was the owner of the small *monte di pietà* where I often pawned the boss's books. It was the first name that came to me. I prayed he had never heard of it. "On the Via della Lungara," I added to cover my confusion.

He wrote it down.

"And the name of the other professors you will interview, please?"

I groaned inwardly. This time I really had to think fast. Who the hell knew the names of philosophy professors? He did. And he would catch me if I lied.

"Signore Spada was still compiling the list when I left. I expect the names of the others to arrive in the mail any day. When it does, I will certainly be happy to supply you with a copy. Truthfully, I left Rome with only two names. Yours was one."

"The other?"

Here goes, I thought. He had taken the bait.

"The other is really something of a question mark. I neither know where to find him nor much about him. It is possible that some of his books are no longer even available. I believe he was a student of yours here at the university many years ago. My employer has asked that I inquire further with you about this man. However, since I arrived I have learned that there was some sort of trouble between you and this man, and I am therefore reluctant to..."

De la Faye was hooked. But impatient.

"The name of this former student?"

I took a deep breath.

"Giordano Bruno."

He frowned, but did not respond.

I squirmed uncomfortably under his steely gaze, but I did my best to return it with as much innocence as I could manage, as though I had absolutely no idea of the nature of the "trouble" to which I had just alluded.

His response came at last. He lifted a small bell from his desk and shook it with obvious irritation.

"This interview is concluded," he said, his voice seething with rage. "I do not know what your game is, Monsieur, but I intend to find out. If there is a bookmaker in Rome by the name of Strada who prints Aristotle, I would most certainly have heard of him. As for that *hérétique*... that *imbécile*... that *punaise repoussant*... that... that... that..."

So great was the uncontrollable rage I had triggered in him by the mention of Bruno's name, that he began to stutter:

"I w...w...will not hear his n...n...name s...s...spoken in m...m...my presence, do you hear? Out! Out! Out!"

He was ringing the bell so violently that I flinched, expecting the clapper to come flying off in my face. His secretary burst into the room. He sized up the situation in an instant, took me by the elbow, and propelled me toward the door with a worried look on his face. This little favor to Baroniti was going to cost him plenty!

"And your story had better be a good one, because I mean to investigate it immediately, do you hear?" de la Faye screamed after me. "Immediately! We do not tolerate papist scum in Geneva! I am a p...p...personal friend of Theodore Beza! How d...dare you m...m...mention that m...m...man's n...name to m...m...my face! You...you...!"

The secretary closed the door quietly.

"I do not know who you are, Monsieur, but I know the professor. For Nicco, I give you this advice: get out of Geneva while you can. No matter if you are who you say you are. No matter if your story is above reproach. Unless Beza is your mother's brother, leave Geneva. Do not even think about it. Just leave."

I did. The very same day.

*C*hapter 9

aprile 1597
Hôtel d'Épernon
Rue de Foin No. 4
Paris

I WAS UNIMAGINATIVE as a young man. I took everything literally. It would never have occurred to me in those days to analyze why things happened the way they did. I took things as they came and never gave them very much thought. Now that I am old and nothing much goes on in my life anymore, I find myself being drawn more and more to my past, to analyzing which of the events of my life were directed and which were not.

The church teaches that God has a master plan, that everything is decided long before it happens. So, is all of life *a destino* then? Not so, says the church. The individual has a choice. *Di scelta.* But how can there be choice, when that choice is already a part of my destiny before I choose it? Such a possibility is confusing to think about. What helps me is to believe that God has left room for a third possibility, out of both of our hands, so to speak: that some events occur *per caso,* by accident.

As an instance of this: God surely had much more important events to plan than my entrance into Paris that night. As I think about it now, there were so many ifs along the way that I feel certain neither destiny nor choice were operating. It must have been pure accident that placed me on rue de Foin at precisely the moment that d'Épernon needed help. The way it all turned out, I do not think even God could have planned it better for my purpooooi d'Épernon's either, for that matter.

Toward dusk on the road to Paris, I intended to find a place to stay the night and to proceed into the city in the morning. Yet, I was so excited at the prospect of returning after seven years — I never expected to see Paris again when I left, nor did I think I would ever want to — that I kept thinking, well, I will go just a little further. I went a little further and a little further, and by the time the sun was down I could see the Pont St. Jacques in the distance.

St. Jacques being the southern gate through the town wall of Paris, I thought that since I had come that far, I might as well keep going.

There was a small auberge just inside Pont Châtelet, near the Hôtel Dieu where I stayed with Bellarmine during the siege, almost in the shadow of Notre Dame de Paris. I decided I would take a room there for the evening and then find a more suitable place in the morning.

It had been a long day. We were tired and hungry, my animals and I. I was looking forward to a good meal and some rest. That was all I was thinking about as I rode north along rue St. Jacques toward the Seine.

As I reached the rue de Foin, I thought I heard a faint cry for help down that dark street. At the time I was not sure whether I had actually heard something or whether it was merely my imagination. Many times on the road I imagined all sorts of things when I was tired, especially in the dark. But this time I had a strong compulsion to investigate.

I no sooner turned down the street when I came upon three *giovinastri* attacking a gentleman. The gentleman was alone and well dressed; he was obviously being beaten and robbed.

"*Arresto!* Let him go!" I yelled, leaping off Cammello.

The three thugs probably did not understand Italian, but they knew the meaning of my words well enough. They threw down the man they were beating and turned to face me. One had a pistol and the other two had knives.

"*Décharge!*" I heard one of the knives whisper hoarsely to the pistol, as all three began to advance on me.

I was armed only with my stiletto, but I had a hunch what *décharge* meant and I was not about to remain a stationary target. If I learned one thing from the Corsicans of Ripa, it was that you never wait for your opponent to do something. You do it first.

I moved in fast on the big one with a knife. Feinting a low stab, I slipped inside his parry and slashed upward, ripping open his cheek from mouth to ear. He cried out in pain and dropped to one knee, blood gushing from his face.

His smaller partner hesitated for just an instant, but it was enough. I kicked him in the groin, and when he doubled over, I came down hard on the back of his head with my fist.

I turned to face the third guy, the one with the pistol. He was backing away, uncertain what to do now that his partners were out of action. I made a move toward him and he decided. He raised the pistol and fired.

My ears rang from the noise of the shot. I felt a searing pain tear through my left shoulder. I staggered toward the shooter.

He dropped the gun in terror and turned to run, but he was too slow.

I buried the stiletto into the middle of his back. He pitched forward and fell. I fell on top of him, still holding onto the stiletto.

The last thing I remembered was the sound of a crunching crack to my head and an awful headache.

✳

"How are you feeling?"

I still had the pain in the shoulder and the headache. I was lying in a huge bed, propped by a number of very soft pillows. I remember it felt like being on a cloud. The entire bed was filled with the softest goose down. Very elegant, but I hurt like hell. My shoulder was tightly bandaged, with my arm in a sling of blue silk. I could feel that my head was bandaged as well.

The sun was streaming in through glass doors that opened to a garden filled with flowers and singing birds. The room and the garden seemed to merge into each other like an overlapping vision of Eden, until I realized that there were flowers and birds in the room as well!

I looked in the direction of the questioner and found a man standing at the side of the bed. He repeated his question, smiling a crooked smile because one side of his face was badly bruised and swollen. Otherwise, he was strikingly handsome. I recognized him as the gentleman being beaten and robbed in the street — was it last night? — only now he was wearing a green brocade dressing gown that reached to the floor and had a coat of arms over the breast.

"I'm hungry," I responded, though more to myself than to him, and more in wonderment than demand, that I could feel so rotten and still think of food. Then the night before flooded back into my memory and I began to fire questions at him.

"My animals, have they been cared for? Where am I? Who are you? What happened to those damned *giovinastri?* Was I knocked out? That's the first time in my life! Did they get away? That *bastardo con pistola* shot me! *Dio,* another first! Ah, but he carries my stiletto. I'll know him if I ever see him again."

Talking hurt my head.

"*Dio,* what hit me?" I asked, feeling the back of my head gently. There was a lump the size of an orange under the bandage.

My host laughed pleasantly.

"The thug with the pistol will trouble no one again, *mon cher,* since you killed him quite dead last night," he said, laying the stiletto at my side. As for your head, I fear it may continue to hurt for a time. The smaller one did that to you with a rock, before the two of them made their escape. I think they will not soon forget meeting you, however. One will bear your scar on his face for the rest of his life. The other is now a eunuch with a great bump on the top of his head. *Mon Dieu*, you made such quick work of them! With a sword you would be unbeatable. We could have used you in the old days.

"*Alors, mon cher*, I owe you my life. You shall have a friend in d'Épernon for the rest of yours. Allow me to introduce myself: I am Nogaret de la Valette, duc d'Épernon, late admiral of France to King Henri III, may his troubled soul rest in peace, and currently at service in the court of his most Catholic majesty, King Henri IV, long live the king!"

He bowed deeply, but smiled throughout this self-introduction as though it were all a great joke; one which I failed to share at the time, though I understood it later.

"My name is Pietro Guidotti, no title. I am from Rome and I am hungry as a bear because I missed my supper last night," I replied in a serious tone. Then I laughed to let him know that I did not take myself too seriously either.

D'Épernon clapped with delight.

"And so you shall eat, Pietro, my friend!"

He pulled on the cord next to my bed and within minutes servants entered with more food than I could consume in a week. One thing I discovered on this second trip to Paris: when it comes to food, the French can out-eat all of Europe.

Their consumption is colossal. They eat four, five, even six times a day. Beginning with a breakfast of fried tripe, ham, grilled beef and kid, thick soup and bread, they eat their way through the day. Stuffed venison, stag with turnips, drakes with cheese, turkey and partridge, wild boar with chestnuts, asparagus, candied cucumbers, little cabbages, pâtés of all sorts: larks, artichokes, snipe, chestnuts, swan, and goose liver and so forth, sole, salmon and sturgeon from the Loire and the Seine, rooster combs and kidneys (they say that was Catherine de' Medici's favorite), followed by tarts and cakes of every description. And all of it washed down with great rivers of red wine.

A banquet in Rome is no more than hors d'oeuvres in Paris. I tell you, my mouth waters at the memory of those sumptuous feasts at Hôtel d'Épernon! Another month of it and I would have grown as fat as Fuligatti and Baggio combined. Of course, nowadays I partake of such food only from the eyes up. Below the eyes I must content myself with a diet of *polenta con latte*. Occasionally, I take a sip or two of wine against the strictest advice of my physician. How the mighty are fallen! Alas, eating is for the young, when the digestion is strong and your teeth are still in your mouth. As they say, all the good things are wasted on the young, who know not how to appreciate them.

If ever you must get shot, I can recommend the shoulder, especially if the ball passes cleanly through the flesh without encountering bone or vessels. There will be almost no pain after the first day and the wound will heal quickly. Avoid, if you can, a rock to the back of the head, however. In that, I was not so fortunate. (Serve the *vilmente bastardo* right if I did make him a eunuch!) I was left with a tender bump, an enduring headache, and the discovery by the duke's physician of what he called a *fracture de tête*, for which he advised no less than a week of bed rest.

There was no choice. It was three days before I could even stand without dizziness, four before I could make it outside to the garden. Bellarmine later said that it was a small price to pay, since saving the duke's life would count well in the great beyond. He did not use those exact words, but that was his meaning. Clerics often use euphemisms. I was not averse to banking some points for the eventual salvation of my soul. I just did not want to have to wait until then to collect for my efforts. As it turned out, the duke became my almost immediate benefactor.

D'Épernon took it upon himself to entertain me during my convalescence. He was my constant companion. I discovered he was a charming and gracious host and a lively storyteller. For hours on end he entertained me with long rambling tales of court life at the Louvre, explaining also, in a way that I could understand, the wars of religion that had plagued France for so many years.

During my first trip to Paris with Bellarmine and Cajetan, my understanding of these wars was limited. To me it had seemed an uncomplicated matter. A simple battle, I thought, between the Catholics and the Protestant Huguenots, over who would control the souls of the people. I was not alone in this conception. Most of France were similarly limited, encouraged in their ignorance by their rulers and their respective churches.

Has it not always been that way for the people? In my country too. It never suits our rulers for us to be too well informed. We might then begin to doubt the necessity of sacrificing our hard-earned money and our lives, just to suit their lust for power.

The real struggle, as d'Épernon explained it, was for control of the throne, not for the immortal souls of the people, about which they cared little. The battle was between three points of a triangle: duc de Guise and the Catholic League, Catherine de' Medici and her Valois children, and the Bourbons with Henri of Navarre at their lead. In addition there were numerous lesser intrigues within these three camps...and a greater one without. Some kings were pawns, some queens were kings, some knights were bishops. The roles were constantly shifting, as was the outcome of the game until the very end. It was indeed complex.

But not for the people. For the people it was simple, as usual. The people, Catholics and Protestants alike, believed they were fighting for good against evil, and that they would be rewarded for their loyalty and zeal. So their leaders assured them. And reassured them. Well, they found their reward — irrigating the battleground with their blood so as to nourish future fields of flowers.

The labyrinth of high-level political intrigue within the three camps, combined with that of the outside manipulators — Elizabeth of England, Philip of Spain, and not to forget a number of successive popes in the Vatican who more often than not played each of the combatants off against the others — proved more devious than I could follow, even with so expert a guide as d'Épernon. What I learned is that in politics, the straightest line between two points is most often a circle. Had I to earn my living at it, I should surely have starved to death in politics.

I really could not complain. I was sleeping in silks on satin and down, I was eating my fill of rich food, I spent my days relaxing in the garden outside my bed chamber on a warm spring afternoon, and I was treated to the experiences of a member of the French peerage as though I were his bosom pal. It was a dream I was not anxious to end. But end it did, abruptly and unexpectedly, and once again I was immersed in my mission.

D'Épernon was describing the relationship between Henri III — who sounded more like one of the entertainers at the carnival on Monte Testaccio than the king of France — and his *mignons*, his darlings.

"Imagine it, *mon cher*, what it was like for us to be the favorites of the king. We were young and daring, barely in our twenties and totally inexperienced. We were flattered by his affection, made bolder by it, willing to risk anything to keep it, ready to follow his lead anywhere, to do anything, on the spur of the moment.

"If he wore earrings and aigrettes, we did also. If he wore a little velvet bonnet, then we all wore little velvet bonnets. Life was a *mascarade* in which each of us tried to outdo the other, though no one could outdo the king because it was his lead we followed and no one could predict where that might go. The more outlandish the costumes he designed, the greater the challenge to exceed them. Jewels, plumes, ribbons, and lace. We used purple powder on our faces for rouge, exotic perfumes, beautiful wigs of long curls, *mon Dieu*, I have to laugh when I think how ridiculous we must have looked! But of course, it was all *très drôle, n'est-ce pas?* We never took it seriously.

"Once, he had us all wear dresses to a ball. There we were, young stallions wearing dresses and dancing with ladies who were wearing dresses. Oh my! You doubt me? *Mais certainement! Le roi* himself! Henri often wore gowns at state affairs, low-cut ones, with enormous jeweled necklaces. At other times we all had to wear those awful starched linen muffs that stuck out from our necks and made us look like so many heads of John the Baptist on platters. There were so many changes of fashion under Henri, your head would spin. I once owned thirty-two outfits and wore every one of them in the space of as many days!

"We drank and we whored ... oh, *mais oui*, though there were those among us, true enough, who preferred their 'ladies' with cocks between their legs. Nothing was frowned upon in that department. We caroused in the streets at night with our king, whistling and jeering and shouting *'piou! piou!'* until the morning sun. Or he might suddenly take a notion that twenty or thirty of us should accompany him on horseback to the Midi somewhere for a taste of the first ripe melons of the season. You never knew what he might do next or when. We used to make wagers about it.

"There were balls and ballets and masquerades, always some occasion to be celebrated with tourneys and jousts. Oh, yes, *les mignons* were most adept at sword and lance! Too adept for their own good, I fear, more's the pity, poor dears. D'Arques and I did not consider ourselves true *mignons*. We were older than the others, and the king's favorites. So we placed ourselves above the baser foolishness. I am certain it was the reason we lived longer than the rest, though D'Arques — duc de Joyeuse — fell in battle ten years ago, and I am now the lone survivor. Few of them lived to see thirty. Quèlus, Saint-Luc, young Mésgrin who was attacked by thirty men one night outside the Louvre for having had the audacity to sleep with the wife of duc de Guise ... oh, so many beautiful young men! If they were not fighting wars, they were fighting duels. Forever being discovered with another man's wife or some other stupidity.

"The people despised and mocked us. Fornicators, adulterers, *fruits en compote, les grands gommeux,* they had many names for us, all bad. We laughed at them. After all, we were *les hommes de le roi,* the king's men. We served him, not the people. What did we care what they thought of us? Young, brash, impulsive, we were simply not prepared to accept responsibility for the nation.

"When D'Arques was made duc de Joyeuse and married the king's sister-in-law, he was only twenty years old. There were no less than seventeen parties given in his honor. Jousts, tourneys, music, entertainment and dancing, gifts from the king for everyone. The Louvre was ablaze every night for weeks. Within a year, D'Arques was admiral of France. At twenty-one! I myself was raised to the peerage, became a colonel-general and then admiral of France, all while I was still in my twenties.

"Some said we were too young. Even the king was only three years older than I, twenty-three when his brother King Charles died and left him the throne. Poor Henri. No one really understood him. He was *une énigme.*

"Imagine inheriting that much power at twenty-three. Suddenly you are king of France. You can do anything, say anything, and no one dares criticize you to your face nor deny you the right. Are you lonely? Give a party! Bored? Fill the Louvre with lap dogs, with parakeets, monkeys, and lions and as many wild animals as you wish. Are you restless, Monsieur le Roi? Ride south, ride north, ride west to one of your castles. Or build another! Feeling poor? Tax the people. It is so simple. But does that make you feel guilty, worried about your soul? Equally simple! Fast for a week and repent. Better yet, dress up in a white linen sack with two holes in it for your eyes and join the procession of barefoot penitents in the rain. Chant the litany with them. Fall on your knees at Notre Dame and sing the "Salve Regina."

"The wonder of it was there were times when he could rise above all that, when he was *un roi juste,* a proper king. I remember him before the Estates General, he was but twenty-five, in his white doublet and cloak of purple velvet, looking every inch the majestic king. His speech that day — *un roi, une foi, une loi!* ... 'one king, one faith, one law!' — was the most eloquent address ever delivered by a prince of Europe. In moments like those he had enormous charm and dignity, my king, and, though I suppose history will remember only the pampered eccentricities of his reign, he actually accomplished many things for France.

"For one thing, he held on to the crown and managed to pass it on to Navarre, who, if I am any judge, has the makings of a great ruler. Guise would have made a disastrous king. So would Cardinal de Bourbon or Cardinal de Guise. And God help us if Henri's brother, duc d'Alençon, that scheming chameleon, had lived to make it to the throne or had succeeded in his courtship of Elizabeth. Henri Trois made many mistakes in his lifetime, but selling out to the League was not one of them, we owe him that. Neither Elizabeth nor Philip had their way with him either, though they certainly tried.

"I claim no credit for these things on the part of the *mignons*. We were all too busy playing with yo-yos to worry about politics. Yes, yo-yos. Can you imagine? The king of France and his *mignons* playing with yo-yos for a whole summer, like small children. No, I credit his advisors. Old de Bellièvre, and Villeroy, and of course 'Maman'...Catherine de' Medici. Say what you want — I hate to admit it myself — but that shrewd, fat, bloodthirsty, scheming old bitch, who was behind every murderous, treacherous act in France while she lived, including the St. Bartholomew's Day Massacre, managed to hold this country together as regent after Charles died, saved France on any number of occasions from Guise, and somehow preserved Navarre for our future king. The stories I could tell you about that 'Florentine Shopkeeper,' damn her selfish soul! Remind me to tell you some of them, *mon cher.*

"Are you still awake? You poor dear, I am talking your ear off! Perhaps you would like to rest. No? Very well then, I will continue. As I was saying, my king was unpredictable and not an easy man to understand. He was moody. He was frivolous. He was sometimes a religious fanatic. He was under his mother's thumb when it came to politics, but when it came to governing he was a wise and intelligent man, a man of culture and refinement when he chose to be. His tutor was Jacques Amyot, who prepared him well in languages, of which he spoke several fluently, including yours. He was also learned in ancient Greek and Roman philosophy, in science and in mathematics.

"Few people were aware of this side of him. He supported the university, even when that left him little money for other things. He endowed a wide number of scholars, writers, and lecturers. At least twice a week at the Louvre, after dinner, he would retire to a closed room with several of us, and discussions and debates would be held that might last for hours. One of us would choose a topic on which to speak and then the others would criticize, or on occasion his majesty would summon a famous philosopher from the Sorbonne or perhaps a visiting professor from another country.

"I remember one occasion in particular, when the king invited one of your countrymen to the Louvre to give us a demonstration, one Jordanus Nolanus, recently arrived in Paris from Geneva. This professor was at the time delivering a series of lectures on the thirty divine attributes as expounded by Thomas Aquinas. I remember him because his demonstration was so unusual. Word had reached the king of this professor's remarkable memory, and the king had sent for him to..."

The duke's stories had indeed been lulling me to sleep. I had been dozing, off and on, waking with a start and then nodding off again. But when he mentioned that name, I was jarred wide awake with all my senses quivering.

"What did you say the man's name was?" I asked, doing my best to contain my excitement.

"Nolanus. Nolano. Something like that, I think."

"Could it have been Giordano Bruno, who called himself 'the Nolan'?"

"You might think I would remember, since it was a demonstration of memory. And I did see him on a number of occasions after that. Let me think now...(Oh, the suspense!)...Well, yes, I believe that was one of his names. Now I recall, he used several. Jordanus Nolanus was the name he used in connection with his lectures. Yes, it comes to me now. Bruno. I remember. It was quite a number of years ago, you understand. I do not even know what made me think about it just now. Just rattling through the old days, and I remembered that demonstration. Fifteen or twenty years ago, I wager, yet he sticks in my mind. He was so...so... *audacieux* is the only way I can describe him. He was remarkable, all right. I wonder what ever happened to him?"

D'Épernon eyed me closely.

"Did you know this Bruno Nolano, *mon cher?*"

"I'll tell you later. Go on with your story. I'm interested, Duke."

✠

The king was growing impatient.

The others conversed among themselves in hushed tones, but there was an air of nervous expectancy among them as they waited for him to explode. As, sooner or later, they knew he would. His foot was the telltale sign. When King Henri was about to explode, his foot began to tap out the message in advance.

Merde! Why must Maman persist in doing this to him? He was the king, dammit!

Twisting in his chair, he looked again behind him toward the Louvre. Still no one in sight. Pouting, he slumped in his chair and glared at the others over the top of his fan. Probably they were talking about him, laughing even, at a king tied to his mother's skirts. Some day he ought to kill her, that's what he ought to do. Poison. He ought to poison her damn food. She ate enough for a horse. He would watch her writhe in agony, and she would plead with him, help me, *mon petit!* Call the physician, *mon petit!* And he would say, Wait, Maman, wait until I am good and ready, the way you always made me wait for you. Then he would let her die, waiting. Wait, Maman, wait until hell freezes over!

He chuckled wickedly at his thoughts, fluttering his fan excitedly. The thought of doing his mother in always excited him.

The foot continued to tap.

"*Il fait trop chaude,*" he sighed to no one in particular.

De Pibrâc's idea, meeting out here in the garden tonight. His own apartments were stifling. Even here there was so little air. This heat was oppressive! If only Guise were not so disagreeable, he might have taken the mignons and gone north, gotten away from Paris and the heat and the damnable plague for a while.

Oh, where was she?

He belched. He should eat less. He would grow fat like Maman. The thought of food and Maman rekindled his fantasy for a moment. What would he use? Belladonna? Hemlock? Black hellebore? Amanita? Yes, amanita! The idea of poisoning his mother with toadstools amused him. He tittered, then glanced guiltily at de Pibrâc, as though the latter might have overheard his dark thoughts.

"Are we all here, de Pibrâc?"

"*Oui, majesté.*"

Guy du Faur de Pibrâc, advocat général du Parlement, had also been appointed by King Henri years ago to be gérant d'Académie, manager of the Academy. Dear de Pibrâc, he really was most responsible for the success of these twice weekly meetings. We shall have to remember to do something nice for him, thought the king.

If only Maman would make her grand entrance already, we could begin the meeting! His foot increased its rhythm.

No one else in the small group that was assembled in the garden appeared concerned by the delay. In tribute to their courtly inscrutability, they pretended not to notice their king's ire. Possibly they were impervious to it by now. They stood in clusters of animated conversation. Jaymn, Ronsard, and Tyard stood together in one group, circled around Calude-Catherine de Clermont, Maréchale de Retz, who at the moment was enjoying the attention of these famous poets. The other female member of the Academy present was Madame de Ligneralles. She, too, had her set of admirers: the Maréchale's husband, duc de Retz, de Nevers, Antoine de Baif, whose Académie de Poésie et de Musique had now been joined with the Palace Academy at King Henri's insistence, Mauduit the composer and young Jacques Davy Du Perron, the enfant terrible of the French poets.

Old Dorat stood off to one side, chatting quietly but insistently with Philippe Desportes, the philosopher. And rounding out the evening's assortment of academicians were King Henri's favorites, D'Arques and la Valette, both of them decked out in mignonesque finery and just now mirthfully enjoying the latest in a rash of lewd jokes that had been making their way through court.

It was, Henri decided with a touch of pride, an exquisite gathering of some of the finest minds in France. For this evening's program, he had planned with de Pibrâc a mental demonstration, one that would depart from the usual debating of moral virtues. None of those present was aware of the nature of the program. Henri was looking forward to springing his little surprise on them. At least his friends appreciated what their king was trying to accomplish with this Academy, if no one else did. He was still smarting over Passerat's rebuke in Parlement, that the king might better learn his duties as sovereign from the verses of Virgil than from the empty discourses of some academy.

It was Du Perron, a supporter of the Copernican opinion and himself possessing a remarkable memory, who had first brought to Henri's attention the memory feats of this Italian professor newly arrived in Paris. From what Du Perron claimed to have witnessed during the Italian's lectures, they were to be treated to a rare experience this evening.

C'est assez, Maman! Par exemple!

"Has the Italian arrived, de Pribâc?"

"Oui, majesté. He awaits your pleasure in the alcove. I have asked Delbene to keep him company. I thought one of his countrymen might help the professor feel more relaxed, since I understand that he speaks no French."

"Très bien. But where is Maman? This is most unpleasant!"

"Forgive me, *majesté.* The queen mother arrives."

Henri twisted in his seat to see his mother being carried through the gardens in a chair. She had one husky attendant on each side, while a third proceeded backward in an awkward posture, holding an ottoman on which was supported her swollen foot, swathed in bandages and decorated with strands of pearls. Catherine was no light load. Despite their size, the attendants set their regal burden down next to the king with indelicate grunts that could be heard by everyone. No matter. The imperious woman, her shrewd mouth hinting a smile, while her opaque dark eyes coldly surveyed the scene, dismissed them with a pudgy wave and leaned toward her son.

"Je regrette, mon petit. La goutte . . . (she pointed to her foot) . . . or I should say, *le gotta* in deference to our guest. We should all be speaking Italian tonight," she said, raising her voice for all to overhear. "After all, we should make our Neapolitan memory expert feel at home for his demonstration. Is something wrong, my son? Your face is flushed. You are not cross with me for keeping you waiting? You know how I suffer with this foot."

He would poison her. He would!

"Cross with you, Maman? *Mais non!*" He was smiling, but his eyes glistened with his hurt and anger, that she had thus spoiled his surprise. "The king waits for no one. It is our pleasure to begin when we choose."

The conversation among the guests had ceased upon the queen mother's arrival. Now they all waited to see how she would respond to the king's sarcasm. Catherine's temper was even more explosive than that of her son's.

But she laughed lightly, dismissing the remark.

"*Bene, caro mio,* then let us begin. De Pibrâc..." She gestured to de Pibrâc to summon the Italian professor.

It vexed Henri even more that his mother would attempt in front of his friends to take charge of the evening.

Diplomatically, de Pibrâc hesitated, suddenly finding reason to adjust his boot. He was loyal to his king, though he too was aware who pulled the strings in the royal household. A moment was all Henri needed. He straightened up in his chair, tossed his head, and gave de Pibrâc a royal nod, the smirk on his face indicating that he was content to believe that it was his command, not Maman's, that de Pibrâc obeyed.

"Your Majesty," the Italian began, speaking awkwardly in faltering French, "I am greatly honored that you have sent for me. I dared hope that I might some day have this opportunity to plead my status directly to you. I am an academician without an academy, a teacher without students, a writer with no printer, a philosopher with no patron, a patron with no funds, a stranger to your language as you can see, but no stranger to your warm and generous..."

"Yes, yes, enough of that," the king interrupted impatiently. "Your French is impossible. We understand your language. You may as well use it or we will be here forever. As it is, we have been waiting so long for this demonstration of yours that our rear end has grown blisters! Stay in Paris as long as you wish; you have our permission. With luck you will not die from the plague. Let us dispense with formalities in this heat.

"We understand from Du Perron here that you profess expertise in mnemotechnics. What we wish to know first is whether this memory system of yours is the result of natural or magical causes? We have enough trouble with the League already. We do not wish to inflame them or the Holy Father in Rome by embracing magic in our court. Be forewarned that magic is a subject on which our mother is herself something of an expert, are you not, Maman? Astrology, the use of talismans and the like. She will be the first to detect any hint of magic. As for memory, we are not

unschooled in such matters ourselves. Du Perron has already dazzled us with feats of memorization. Can your system do better?
We shall see. Come, fellow, is your system natural or magical?"

Henri enjoyed taking charge. The awkward little Italian (his
eyes were as dark as those of Maman, he observed) had properly been put on notice. There was drama in Henri's introductory
speech, and he was pleased with the effect.

Giordano drew himself up, rising on his toes as though seeking
to stretch his short height to its maximum, and responded in a
clear and assured manner. When it came to mnemonics, he was
not to be intimidated, not even by the king of France!

"Sire, my system is natural and scientific. My system is unique.
My system is such that I can easily teach others to use it. My
system is..."

He trailed off, responding to the king's dark look of annoyance.

"...Your Majesty, I have prepared a suitable and I think
appropriate demonstration for you of my system."

(*Mon Dieu*, Henri thought, this fellow is a bore!)

"Yes, yes, why else do you think you are here, Professor Jordanus? Proceed, proceed, by all means. This had better be good,
Du Perron, or you may have seen your last crown from us."

Du Perron acknowledged the threat as though it were a joke,
with a knowing smile.

"When I was studying in a convent ten years ago," Giordano
began, "His Holiness Pope Pius V sent a coach for me that I
might come to Rome to give a demonstration of *ars memoriae*
similar to that for which you have summoned me this evening."

"De Pibrâc," the king interrupted, turning to his gérant
d'Académie with a wink, "see to it that the professor is driven
to his rooms in our coach after the meeting. Let history record
that the Catholic king of France was no less gracious a host than
a dead pope."

Dutifully, the listeners applauded their king's witticism. The
two ladies nodded appreciatively behind their masks.

"What I did at that demonstration," Giordano continued, "was
to recite the Psalm Fundamenta in Hebrew."

The king looked perplexed.

"I did not understand a word of Hebrew, Sire."

Henri mouthed an "oh" and nodded enthusiastically.

"Yesterday, when Signore de Pibrâc approached me with your summons and described the nature of your command, I went immediately to the Abbey St. Victor, where I am acquainted with the librarian, Father Cotin. With his assistance, I selected a portion of an old manuscript to recite for you. I do not know whether Your Majesty is familiar with this particular manuscript. I myself was not. It is written in French. I neither speak nor understand French. Under most systems of memory, knowledge of the language would seem essential. With my system, it is not. While my system is complex to some, and may be understood in its entirety only by a sturdy intellect such as Your Majesty's, I can, I assure you, teach it. And I am currently writing a book on this subject, which, if it please Your Majesty, I intend to dedicate to you."

(How tedious.)

Henri yawned.

Catherine made a clicking noise of sucking through her front teeth.

D'Arques and la Valette exchanged sniggers.

But the Italian was impervious.

"What I selected at the abbey library was the manuscript of a meditative prayer written by Christine de Pisan for Charles III of Navarre more than a century ago, *Les sept psaumes allégorisés*, which Father Cotin indicates is an allegorical interpretation of the seven penitential psalms, 6, 31, 37, 50, 101, 129, and 142."

Henri shifted uncomfortably.

It was the listeners' turn to be perplexed. Not only was this Italian pedantic and verbose; he was also recondite! A fifteenth-century prayer?

Du Perron, being quicker than the others to spot what was coming, smiled to himself. Damned clever!

"Father Cotin has told me something of Your Majesty's proclivity toward penitence. Thus the selection seems appropriate. I hope you will agree. As you know, the number seven has symbolic significance, adding I hope further virtue thereby. There are seven planets. Seven stars in the Great Bear. The seven days of Creation. Christ's last words numbered seven. There are seven branches of the Babylonian tree of life, seven branches also on the Hebrew menorah. 'I will punish you yet seven times for your sins' – Leviticus 26:24. St. Augustine divided the mysteries of the faith into groups of seven. Pythagoras ascribed to the number seven, which is the combination of the first odd with the first even number, the attribute of infinity... universal harmony. There were seven pillars to the Temple of Solomon. There are seven liberal arts, seven continents, seven heavens..."

D'Arques and la Valette feigned loud snores.

Catherine had fallen asleep with her mouth gaping.

But Henri was wide awake and fascinated. He glanced at Du Perron, Du Perron smiled, nodding sagely. The others too were becoming caught up in the drama unfolding before them. La Valette noticed, nudged his friend, and the two of them grew silent as well. The Italian had them now.

"...And so, Your Majesty, I have selected for this demonstration the Litany of the Saints, inscribed at the conclusion of this most spiritual manuscript of penitence. The litany is in French, which, as you have perceived, I do not speak. Father Cotin has assisted me only in the correct pronunciations. I have never seen this manuscript before yesterday afternoon...

Kyrieleyson
Xpisteleyson
Kyrieleyson
Xpiste audi nos.
O Père, O Dieu des cielux, ayes merci de nous.
O Fils, Redempteur du monde, douls Dieu, ayes merci de nous.
O Saint Espirit, doulx Dieux, ayes merci de nous.
O Sainte Trinité, un Dieu, ayes merci de nous.

Sainte Marie, prie pour nous.
Sainte Mère de Dieu, prie pour nous.
Sainte glorieuse Vierge des vierges, prie pour nous.
Saint Michel, prie pour nous.
Saint Gabriel, prie pour nous.
Saint Raphael, prie pour nous.
Saint Uriel, prie pour nous.
O vous benois angels et archangels, pries Dieu pour nous.

Saint Jehan Baptiste, prie Dieu pour nous.
Tous sains patriarches et prophètes, pries pour nous.
Saint Pierre, prie pour nous.
Saint Pol, prie pour nous.
Saint Andri, prie pour nous.
Saint Jacques, prie pour nous.
Saint Philippe, prie pour nous.
Saint Barthelemy, prie pour nous.
Saint Barnaba, prie pour nous.
Saint Jehan, prie pour nous.
Saint Mathieu, prie pour nous.
Saint Symon, prie pour nous.
Saint Jude, prie pour nous.
Saint Marc, prie pour nous.
Saint Luc, prie pour nous.
Tous sains, apostres et evangélistes, pries pour nous.

Tous sains disciples de Dieu, pryes Dieu pour nous.
Tous sains innocens, pries pour nous.
Saint Estienne, prie pour nous.
Saint Line, prie pour nous.
Saint Clete, prie pour nous.
Saint Clément, prie pour nous.
Saint George, prie pour nous.
Saint Fabian, prie pour nous.
Saint Sebastian, prie pour nous.
Saint Laurens, prie pour nous.
Saint Vincent, prie pour nous.
Saint Denis avec tes compaignons, prie pour nous.

Tous sains martirs, pries pour nous.
Saint Silvestre, prie pour nous.
Saint Léon, prie pour nouse.
Saint Grégoire, prie pour nous.
Saint Jerome, prie pour nous.
Saint Ambroise, prie pour nous.
Saint Augustin, prie pour nous.
Saint Bernard, prie pour nous.
Saint Bernabe, prie pour nous.

Saint Benoit, prie pour nous.
Saint Germain, prie pour nous.
Saint Martin, prie pour nous.
Saint Yves, prie pour nous.
Saint Marceau, prie pour nous.
Saint Louys, prie pour nous.
Tous sains confesseurs, pries pour nous.

Sainte Anne, prie pour nous.
Sainte Marie Magdalene, prie pour nous.
Sainte Maie Egypciane, prie pour nous.
Sainte Katherine, prie pour nous.
Sainte Margarite, prie pour nous.
Sainte Agnes, prie pour nous.
Sainte Cecile, prie pour nous.
Sainte Agathe, prie pour nous.
Sainte Genevieve, prie pour nous.
Sainte Petronille, prie pour nous.
Sainte Anastasie, prie pour nous.

Sainte Foy, prie pour nous.
Sainte Esperance, prie pour nous.
Sainte Charité, prie pour nous.
Toutes saintes vierges, pries pour nous.
Tous sains et saintes,
Soyes nous propice et nous espargne, Sire.
De tout mal deffens nous, Sire.
Des agais du deable delivre nous.
De soubdain et impourveue mort delivre nous, Sire.
De yre, de haine, et de toute male voulenté, delivre nous, Sire.
De l'espirit de fornicacion, delivre nous, Sire.
De fouldre et tempeste, delivre nous, Sire.
De mort perpetuelle, delivre nous, Sire.

Par la vertu du mistere de ta sainte incarnacion, delivre nous,
   Sire.
Par la vertu de ton saint avenement, delivre nous, Sire.
En l'onneur de ta nativité, delivre nous, Sire.
Par la vertu de ton baptesme, delivre nous, Sire.

En l'onneur de ton saint jeune .xl. jours et .xl. nuis, delivre nous,
   Sire.
En l'onneur et par la vertu de ta passion et de ta mort, delivre
   nous, Sire.
Par la vertu de ta sainte croix, delivre nous, Sire.
Et en l'onneur de ta sainte resurreccion, delivre nous, Sire.
Par ta tres marveillable ascencion, delivre nous, Sire.
Par et en l'onneur de l'avenement de ton Saint Espirit, delivre
   nous, Sire.
Au jour du jugement, delivre nous, Sire.

Nous tres miserables pecheurs te prions que tu nous vueilles oir.
Que tu nous vueilles donner paix, nous te prions, Sire.
A ce que remission de tous nous péchés nous vueilles donner,
Nous te prie que tu nous vueilles oyr.

Et que tu humilies les ennemis de sainte Eglise et perturbeurs de
   sainte Xpianté, nous te prions que tu nous vueilles oyr.
Et que a tout peuple Xpien, paix et union par vraye concorde
   ottroier vueilles, nous te prions, Sire, que tu nous vueilles oyr.

Et a ce que nos pensees soient eslevees aux celestieux desirs,
   nous te prions que tu nous vueilles oyr.

A ce que tu nous vueilles donner fruis de terre de quoy tu soies
   servi et pour la sustentacion de tes creatures, par lesquelles
   tu soies loué et regracié, nous te prions que tu nous en
   vueilles oyr.

Pour tous nos biens faicteurs, que tu leur vueilles retribuer
   pardurables biens.
Et que tous les loyaulx deffuncts tu vueilles donner repos
   pardurable.
Et que tu nous vueilles exaussier, nous te requirons que tu nous
   vueilles oyr.
Nous enfans de Dieu (.iii.) te prions que tu oyes notre prière et
   nos requestes.

Agnel de Dieu qui ostes les péchés du monde, exausse nous,
   Sire.
Agnel de Dieu qui ostes les péchés du monde, exausse nous,
   Sire.

Agnel de Dieu qui ostes les péchés du monde, ayes merci de nous.

Kyrieleyson
Xpisteleyson
Kyrieleyson
Pater noster
Et de nos
Sed libera
Sire, exausse mon eroison, et mon cry a toy viengne.
Oroison

O doulx Dieu, au quel propre chose est pardoner par ta pi-
teuse misericorde toutes les fois que le pencheur se repent et
requiert mercy, veuilles prendre en gré nostre prière, à ce que
ceulx lesquieulx le chaine de pechiés a constraint, la misericorde
de ta doulx pitié vueille delier et pardonner et absouldre. Per
Xpistum Dominum nostrum. Amen.

✠

"I remember I was profoundly moved by this recitation," d'Épernon went on. "We all were. Even now, I recall it with *chair de poule*, with goose flesh. The king, who was *très émotionnel* anyway on the subject of spiritual penitence, was moved to tears. We had witnessed far more than a simple feat of memory, though that alone was astounding, to remember not only the words of a language you do not understand, but the pronunciation as well, and after only one day! But the choice, *mon Dieu!* And the way he recited! It was clear to us all that he was like no one we had ever invited to the Academy before.

"In what way was he different?"

The duke thought for a moment before replying.

"It requires a depth of understanding to consider a man's ideas separately from the man himself, since the one is so often an extension of the other. The Italian was far more complex that any of us at the time imagined. On the surface, he appeared to be a pompous, overblown ass. Utterly lacking in humility or in social graces. He was stubborn and self-centered, as though no one else's ideas were worthy, only his.

"The majority at court were at best amused and at worst annoyed by his behavior. D'Arques and I poked fun at his boring speeches.

The *mignons* mimicked his affectations. Members of the Académie, the Sorbonne, and the Collège de France were frankly irate. They called him *le fléau,* the Nuisance. Eventually, even the king wearied of having him around. He was an embarrassment.

"On the other hand, when he actually got down to it, as with that first incredible demonstration of memory, or in a discussion of his theories, or with a demonstration of one of his various systems — if you could manage to overlook his personal style, to listen beyond the bombastics to what he was really saying — why, then the Italian's ideas were daring, provocative, absolutely brilliant.

"Of course, few of us were capable of such objectivity. As a result, he was often a subject of scorn and ridicule. In retrospect, I realize we were wrong. But we were young, headstrong, and immature. His philosophy was of little interest to us then, especially as it often con-tradicted accepted theories. The only philosophy that impressed us in those days was that of Epicurus, not Plato or Aristotle. We were too intent on having a good time to be serious. On the other hand, Bruno was never anything but serious."

"Were the Nolan's ideas only philosophical? Were some religious?"

"Religion was not a subject discussed at court, nor in the Palace Academy. Catherine de' Medici was determined to reunite the reli-gious factions. Most of her schemes, aside from keeping her favorite son in power and killing off his opposition, were to that end. She im-pressed her desires on her son as well. So the king sought to walk a middle road. There were at court representatives of each of the fac-tions, there was even a Huguenot or two in the Académie. To allow the subject of religion to be discussed, therefore, Le Roy would have had to acknowledge the issue in public debate. As we were then at peace, he could not afford to do so.

"Bruno was rumored to have been a priest, not favored in his own country. There was some talk of trouble with the Holy Office. The king chose not to question him on these rumors, so as not to 'know' anything about it. As I recall, he never referred to his religion, nor did he expound on purely religious themes. We took him to be Catholic. Beyond that, no one questioned him. Once or twice, I overheard him in discussion with Du Perron on the subject of Copernicus. At other times with Tyard against the teachings of Aristotle. These discussions were beyond my comprehension or interest.

"In the beginning, most of his ideas related to his memory system. I was fascinated with that, despite the fact that I found it complicated and difficult to follow. That first evening in the garden, after he completed his recitation of the litany and we were all so impressed, the king put him to a test."

✠

The king was overcome with racking sobs. The queen mother attempted to calm him, to restore him to some semblance of kingly comportment, while the others, thrilled with the Italian's recitation, broke into spontaneous applause. Even Du Perron, who had seen the mnemonist in action before, was impressed with this surprising achievement.

The clapping brought Henri back.

"Well done, Jordanus Nolanus!" he exclaimed enthusiastically, as though he had just been purged. "A remarkable demonstration. Now, can you do as much without preparation? Improvise? Let us see. We have in mind a test. Each of us shall give you something to remember. When we have all had a turn, then you shall repeat everything in the order in which it was given. How say you to that? Can you do it?"

Bruno bowed low, smiling.

"Your Majesty, it is mere child's play. My system is the perfection of all others. There is no feat too taxing for my system. I have lost count of the number of things it can hold, so great and so powerful are the number and kind of memory places in my system. A thousand times a thousand, perhaps a thousand thousand times a thousand. In theory, it is without limit, and only I . . ."

"But is it not merely based on the system of Ramon Lull?' asked Du Perron.

"No. I understand Lullism better than Lull did himself," was Bruno's response. "My system surpasses those of Democritus, of Simonides Melicus of Ceos, of Cicero and Quintillian and Petrarch and Tullius, of that found in the *Ad Herennium*, of Metrodorus of Scepsis, of Hippias of Elis, of Appolonius of Tyana, of Martianus Caprella of Carthage, from the ancient Egyptians, Hebrews, Greeks, and Romans, to Albertus Magnus and St. Thomas, to Johannes Romberch and Petrus Ravennatis, I have studied them all, improved upon them, and added a special scientific aspect — of which I shall write in my *De umbris idearum*, which I shall dedicate to you, Majesty — that is my own, and no one else's, unique and perfect memory system."

"Mon Dieu, the man's tongue is wired with springs!" exclaimed King Henri. "Very well then, to the test! I shall be first . . . "

✱

D'Épernon smiled as he recalled the scene in the Louvre Gardens that night.

"The king recited a riddle, in the English tongue. It had to do with the English queen and his brother, duc d'Anjou, whom she called 'her Frog.' I cannot remember it exactly. Several of the poets recited portions of their poems. The Italian had them each repeated, slowly. As I recall, the ladies demurred. Ronsard sang his *'Mignonne, allons voir si la rose,'* which Guilauime Costely had put to music, and Mauduit whistled a tune to accompany Baif, who recited one of his famous psalms. The queen mother went last, reciting the complete prophecy of Nostradamus, which she of course knew by heart, but of which I recall only this short passage, the one which correctly prophesied the death of her other son, King Henri II:

> The young lion will conquer the old
> On the field of battle in single combat;
> In a golden cage he will pierce his eye,
> This the first of two smashings,
> then comes a cruel death.

That was five years before Gabriel de Montgomery's broken lance accidentally pierced the king's eye in a tournament and caused his death."

"Was the Nolan able to do it?" I asked.

"Exactement, even down to the incorrect English grammar inserted deliberately by the king. *Formidable!* The king was so impressed, he immediately named the Italian to a reading post at the Collège de France. The king knew they never would have accepted an ex-priest at the Sorbonne, not even at his request. No matter. The Italian was thrilled to have a post, any post, even at the Collège de France. The meeting ended, and, true to the king's word, the Italian was driven home in the royal coach."

"I gather you had other exposure to his memory system. Did you ever learn it?"

"Jamais. Never. I understood the theory behind the memory places for remembering names and events. I understood the reason for us-

ing familiar places, like my home, my church, other similar buildings, and places within them on which to attach things that I wanted to remember, then to retrace my steps from the beginning and to retrieve those things in their proper order. That much I was able to digest, but from there the system become far more involved than I could handle. There were wheels and charts with figures and letters of the Greek and Hebrew alphabets, as well as from ours, moving and concentric, divided into segments, the segments into divisions, the divisions into subdivisions. The signs and images of the decans of the zodiac were used, images of the planets, the mansions of the moon, the houses of the horoscope, stars and constellations of the heavens — it was all a dazzling myriad of detail. I could not have learned that system in a hundred years! Du Perron was the only one among us who could even begin to understand it.

"I tried to read his books, but for me it was much like playing chess: you can hold only so many moves in your head at one time. Try for one more, and you lose them all and have to begin again. To understand his system was to hold more moves in my head than I had capacity for holding, *tu comprendre?*

"Let us, for the sake of discussion, say that I am capable of holding five or six moves. Du Perron's capacity was greater, he might perhaps have the ability to hold as many as ten moves in his head. But at least I could still be competitive in a game with Du Perron. The Italian was in a class by himself. With him the difference was more than quantitative; it was qualitative as well, *tu comprendre?* On the social level he may have been *le fléau*, but on the level of his ideas he was *un génie*, a genius. I never pretended to that level of play."

✠

It requires a depth of understanding to consider a man's ideas separately from the man himself.

That thought disturbed me. When my master had given me this mission, he said it would help him to understand the Nolan's ideas if he could understand the Nolan. That made sense to me at the time. The church says we are as responsible for our thoughts as our actions, and that God holds us accountable for both. Our ideas are the sum of us. In Campo Marzio, we had a proverb: A deaf mute does not compose music.

But after listening to d'Épernon, I was not so sure anymore. How many times had someone guilty of a crime been set free just because he looked innocent or sounded innocent? And how many times had an innocent bystander been nailed because he looked or sounded guilty? We judge the contents by the package. That is our nature. We think we can keep them separate, we even try, but we don't know how. So the one influences the other, and we are not even aware that it happens, because we think we are being objective.

What would it take to appreciate the thoughts of an obnoxious genius? "A depth of understanding," d'Épernon had said, and a level of play to which he did not pretend. What about Bellarmine? Did he have that special kind of understanding? Did he pretend to that level of play? I thought he did. After all, my master was also a genius. But could two geniuses play the same game by different rules? And would it then still be the same game?

If the Nolan was "a pompous, overblown ass, utterly lacking in humility or social grace," what chance did he have against the Sant' Offizio?

Bruno was no sweetheart. No supplicant ready to roll over and play dead. He was a man who rubbed everybody the wrong way, a man with a big mouth, a man who knocked everybody's ideas but his own, a man with all enemies and no friends, a man already imprisoned and on trial for the last five years. There was no such thing with the Sant' Offizio as their having to prove guilt. If you were accused of heresy, you were guilty as hell, trial or no trial.

It made little difference whether one was recalcitrant or repentant. The only variables were how long a trial, how much torture, how big a sentence. With Bruno's personality, he was cooked. Bellarmine was his only hope. Bruno had better pray that my master had the depth of understanding it was going to take to separate the ideas from the man, because what I had to report so far was not going to do him very much good.

Still, I had to give him the benefit of doubt. So far, I had only traced Bruno to 1581. The Nolan had sixteen more years to improve his personality.

✠

"Who are you, Guidotti?"

"The man who saved your life."

I had been expecting the question. I was ready with the answer.

My shoulder and the crack to my head were both healed. I was no longer confined to the hôtel and gardens of my host, and d'Épernon — "Nogie" by now — had undertaken to show me the Paris

I had missed on my first visit with Bellarmine, a Paris I had not even imagined existed. For the past three days I had hardly slept at all.

Mornings, Nogie walked me through the narrow streets and back alleys of the city from one end to the other, across every one of the sixteen bridges, in and out of half the cathedrals, palaces, and hôtels, and up and down most of the towers to point out the sights. The noise and the filth of the streets were as bad as Naples or worse. So were my hangovers. Not Nogie, who had the enviable ability to pour brew down him at prodigious rate and yet suffer no effect whatever the next morning! At midday we would begin to eat our way through enough solid food to settle my stomach, and enough liquid — *capello de le cane,* we called it in Campo Marzio, the hair of the dog that bit you — to quiet my head. By late afternoon, I would be feeling myself again. But by evening, Nogie would have me just drunk enough to forget what I was going to feel like the next morning, and I would do it all over again. I could not decide whether this was the way he always spent his time or if he was just doing it to entertain me, but I was beginning to think I could do with a little less entertainment. This pace was killing me!

Weary as I was though, I found these daily wanderings through Paris most interesting. I saw common street stalls like the ones we had in Rome, except these sold a much higher grade of goods. Rich things, gold and silver and jewels, rare silks and satins, goods from the Orient and from the New World.

The owners of these stalls were shrewd traders. Unlike those in Rome, whose attitude was this is what we sell, take it or leave it, these would go out of their way to produce for you whatever they did not have. You had only to express an interest; they would be gone in a flash, reappearing minutes later with the exact item. Rome was a sellers' market, where the traders grew fat and lazy on an overabundant supply of tourists and pilgrims. In a buyers' market like Paris, these traders could not afford to get lazy or they would be out of business. A similar comparison might be made with the church. The pope would do well to study the methods of the Paris traders, not just those of Rome.

Equally fascinating were the bookshops of the Boulevard St. Germain. Lined one after the other for blocks, each boasted an inventory large enough to stock a college. They had books in every language and on every subject imaginable, from illustrated sex manuals of the Orient to rare religious manuscripts hand illuminated by obscure

Benedictine monks. I do not exaggerate. The bookshops of Paris put those of Rome to shame.

On the third morning of our rounds, Nogie took me to the Louvre, where I briefly met King Henri IV on his way to a hawking. The king invited us to join his group, but d'Épernon declined, explaining that I was only recently recovered from wounds suffered in his defense and thus unable to sit a horse. Immediately, the king demanded the details of this infamous attack on one of his peers, whereafter he swore an oath he would see the villains drawn and quartered who would dare to attack a Knight of the Holy Order of the Spirit and a colonel-general of France!

This king was a pleasant surprise. I would have expected someone more reserved, someone more ... regal, I suppose. Instead, he was a stocky little man, bald, with a furrowed brow, a great hooked nose, and a square grizzled beard. He had a powerful stink of garlic about him — Nogie said he munched the stuff like apples — and of sweat. He was one of those men who believe that in their natural odors lies their sexual power, like a great wild beast, and they fear to wash and lose it.

I took an instant liking to him. He had a way of meeting me eye to eye, as few men do. I liked that. It gave me the feeling we understood each other.

He laughed and swore and swaggered like a mountain man, and gave the impression of being happy and sad at the same time. Wise and stupid too. Above all, he seemed a caring and unpretentious man — he dressed simply, in plain gray with a doublet of taffeta that had no trimming of lace or sash — yet he never left you in doubt that here was a king, a ruler, a champion of the people.

Donning a wide-brimmed hat with the sweeping white plume that was his trademark in battle, he mounted his stallion from the block, wheeled, and galloped recklessly toward rue St. Honoré with his companions racing to catch up, all tearing madly around the corner together, that white feather bobbing up and down like a banner, and I was struck by a sense of loss, I feel it now, that had we only met another time, under other circumstances, we might have been close friends. I had that feeling. Perhaps others had it too. Perhaps that was how he managed to inspire loyalty and devotion in his followers and to put an end to the civil wars that had torn his nation apart for so long. He was "Henri le Grand."

Nogie and I spent the rest of our afternoons making the rounds of his cronies, who never seemed to do anything but gamble at dice and play billiards, that is, when they weren't eating and drinking. Evenings began at elaborate palace parties attended by the most elegant and distinguished personages of Paris; shifted in the small hours of the morning to cheap hostelries like "Les Rats" and "Les Trois Pigeons," where I met some of Paris's less elegant but no less distinguished citizens — painted ladies of the evening, possessing a knowledge of fornication more lively and extensive than any I had known in my old pimping days in Campo Marzio; and concluded staggering drunkenly back to l'Hôtel d'Épernon as the morning sun began its day glistening on the River Seine, finally falling into bed for a few hours' sleep before Nogie had us off again.

In all this time, despite my own persistent probing on the subject of Giordano Bruno, the duke never once questioned me about my personal life, who I was, where I came from, what I was doing in Paris. I knew he must be burning to know. And at last, he was able to stand it no longer.

We were sitting in the corner of his salon. The room was filled with the very same people who had been attending the other parties all week long and were now attending his. None of these people appeared to work. As far as I could see, life was one continuous party which simply shifted from one location to another.

I was drinking a strong concoction called "brandy," made from distilled wine in Gascony — heady stuff that was all the rage in Paris, what with having a Gascon for a king — smoking Virginia tobacco, and enjoying the music of the duke's friend, Claudin le Jeune, who played a "violin," a bowed instrument invented, some said, by a certain Amati of Cremona.

"Yes, but who are you really?" d'Épernon wanted to know.

"Nogie, I am the man who saved your life two weeks ago. Isn't that enough?" I responded calmly.

I closed my eyes and blew smoke lazily toward the ceiling. This was the life!

"*Certainement, mon cher,* and I shall never forget it. But dammit now, you really must tell me who you are. I shall not sleep until I know. You can trust me. I would not tell a soul. Are you a spy? I know you are hiding something. Has it to do with that crazy Italian? I won't give up, you know. It piques my curiosity. Be reasonable, Pietro, I am your friend, I swear it."

Now that it was loose in him, he would never contain it. His voice grew louder, as he insisted on knowing. Others had shifted their attention from the music to our conversation. It was obvious he was not going to let go of the subject.

"All right, but not here," I said, eyeing our eavesdroppers. "Let's go outside."

I still was not sure how much to tell him. My mind sifted through the events of the past few months as we left the concert and went into the garden to be alone. Why was I going to tell him anything? Was it because of his insistence that I trust him? Or was it because I was as anxious to share my secret as he was to learn it? Or was I just out to impress the duke with my importance? Nicco Baroniti had been right in Geneva. I was an amateur.

The thing was, deep down I knew I could not keep up this kind of life indefinitely. Sooner or later I was going to have to get back on the Nolan's trail. It was nearly summer already. When I did, I could use an ally. I had a list of names, and Nogie knew everybody in Paris.

There in the garden in the moonlight, amid a blend of crickets and violin music, I told Nogie la Valette everything I knew. About me and Bellarmine and Bruno and the Inquisition. I did exactly what the boss had warned me against doing. I took a chance and placed my entire mission at risk because I could not keep my mouth shut. But I decided if you can't trust a man whose life you saved, you can't trust anybody.

We strolled along in silence. I will say one thing for the duke. He knew when to keep *his* mouth shut. He made no comment, asked no questions. I could not begin to guess what he might be thinking. Was he shocked? Would he throw me out? Would he turn me in? What did I really know about him anyway? I remembered how wrong I had been about Baroniti. These people were experienced in diplomacy and intrigue. I was just Pietro Guidotti, son of a bone setter.

D'Épernon's silence made me nervous. This was a very different reaction than the one I had expected. It could be I had just made a terrible mistake. And in this business you did not make mistakes.

The music was concluded. We heard the applause.

"Allons," the duke said quietly. "My guests will soon be departing."

And we went inside.

The duke began to circulate among his guests, chatting here, joking there, smiling and making his way smoothly from one to another. His face was a mask, showing nothing of our conversation in the garden. I saw him pause briefly in animated conversation with two extremely attractive young women. They were without question the most beautiful I had yet seen in Paris. All evening their male admirers had circled them with the kind of unconcealed eagerness of male dogs sniffing at a bitch in heat. I had smiled at the obviousness of these young men, yet envied them in their quest. Another time, another place, I might have joined them. Just now, I was far too concerned about the duke.

He returned to my side.

"Do you notice those two young beauties over there, the ones I was talking to a moment ago?" he asked in a confidential tone.

"Does a bull have balls?"

"They wish to meet you. The one on the left is Diane d'Estrées, marquise de Villare. She is the sister of the duchesse de Beaufort, Gabrielle d'Estrées, the king's current mistress. The dark one is Ariel Sardini, daughter of Scipio Sardini, the king's banker. Her mother, Isabelle de Limeuil, was once a member of Catherine de' Medici's *escadron volant*, those ladies who used their feminine charms to obtain political secrets for their mistress. They say Isabelle was the best, until she retired and married Sardini for his wealth. Of course, she may still have been working for the queen mother even then, who knows?"

"Why all this history, just to meet two ripe plums?"

"Because, dear Guidotti, it was rumored in court at the time that your little Italian doctor was bedding Sardini's wife on the sly. It may be that her daughter will remember him. Ariel would have been only nine or ten at the time, but with Isabelle de Limeuil for a mother, my guess is she was nine or ten going on twenty. She has already surpassed her mother in reputation. Believe me, the two of them are a pair of minks. Come, *mon cher*, you shall meet them. D'Épernon pays his debts. Perhaps this shall result in some help to your mission. If not, I promise they will provide at least an amusing diversion."

My concern about the duke disappeared. I had not made a mistake after all. A pair of minks? *Ecco*. Information or diversion, either way I could not lose.

D'Épernon introduced us and wandered off almost immediately. There ensued a brief but surprising conversation. They talked; I listened. In a few minutes I was treated to a dizzying range of topics, from the breeding practices of Arabian stallions to the size of summer cucumbers in the Midi, receiving a quick lesson in what the genteel French refer to as *double entendre*. They were amused by my confusion.

Now, I was no stranger to lewd talk from women. It was the customary manner of speaking used by prostitutes in Campo Marzio. And I was no prude either. We Romans believe in straight talk, no beating around the bush. But these were not prostitutes; these were refined young ladies of the French peerage. I was simply unsure how to respond. In the course of ten minutes, these two had conveyed to me an invitation to share with them a variety of sexual pleasures, the nature of which was unmistakable, and yet had not uttered one off-color word. By the end of the conversation, I was left in no doubt of their meaning. The bulge beneath my codpiece served as ample interpreter.

Sometime later, they departed with several young escorts. As they brushed past me, Diane d'Estrées, with a look that required no explanation, contrived to hand me a card on which was printed:

D'Estrées
Rue Cortot No. 20
Paris

beneath which a postscript had been hastily added:

midnight tomorrow, rear entrance
D & A

The postscript may well have been yet another of the ladies' double meanings. I spent the night dreaming of cucumbers and melons.

My decadent meanderings through Paris with Nogie ended that night. The following day, he was all business. One thing I discovered about d'Épernon, he was an organized and systematic thinker. And his word was as good as gold. He said he would try to help me, and help me he did.

First, he had me review with him my notes on our talks about Bruno. He was looking for cues that might stir new memories. I had begun recording these notes in Geneva when I had decided there was going to be too much for me to remember until I got back to Rome. The Nolan may have been a memory expert, but I was not. I needed something on paper, despite my master's warning to put nothing in writing.

I thought it would be safe if I used some kind of code, something only I could understand. So I used only first letters for names, ab-breviated key words, substituted numbers for letters. At least I made an attempt to do that, when I had the patience and was without a hangover. Occasionally, I even threw in symbols of my own devising. The result, I was certain, would give anyone reading these pages an impossible task to decipher their meaning. Besides, I had little doubt the master had exaggerated the need for such secrecy in the first case.

It was just the kind of thinking that proved Baroniti's point about amateurs, but I didn't know it at the time. If I had had the slightest inkling of the trouble these notes were going to cause me one day, I never would have started them, code or no code.

✖

The review of my notes produced only one possibility: the librarian Cotin from the Abbey St. Victor. If he was still there, I would try to talk to him. Of the other names on my list, Nogie recognized several, but they had been foreigners, in Paris on mission for their governments at the time the Nolan was there, and now long gone.

Next, we scoured the bookshops, hoping to locate some of the Nolan's works. The dedications were what we were after. It was d'Épernon's idea and a good one, except it turned out that the people he had dedicated his books to were either dead or no longer in Paris. The most important of these had been Michel de Castelnau, marquis de Mauvissière. He was on my London list. Mauvissière had been Henri III's ambassador to the court of Elizabeth at the time Bruno was in England. D'Épernon said the ambassador had been recalled to Paris in '85 and that the Nolan had been among his household. Mauvissière would have been perfect, another patron like de Vico. But, like de Vico, he was dead.

A second book we found contained a dedication to Henri de Valois, duc d'Angoulême, signed by Jean Regnault, the duc's councillor. Both of them were dead. Regnault had been a friend of John Moro, an ambassador from Venice. We made the gambling rounds for the rest of the afternoon, hoping that one of Nogie's friends might know what happened to John Moro. None did.

It gave me a peculiar feeling, coming across those two books by Bruno. This was the first physical sign of him having been somewhere before me, like a footprint or a cold campfire along the trail. For some reason it made me feel like an intruder, as though I were eavesdropping on a private conversation, though of course the books were public. Could it be that I was beginning to feel some attachment to the man? He was a real person now, no longer simply a name, not just someone I had never heard of whom my master wanted me to find out about, but a man who had eaten and slept and gone to parties in Paris, just as I had, and perhaps had hangovers the next morning, just as I had, a man who had written books, had dedicated them and had them printed, and now years later two of his books were on the Boulevard St. Germain and I could leaf through them and see his thoughts laid bare on a printed page.

It did something to me, to realize that somebody wanted to fry the poor guy for these words that I was looking at. Maybe there was something out there I could discover about Bruno, something good that I could report back to my master that might somehow save Bruno's skin! That made me nervous. It excited me, but it made me nervous, because what if it was there and I failed to find it?

For the first time, I realized the full importance of my mission: I was responsible for Giordano Bruno's life. This man, who I had never met and about whom I had known nothing when I first left Rome, this man, who d'Épernon thought a genius but just about everyone else had considered at best a crackpot and at worst a heretic, this man could live or die based on what I might discover or not. Having power over another man's life is a serious business.

✠

An idea struck me at dinner that night. I wonder why it had not occurred to me sooner. Crazy, but maybe it would work. We had been talking in general terms about Bruno's plight, the plight of anyone in fact who got into trouble with the authorities, whether secular or religious, state or church, concerning ideas that threatened established thinking. Nogie said he could sympathize with the Nolan, that he might have been peculiar and a pain in the ass, but that he had also had a daring intelligence and was most certainly not a heretic. That was when I got the idea.

"Let me ask you something, Nogie. Would you be willing to stand up for Bruno?" What I was thinking was really crazy!

D'Épernon did not at first understand my meaning.

"Mais certainement! Have I not just done so?"

"Not with me, with the Sant'Offizio. What I mean is, would you be willing to come to Rome with me, go before the tribunal as a volunteer witness and tell them what you just told me, that you, duc d'Épernon of his majesty's service, colonel-general of France, knew Bruno in Paris, respected his intelligence, and do not believe him to be a heretic."

Nogie shook his head vigorously.

"Parfandious! Are you mad?"

"Why not? Are you afraid of the Inquisition? Are you afraid to risk your reputation? What?"

"None of those. I would do it for you, *mon cher,* and without a moment's hesitation. Do you know why? Because you would do it for me. Have you not already done so, and without even knowing who I was? Bruno would not risk himself for anyone, stranger or friend. I said that I respected his intelligence, not him. The thing I remember most about this man was his narcissistic singlemindedness. Whatever he did, he did for himself. He would stop at nothing to further his own ideas and would not lift a finger for anyone else's. He cared for no one and used whoever he could. I do not trust a man like that. I would not risk myself for such a man."

I could understand his reasoning. But I resolved that if ever I found a friend of Bruno's, I would raise this issue again. Surely there was someone, somewhere, who would stand up and be counted for him. There was still time for me to find that person. And when I did, I would bring him back to Rome with me. This could be the way to save the Nolan.

Chapter 10

maggio 1597
Rue Cortot No. 20
Paris

I LOST MY VIRGINITY at the age of eleven when a fourteen-year-old miller's daughter who had lost hers at ten stuffed me into her under the Ponte Fabricio by way of demonstrating that a sin of the flesh was too much fun for God to have meant it to be a sin. I was easily convinced. Over the next years, I had many opportunities to reconfirm her theory. What I mean to say is that I was hardly inexperienced.

Then why was I feeling just like a nervous young kid? I admit I was stimulated by Nogie's gossip. A midnight rendezvous with two seductive young Parisian noblewomen would be a new experience for me. There was additional novelty in that one was the sister of the king's paramour. Nothing so quickening to a man's pulse as the combination of sex and danger.

I bathed not once but twice. I used d'Épernon's cologne. I warmed my insides with a stiff brace of his brandy. By the time I was dressed, I had a good glow. Not even my host's steady barrage of teasing dulled the edge, as I finished preparation for my tryst with "D & A" at No. 20 rue Cortot. With Nogie's good-natured laughter still ringing in my ears, I set out alone through the dark and narrow streets of Paris.

More to heighten the excitement than to calm it, I pretended to myself that this was to be strictly business. Nothing sexual was going to happen. I was interested only in doing the job that I had been sent by my master to do.

Who was I kidding? There was little doubt what kind of business was going to be conducted at this hour, not after that little conversation at the duke's party the other night. Remembering that, I sped my pace.

I thought, too, about Giordano Bruno, locked away in a dungeon at Sant'Angelo. Frightened, lonely, without hope, poor guy. I decided to dedicate this evening to him, the way he had dedicated his books. From what I already knew about him, I imagined him urging me on. "Do it once for me, Guidotti!" he would shout. Laughing at the thought, I doffed my hat to him in the empty street, and hurried on.

Thoughts of my master fleetingly crossed my mind. I imagined him frowning at me, then turning his back so that I would not see him stifling a smile. There was plenty I did not tell my master, but not much that he did not already know. I never pretended to be like him; he never asked me to be. (Fat chance if he had!) He accepted me for what I was and did not try to change me. I always appreciated that. It made life simpler. But he did make a point to let me know he was not interested in hearing the lurid details of my private life.

I doffed my hat again: Boss, here's one more detail you won't hear. About now, I was feeling as good as I know how to feel.

✠

A nearby cathedral tolled midnight when I reached rue Cortot. Right on time. There was no moon. No street lamps in this section either. The old street was so dark I had to trace with my fingers the number on the gate, to be certain I had arrived at the right address.

Number 20 was a tall, steep-roofed wooden house, separated from the others by a high wall. The gate was locked. Wrong house? Wrong night? Or was it a test? More likely a tease, I decided. I went over the wall.

The house was as dark as the night. All the Venetian blinds were drawn. Groping my way through the garden, I reached the rear of the house. I stood before the door, listening. I thought I detected something stirring on the other side. Then I heard whispering. As I tried the handle, the door suddenly opened from the inside. Hands grabbed my outstretched arm and pulled me in.

I could not see a thing. Yet, there was no mistaking their presence. The warmth of their bodies. Perfume. The scented smell of freshly washed hair. The sensual pleasure of small soft hands clasping each of mine in the darkness. The wisp of gossamery material brushed my face as I ducked through the doorway, and now there was the feel of firm hips wedging me between them as we stood just inside the door.

"Diane? Ariel? Is it you?" I asked.

"Ssshhh!"

This warning was whispered into both my ears at the same time, their lips lightly brushing me in the process. One of them had the faint odor of oil of mint on her breath. My heart was pounding with excitement.

One of them let go of my hand and stepped behind me. I felt a blindfold being loosely tied over my eyes.

"Wha...?"

"Trust us," she whispered. Then she took my hand again in hers. Was it Ariel or Diane? I couldn't tell.

Giggling, they led me through what seemed a long hall and then up a winding staircase. They had no difficulty navigating in the dark.

Another set of stairs, straight up this time. We stopped. I sensed something in front of me, a wall or a door. Door, probably.

"Wait," whispered one.

I did as I was told.

I felt a rush of warm air on my face as a door was opened. I was led inside and heard the door close softly behind me. A dozen paces forward, stop again.

"Stand here."

I stood, feeling a little foolish by now. Looking so too, I imagined. But, if they wanted to play, I could play.

I heard them scurrying about, heard their breathing, the swishing of their gowns. There was light in the room, I could distinguish its flickering through the space beneath the blindfold. The room exuded the subtle aroma of burning incense.

Now they were near me again, whispering excitedly to each other. My hands were brought behind me and bound lightly with a piece of ribbon. I could easily have broken it or slipped my hands free if I wished. I chose not to. The game was amusing them, and it was arousing me. Why stop it?

"You must keep your eyes closed until we tell you to open them," was the next command as the blindfold was removed.

Everything was done and said slowly, seductively.

From the other side of the room now, they chanted softly, in unison: "We are the daughters of Aphrodite Pandemos. And you are the son of Adonis. You are our captive and must obey our commands. You may open your eyes."

Words fail me. I can see that room now, just as if I were standing in the middle of it again. If only I had the power to describe it, to describe the sensations that it generated in me. The immediate impression was one of total sensuality and eroticism. It resembled the pistil deep inside a dark red rose. The color, red; the texture, velvet. Plush Persian rugs, brocaded draperies of heavy silk. The ceiling was entirely mirrored. Upon the walls were painted nudes in provocative poses, many in the act of copulation, in couples, in trios, in groups, in various combinations of age and gender.

Against one wall there was a great canopied four-poster bed, upon which were thrown dozens of satin-covered pillows decorated with cupids. Red candles were burning in alcoves of the room, casting dancing shadows on the walls, which seemed to lend action to the nudes. The flames were reflected in the mirrors on the ceiling.

This room made Silvia Gandini's salon look like a confessional.

✠

I spotted them on the ceiling first, then lowered my eyes to the room. They were reclining on matching divans of deep red velvet. The daughters of Aphrodite. Long tresses braided with flowers. One blond, the other raven-haired. Voluptuous young bodies clad in layers of delicate gauze that I could almost but not quite see through. Diane in black. Ariel in white. They were a feast to stir my juices.

They glanced at each other slyly, then at me, and smiled. They were pleased with the effect they had created, as well they might be. Never in my dreams had I ever imagined anything like it, nor have I ever seen anything to match it again. I was grinning like an idiot, waiting to see what would come next.

"Come closer, son of Adonis."

The divans were placed in the form of an inverted V, like a pair of legs spread open and awaiting my entrance. I approached until I could go no further and was looking down at the daughters of Aphrodite on either side of me. How I longed to have my hands free of their bonds, to tear away their clothing and have them both there and then! But the game was still young. I was the captive, and patience would have its rewards.

"How may I serve your Highnesses?" I asked politely.

"Oh, we'll think of something," Diane answered with feigned indifference, running a languid hand up the inside of my leg and down the other.

"Yes, something," Ariel added, looking up at me. "There might be something you could give us."

"What have you got?" asked Diane innocently.

"Shall we look?" Ariel asked before I could respond.

"We may as well, I suppose."

"But my hands are tied," I complained.

"Why, so they are," Diane observed. "What a pity. Now we shall never know."

Ariel giggled.

"But look at his drawers, dear," she said. "There is a fellow trapped in there, I believe. Ought we not free him?"

"I wish you would," I said laughing. "It's not his fault, you know, that you have gone and got him excited."

They frowned, indicating that I was to remain a passive captive.

They reached up and together began to unfasten and remove my drawers and underclothing. I could barely contain myself, so anxious was I for them to speed the process.

But it was torture they had in mind, not speed. They pretended to have difficulty with a fastening. I slipped a hand free to help them. It was resoundingly slapped. I put my hand behind my back again and shrugged. My turn would come.

Now they had me completely exposed below the waist. They proceeded to stroke my member, discussing it between them as though it were a separate object and I were not even in the room.

"How big it is!"

"What does it do, do you think?"

"I cannot guess. It certainly is hard. Perhaps it rams things or is used as a club."

"Or to poke holes in things?"

"Why does it quiver so? Is it frightened?"

"I do not think so. Look at its color! It is purple with rage."

It was beginning to throb from all this attention, and I worried that it would too soon spit its juice. I fought against the sensation.

They looked at each other knowingly. Suddenly Ariel dealt it a stinging blow with a flick of her fingers.

I howled!

And it went immediately limp.

"Now see what you have done, Ariel. The poor thing! Is it dead, do you suppose?"

"No, I do not think so. Only sleeping. Let us awaken it."

But when they succeeded in doing so, Ariel only flicked it down again. I was beginning to tire of this game.

The room was warm, and I was hot. I requested permission to remove the remainder of my clothing. Granted. Might I remove theirs? Denied.

Go to bed, I was ordered.

I went to bed. This time the daughters of Aphrodite bound me hand and foot, loosely as before, one appendage to each of the four posts. In a sitting position, propped by pillows.

Diane stretched out beside me, caressing my body lightly with her fingertips. Ariel stood at the foot of the bed and provocatively removed the flimsy fabric that covered her body, one layer at a time until the last layer was gone and nothing of her beauty was hidden. My tool once again came erect with anticipation.

Diane produced a flagon of red wine and held it to my mouth. I drank deeply, feeling the warmth of the liquid spreading inside me, until the flagon was drained. She licked the remaining drops from my lips with her tongue.

Now it was Ariel beside me in the bed, rubbing my body with hers as Diane disrobed.

They were the true daughters of Aphrodite. Never had I beheld such beauty. The temptation was impossible to resist. I could no longer remain passive, playing their game. It was expecting too much! After all, the natural urges of the body are too strong for the mind to contain. Laws may govern our behavior in public, but in this chamber of love there could be no laws. The end of this match was known from the beginning, and it was only a challenge to see how long I could hold out against their teasing. Well, I had to have them...now!

✠

I roared, broke my restraints, and leaped to my feet on the bed! I roared again, beating on my chest. Then I dropped, intending to nail Ariel beneath me, but she was too quick. She was off the bed in a flash. Now the two daughters of Aphrodite squealed and raced around the room, dodging behind pieces of furniture, the son of Adonis chasing after them, awkwardly grabbing first for one, then for the other, only to come up with thin air as they squirmed elusively out of reach.

It was a wild naked chase! Over the bed, around the divans, with me just behind them, their full breasts bouncing gaily, long legs thrashing, rounded asses only inches away from my stiff sword, then wheeling suddenly to reveal patches of tawny bush glistening moistly as they raced by me, taunting, shrieking gales of laughter!

And then the chase ended. Suddenly. As though by mutual consent. We stood facing each other, panting. A look of open invitation spread across their faces. They backed away from me toward the bed. Slowly. Slowly. Caressing themselves between the legs with both hands. Lips parted. Eyes flashing in the candlelight.

I followed at the same pace. Slowly. Slowly. My eyes were fixed on them. My breath came in quick bursts. My half-lowered staff rising yet again, this time its use certain.

They reached the bed and stopped.

I continued until I was almost upon them. I could smell the musky sweetness of their excitement. I...

Suddenly, the door burst open and a lusty voice bellowed:

"Ventre Saint-Gris! How are we expected to sleep with all this noise!"

We stared, wide-eyed.

Gesù Cristo it was the king! There stood Henri in the doorway, dressed in his nightshirt and cap, legs spread and hands on hips, peering into the room and trying to digest the sight of two naked women and a naked man.

As he did, he threw back his head and roared with laughter. Then, abruptly, he stopped. He was staring hard in my direction.

"Mordieu, it is Guidotti! And right over my head! *Cap de Bious!"* he exclaimed. "You do get around, don't you, you rogue?"

Placing his finger to his lips, he turned and shut the door quietly.

"No need to wake your sister, Gabrielle, is there, my dear?" Henri said, winking broadly to Diane. Then to me: "You intend to share them with me, Guidotti, do you not? I am the king, remember."

He chuckled at his joke. Then he quickly pulled off his nightshirt, leaving the cap on. It gave him a comedic look, standing there naked with his nightcap on. Numerous battle scars were visible on his chest. His body hair was completely white. But it was already apparent that the royal plough was neither too old, nor was it — after fifty mistresses and with yet another sleeping in the room below — too worn to cultivate such fertile ground, which, by royal decree, we were about to share between us.

It could have been worse. As he said, he was the king. He could have chosen both. Instead, he gave me Diane.

✠

"Guidotti, I will wager I can outlast you."

We were sitting side by side on the bed, the daughters of Aphrodite with their heads between our legs.

"Your Majesty, I lack sufficient funds for such a wager."

Henri took a long swallow of wine and passed the bottle to me.

"Under the circumstances, we can suspend formalities, Guidotti. Call me Henri."

I passed the bottle back.

"Henri, I'm broke."

"Very well. In the morning I shall give you *cinq cent écus.*"

"I appreciate that, Henri."

"Guidotti?"

"Yes, Henri?"

"How much do you wager?"

"Two-fifty."

"Only two-fifty? *Ventre Saint-Gris!* But I just gave you five hundred!"

"Well, Henri, this way if I lose, I will still have two-fifty."

"It is a bet then, you rogue."

Without slackening in their tasks, the daughters of Aphrodite now entered into a silent wager of their own: their skills against our resistance. Ours a wager to prolong, theirs to hasten. The pace quickened.

I looked at Henri. His face was blotched red. His mouth was tightly set and determined. His brow was creased with concentration.

I was drenched in sweat. I tried to put my mind elsewhere. The trick was not to think about it, to think about something else. It was less easy than it sounds.

My eyes strayed to the ceiling. Mistake! I had forgotten the mirrors. I would never win this bet.

I looked at Henri again. He looked at me. Each saw in the other's desperation his own, and looked away.

The daughters had not relinquished their control after all. This was just one more game.

No use. It would be over in seconds. The tingling sensation had already begun, deep, deep down, now irreversible.

Henri rolled his eyes upward and groaned.

I did the same.

"Merde!"

"Merda!"

The room was filled with heavy breathing.

"Guidotti?"

"Yes, Henri?"

"You win," he sighed ruefully. There were tears in his eyes.

"Your Majesty?"

It was Diane.

"Madame?"

"Your Majesty, Mademoiselle Sardini and I have conferred. It was a tie."

Chapter 11

"WAKE UP, PIETRO!"

D'Épernon was shaking me awake as though from the dead. Which is about how I felt when he finally succeeded... dead.

After King Henri had returned to the bed of Gabrielle d'Estrées the night before, the daughters of Aphrodite and I continued from where we had left off, only this time it was a game of my choosing. Several hours and was it one or two bottles of wine later, with much coaxing — I was not that anxious to leave — Diane and Ariel had managed to get me out of the house and over the wall again, the gate being still locked.

It turned out that only Henri had a key to this gate. He locked it every evening when he arrived and unlocked it in the mornings when he left for the Louvre. Evenings on which he did not attend the duchesse de Beaufort at her house on rue Cortot, one of his body-guards performed the gate-locking ceremony. This was told to me by her sister, Diane. Henri might have fooled around upstairs, and plenty of other places too on occasion, but he had remained otherwise faithful to Gabrielle for many years. The locked gate? Why, to insure that she was equally faithful, of course.

I had staggered home somehow, feeling like a soldier returning from the wars, had fallen into bed with my clothes on, and now, though it seemed barely minutes later, it was well into the afternoon when Nogie was shaking me awake.

"Nogie, go away!" I groaned. My fogged brain screamed for sleep. "I will tell you all about it later, I promise. Just let me sleep another hour or two."

I stuffed a pillow over my head.

"*Parfandious!* You will sleep at the Place de Grève tonight if you do not get up now, this instant. Wake up, *imbécile,* you are in big trouble!"

Place de Grève? People were separated from their heads at Place de Grève! Drawn and quartered. Tortured. Only last April, someone named Charpentier had been broken on the wheel at Place de Grève for carrying messages against the king. Nobody makes jokes about Place de Grève.

I sat bolt upright.

"What's the matter?"

D'Épernon had a grave look.

"Montmorency's men are inquiring for you all over town. They have not come here yet because the constable owes me many favors. This is his way of giving me time to get you away from my house so that I will not be connected with your arrest. You must leave Paris at once!"

"But what is it all about? What would Montmorency want with me?"

What a hell of a way to have to wake up after such a beautiful night!

"Montmorency is the king's man. Therefore, the king is behind this. What I do not understand is that you have been here three weeks, so why now? What could have suddenly aroused the king's suspicions?"

"Henri? You must be mistaken. Henri and I are pals. Why, last night he said..."

"Last night?" The duke eyed me with suspicion. "You were with the king last night? I thought you were with the two ladies?"

"I was. But I was with Henri too. Listen, Nogie, last night was a night such as you would never believe," I said, grinning broadly.

I gave him the highlights.

"...So you see, Nogie," I finished, "you must be mistaken about Montmorency being after me. Henri and I are *amici*. Buddies."

D'Épernon shook his head sadly.

"You have much to learn about Frenchmen, *mon cher*. What goes on between the sheets has nothing to do with friendship. And with a king, there is no such thing at all. He is *le Roi*, you understand?

"Yes, he may drink with you, yes, he may whore with you, yes, he may even allow you to address him by name, but when it comes to *les affaires d'État, il est suprême*. He will have your head — zzzttt! — without blinking an eye, if he so much as suspects that you pose him a threat. Who knows what goes on in a king's mind? You were in the house of his mistress. Perhaps he is jealous. He was asleep one floor beneath you. Perhaps he fears you are an assassin. Perhaps he has learned that you work for Bellarmine. L'Estoile and others loyal to the throne always suspected that the papal legate Cardinal Cajetan and your master were in Paris during the siege only in order to stir the fires of sedition.

"Remember also that the king banished the Jesuits for their political plottings against the throne. Perhaps he suspects that you are a Jesuit spy. Or it may just be that the king knows nothing about you, and that knowing nothing makes him suspicious. It can be very dangerous for a king to know nothing about a man with whom he has shared wine and women.

"Whatever the case, the fact is that le duc de Montmorency is looking for you and that his men will be here soon. They must not find you."

"But he owes me 750 *écus!*"

D'Épernon shrugged.

"Easy come, easy go," he punned.

✠

I packed my belongings, including the new clothes the duke had bought for me — no telling what I was going to need in England — and took my leave of Nogaret la Valette. In the three weeks we had known each other, I had come to look upon him as a friend. I had not misplaced my trust in him. He had been faithful to his word. That counted for something with me, much more than clothes and good times.

La Valette had been my nurse, companion, mentor, and friend. Despite his high rank, he had treated me as an equal, and I learned from him things that one with my background might otherwise have never hoped to experience. More importantly, he had been a tremendous source of information and insight regarding the Nolan. Though I lingered longer with him than with anyone else on my journey, it was in every way time well spent. I would miss him.

✠

Montmorency or no, there was a stop I was determined to make before leaving Paris: Guillaume Cotin, the librarian of the Abbey St. Victor. Cotin was the only name d'Épernon had come up with that was not on the master's list. I had to see him.

It was nearly sundown. When Montmorency's men arrived at hôtel d'Épernon and found me gone, they would postpone their search until morning. With any luck I could see Cotin and be on my way to Pas de Calais by then. From Calais, I would cross the Channel to England.

If things did not go well, there was a chance I might have to leave Paris in haste. Taking both animals would slow me down. Cammello was the faster of the two — which was not saying much, to be sure — so I made a gift of the mule to d'Épernon's stables. I set out afoot, leading my horse.

I kept as close to the buildings as I could, in order to take advantage of the growing shadows, heading east along rue Galande to

Place Maubert, thence along rue St. Victor to the town wall. I was worried that Montmorency's men might be watching the gates, so I approached Porte St. Victor with caution. I must have stood in the alleyway for the better part of an hour, watching that gate for anyone suspicious-looking. But it seemed to be deserted. I passed through quickly and proceeded to the abbey.

The Abbey of St. Victor is an ancient and imposing monastery. It is by far the largest I have ever seen and one of the biggest in France. Situated a short distance east of the town wall, it rests in a beautiful and tranquil section that overlooks the River Seine. As I approached, I watched the last of the day's river barges being towed downstream, each by a single mule trodding slowly along the riverbank. The abbey was surrounded by a stone wall on three sides, with the river constituting the northern boundary, though there was a considerable expanse of woods and field separating the river from the abbey church. The main gate was always kept open, since both the church and the library were available to the public.

I arrived shortly after the conclusion of Vespers. Inquiring after Brother Cotin, I was directed by one of the friars to the library, a long building situated between the church and the dormitory. But as I approached the library, I hesitated. What was I going to tell him? What story should I use? With Montmorency searching for me, it could be dangerous for me to use my real name. Nor ought I to reveal my true purpose in coming. This was no cloistered convent. The public was openly admitted. My presence at this hour had not been questioned, but there could be spies. I was remembering Geneva and thinking that I should have a cover story. But what?

I was still undecided as I reached the building. The door was open. I stepped inside and paused to gain my bearings. Dusk had arrived and there was little light entering through the windows of this long, high-ceilinged room. No lamps were lighted yet. It was difficult to see at first. Gradually, my eyes adjusted to the semi-darkness.

The room contained a series of long reading tables in the center, with low benches on either side. The walls were lined with books, rows and rows of them, with a number of ladders propped against the walls so that one might reach the higher shelves. At either end was a short circular stairway leading to a kind of catwalk that ran the length of the long walls. More shelves of books extended above these catwalks, all the way into the eaves of the roof. A door at the far end of the room led to a similar long room of books, and still the length of the building had not been spanned by the combination of these two rooms, so that there must have been at least two, perhaps three more such rooms. That was a lot of books!

There was no one in the first room. I proceeded to the second. So many books! I love libraries. Not that I have been in so many or read so much. In those days I had enough to read in my work for the master to keep my eyes busy during my working hours. As for reading for pleasure in my spare time, well, there were other of my senses that I took greater pleasure in pleasing than my eyes. Only in recent years, with those other senses fading into memory, have I been able to turn to books for enjoyment. Yet, even in my youth, whenever I was in the presence of large numbers of books, I experienced that particular sensation of smells and sounds that I now associate with feelings of inspired tranquility. In that sense, libraries resemble wombs. You never quite forget the peace.

I was caught up in that sensation of the books and so had not noticed there was someone at one of the long reading tables, bent over an open book in the darkened room.

"*Pardon, monsieur, mais la bibliothèque est fermée,*" said a gentle voice.

"*Je cherche Fra Cotin,*" I responded.

"*Je suis Cotin. Que désirez-vous?*"

"*Je voudrais...* uh, listen, I just used up most of my French, and I'm not sure how to say this, but are you...?"

"I am Brother Cotin. How may I serve you?" he said in a perfect Roman dialect.

"You have an ear for accents," I observed.

"I have been a librarian for many years," he said, as though that explained it. I suppose it did. "Oh, but forgive me, please! I have been so engrossed in my work that I failed to notice how dark it has become. Let me make a light so that we will be able to see each other at least. Come, sit down. Tell me how I may help you."

While Brother Cotin busied himself lighting several candles in a candelabrum on the table, I had my first opportunity to study the man. He was thin and cadaverous looking, with a sickly pallor to his skin. He seemed permanently bent over. He held his hands in front of his chest, not in a monk's prayerful attitude, but rather as though he were holding a book. Only there was no book in his hands.

He was old. There were large liver spots on his face and on the backs of his hands. What remained of his hair was thin and snow white, and he wore thick lenses that greatly magnified his nearsighted gray eyes. One had the impression of a bookish mole who rarely emerged from these musty rooms into the clear light of day.

Librarians all look alike. I wonder whether they do so because the job eventually transfigures them, or does that sort of work appeal only to people who look like librarians?

But he had a disarming smile. And a gentle voice that put me at ease.

"I have come to ask you about Jordanus Nolanus, whom I understand you once knew."

I said it without thinking. But I would be leaving the minute our conversation ended, so where was the harm? Anyway, what could he tell anyone about me that they did not already know?

To his credit, he asked no questions. Not even my name. He merely nodded as though he had just seen the Nolan yesterday, not almost twenty years ago, or as though I might be inquiring about one of his books. He said he would be happy to discuss Jordanus with me. But first, would I not join him in a simple supper? And he promptly produced cheese, bread, fruit, and wine, which we ate and drank in silence, Cotin smiling gently from time to time, encouraging me to eat more of this or that, while he himself ate sparingly and drank hardly at all. I suspected that he slept in the library as well, that it was in fact his home. From the way he was treating me, I had the impression he did not often have a guest to entertain.

✠

Cotin was more than a little flattered. The Italian doctor not only saw him as one in whom he might confide — a chief librarian was, after all, frequently called upon in this fashion, and Cotin accepted the responsibility with the ethics of a confessor — but also as one with whom he might freely discuss work in progress. Though clearly, as dazzling as these ideas were, some were beyond Cotin's grasp, while others were of the most dangerous sort and therefore frightening.

For an ex-Dominican priest, Jordanus had a disturbing knowledge of occult mysticism. Not only did he know intimately Ficino, Della Mirandola, Agrippa, and other contemporary magicians, but he was familiar with the works of the ancient ones as well, Trismegistus, Zoroaster, Pythagoras, the Corpus Hermeticum, the Asclepius, the Cabala, and so forth. These were dangerous works, many of them forbidden by the Holy Father. Cotin himself had never dared read them for fear of corruption.

Moreover, these ideas of which Jordanus spoke were radical (though admittedly daring and imaginative), such in fact as could land Jordanus in serious trouble were Cotin ever to reveal his confidences to others, which of course he would never do. Guillaume Cotin was not one to betray a trust.

Cotin's predecessor had not understood this responsibility. Instead, Father d'Aubrées had been a positive tyrant as chief librarian, smug, self-important, insufferably self-righteous and patronizing. Possessive too, oh, yes! Exactly the wrong qualities for this job. Never mind that the institution was open to the public, the very first public library in Paris, if d'Aubrées took a dislike to you — it could be your looks, your dress, a not suitably deferential attitude — whatever it was, if he disliked you, you did not get to read his books. Imagine, *his* books!

Well, Father d'Aubrées was no longer chief librarian here (In nomine Patris et Filii et Spiritus Sancti!). It was Cotin's turn. He had worked hard to restore the tradition that had been interrupted by d'Aubrées, and, God willing, he would live long enough to ensure that it would never happen again that the public would be denied free access to all books.

Cotin was not altruistic, oh, no, there were plenty he would rather not see here, the ones who licked their thumbs to turn the pages, for instance, or bent down the corners to mark a place. The ones who took books to the reading tables and never returned them to the shelves when they were finished, or even worse, returned them to the wrong shelf, thus rendering the catalogue useless. The ones who wrote question marks in the margins, or wrote *Ave Maria!* — as though using a holy name could somehow negate the sacrilege of defacing a book! No, these were certainly undesirable types, but they needed to be controlled, not censored. Cotin believed strongly that this was the people's library, not his, and that a public library must make its books available to everyone, not just a select few.

In fact, he had recently devised a system whereby books might be borrowed, taken home rather than having always to be read here in the library. It was a novel idea, and he had managed to convince the abbot of the merits of his system despite the certainty that there would be occasional abuses. Of course, one benefit of the new system that Cotin had not anticipated was that now the library was a far quieter place for him to do his own work, the complete cataloguing of all books and manuscripts, a monumental job to which he had devoted himself for over twenty years.

The Abbey of St. Victor had remained a bastion of intellectual exploration and philosophical pursuit all through the dark years of the thirteenth, fourteenth, and early fifteenth centuries. Now that there was support for intellectual dialogue — the abbey was literally surrounded by educational institutions, Hôtel Baif just down the road, the various colleges of the University of Paris just inside the nearby town wall — the abbey had assumed the obligation of continuing its tradition as a Platonic Academy by leading the way toward new ideas. Cotin saw the library, with its rich collection of books and rare manuscripts, as the focal point for that leadership.

No wonder then that this erudite Italian, just returned from England, fascinated him so. Cotin had first met Jordanus some years before. He had come to the library seeking something with which to impress the king in a demonstration of the Italian's mnemonic system. Cotin had assisted him, since Jordanus spoke no French, spoke none still, though his Latin was superb, by selecting for him a thirteenth-century French litany from *Les sept psaumes allégorisés* of Christine de Pisan, a work that had always been a personal favorite of his.

The demonstration had been so successful that the king had awarded Jordanus a position as Reader at the Collège de France, and by way of thanks Jordanus had periodically given Cotin copies of his books on mnemonics as they were printed. He had also given him a copy of the play that had aroused half of Paris against Jordanus, *Il candelaio* (The Torch Bearer), a comedy that had made little effort to disguise its ridicule of characters from Jordanus's convent days, but had as well poked fun at many too easily recognizable doctors from the university. Cotin had always suspected that *Il candelaio* had been the principal reason for Jordanus's sudden departure from Paris.

In England he had written six more books, but having fared no better among the Protestants of England — "pedants and pedagogues," he called them — he had returned again to Paris. For a number of months now, he had been spending a great deal of his time at the library, researching for his new books. Occasionally, he would spend an evening like this one, conversing at length with Cotin in the latter's little hideaway office tucked between Room Three and Room Four, overlooking the botanical gardens.

✳

"I tell you, Cotin, the heretics in England are no better than those in France! They despise good works. They countenance only what they themselves have been taught. They do not even understand their own master, Aristotle! You see, Cotin, to think is to speculate with images. The Nolan has stripped nature of false veils and coverings to make her naked again, given eyes to moles and illuminated the blind. Yet, even then, they do not see!

"If only they would follow the advice of St. Thomas in *Summa contra Gentiles*. The scholastics made too much of the sacraments, with their pretended subtleties of the Eucharist. Why, even St. Peter and St. Paul ignored the Eucharist, knowing full well that *hoc est corpus meum*. These troubles between Catholics and Reformists — Calvinists, Lutherans, and the rest — would easily be ended, if the questions of the sacraments were just removed! But of course they will never do so. They would rather hide the truth than stand before it.

"Navarre . . . some day Navarre will unite them. I am convinced that he is the only hope."

"Jordanus, do you realize that you could be imprisoned just for thinking such thoughts? Let alone speaking them out loud. I worry about you, my friend. And I caution you to control that wild tongue of yours. Not all of those to whom you speak so frankly will be as solicitous of your welfare as I, nor so understanding of your sincerity," Cotin advised.

"I know, I know," Giordano responded, shaking his head in disbelief. "It seems to be my fate. Have I not been hounded from Naples, driven from Rome, thrown out of Geneva, and asked to leave Toulouse? Forced out of Paris, fired from Oxford, escorted from London? And now, with the League gaining control of Paris, I shall have to leave here again soon too. Everywhere I go, I am persecuted by religious pedagogues and university pedants!"

"Perhaps you should consider toning down your religious . . . er . . . deviations?" Cotin suggested gently, seeking the least offensive word with which to describe Jordanus's revolutionary viewpoint.

"You don't understand yet, do you?" Giordano was exasperated. "No one does! Read my books. Listen to what I say. My ideas are not 'religious deviations.' They are not even religious. I care nothing about religion. Practice whatever religion you wish, believe whatever you want to believe, only do not force your beliefs on me!" Giordano pounded his fist on Cotin's desk, frightening the frail librarian. "My ideas are philosophical and scientific, not religious! They do not conflict with the church!"

"But they do, Jordanus," Cotin insisted firmly. "Surely having trained for the priesthood in a Dominican convent, you of all people should understand that your ideas are in direct contradiction of church teachings."

"There! That's another thing! I have said over and over, it was a mistake. I was not intended for the priesthood. I do not belong in the order. But I am no less a Catholic for that. Last week I went to see Mendoza, Don Bernadino de Mendoza, the Spanish ambassador whom I met in London. I asked him for an introduction to the nuncio. He said what for? And I told him, because I want to go to Mass. He asked was I ready to go back to my order? And I said no, I just want to go to Mass, not be a priest. He said in that case he could not give me the introduction. But when I agreed to think about it, he gave me a letter.

"Yesterday I had an audience with Ragazzoni, bishop of Bergamo, the nuncio. I said, Eminence, I wish to be absolved so that I can partake of the Sacrament of the Mass, and I wish to be received back into Mother Church.' You see, Cotin? Is that a 'religious deviation'? I am a Catholic!"

"How did the bishop respond?"

"He asked if I was prepared to return to my order in Naples!" Giordano struck his forehead with the heel of his hand. "*Dio!* One hundred and twenty-six counts of heresy. If I live through that, I have to be a priest for the rest of my life. For what? Just so I can say Mass? Now do you understand? They are not interested in my faith, but my compliance. They will not absolve me to be free to think, to teach, and to write as I wish; they will absolve me only if I agree not to be free to think, to teach, and to write as I wish.

"You know," Giordano mused facetiously, "I should really found an order of my own somewhere, like Luther and Calvin did. The Nolanists, I could call us. At least then I could be free to be a Christian."

"Ah, but neither Luther nor Calvin managed to free himself that way," Cotin observed. "By contradicting Scripture and the teachings of the holy fathers, they violated faith, and thus committed heresy. Hardly a way to 'free' oneself, Jordanus. The fundamental tenets of the church may not be denied, no matter how much we may personally disagree with one or the other of them. You must see that."

Giordano rolled his eyes toward the ceiling.

"You see? Religion again! My books, the ones written in London and the ones I have plans to write, especially what I have written in Italian rather than in Latin, so that more people may read them, treat of cosmology, of astronomy, of the validity of the Copernican figures. They discuss the infinity of the universe, the power of the sun, the rotation of our planet, the infinity of planets inhabited with people, the wisdom of the ancient Egyptian mathematicians and astronomers. These things are not religious! Take my work on Copernicus, for example. The church has no understanding of Copernicus, no more than did the Oxford pedants to whom I tried to explain him. Even Copernicus did not understand Copernicus!

"We owe him so much. He was a genius. I would be the first to proclaim him so. But being only a student of mathematics, he simply could not transcend his own discovery, whereas the Nolan has penetrated far deeper than anyone the divine truth his figures have revealed. One day soon, I shall demonstrate this to His Holiness Pope Sixtus himself, who will then reward my efforts and cancel this misguided foolishness of the Holy Office.

"Read my *Cena*, read my *Spaccio*. You will see that my work is not religious! Regardless of what people may say, regardless of what my fate holds in store for me, Cotin, I am nourished by my high enterprise. I will continue at all costs."

Cotin had respect for the Nolan but found his emotional intensity exhausting. The library was a peaceful haven. It was possible here to sustain contemplative silence sometimes for days without interruption. But when Jordanus was here and wanted to talk, that inner quiet Cotin so enjoyed was shattered. The man was in a constant state of agitation and nervous energy. While this appeared to help Jordanus to accomplish his work, it interfered with Cotin's concentration to such a degree that he could accomplish nothing. Without putting it in so many words, even to himself, Cotin sincerely longed for the Nolan's departure. Yes, yes, in spite of the realization that it was a most un-Christian wish to have, he hoped to wish Jordanus away. But though it was, he could not help having it. Perhaps this Mordente business would hasten the departure.

Fabricio Mordente of Salerno was a mathematician living in Paris. He had recently invented an eight-pointed compass with an adjustable device on its arms. Jordanus said this compass was capable of producing wondrous results. So struck by the immensity of Mordente's invention was he that Jordanus had written and published in Latin a work explaining the compass, since Mordente knew no Latin. But Mordente, instead of being grateful for the Nolan's efforts, was incensed that he had the audacity to presume to interpret Mordente's work, and Mordente was now buying up the edition all over Paris.

"What is the latest in l'Affair Mordente?" Cotin asked.

Giordano assumed a pained expression.

"I do not understand what possessed him to such ingratitude! My only desire was to help him. Mordente is a god among geometricians! His only problem is that he does not see the full meaning of his own divine mathesis. But I do! Now, however, instead of appreciating what I have done for him, to explain his invention to the whole world for him, he is all in a rage. He has not only bought and destroyed almost all of the edition that I had printed (at my own expense, I might add!), but Del Bene tells me that Mordente has now gone to the duke of Guise himself to complain about me.

"Have I not already enough trouble in Paris without the Guisards against me too? You know, Cotin, that I do not even go out anymore? I no longer socialize, not even with my few friends, if I may call them such. There is still so much for me to do! And who knows how much time I have left in which to do it? That is the reason I am so grateful to you for the use of your library, and for your counsel and support. No one has lifted a finger in this town for me since I returned. Only you. I shall never forget it."

✳

"Was that the last time you saw him then, in December 1585?" I asked.

Brother Cotin consulted his diary.

"No. That was the 12th of December. He was here twice more that month. We talked only briefly on both occasions. But he was here again... (he thumbed through the diary until he found the spot)... in early February of '86. He talked then mostly about his childhood. Nothing about the matters we have been discussing. That was the last time we met."

He closed the diary and replaced it on the shelf behind his desk. There were many other volumes there. Cotin was a methodical diarist.

"Did he leave Paris after that?"

Cotin frowned, as though recalling something distasteful.

"Not immediately."

He had become less communicative.

"Brother Cotin, is something troubling you? You seem... annoyed or distracted about something."

He looked surprised.

"Oh, my! Yes, now that you mention it, I suppose I was. I was remembering the last time I spoke with Jordanus. I told you that we talked about his childhood, and that was true, but afterward we walked through the garden, talking. At some point he spoke rather sacrilegiously, I do not recall the precise reference, and I chastised him for such manner of speech on the grounds of a sanctified abbey. He was annoyed with me, and we argued. He accused me of being a religious pedant like all the others. I resented that. We parted coldly. Jordanus was an obstinate, opinionated, and garrulous man. Quarrelsome to the extreme. But I was very uncharitable to him that day, and I have regretted it ever since."

"Speaking of charitableness, Brother Cotin, let me ask you what may seem a strange question: If you had the chance to go before the Sant'Offizio in Rome to testify on behalf of the Nolan, to explain his philosophy, which you claim you understood and they did not, would you do it? Would you testify for him?"

My question greatly disturbed Cotin. He sat there for a while, stunned. Then he got up and began to pace the little office. Once he stopped to open the door. He peered intently into the reading room for a moment, listening. Then he closed it and resumed his pacing. Finally he seemed to arrive at a conclusion, for he stopped his pacing and sat down. He wore a troubled look. If you ask me, he was unhappy with his conclusion. He would have liked himself better had he been able to answer in the affirmative.

"Let me answer your question with a brief story," he began. "Jordanus circulated an invitation to the royal lecturers and doctors of Paris to attend his disputations at le Collège de Cambrai on Wednesday of the week of Pentecost 1586, on the subject 'One hundred and twenty articles on nature and the world against the Peripatetics.'

"These disputations had been printed and circulated by him some weeks before. I had a copy from him personally. They were a rehash of his books from England, relating to the infinity of the universe, the majesty of truth, the feebleness of the arguments of the peripatetics, et cetera. His protégé, Jean Hennequin, read these disputations from the Great Chair, while Jordanus occupied a little chair next to the door to the garden.

"When Hennequin completed the reading, Jordanus stood and challenged the doctors to debate his disputations if they could. No one responded. He issued the challenge a second time, this time louder and more tauntingly. At last a young advocate, identifying himself as 'Rudolphus Calerius' — this was Raoul Cailler, a poet of the Vincennes group and a friend of Du Perron, and through Du Perron of the king — accepted the challenge. He prefaced his remarks by stating that no one had responded until then because they did not deem Jordanus worthy of response. He then challenged Jordanus to open debate. Jordanus did not reply. Instead, he made to leave through the garden. Some students forcefully detained him until he promised to return the next day to debate Calerius.

"When the audience reconvened on Thursday, Calerius now occupied the Great Chair. He responded forcefully in defense of Aristotle. Young Hennequin did his best to refute these arguments, or at least the first one, but he was no match for Calerius. Where was Jordanus? He did not even appear. Nor did anyone ever see him again in Paris.

"My point in telling this story is this: Jordanus deserted his own protégé, whom he left to defend *his* disputations, rather than face Calerius himself. I have no doubt there were reasons — not the least of which was the animosity of Guise and now, because of Cailler, that of King Henri as well. But notwithstanding these reasons, he had promised to return and did not.

"Jordanus had one set of principles for himself and another for the rest of the world. He held himself apart. To some measure, I am prepared to believe that this may be necessary to accomplish great work. I cannot judge such things. Jordanus may indeed be a great man. But I cannot condone his failure to appear and defend himself at Cambrai that day, to subject Hennequin to such humiliation as though he were simply expendable.

"Therefore, I am no longer so certain that I understood Jordanus and his philosophy. I could not truthfully and in good conscience — *would* not — so testify in your hypothetical case before the Holy Office. I am sorry. More than you can ever know. I hope that answers your question."

Poor Bruno.

C*hapter 12*

luglio 1597
Shoe Lane, St. Andrew's Parish
London

I FELT NO MORE than a shadow of myself when I finally reached the shores of England. Weak, weary, more a stranger in this land than in any other yet, I felt awkward and foreign, and I wished I were back home again in Rome where I belonged. My eyes were dull and stared out from sunken sockets. My skin was sallow, my beard was no longer dark but graying, and my legs had been reduced to quivering sticks barely able to support a frame that had itself been reduced by a good two-stone over what it had weighed in Paris only six weeks before. Ah, but I would not have wished those weeks on my worst enemy.

On the second morning out of Paris, I had awakened with a slight fever and a raw throat. It would pass, I thought. I had rarely been sick in my life. But by afternoon I became suddenly and violently chilled, and I swooned from my horse. I would have died there, sprawled in the middle of that lonely road and covered with dust, were it not for two priests who came upon me on their journey. They managed to transport me on a makeshift horse litter to their monastery, Notre Dame de Lorette, somewhere north of Arras in the Pas de Calais; and there I spent the entire month of June at death's door with the plague. I was out of my mind with fever and delirium for many days. I survived only by dint of the brothers' constant care and by the miraculous powers of the abbey's herbalist, who for my money had to be one of the great magi in all Christendom. Would that I had been able to keep him with me when I left the abbey, however, for I no sooner recovered from one plague than I was beset by another — the sea.

Oh, Lord, I am no sailor! Rome is on land, after all, and I had spent my entire life with both feet solidly upon it, not on the swaying deck of a ship. Working on the docks of Ripa was the closest I had ever been to the sea, and even then I sometimes became queasy. To be captive to the sickening roll and pitch of a vessel at sea with no way to get off is to suffer the tortures of the damned!

Three times we set out from Calais, and three times we were turned back by an angry storm blowing down from the North Sea. When I wasn't puking my guts over the rail, I was pleading with the captain to go on, not to turn back. I reasoned that I would be just as sick, storm or no storm, and the thought of having to undergo such agony for nothing was the worst torture of all. But he was a stubborn Norwegian. He understood not a word of Italian and would not have changed his mind if he had. If anything, my indisposition seemed to amuse him.

Our fourth attempt to cross the English Channel was successful. The storm abated, the weather cleared, and with a fair wind behind us, we reached Dover in five hours. But of course I was sick as a dog the entire voyage, sicker for the knowledge that I would yet have to make my return to the Continent in the same fashion.

I later learned that the same storm had forced the English fleet commanded by the Earl of Essex, along with Vice Admiral Lord Thomas Howard and Rear Admiral Sir Walter Ralegh, back into port at Plymouth and at Falmouth with many ships badly damaged after four stormy days at sea in an aborted attack on Calais. Fifteen of the queen's ships, two Spanish prize-ships, twenty-two men of war of Holland, twenty-four fly boats and hoys, four thousand pressed men, and twelve hundred musketeers, all floundering around for four days in that same terrible storm!

I had cursed the stubbornness of my Norwegian sea captain and his *maledetto barcaccia* for turning back three days in a row, but when I heard this story I had to admit that he had been smarter than I, smarter in fact than the whole English navy.

✠

What I needed most when I arrived in Dover was rest and nourishment to get back my strength. I slept straight through two days and well into the third. I awoke famished. Not even the uninteresting table fare — the English use lard instead of oil, scant seasonings, have no pasta and poor bread, indecent wine and bitter ale, and they are thoroughly lacking in table manners of any sort — stayed me from eating so prodigious an amount as to amaze the innkeeper, who decided that I must surely be mad to think his wife so good a cook as that!

Refreshed and feeling stronger, I dressed myself in work clothes, draped a bale hook on my shoulder (borrowed from the Greek sleeping off a drunk in the bed next to mine), and wandered the docks looking for information.

In France d'Épernon and his friends had all spoken a number of languages, including Italian and Latin. Even the common people spoke a language I could begin to understand. But these English had a whining island tongue, as much expressed through the nose as the mouth, and it was beyond my comprehension. As was my Italian beyond theirs. The result was I had been unable to learn at the inn how to even get to London.

I fared better at the docks. On the docks of any port you are likely to hear a dozen different languages spoken by stranded sailors. Having jumped ship, or had one too many brawls, or maybe overslept a drunken binge, they would now work around the docks until they could pick up a new berth. One has only to use one's ears. Sooner or later, you will overhear a countryman speaking a language you understand. In no time at all, I befriended an old salt from Messina, who for two pints told me all I needed to know.

Two days later, after riding in an open coach through Canterbury and Chatham, I arrived in London.

✠

No amount of warning from the Messina sailor in Dover prepared me for London. The noise was so deafening it made the *Mercato* of Napoli seem tranquil as a country church. Not even the swamps of Circus Maximus could compete with the stench of London's streets. And even on my hungover morning tours with d'Épernon, the back streets of Paris seemed almost straight in comparison to the rabbit warren of narrow, twisting, congested streets, lanes, and alleys that comprised the City of London between the ancient crumbling Roman walls on the north and the River Thames on the south.

But of all that was despicable about London, the people themselves were the worst. The coach had let me off on Thames Street, between the Tower and London Bridge. Thinking to learn the lay of the town by walking its streets, and perhaps to find someone who might know enough Italian to at least direct me to those with whom I might converse, I wandered in a zig-zag fashion through Cornhill, Poultry, and Cheapside. I found myself back on Thames Street again and tried to make my way generally toward the western boundary at Temple Bar. All the while, I was smiling at everyone and inquiring whether anyone spoke Italian.

"G'way, ye trait'rous furr'ner, 'fore ye gets bashed 'n yer 'ead!" was the typical response, as near as I could make it out. A few of the larger ones went so far as to brandish clubs at me and spat at my feet to emphasize their meaning.

They stank as bad as their streets, too, and foreigners were not the only ones singled out for their distemper. They pushed and shoved at each other as well, spat and swore and picked fights for no reason at all, ending only when one or the other lay half-dead in the muck of a drainage gutter. The only thing that seemed to humor anyone — and that, to a hot fever — was a game called "football" played in nearly every street.

London was a place of savages.

✠

I had been traveling for almost seven months. You learn a thing or two about survival in that much time, tricks of the road. One such discovery was that the safest place of all — safest, but also the cleanest and quietest — a place where you can rest, wash, and obtain a warm meal, a place where you can be assured that someone will understand, if not Italian, then at least Latin . . . is a church. It is helpful, though by no means imperative, to know the particular denomination of a church before you enter it, so as not to step on any toes and possibly to save your own from being stepped on, but should you be uncertain as to that, why then, you can always fall back on a neutral: Padre, I am a poor sinner come to God's house for forgiveness! It will be enough.

Whatever your needs, the church will gladly provide. I have learned that they all have that in common, that they will grant you almost anything to save your soul. I myself have had my soul saved by half the churches of Europe. And my belly filled as well. For travelers who may have not yet discovered this essential truth on their journeys, I gladly pass it on: If you find yourself in a strange, lonely, or threatening place, whether it be a large town or a country village, go to church and let them save your soul. On this particular day, I found myself opposite Old Bailey on Fleet Hill; and as luck would have it, I wandered up the hill until I came upon St. Andrew's Holborn. I was hot, I was tired, I was hungry and confused. Time to have my soul saved.

I went inside. Now, I was not so ill informed as to expect a Catholic church in London. The Act of 1584 had destroyed Catholic missions in England. The Jesuits had been given forty days to leave England or suffer arrest for treason. Priests who had been trained abroad were jailed. Papists were judged heretics. But, this being my first English church experience, I was unsure whether they genuflected or not upon entering, so I grabbed the first hand in a robe I came to, fell on my knees and kissed it, crying: *Padre, perdona mia!*

"*Vieni, mi figlio, ti aiuto io,*" he said softly, urging me to my feet.

"*Alla buon'ora!* You speak Italian!"

"*Si.*"

"Thank God!" I exclaimed.

"No, thank my mother. She may have married an Englishman, she always used to say — my mother was from Parma — but her children were going to be raised Italian and Catholic." He looked around the church and smiled ruefully. "Well, at least I can still speak the language. Happily, she did not live long enough to see my 'conversion.'"

Bartholomeo Matthews was the deacon of St. Andrew's. He was a solitary man, given to a disgruntled cynicism that was more the result of disillusionment in himself than in the rest of the world. He was too English to be Italian, but too Italian to be properly English; a Catholic unable to avow his religion, and thus a deacon who could never rise to priest. His life existed in a space between here and there, and his adjustment to that space was now so complete that he despaired he could ever leave it. For all that, he was kind and congenial, offering me a warm meal, a hot bath, and a bed for the night. And for once I was not required to offer my soul to be saved in exchange.

Matthews had long ago fashioned himself a kind of living quarters out of two small connecting rooms behind the sacristy. He rarely went out from the church except to buy food and other necessities. And yet I found him surprisingly well informed on events in the world, and there was little he did not know about what went on in London.

Later in the evening, as we lay on a straw mattress in the dark, he offered me some sound advice:

"Guidotti," he said in a grave voice, "London is not a safe place for you. Even though you have not told me who you are or why you are here — and it is wiser that you do not — I have already guessed some of it, and if I can, so can others. Your dialect is Roman but your clothing is French. By not immediately stating your business, you narrow the possibilities and encourage speculation: an Italian, a stranger, most likely a Catholic. To suspicious minds at court, in Parliament, and in the hierarchy of the church — and, believe me, such suspicions these days are in no shortage of supply — that could easily spell papist spy.

"Your every move will be watched. Trust no one. There are as many spies in London as church mice. Everyone suspects everyone else. The older the queen gets, the more plots there are, real and imagined. The situation is worse even than when Mary was held captive at Fotheringay Castle. Tell me this, will your business take you to court?"

"I honestly don't know," I answered. "Look, you have been frank with me, I may as well be straight with you. I am here only for some information about a man, a countryman who lived here

for a while about twelve years ago. It is not political. I am not
a spy. The...uh...person I work for needs this information for
a...uh...court case in Rome. It has nothing to do with England,
I assure you. My problem is, I don't know my way around London. I
do not speak the language. I am not sure where to begin, and I certainly do not need any trouble. All I want to do is find a few people
who knew this guy, ask a couple questions, and then head for home. I
have been on the road a long time. This is not my kind of life. *Non é
la via dell'orto,* you know what I mean. I am not looking for trouble."

There was a moment's silence. Matthews was thinking.

"This man about whom you inquire, this countryman of yours, was
he important? Would he have had access to court?" he asked.

"I think so, yes."

"To her majesty as well?"

"That I do not know."

"Then you must be doubly careful who you discuss this man with,"
he warned. "You have no idea how easy it is to meet the hangman at
St. Giles Fields these days. Things are greatly changed at Whitehall.
Leicester is gone. Walsingham is gone. Essex and Ralegh vie for the
queen's favor now, and young troublemakers like Southampton feed on
the scraps. Though Burghley, that old fox, still holds the real power.
Any one of them would not hesitate to arrange your hasty departure
from life, should he suspect that your presence even remotely threatens
his position.

"You think that far-fetched? It is an everyday practice. These are
desperate and suspicious men. They do not ask questions of strangers;
they merely dispatch them. This country is only recently become
civilized. We are unused to so new a cloak.

"I do know of one who might help you. He is an Italian Englishman like me, a writer and lecturer who associates with these people.
He is at court. He travels in their circle. They accept him. He may
even have known your man. If not, then he will most likely know
who did. The Italians in London are a tight group. We all know each
other. This fellow lives in a house near here on Shoe Lane. Tomorrow
I will take you to him."

"Non so come ringraziarti," I murmured gratefully.

"There is no need, Guidotti. We Italians must do what we can for
each other. And we English..." he added caustically, "...we English must learn to be less suspicious of Italians. Now get some sleep.
'Il mattino ha l'oro in bacca.' You will need your wits about you in
London, my friend."

"*Buona notte.*"

"*Buona notte, Guidotti.*"

Several minutes later, on a crazy whim, I whispered tentatively:

"Deacon Matthews, are you awake?"

"Ummm...?"

"'My helmet is Salvation.'"

There was no response, save his regular breathing.

"Deacon Matthews?" I whispered again.

Silence.

Then: "Guidotti, to be a slow learner in this town can sometimes be fatal. Go to sleep."

✠

The following morning I accompanied Deacon Matthews to the house on Shoe Lane. He had been close-mouthed and deep in thought since rising. Whether this was his usual demeanor in the early morning or the result of our conversation of the evening before, I could not tell. He made no reference to the biblical quotation from Ephesians and neither did I, but the feeling that perhaps he was a Jesuit agent not on my list persisted. If so, though, it was puzzling that he had not acknowledged the password. Was it that he did not trust me, or was he telling me not to trust him? True, I was a stranger. But equally true, he was a man of divided loyalties.

Well, I was no longer the amateur I had been in Geneva. I would wait and see what game was being played here. Meanwhile, I would take his advice and trust no one.

I shifted my attention to our surroundings. It was but a short walk down the hill to the house, as St. Andrew's was located at one end of the lane and the house at the other, near where Shoe Lane joined Fleet Street. The morning was clear and bright. It was already quite hot, though not so humid as Rome in the summer. From the hill as we walked I could see the River Thames, already teeming with sailing vessels, cargo barges, tilt boats, and wherries, the latter being those small for-hire oar boats that ferried passengers up and downstream between Westminster and the Tower. Across the Thames were open fields and neatly rowed orchards. Next to them, I could see the bull baiting and bear baiting rings, and after that the cluster of houses that ran along St. Toolys Street to the start of London Bridge.

Observing all the activity on the river, I was struck by the importance rivers must play in the commerce of the great cities I had seen — the Tiber of Rome, the Po of Torino, the Rhone of Lyon, the Seine of Paris, and the Thames of London. It had never occurred to me before. Nor had I stopped to consider until now that each was also a source of drinking water and of irrigation, of food as well, and that each was a mighty road on which were transported goods and passengers that were vital to the life of the city.

The whole of London depended on that river down there, would wither and die without it. The same for the other cities and their rivers. And yet, if I was any example, people just took their rivers for granted, clogging them with refuse and garbage of the worst sort, even the bodies of the dead, as though their rivers would run forever, forever clean. Already the Tiber was all but undrinkable. I wondered if Londoners had any idea that their Thames, their sweet-tasting Thames, might one day not be so sweet, might one day even taste like the Tiber?

As a young man, I imagined that the whole world must be exactly like Campo Marzio, or at least like Rome. Now I was acquiring a traveler's perspective, comparing one place with another, one people with another, one set of customs with another, and I was beginning to see the difference between them. Imagine God's perspective then, I thought, to see them all at once!

Shoe Lane itself was a quiet little street, far removed from the noise and confusion of the center of town. Tidy rows of oaken houses, each with a brick or stone chimney, and each right next to the other on both sides of the narrow lane. We stopped at a door no different than all the other doors, which upon knocking was opened by a man whose face, for the life of me, I cannot remember.

Is it my age, that I can remember some people so vividly and others not at all? Not even my notes from that period are of any help. I wrote nothing down about the looks of John Florio, save that his looks were 'average and undistinguished.' What I do remember, even without my notes, is that nothing else about him was. Of all those I interviewed, his recollections of the Nolan were the most complete.

✠

At first Florio was not very communicative. Deacon Matthews introduced me and then hurried back to church for Terce. As he left, I saw him give Florio a meaningful look which I do not think I was meant to see, as if to say to Florio: I don't vouch for this man; you are on your own. Since I was not about to trust him either, we were off to a slow start.

We talked for almost two hours and said absolutely nothing. About Italy, mostly. Background stuff. I learned that his parents, both dead now, were from Florence. That his childhood had been spent in the tenements of Upper Thames Street, his student and teaching days at Oxford. He wrote textbooks on the Italian language. Empty talk. Circling and sniffing, like a couple of wary mongrels.

Finally, I said, *"Ma questo, scusa, Signore Florio,* but this is getting us nowhere. You are suspicious of me. That makes me suspicious of you. Then my suspiciousness confirms your suspicions and you become even more suspicious. Do you see where this leads? We will end up quarreling, and I will leave. That is not what I came for. Deacon Matthews may be a little suspicious of me himself, but at least he did put us together. He must have had a good reason, no? He told me that we Italians have to help each other."

"He said that? Matthews said that?"

"Si. But he also told me to trust no one, and see what that gets us. Here we are, wasting time when we could be helping each other, all because neither one of us will trust the other first. So here is what I propose: I will take the first chance. Not a big one. Just enough to show you I am willing to risk something for your trust. Then it will be your turn to take a chance. Tell me something, anything to help me trust you. We will continue that way until we trust each other completely. But if I tell you something and you tell me nothing, then I will tell you nothing further. I will know that I was wrong to trust you even a little bit, and I will leave. The same rule can apply for you with me, and in that case I will also promise to leave. What do you think?"

"Sono affari tuo," he said with a shrug. "What you decide is your affair."

But I could see that I had aroused his interest. Someone tells you "I will go first," what have you got to lose? You might just learn something interesting.

I took a deep breath.

"I am looking for information about Giordano Bruno."

Florio's eyes widened just for an instant. He made no other sign of recognition. But his lips were set as tight as a frightened clam, and I could feel a wall slam down between us.

Without another word, I gathered my things and prepared to leave.

"Wait a minute," he said.

I sat down again.

"Giordano Bruno was my friend," he said in a low voice tinged with excitement. He had taken the bait.

My turn again.

I leaned toward him and said, "The Nolan is being held in Castel Sant'Angelo by the Roman Inquisition. He is on trial for heresy. I mean to help him if I can."

A small lie. Or was it?

Florio was catching the mood. He was less suspicious now and not so tense. Excited, even. Without realizing it, he had been drawn into the game.

It was like a long rally in a tennis match, only more dangerous. I had served, he had returned my serve. I returned his return with a harder shot. The ball was in his court again.

Almost eagerly, he volunteered: "My father and mother were Jews. They converted, were baptized, then they reformed. My father was arrested by the Inquisition and held in Rome for two years. When he was released, they fled to England!"

He beamed proudly.

His mother and father were Jews? *Sai che roba.* Big deal! Who cared about his parents? Bruno was who I wanted to hear about! There you are, release a dam and the water never seems to follow the direction you expect. I had to get Florio back on the right path without insulting his parents.

I took a big chance. To convince him that he could really trust me with important information, I would have to trust him with something just as important. *Bere affogare,* I thought, here goes.

"Signore Florio, I trust you. I can tell you this much: my master is connected with the Holy Office. It is for him that I gather this information, and it is he whom I must convince of your friend's innocence. I cannot do that without your help."

Florio nearly lost his composure on that shot. He was sweating profusely. I heard his wife calling him to lunch from somewhere in the house. He ignored her call. I heard his young daughter call to him. He ignored her too. He was wrestling with himself over a big one now. Should he or shouldn't he? I waited patiently. At last, he decided.

"I lived with the Nolano for two years in the house of Michel de Castelnau, Marquis de Mauvissière and ambassador of France to her majesty, Queen Elizabeth. We lived and worked together in that house on Butcher Lane near the Strand, from 1583 to 1585. I know everything about him for the entire time he was in England."

It was big, all right, but was it the biggest he had? So far, everything I had told him could get me into trouble, but all he told me was public knowledge that I could have found out eventually on my own. I was after something bigger, something private that no one else knew, something that would equalize the trust factor.

There was only one way to do it. In a slow voice (I tried to make it as dramatic as possible) I gave him my best shot:

"Signore Florio, I will go all the way with you. I place my fate in your hands, to prove to you my sincerity. The name of my master, soon to be cardinal, soon to be an inquisitor general, is...Robert Bellarmine."

Florio gasped! Naturally, he recognized the name. All England knew my master's reputation. He must have groaned inwardly when he heard it. That I would make such a confession to him was an expression of greater trust than he had been prepared to reciprocate, even in his state of heightened excitement. But now the ball was in his court again, and it was up to him whether to return it or concede that his trust was not equal to mine.

Wiping his brow with his sleeve and leaning forward on the edge of his seat, his eyes glazed from the enormity of what he was about to reveal, he said in a croaked whisper:

"I was Walsingham's spy in Mauvissière's house!"

The game had ended in a draw. We were both exhausted. Though I had an idea this final revelation was not that dangerous for Florio, to him it was a confession of the first magnitude and it sealed our trust. Each of us now knew the other's secrets, but also knew that the other knew his. We were stuck with each other. I cannot say that either of us was pleased about that, nor really that we even liked each other — how can you like someone who holds your life or reputation in his hands? — but I will say that it produced a good working relationship.

Florio kept the bargain. He gave me everything I needed, including Ralegh and Fulke Greville. And I am pretty sure it was he who saved me from the Tower and interceded with the queen, though she never told me that in so many words but only hinted at it. What I learned from him and the others about the Nolan was enough to convince me that I had to return to Rome as quickly as I could so that I might explain to my master that Santa Severina was dead wrong about this case and must be stopped.

Chapter 13

agosto 1597
Durham House
London

WE HAD BEEN AT IT for two days. This interview was like extracting blood from a stone! Not for nothing did he refer to himself as "Florio the Resolute." Florio was resisting the role I had thrust upon him. It was against his nature. His motto had always been: *Non andare in cerca di guai,* Don't ask for trouble. He saw no reason to change that now.

He was committed to helping me, yes, because I had tricked him into revealing things about himself that he did not wish known; but he answered my questions reluctantly and did not make things easy for me. He also did his best to make me feel uncomfortable in his house. He, and his grumbling wife, and even little Joane, treated me with cold formality. I was an uninvited guest, they wished to make clear, and I had already overstayed.

Grudging as he was with detail, I was at least successful in dragging from him this rough sketch of the Nolan's two-year stay in England:

Bruno arrives in London in the spring of '83. He connects with some of the Italians (speaking no English himself), including Florio, who suggests that inasmuch as he himself is lecturing at Oxford, he will try to help line up a lectureship there for the Nolan. At Oxford they become friends. Bruno lectures on mnemonics from April until June, during which time he also becomes cozy with Florio's friends.

On the eleventh of June...trouble. Bruno wangles an invitation to take part in disputations at the Church of the Holy Virgin in honor of a Polish nobleman, Albert Laski, Count Palatine of Siradia, then visiting England on a diplomatic mission. The Nolan ends up in a fearful debate with the Reverend Doctor John Underhill, rector of Lincoln College. Bruno defends Copernicus, attacks Aristotle, insults Underhill and the entire Oxford faculty, and promptly gets canned from Oxford. He is escorted to the gates, his lectureship cancelled forthwith.

So much for Oxford. The Nolan finds himself back in London with no job, no money, and no place to stay. But what he does have is a letter of introduction to the French ambassador from Henri III.

Mauvissière takes him into Beaumont House and puts him on the payroll as a sort of gentleman companion. Bruno then puts in a good word for Florio, who lands a job tutoring the ambassador's little girl, Katherine Marie. Now both of them, Bruno and Florio, are living at the French Embassy on Butcher Row near the Strand, and they are accompanying the ambassador to court on numerous occasions. The queen, it seems, prefers to converse in Italian rather than French, and Mauvissière's Italian is terrible.

Florio knows many people at court. Through him, Bruno gets to know them too. At first, they are all very impressed with the Nolan. The English believe they have a lot to learn from Italians. (From what I had already observed, I could agree.) Bruno, after all, is a very bright fellow. Opinionated, but with new ideas. And these people are hungry for new ideas. True, some of these ideas are wild, risky too, but then, they are not afraid of risky ideas, these people. They have a few of their own.

So far, so good. But now the Nolan begins to write books about these ideas, and in these books he waxes sarcastic about Englishmen and English life. He makes fun of them. He drags up the whole incident at Oxford and insults the faculty all over again. This rubs everybody the wrong way, especially Florio's important friends. Once again, the Nolan is out on a limb. *É matto da legare!* No one will have anything to do with him.

About now — this is toward the end of '85 — Mauvissière is re-called to France. No more job for the Nolan. No more patron, no more protector. But by now the Nolan is homesick anyway. (I know the feeling!) He wants to go back to Italy. He has the idea he can write a book that will convince the pope he should forgive the Nolan, offer him a chair in philosophy in Rome instead of a cell in Sant' Angelo. This he tells Florio in strictest confidence. So he decides to leave England with Mauvissière, return to France, and work on this book. And that is the last Florio sees of his pal, the Nolan.

Did he have any friends? A few, mostly Florio's. Any women? Here and there. A widow or two, now and then a lonely woman at court whose husband was off fighting on the Continent or trading with savages in the New World. But Florio the prude is short on detail.

What about pastimes then, did he hunt? play games? dance? what? Nothing. This was a serious man. All he did was think and discuss his ideas and write books about them. Six books in England, all in Italian. Why in Italian, why not in Latin? Because everybody who was anybody at court could read Italian, but no one could at Oxford.

Was he religious? No. Was he sacrilegious? No. Was he an atheist, then? No, not that either. What the hell was he? A philosopher. A scientist. A genius.

During the two days of conversation with Florio about the Nolan, a lot of names were dropped. Many of them bore a "Sir" or "Lord" or "Doctor" in front of them. These were influential people, and they had known the Nolan. A few, such as Sidney, were dead, but some were still around. Would it not be a good idea for me to get their opinions? I thought about it. It would not just be good, it could be important, I decided. I should hear what these people might have to say about Giordano Bruno. That was when the idea came to me.

It was unreasonable, I knew that. Florio was certain to resist; and even if he did finally agree to try, I was not sure he would be able to pull it off. But it was a gem of an idea, so I broached it.

He squawked like a wounded chicken, of course. Turned red in the face and sputtered. He was such a cautious man, really, not at all prone to taking chances. On the other hand, he wanted nothing more than for me to be gone, the quicker the better. It was all he could think about. He wanted me out of his house, out of England, and out of his life. The more I pressed him on this idea, the more he began to sense that it might be what it was going to take to get rid of me. Also, that he might be able to turn this to his advantage. It could later be made to appear to suspicious minds that he had done this to strike a blow against the papists. No one would fault him for that. Florio would be a hero! At least that was the seed I planted within him.

Two days of facts, yes, but never anything intimate. I still had no idea how they got along, or how the Nolan got along with these other people Florio had been talking about. What did they say to each other? What did they talk about? What was an average day like? What was the Nolan's relationship with these people? Was one of them capable of testifying in his behalf before the Inquisition?

"Listen, Florio, what about getting some of them together for me, so I can ask them about the Nolan?"

"What? Who are you talking about?"

Florio had that absent look again. I could tell he was not paying attention to my questions. I had overheard his wife give him an ultimatum after supper: "Either this Roman lout leaves or I do!" I swear she deliberately said it loud enough for me to hear.

When Dame Florio was not scowling at me, she was whining to her husband. She was an awesome complainer. And what a terrible cook! Overcooked meat and stale ale, she did not know how to cook anything else. I was sick to death of it. What I would not have given for a big salad with some decent olive oil, or a heaping bowl of pasta, some fresh Italian bread, and a bottle of red wine! Too bad Florio had not married an Italian. Well, Dame Florio, on that much at least we agreed: I was as anxious to leave these two as they were to be rid of me. If this idea worked, we would all be happy.

"Ralegh, Dee, Greville, this fellow Gilbert, people like that," I answered blandly.

"Are you mad? *Dio ce la mandi buono!* You will get us both thrown into the Tower! I would not even consider approaching such people with an idea like that! Are you trying to get me into trouble? Why don't you leave? Haven't I told you enough? Must you have more, always more? Oh, it is too much!"

"Don't get yourself worked into such a lather. I am not asking so much, after all. A few people to get together, that's all. What kind of trouble? I would take my chances on their knowing about me. And I would not say a word about your being a spy for Walsingham, if that's what you're worried about. I just want to talk to them about Bruno. What's the big deal?"

That was a low blow. I knew it when I said it. It did not matter that it was Walsingham he had spied for. That was a long time ago. Anyway, Walsingham had been on the queen's side, so no harm done. No, what mattered was that he had been a spy at all, because his friends would never trust him again if they knew that.

Suddenly his whole reputation was on the line. That really frightened him. His position as an Italian Englishman had always been a delicate one, and he had studiously cultivated a non-threatening reputation in order to associate with people like Ralegh and Greville. Now that reputation was hanging like a thread, and I was holding a knife to that thread. Small good it would do him to hold one to mine if I was willing to risk having it cut. He was not.

The flaw in our deal was at last made plain to him. If one of the parties did not fear the exposure of his secrets, the risk of exposure to the other became greater. The end of *quid quo pro*. Thus did mutual trust convert to blackmail. *His secret was no longer safe!* "Sleep on it anyway, will you?" I suggested. "You might change your mind."

He did, of course. And that was how we came to this meeting.

Chapter 14

THE MEETING WAS HELD at Durham House, Ralegh's place, under the guise of a small dinner for a few of his friends before leaving aboard the *Warspite* on his islands voyage. This part had been my idea. Ralegh's arch rival at court was Robert Devereaux, the Earl of Essex. Florio was friends with Southampton, who was closest to Essex. Ralegh was the fox. By doing this favor for Florio, Florio would be obligated to Ralegh. Then Ralegh could feel free to exploit Florio's connection with Essex through Southampton. Ralegh was a survivor. He was an old hand at such intrigues. The fox took the bait.

I was beginning to understand that though high-ranking people spoke in different languages, their minds worked in the same devious fashion. Vatican prelates or English noblemen, there did not seem to be very much difference. My own survival skills from Campo Marzio might work as well with either.

Durham House was a gift from the queen to her then-favorite of some years before. It was a huge place running from the Strand to the Thames, and situated between The Savoy and York House. To reach it, Florio hired a wherry after dark from White Friars Steps, and we were rowed upstream with the incoming tide.

We were the first to arrive. The dinner took place in Ralegh's apartments high up in one of the little turrets overlooking the Thames. I pitied the poor servants who had to lug all that food up a couple hundred circular stairs from the kitchen far below. They were at it half the night.

What a feast it was! The first course consisted of a choice of roast mutton, lamb, veal, kidneys, venison, "chicken bake," and conger eels. The second course had a choice of boiled beef or roast kid, swan, larks, quail, cocks, sturgeon, and gurnard. There was the usual sour wine, flat beer, and bitter ale to wash all this down. Manchet, custard, and fruit with cheese. As usual, bones were thrown on the floor, mouths were wiped with sleeves or the back of one's hand, food was eaten with much slurping, and there was a steady chorus of loud and frequent belching. English gentlemen at table have the manners of pigs in a sty at feeding time.

Afterward, we talked. I had been introduced as "Florio's cousin Guidotti from Italy." I was protected to some extent from further questions by virtue of my place between our host at the head of the table and Florio on my right. Seated on the other side of Florio was his friend Gwinne. Then Gilbert, Gentili, Dee, and finally Greville directly across from me. Florio had earlier briefed me on each man:

Doctor Matthew Gwinne, thirty-nine, a Welshman. M.A. and M.D. from St. John's College, Oxford. At the time Bruno and Florio were at Oxford, he was lecturing on music at St. John's. He was currently writing bad Italian verse, which he signed "Il Candido."

Doctor William Gilbert, fifty-seven. M.D. from St. John's College, Cambridge. Lived and conducted a large practice at his house at St. Peter's Hill near Upper Thames Street, London. A distinguished physician and scientist, Gilbert did revolutionary work in "magnetism," whatever that was.

Professor Alberico Gentili, forty-five, an Italian in England since 1580. One-time protégé of Sir Francis Walsingham. Formerly Regius professor of civil law at Oxford, lately a practicing advocate in London and awaiting admission to Gray's Inn, one of the four Inns of the High Court of England. I had no idea what any of that meant.

Warden John Dee, seventy, warden of Manchester College. Astrologer, mathematician, geographer, crystal gazer, and occultist. At one time, Dee had been Queen Elizabeth's favorite astrologer and alchemist; at another, that of Albert Laski. One-time friend and neighbor of Sir Francis Walsingham at Mortlake. Dee had also formerly been advisor on navigation to Sir Francis Drake and Sir Walter Ralegh. He was a very strange fellow.

Sir Fulke Greville, forty-three, from Warwickshire. A lifelong friend until his death of the late Sir Philip Sidney, the famous son-in-law of Sir Francis Walsingham. Educated at Cambridge, attended court since '75, an experienced sea captain, currently involved in preparations for Rear Admiral Ralegh's impending voyage. And, some said, the next Treasurer of the Navy. Greville was a friend and distant cousin of Essex, but no less a friend and supporter of Ralegh, which marked him at the least as some sort of diplomat.

Sir Walter Ralegh himself, forty-five, rear admiral of her majesty's navy, world traveler, explorer, in his youth a dashing figure who so caught his queen's eye with his gallantry in placing his cloak in the mud to protect her path that she named him Captain of Her Guard the very next day, though she did not hesitate some years later to clap him into the Tower for having so insulted her favor as to get one of her maids, Elizabeth Throckmorton, with child. In and out of Elizabeth's favor ever since. Out, at the moment.

And Florio. And me.

Eight in all.

Sir Walter leaned heavily on his walking stick to ease the burden on his game leg — (wounded by the Spanish at Cadiz last year, Florio whispered by way of explanation) — belched for attention, and picked up a large cup of wine. Holding it before him, he recited through half-closed eyes:

> Prais'd be Diana's fair and harmless light,
> Prais'd be the dews wherewith she moists the ground;
> Prais'd be her beams, the glory of the night,
> Prais'd be her power, by which all powers abound.

"God save the queen," he concluded, solemnly raising his cup high. Ralegh drank deeply, passed the cup to Greville, and sat down. The cup made its way around the table, as each man took a swallow and echoed: "The queen!" When the cup reached me — barbaric habit, these English have, all pressing their lips to the same cup — I drained it and passed it back to Ralegh. (*Paese che vai, usanza che trovi*, When in England, do as the English do!) But I said nothing about their queen.

Ralegh took several minutes to light his foul-smelling silver pipe. It was one of the affectations he had brought back with him from the New World. Florio told me that because of Ralegh, smoking a pipe was now all the rage at court. I found myself drawn to this swashbuckling adventurer. To begin with, he was far away the most elegantly dressed man I had ever seen. The rumors were that he was nearly broke, but you would not know it from his wardrobe. His clothes must have cost him a fortune. If this was the way he dressed at home, I could only guess what he might wear to court.

Satins, silks, and brocades, all merged into one peacock of an outfit, then trimmed with pearls and edged in gold thread. A single large black pearl dangled from his left ear. His dark hair and neatly trimmed beard had streaks of gray through them, and there were age lines gathered at the corners of his heavy-lidded blue eyes, but he was every bit as handsome in middle-age as he must have been as a young man when he first caught his queen's fancy. Ralegh was a courtier, a scholar, and a poet, but he had more the rakish look of a successful pirate. One could not help but like and admire him.

Nearly enveloped in a cloud of smoke from his pipe, his west country burr adding a touch of humor to his otherwise flawless Italian, he made a little speech:

"I'm everlasting pleased by your company this night, my friends.

I mind the time we held dinners like this more regular. God's belly, that's a long time ago!" he said, slapping the table with his hand as if remembering the good old days. "Aye, and a fellow has sore need of friends nowadays, comes to that. There are those would turn a Lady's heart to stone toward this Ocean whilst he be away on Her business. There's a bitterness on it! Sir Arthur and me hie to engage the Spanish at Ferrall, thence to the Indies at great risk to life and limb, aye, and to purse also, I might add, with me in debt to me eyeballs already for queen and country, whilst betimes these schemers, these blackhearts, wouldst meantime do their best to pave our way to the Tower again, given half the chance! Why, in war the danger is more to your back than your front!

"How think you about that, Signore Guidotti? Dost call that proper reward for twenty years' loyal service? Nay, hardly! Well, well, we've kept our head so far; we will keep it a while longer, eh? God willing, this damnable weather'll steady down long enough for us to slip away on the tide one morning soon, and then let them do their worst and to hell with them! *Warspite* is trimmed out at last. *Ark Royal* and the other ships as well, though I hear m'Lord Essex may be another two weeks getting the new mast stepped on *Due Repulse*. Well, we have need of only one Plantagenet on this voyage anyway, comes to that. Essex will just have to catch up as best he can, eh?"

He laughed heartily. There was obviously no love lost between the two commanders.

Ralegh paused to relight his pipe. The others at the table grew restless. No one really understood this invitation to dinner. They had never actually been a part of Ralegh's inner circle, his "School of Night." They all knew him, of course. And they were all flattered to be included on this occasion. Dee had come all the way from Manchester and Gwinne from Oxford. But a few were worried that Ralegh was seeking financial backing for this voyage — it was no secret that he was badly in debt — and that they might now be called upon for contributions. Others, especially Greville, were nervous it was some scheme to recover the queen's favor at the expense of Essex, using them as go-betweens. Such a scheme would place them in an awkward position, since it was unclear which of these two would emerge victorious. If one chose to back Ralegh, one could easily be on the losing side. It was better to stay neutral when it came to wagering on the queen's whims. Thus, all waited impatiently for Ralegh to come to the point.

"Signore Guidotti here, John Florio's cousin from distant Italy, has been enquiring about a countryman of his, one whom some of you may recollect. He was, I believe, a friend to some of you. I know that he was of yours, John, and yours, Matthew. And Fulke, if I am not mistaken, did not you and Phil Sidney bring him round to one of our 'School' meetings? Dazzled hell out of 'Wizard Earl' Henry Percy, I recollect," he said, chuckling to himself.

Florio looked away, embarrassed. The others were puzzled. Dee, a trumpet to his ear, waited for Gentili to finish translating. Dee was the only one present who spoke no Italian. As Ralegh had set the pace by speaking Italian and had indicated thereby that the others do the same, Gentili had volunteered to translate for Dee.

"Who is Walter talking about?" Dee asked in a loud voice.

"He has not yet mentioned the man's name, Doctor," Gentili responded, glancing questioningly toward Ralegh.

"Why, 'tis true, so I haven't," Ralegh agreed, puffing away. He raised his voice and spoke directly to Dee in English. "Talking about Giordano Bruno, John. The Nolano. Remember him, d'ye?"

There was an immediate reaction from Greville. He frowned angrily. Whatever triggered it though, he held his tongue. The others seemed nonplussed. Bruno was a name that had not crossed their minds in a dozen years or more. For Ralegh to dredge it up out of the blue was a bit like drinking water when you were expecting wine. A surprise to the senses that took several moments to even register. Doctor Gilbert was the first to respond.

"I never actually met the man, Walter, although I remember him well enough. I have read his books, of course. *La cena de le ceneri...* (he glanced curiously at Greville, as if there were more to that but he wasn't saying)...*De la causa, principio et uno,* and *De l'infinito universo e mondi.* I was much stirred by *De l'infinito* in particular. Discussed it straightaway with Hues and Hariot.

"These were mathematician friends of Sir Walter's, Signore Guidotti," he explained, turning to me, "and of mine. I have for many years conducted experiments with magnetic bodies and with what I call electrical attractions. This work has led me to study the size and structure of the universe, which now appears to bear the possibility of infinitude. You see, Aristotle claimed that the infinite cannot be an actual thing and a substance and a principle, but your countryman Bruno did not agree. And now, I do not agree either. In *l'Infinito* he said: 'I call the universe infinite because it has no margins, limit, or surface; I do not call the universe totally infinite because He excludes from Himself every term, and every one of His attributes is one and infinite: and in each part of it totally and infinitely.' Now, I take that splendidly phrased!

"Now then, in my opinion Doctor Copernicus was correct in his findings that our world rotates on an axis and does not stand immobile in the ether like a great stone at rest. This concurs with the Nolano's own conclusions. But as to the Nolano's conjecture that there are many such worlds as ours — 'an infinity of peopled worlds' is what he proposes — I am certainly not prepared to accept that on the strength of his speculations. We must wait until this can be proved experimentally, scientifically. Hues and Hariot agreed with me. They were of the belief that the Nolano's mathematics were weak and imperfect. Probably his physics as well, although Doctor Gwinne would know more about that than I. On the whole I would say I found his ideas stimulating, challenging, and provocative. Would that I had met him personally, as there are many questions I should like to have put to him. Let me ask, Signore Guidotti, are you a scientist? What is your connection with the Nolano? Is it possible that I may address my questions to him through you?"

I was saved the awkwardness of explaining my connection with Bruno by the momentary commotion at the end of the table as Gentili completed translating Gilbert's comments to an impatient Doctor Dee. When that shouting match subsided, it was Gwinne who then took up the discussion.

"I cannot quote from the Nolan's books as ye have done so admirably, Doctor Gilbert," the Welshman began, "but I have read them and did get to know the author, first at Oxford and later here in London. 'Twas me, alas, contributed to that unpleasant imbroglio in the Church of the Holy Virgin, when the Nolan disputed with the Reverend Doctor Underhill and others before the Palatine Laski. My rector at St. John's had invited me to partake in the disputations. My topic was to be 'Whether males live longer than females.' I contrived at his request for the Nolan to be invited to join these disputations, knowing nothing at the time of the subject he might choose.

"'Twas a mistake. I knew it from the start of his speech. The good doctors were ill prepared for the likes of the Nolan. Aye, and 'twere naught but ill could come of his telling 'em they knew more about beer than about Aristotle!"

Ralegh chortled at the thought of anyone so accusing the stodgy doctors of Oxford. Greville, however, frowned darkly and his face turned an angry color. I noticed that Florio, meanwhile, was busily inspecting a pile of crumbs he had made on the table before him.

"Nor did 'e stop at that," Gwinne continued. "Methinks 'twas his greatest failing, that he never knew when to be shut of an argument, but rather would go on and on *ad nauseam*. No way 'twould end otherwise but to have his lectureship withdrawn, which they accomplished within a fortnight. 'Twas then he entered the employ of Mauvissière, the French ambassador. And aye, Walter, ye recollect rightly, 'twas indeed Fulke and Phil brought him round to Leicester House for a meeting of the 'School.' John and me were present that night, the night he wondered everybody w' his soaring poetry."

"Oh? 'Soaring,' was it? Soaring, me arse!" Greville grumbled, unable to contain himself any longer.

"Oh, oh!" cried Ralegh in mock horror. "Now see what ye've done, Matt! God's teeth, ye've gone and upset Il Candido!"

"Joke if you will," sniffed Greville, "but there is naught to joke about where that ungrateful monk's concerned."

Dee put his trumpet to his ear.

"Monk? Did he say 'monk'?" he shouted at Gentili. "What monk? What monk?"

"Monk is what he was, *sans habit*, monk or priest, they're all the same," Greville continued, ignoring the interruption. "I grant you, William, his theories on the universe were recondite. He was also passable smart on the ancients, the Egyptians, Hermes and that lot, though George Abbot said that lecture in the Church of the Holy Virgin was mostly filched from the works of Marsilius Fininus. But a soaring poet, say you, Matt? Nay! Say, rather, a plummeting one. A clever and tricky poet, all right. Nor yet, even then, a true poet, much less a *soaring* poet! Say, instead, that he was a clever little man, a crafter of words, a rhymer, a sonnetizer, a verser, aye, and worst of all, a cabbalist, this Philotheus Jordanus Brunus Nolanus. "Mark, I nevertheless raise no objections on the basis of any of these grounds, save only that he dared presume to lecture Sir Philip Sidney on the structure and meaning of poetic love. Why, the man lacked not only humility but common sense! Lecture Sidney? Lecture one of this country's finest, noblest, and most gifted poets? How dared he speak of Phil's as 'vulgar loves,' whilst only he, the great No-lan-o, might address the higher Cupid! Is that your sign of a soaring poet? — (he dragged the word out sarcastically: . . . soarrring) — Well, I say he was a *sore* poet, I say *sore* friend too! After what Phil and I did for him at court? We welcomed him into our group, introduced him about, even brought him together with Phil's father-in-law — would you have managed even that little lectureship at Oxford, John, were it not also for a word in the right place from Leicester? — and look what he did in that book of his, that *Cena*. Made me the laughing stock of England, he did! Insulted me beyond forgiveness..."

✠

"*Bella roba!*"
"Does that mean you like it?"
Oblivious to the edge of sarcasm in Florio's comment, Giordano beamed with pleasure at what he chose to interpret as a compliment.
"What it means it that this time you have gone too far," answered Florio, putting the book down with a sigh and a shake of his head. "What in the world possessed you to write a thing like this?"
"A thing like what, Giovanni? *Non capisco!* What have I written that is so terrible?"
Giordano was confused. For him this had been a prideful time, to have his most important book finished, printed, bound, and ready for the whole world to read. Well, not the whole world, only that part he cared about.
The Ash Wednesday Supper was his first book to be published in England, his first in Italian instead of Latin, and his first major attempt to elaborate on the theories of Copernicus. It was his intention to use Copernicus as the theme by which he would bind together the issues of reunification, heliocentricity, and the infinite oneness of all things, bind them together into one coherent philosophy of Universal Unity. Already he had begun work on the next book in the series and had formulated plans in his head for the one after that.
He was on the right path now, he was certain of it; and when the right people read the *Cena* and the books to follow (not those narrow-minded pedants at Oxford, but the *true* intellectuals of England!), they would all recognize his genius and accept the wisdom of his true philosophy!
So filled with excitement had he been with the completion of this book that he had rushed home from the printer with the very first copy, thrust it into his friend's hands to read, and then hovered over him making impatient noises as he waited eagerly for an

opinion. And yet Florio, having read not even a quarter of the way through the book, had just put it down with a shake of his head. Why? What could be wrong? If Florio, who was more English than he was Italian, did not understand *La Cena*, than Giordano might have missed his intended audience altogether! Giordano's confidence was badly shaken.

"In uno battibaleno," Florio explained, affecting that same flat tone and patronizing manner he used when lecturing his six-year-old pupil, "in one flash, you have alienated half of London. You show contempt for their manners, their dress, their town. You then resurrect that whole *vistoso e di cattivo gusto* of an affair at Oxford last June, in such a fashion that the good doctors must swallow the same *pillola amaro* from you all over again. And then, worst of all, you insult a friend who is one of your most important contacts at court, Fulke Greville. You accuse him of being a thoughtless, insensitive, and vulgar host. Moreover, this supper which I happen to recall — and I have no doubt Greville, Sidney, Gwinne, and the others will also — took place, not at Greville's, but right here on Butcher Row!

"Your book is full of insult and distortion. I seriously advise you to consider destroying it," Florio finished emphatically. But immediately he softened his tone when he saw the pain and shock on his friend's face. "Look, Giordano, I am your friend. I tell you plainly, I am afraid that this book would be your ruination in England. If you distribute this book, I think not even the Marquis de Mauvissière would come to your defense."

This was harsh criticism. *Dagli amici mi guardi iddio, che dai nemici mi guardo io?* (With friends like these, who needs enemies?) Clearly this was not what he wanted to hear from Florio.

"But you don't understand!" he cried in exasperation. "The supper is allegorical! Literary license, nothing more! Surely you understand such things, even in England. What does it matter that I place the supper at Greville's and not here? Who cares? What difference does it make if I poke a little fun at the common people, at their stupidity and ignorance, at the filth of their streets? Everybody at court, yourself included, is forever expressing the same annoyances. It is a way for them to identify with me instead of regarding me as a foreigner. How many times have

I heard even you curse those ill-mannered and thieving Thames wherrymen? Come now, Giovanni, Greville and the others are intellectuals. I have not poked fun at them. They will be amused, not insulted. Surely you are wrong?"

But Florio was unconvinced.

"I was born in England. For me to criticize my countrymen in private is one thing. But you are not English. Like it or not, you are a foreigner here, an invited guest in the house of the queen. You delude yourself; they do not forget your birthplace. So for you, a foreigner, to make such criticisms publicly in a book, that is quite a different thing. I am telling you, they will not tolerate it."

"*Per carità*, what a turd you are! You defend those pigs at Oxford? What do those 'good doctors' of yours understand of cosmology or philosophy? You could put what they know in your left eye! Remember, please, it was they who insulted me, not the other way around. What is so wrong with my stating my side of the case?

"Listen, Giovanni, I think you are focusing on petty details — the streets of London, the Oxford doctors, where a supper happens to take place or who I choose to place around a table. These are insignificant matters, decorations, like flowers in a room. It is the room itself that counts! The substance of this book is the Dialogues. Tell me, minor objections aside, what do you think of the Dialogues?

"What about in the Third Dialogue, the proof offered by Teofilo that a small luminous body can illuminate more than half of a distant opaque body? What about the 'Ship Experiment'? Did you get to the part yet in the Fourth Dialogue where I demonstrate the error of Nundinio and Torquato, and where I prove that Copernicus showed the earth and the moon are contained in the same epicycle? Or in the Fifth ... no, no, of course not, you have not read that far. You were too busy anticipating Sir Fulke Greville's reaction.

"You worry too much, Giovanni. Let me worry about Greville. I can handle him, I assure you. Go back to the *Cena*. Read the Fifth Dialogue, where I describe the four motions of the earth as it travels around the sun. No one has ever described them in this fashion!

"These are the important elements of the book, not the petty concerns you have allowed to distract you. For a minute you had me worried! Who cares about the common people? They do not even read! Who cares about those Oxford pedants? Hell will freeze before they change their minds about anything! Who even cares about Greville or Sidney or anybody, even you or me? Can't you see? These are revolutionary concepts! My philosophy will change the world. It will bring people together, churches, even nations! Don't you see that world peace is more important than whether someone's feelings are hurt, that world unity is more important than a few ruffled feathers?"

Giordano was flushed with renewed enthusiasm. He was always like this, never down for very long. He had the ability to stoke his own fires, to generate excitement for his work even in the face of the meanest criticism. Who could resist such enthusiasm. Not Florio.

"You win, Giordano," he said with a weak smile. "I do agree that these are exciting ideas. And of course I will read the Dialogues. I only pray for your sake that you are right about Greville being amused. I do not wish to see you in trouble again. Greville is not without influence. (He held up his hand in mock terror.) All right, all right! Don't start in again! I will be good, I promise!"

✠

Giordano of course did not curtail distribution of *La Cena,* as Giovanni Florio had originally suggested. Nothing of the kind. Instead, he instructed his printer, John Charlewood (himself so wary of publishing this book that he had insisted it carry a Paris imprint and not his own), to cause copies to be delivered by special messengers to John Dee, Greville and Sidney, to Gwinne, Gentili, and Smith, to Ralegh and to his friends Hughes, Roydon, Warner, and Hariot. He had a copy delivered to Walsingham, one to Leicester, and one to the Lord Treasurer at Theobalds. He had a specially bound copy delivered to her majesty at Greenwich, along with a flowing note that expressed his respect and his gratitude for her princely hospitality.

Finally, there were copies to Thomas Digges (as one Copernican to another), to Alexander Dicson with thanks for his help and friendship, and one to his patron, the Marquis, which he delivered personally. Of the remainder of this first small printing, half went to the booksellers at the Pawn on the upper floor of the Royal Exchange on Cornhill, while the other half would be distributed by Charlewood through his various agents abroad.

No copies went to Oxford. What for? Few of them understood enough Italian to read his book, much less appreciate its importance. Besides, he thought to himself with malicious satisfaction, they would be hearing soon enough from their friends in court about the stupidity of "Nundinio and Torquato." Perhaps now they would realize the injustice they had done him last June.

As for Mauvissière, Florio had been mistaken there as well. The ambassador was more than pleased when he read the dedication to him in the book. He also had understood and appreciated Giordano's reasons for transposing the site of the supper to Greville's. To have had it take place at Beaumont House, as it actually had, would seem to have implicated Englishmen in the taking of the Eucharist at the French Embassy. Though taking of the Eucharist was permitted at foreign embassies, this particular act might easily have been misinterpreted and could possibly have precipitated a diplomatic incident at a most inopportune time for Mauvissière.

Giordano was not unaware of his patron's secret correspondence with the Scottish queen. Florio had hinted about it often. He had long suspected that the ambassador was serving as a conduit for plots and intrigues of which Giordano wished to know as little as possible, certain as he was that members of Walsingham's famous "spy network" were right here in the ambassador's household. Perhaps Florio was one of them. He seemed at times too well informed for a mere tutor and writer of dictionaries. You could be certain of no one. Had he himself not exaggerated King Henri's parting " ... keep your eyes and ears open over there, Signore Bruno ... " into what he broadly hinted to Florio and Mauvissière was a "secret mission for the king"? Who could tell who was doing what for whom? Nobody's hands were entirely clean.

Mauvissière had nevertheless proved an ideal patron. By accepting Giordano into his household, he had assured him a quiet place to work, a small income with which he was able to pay to publish his books, entrée into court where he was free to expose his ideas to leading intellectuals and to influential members of the government, and the diplomatic protection of an ambassador representing a powerful, if momentarily confused, state.

Giordano knew, however, that he was only as safe as his patron's good favor, a status he had become increasingly adept at maintaining. As an Italian, he was much sought after at court — the English still regarded Italians as the originators of culture — and he used this popularity to advance his patron's reputation whenever he could. He was also quick to help Florio with Katherine Marie, and he praised her at every opportunity. Mauvissière doted on his daughter. It was not difficult to find reasons for this praise, since she was extremely precocious and also quite likeable. And even though he doubted that the ambassador really understood the subtleties of his work, he went out of his way to explain it, expounding his theories at great length.

In return, Mauvissière treated him as a friend and as a gentleman, not as an employee. For his part, he too was being just a bit cautious. After all, who knew but that Signore Bruno might not actually be on a secret mission for the king? In Mauvissière's position, it paid to invest in caution.

✱

Giordano was on edge. Allowing several days, say a week, for the books to be delivered, another week, give them two, to read it thoroughly at least once, there should have been some reaction by now. Yet he had heard nothing in three weeks. It was as though the ground had opened up and swallowed *La cena de la ceneri*, all five dialogues!

The waiting was unbearable. So important was this book to him (yes, and he was not too modest to say it, important to the rest of the world too!) that he was ready to humble himself completely by going to some of those on his list for the purpose of soliciting their opinions. Fortunately, Mauvissière saved him that embarrassment with the request that he and Florio accompany the ambassador to Greenwich for an audience with the queen.

Ever since the Spanish ambassador, Mendoza, had been expelled earlier in the year for plotting with Mary Stuart against the throne, and even more so since the assassination of William Prince of Orange and the resulting rapprochement between France and Spain, the French Embassy had been beset with attacks. Broken windows, threats, beatings of the servants on their way to market. Mauvissière had complained to Sir Francis on numerous occasions, but to no avail.

The latest in this conspiracy had come last week. William Gryse, clerk of the queen's stables, had been building himself a house next door on Butcher Row. Now he had interfered with the drainage system and the embassy stank to high heaven! Mauvissière sought redress and was now taking the matter to the queen herself.

The three arrived at court dressed for the occasion: Mauvissière in his finest ambassadorial splendor, Florio in a tasteful if subdued outfit that befitted his neutral nature, and Giordano in the same dark and threadbare doublet he had worn at court for two years in Paris. Besides being perennially short of cash, Giordano was simply too preoccupied to take any notice of his appearance.

They were early. Mauvissière made it a point always to be early, so that he and not the queen should be kept waiting. They sat in the antechamber. Laughter and music could be heard coming from inside the queen's chambers. This aging queen kept a rigorous schedule. Hunting, riding, dancing, game playing until all hours of the night, it was enough to wear out even the younger men! All the same, she was ever abreast of the minutest of details of her kingdom, keeping herself well informed at all times on her subjects and on events abroad. On the few occasions that Giordano had had an opportunity to converse with the queen, he had found her eager for conversation, fluent in Italian and Latin, and conversant on a far wider range of topics than her bishops might have preferred. She was a powerful and important ruler. And not one to be crossed. It was rumored she could be as ruthless and as vainglorious as her father, yes, and that, hands on her hips and legs astride, she could curse as well as him too.

Giordano could not help but speculate that the fate of the world might well take a positive turn were this splendid queen ever to unite with Navarre. Now that was a thought worthy of contemplation!

Florio nudged him from his reverie. Sidney and Greville were just making their exit from the Presence Chamber. Greville spotted Giordano immediately. He scowled, hurried past without a word, his face an angry crimson. Sidney paused to speak with them. After exchanging pleasantries with the ambassador, he drew Giordano aside.

"Signore Bruno, I feel I must tell you that you may have made of poor Greville an enemy for life. He feels you have treated him unkindly in your book. He is a sensitive man, Signore Bruno, with the heart of a poet and the pride of a lion. I cannot seem to budge him on this. He believes he has been gravely insulted. As you must know, we have admired you and your work. It is important work, I recognize that, and so does Fulke. But it does not give you license to abuse friendship. I will do my best with him, but I am not optimistic. You would have done well to consult with him before printing your *Cena*, I think."

Giordano frowned.

"'A city that is set on a hill cannot be hid' – Matthew 5:14. I do not consult with anyone before I publish. Surely you can understand my reasons, Sir Philip. I am in the open for all to see, for all to dispute with who desire to, for everyone to criticize. These are my ideas. I will defend them with my life. But let people debate with me over ideas, not over jealousies and pride. I have no time for vanity. Fulke Greville is too thin-skinned. I am sorry he is upset. I meant him no personal insult. But he will get over it, I am sure. The world is in great and cataclysmic upheaval. My work is at the dawning of a New Age!

"Teofilo says in the Fifth Dialogue of *La Cena:* 'We know that the beginning of inquiry is the knowledge and the understanding that the thing exists, or is possible and fitting, and that one may draw profit from the inquiry.' Tell that to your friend. Tell Sir Fulke to read my book, to study it night and day, and to do his best to try and understand it. Tell him that I do not consider it important whether he likes me or whether even he understands me. Only that he reflect on the ideas in my books. Tell him that, I beg you! *Guardi che siamo alle porte coi sassi,"* There isn't much time, you know!

✠

"...and he had the temerity to suggest to Phil that I should study his insulting book. Imagine! *I* should study *his* damned book! Well, naturally, I instructed my servants that henceforth I was never to be at home to that...that pompous little peacock. I came very close to throttling the ungrateful fellow, I can tell you!"

The subject of Giordano Bruno was more than just a simple sore spot with Greville. It had tapped such a wellspring of rage that his face was now near purple with emotion simply talking about him. As he finished, he grabbed his wine cup with both hands and brought it to his mouth, his eyes darting challengingly around the table and daring anyone to disagree with him. I half expected to hear the wine hiss when it touched his lips, he was that hot.

No one spoke. In the face of Greville's outburst the table was silent for some time, save for the rasp of Doctor Dee's breathing and the sound of the abbey's bells as they tolled the late hour. Finally, Gentili broke the silence.

"Fulke, my dear fellow, we are not unsympathetic. And we do certainly understand the nature of your complaint. But are you being quite fair in your evaluation of the Nolano's worth? May we not also concede that there was more to this man than his regrettable lack of tact?"

Greville scowled, but said nothing.

Ralegh, however, seemed amused.

"It appears the 'accused' is about to be defended by our learned advocate of jurisprudence," he ventured with a sly smile playing at the corners of his mouth. "Tell us, Alberico, are we to be treated to one of your splendid *retorsio argumenti?*"

"De minimus non curat lex, Walter," Gentili responded gravely, "'The law is not concerned with trifles.' With due respect to Fulke's personal feelings in this matter...(he nodded apologetically toward Greville, who merely shrugged)...these are not sufficient grounds for slander, and this sort of grievance would not obtain in a court of law. We must in all fairness, therefore, consider the man's work with at least the same verisimilitude as his personality, obnoxious as the latter

may have been. In this regard I believe I might pose credible argument for his historical significance."

Greville I found boring. *Pieno di sè*. I could not get worked up about his complaint. After my walk through the London streets on the day I arrived, I would say the Nolan's account of the common people and their manners was probably accurate. As for Oxford, what I pictured happening there was that this feisty little Neapolitan did battle in some church with a bunch of stiff-backed *asini* in academic robes. I have seen a few of their sort in my day, and they could not stand the heat. Credit to Bruno for having the balls to take them on. And what was the point of worrying where the supper took place anyway? It sounded as though Greville was making a big deal over nothing. Sour grapes, if you asked me.

Gentili, on the other hand, did interest me. This was one smart fellow. An Italian trained in English law, he was the first one of the evening to suggest that maybe there was something about Bruno that was of historical importance. Thus far, they had all focused more on his mouth than his pen. Gentili's remark about "a court of law" had especially caught my attention, and I listened very closely to what he had to say.

He appeared knowledgeable about the Nolan's work, referring even to some of his books published after his departure from England, from which I inferred that he was either extremely well read or had continued to pay unusually close attention to the whereabouts and do-ings of the Nolan. I wondered why. His argument pointed to Bruno as a sort of link between Catholic theology and the theory of natural law, which he said was emerging from the Protestants. It did not seem that he was placing the Nolan in either camp, but rather somewhere in between.

Gentili had much to say about the followers of Copernicus in Eng-land, who he said persisted in spite of the powerful objections of diehard Aristotelians. He placed the Nolan at the leading edge of those who sought to expand on that concept in order to articulate a new philosophy of the universe.

"Note I said a new philosophy," he added with caution, "not, as some would no doubt have it, a new religion. On the contrary, what I see this new philosophy — science, if you will — accomplishing is a strengthening of traditional religious values, and perhaps ultimately a solution to the current impasse between Rome, Madrid, and Paris on the one hand, and ourselves on the other. Notwithstanding, of course, dialectical differences between various Protestant factions here and on the Continent."

"Do you actually suggest that this fool's work contributes to some sort of reunification? I mean, *really!*" Greville said incredulously.

"I do more than suggest. I believe that his theories, as well as those of a number of others developing similar ideas relating to nature and the universe, will permanently alter our understanding of ourselves, our world, our universe, even of our Creator."

Greville was aghast!

Doctor Dee, I noticed, who had been getting filled in by Gilbert on what Gentili was saying, had been nodding in vigorous agreement. The others seemed only mildly interested and remained noncommittal. Except for Florio. He continued to look down at the table. If he could have disappeared, he would have.

"Signore Gentili," I asked when he had finished, "you suggested earlier that you could make this case in a court of law. *Any* court of law?"

"Well, yes, I think so," he replied.

"Forgive me. My knowledge of these things is limited. Might 'any court' include one in Rome? Say, for example, that of the Holy Office?"

Florio shuddered. Greville's questioning eyes darted quickly to Ralegh, who remained impassive but who nevertheless responded to Greville with a barely perceptible shake of his head. Doctor Dee's trumpet rushed to his ear, while everyone else at the table leaned forward to hear Gentili's response. "I fear not. The Inquisition is a religious, not a secular court. Civil law does not apply. The accused are without rights. They may not be represented by an advocate. They may not know the names of their accusers, nor may they know what they are accused of. They may neither call witnesses in their favor nor hear the testimony of witnesses against them, except such as the inquisitors may wish to have read to them. Contrary to our civil law, they are guilty until and unless the inquisitors declare otherwise, regardless of the evidence that has been presented. Signore Guidotti," he said, staring at me intently, "are you suggesting that the Nolano is on trial in Rome by the Inquisition?"

"Yes."

"Then the Lord have mercy on him, as they will not. There is no one here with the power to save him from that most ungodly of tribunals, least of all me."

"After that part you played in having Mendoza bounced," Ralegh interjected, "I should think it might even be a bit dangerous for you in Rome, eh, Alberico? If there is one thing the Inquisition has, it is a long memory."

"You are no doubt correct. Rome and Madrid hold hands like a pair of lovers having patched a quarrel, though I suspect Clement has no more trust of Philip than we do. Religious politics makes strange bedfellows. On the other hand, what they do not know is that I probably saved Mendoza's life. When the queen solicited my opinion, the Lord Treasurer was all for hanging. Walsingham had already ordered construction of the gallows."

"Speaking of her majesty," Doctor Gilbert interrupted, seeking to ease the tensions of the moment, "have you all heard the story of what transpired in court between the queen and the Polish emissary 26th July last?"

"I heard good Queen Bess gave the Polack what for," Ralegh said, relighting his pipe once more," but I was down at Plymouth. What actually took place, William?"

"I have the account from Harrison, as I was not there personally. The way he tells it, the queen was possessed that this ambassador — a comely gentleman of excellent fashion, wit, discourse, language, and person — intended a proposition of peace. And so the queen received him publicly in the Presence Chamber, where most of the lords and ladies were present.

"He entered in great finery, attired in a robe of long black velvet, well jewelled. He bowed low, kissed her majesty's hand, thence straight retired ten yards off her and began an oration in Latin."

Dee interrupted.

"Did he say 'Matin'?" he shouted.

"Nay, *Latin*, John."

"Ah! Very well. Proceed, Gilbert."

"The thrust of his speech, according to Harrison," Gilbert continued, "was that the king had sent him to put her majesty in mind of past treaties between Poland and England, that the king had ever friendly received her merchants and subjects, but that she had suffered his to be spoiled without restitution, out of mere injustice, notwithstanding particular petitions and letters received. To confirm her disposition to avow these courses, violating the law of nature and nations, because there were quarrels between her and the king of Spain, the ambassador said, she — meaning the queen — took upon her by mandate to prohibit him and his countries, assuming to herself thereby a superiority not tolerable over other princes..."

Ralegh pounded the table with his fist.

"God's blood, sir, the man should ha' been horsewhipped! I'd ha' done it meself, God's me witness! What did she do, man?"

Gilbert raised his hand.

"Wait, he said more! This Polish ambassador continued — in Latin, as he'd rehearsed, so as to embarrass her majesty's lack of it, or so he thought — that his king was determined not to endure further, but wished her to know that if there were no more than the ancient amity between Spain and him, it was no reason why his subjects should be so impeded, much less now when straight obligations of blood had so conjoined him with the illustrious house of Austria. Finally, he concluded that if her majesty would not reform it, the king would."

Ralegh was indignant! He was on his feet, his dagger drawn.

"The bastard!"

Gilbert grinned with amusement.

"So all must have thought who were there. But, gentlemen, this be no dainty damsel in distress who rules us, lo, these thirty-nine years, but a heroic prince of the realm. Much moved to be so challenged in public by this Polish ambassador, and loth to pause even long enough for his speech to be translated for those of the lords and ladies who understood not his Latin, the queen proceeded immediately to answer him extempore in Latin.

"Now this I have had in writing from Harrison, as he noted it, so as to commit it to my memory — oh, it must have been marvelous to the ear! — *Expectari Legationem, mihi vero querelam adduxisti!* and continuing to this effect: 'Is this the business the king has sent you about? Surely I can hardly believe that if the king himself were present, he would have used such language; for if he should, I must have thought that being a king not of many years, and that *non de iure sanguinis sed iure electionis, immo noniter electus,* he may haply be uninformed of that course which his father and ancestors have taken with us, and which peradventure shall be observed by those that shall live to come after us. And as for you, although I perceive you have read many books to fortify your arguments in this case, yet I am apt to believe that you are not lighted on the chapter that prescribes the form to be used between kings and princes; but were it not for the place you hold, to have so publicly an imputation thrown upon our justice, which as yet never failed, we would answer this audacity of yours in another style. And for the particulars of your negotiations, we will appoint some of our Council to confer with you, to see upon what ground this clamor of yours hath foundation.' Et cetera."

To a man, we rose and cheered and thumped the table with our cups. Ralegh sheathed his dagger and collapsed in a fit of laughter.

"Sweet Jesus," he cried, wiping the tears from his eyes, "the woman has style! What I would not give to have witnessed this scene. Oh, I do love that queen! Here, fellows, a drink on it."

He filled the cup, drank, and passed it again.

"Her health!"

"Long live the queen!"

"Hear, hear!"

When they settled down again, some considerable number of toasts to the queen later, Matthew Gwinne turned to Doctor Dee and said, "Speaking of Poles, Warden, were you not also present at Oxford during the aforementioned disputation of the Nolano before the Palatine Laski?"

✠

Dee put his trumpet down and leaned forward to speak, giving Gentili a rest from his translating chores. Florio now translated Dee's English for me. I would sooner Gentili had continued to speak, his being the more pointed exposition from my point of view, but I did listen to what Dee had to say, and I heard more than I expected.

"No, I did not. I was at Mortlake at the time. But the Count did visit me, both before and afterward, and on 15th June he recounted to me of his visit to Oxford and of the Nolano's disputation, of which he was some bemused. I will say that I knew immediately and most certainly that the Nolano was a kindred soul, because that very night I had E.K. consult with the Angel Michael about him."

("Edward Kelley, his skryer," Florio whispered to me by way of explanation.)

"And what did the angel have to say, John?"

This from Ralegh, his face a mask of innocence, but his eyes dancing merrily. By which I understood that Ralegh was not very seriously inclined toward seances between mystics and angels.

"He said the Nolano was a prophet who would not be understood in his own time," he answered gravely, his voice low and rumbling like distant thunder on a summer storm. Dee was deaf and ailing, but he was far from weak. His voice projected an inner strength that belied his age, and the hands that now gripped the edge of the table were powerful indeed. And yet there was a gracefulness about him, and a quiet dignity despite the ludicrous trumpet he held to his ear whenever anyone else spoke. I could see why the others held him with respect despite their skepticism for his mystical side.

"I was abroad with my household during most of Doctor Bruno's stay here, having departed with Count Laski's party in September of '83 and not returning until five years later. By that time, he was of course gone. I have, however, read some of his work, admiring the Latin poems in particular — *De minimo, De monade,* and *De immenso* — and I concur with Gentili here when he says there may be historical significance. I would go further. There is spiritual significance here, as well. I base that judgment not only on the theories he has formulated, but on those being advanced by others who now work along similar lines.

"As one instance, I am in communication with a young mathematician and astronomer in Germany, Johannes Kepler. Young Kepler is about to publish his book, *Mysterium Cosmographicum,* excerpts of which he has sent to me from time to time. Now, Gilbert, this may interest you: Kepler claims that whilst the sun is at rest, yet it is the source of motion, having the force to move the planets..."

"Did Kepler give this force a name?" Gilbert asked excitedly.

"Nay, not that I know of. But it could be that his theory has some relevance to your work on magnetism, do you agree? In a different chapter, he goes on to say that as God the Father creates through the Holy Ghost, so the sun distributes his motive force through a medium which contains the moving bodies. Be mindful that, thus far, Kepler has worked only theoretically. But, were he to affiliate himself with a more experienced astronomer, one such as the Dane, Tycho Brahe, with whom I also communicate — and I have suggested to both that such an affiliation would greatly serve the new science — then he might easily apply his calculations to Brahe's precise observations. Brahe is stubborn. He labors still with a stationary Earth and a revolving sun, though at least he concedes the other planets revolve around the sun. But there is not another astronomer in the world today with planetary observations to match his, both in number and quality. He would be invaluable to Kepler, who would in turn be invaluable to him. The implications of this match would be most profound, most profound indeed."

He looked around for agreement.

Greville seemed perplexed. "I fail to see what all this has to do with Bruno," he grumbled, pouring himself more wine. Fulke Greville was slowly getting drunk. He was beginning to slur his words. Doctor Dee seemed not to notice. Or not to care.

"Bruno lacks Kepler's mathematics; Kepler lacks Bruno's imagination. What a team they would make! Naturally, it is too late for that, but not too late for Kepler to read the Nolano's work, and I have sent some of it to him, all I had to send. It is possible that he will pass these on to Doctor Galileo in Padua, with whom he communicates himself. On the other hand, he may reject my suggestion, neither reading them nor passing them on. I fear these great men can be very insular when it comes to sharing their ideas with each other. Jealousy perverts their common sense.

"The Nolan's work is very complex. There is much in it I neither understand, nor, to be perfectly frank, do I relish understanding. In truth, I have grown too old to battle such complexities. And what would I do with this information at my age, were I able to achieve the understanding of it? Nay, I comprehend not this business of dyads and monads, of atoms and infinity. Gilbert, you have more reason than I to try to understand these matters. And you are younger.

"Perhaps it is true he lacks mathematics. God's truth, he is no astronomer either. And yet I was able to journey with him to the moon in *De immenso*, and it was grand! When he looked back at the Earth, so also did I:

> *Dic: ubi sylvarum species? ubi flamina montes,*
> *Stagna, lacus, urbes, brumce, discremen et aestus?*

Do you see, Gilbert? Now, in *De minimo* he proclaims that as God is manifest in the universe, so the universe is worthy of study, thus to draw nearer to God. This is Kepler also! Do you see? The unity of all matter:

> *Ergo atomam tantum naturam dixeris esse*
> *Perpetur, cuius nulla ont propria una figura est.*

And thus the perfect circle is a creation of the spirit: *Definit cyclum tantum mens.* Do you grant this? Therefore: *Mens super omnia Deus est, mens insita in vebus Natura.* Thus, we can understand how these things connect. If it is your pleasure, we may consult my spirit guide further. What say ye all ... uh ... shall we ... uh ... nay, where is E.K.? ... dead, oh! ... I shall need ... I cannot ... well, you see ... "

Doctor Dee seemed suddenly bewildered, as though not knowing how to proceed. He looked around the table for guidance, but everyone averted his gaze. No one wished to acknowledge that this splendid old man had lost his way. There followed an embarrassed silence, scuffling of chairs, clearings of throats, and so forth, until at last Doctor

Dee decided that he must have finished. He slumped down in his chair and promptly fell asleep.

Greville was not to be put off.

"What is all this about Bruno, Ralegh? Why have we spent the entire night on the bloody bastard?" Turning to stare balefully at me, he demanded to know: "And what's your connection with him exactly, Signore Guidotti, may I ask?"

I too had been drinking too much wine, which, combined with Ralegh's pipe smoke — he had been passing it to me all evening, and I had taken quite a number of puffs of smoke into my mouth — made me feel queasy at this point. I was in poor condition to make my case, but it was now or never, so I made the attempt.

"I am attempting to mount a defense of the Nolan, who is accused of heresy by the Sant'Offizio," I said, haltingly. I was aware that I was slurring some of my words, but you know how it is, part of you is aware the other part is drunk, and it becomes a question of which part gets to control the speech. Alas, the sober part rarely seems to win. "I came here to find out more about him and to see if any of his old friends would be willing to testify for him in Rome."

"Testify? Testify? Be damned if I will!" shouted Greville, standing. "I believe I meet no opposition when I say that I place second to no one in defense of honesty and fair play. But to stand for that ungrateful...that self-centered, pompous...that...that...!"

Ralegh placed a comforting hand on Greville's sleeve and guided him gently back into his seat again.

Gentili turned to me and asked, "Signore, you have not yet answered Sir Fulke's question. Precisely what is your connection with the case?"

Gwinne and Gilbert nodded in silent agreement. Dee was awake again, and he seemed to be listening. But Florio was definitely apprehensive. Ralegh saw the look on his face and raised his hand for attention.

"Gentlemen," he said, before I could answer Gentili's question, "methinks we have had sufficient for one evening. The hour is late. Sir Edward Darcy, who occupies the ground floor of this splendid house — we are both the recipients of her majesty's largess, you see — has lately complained of my besporting with late night drinking companions. I vow he has blabbered as much to the queen. Perhaps it would be wise therefore to end our supper. Cousin Pietro here is in sorer need of a bed at the moment than a continuation of this discussion, and John had best get him home for a good night of sleep.

Doctor Dee, a room has been made ready for you; you also, Matthew; you'll both spend the night at Durham House. 'Tis far too late to be traveling all that distance to home. And as for me, I'm off to Plymouth in the morning, so I could use a bed meself.

"Well then, I bid ye goodnight. Let us all agree at least to say a prayer before we turn in, for the Nolan's safe outcome with the papist inquisitors. Fulke, we know ye mean the man no harm, for all your sulks. Be thankful it were only discussion this night, that we are not in that man's shoes, nor shall we be as long as we have a queen so mighty, so generous, and so fair. And count yerself lucky as well it was not primero we played at this night, Fulke, or ye'd be going home considerable lighter in the purse! I took Southampton for five gold crowns last week at Whitehall. So, goodnight then. Godspeed!"

✠

The cool night air cleared the dizziness in my head, but I was still weak in the stomach. I leaned heavily on Florio. On the ride down the Thames he had little to say, and for once I was grateful for his silence. With a roaring head and a fluttering stomach, I was not much for conversation.

I was disappointed in John Florio though, both as a man and as a friend of Bruno's. He had said nothing all night, never once defending his friend. He seemed instead to be almost embarrassed to have known him, while at least everyone else had contributed to the discussion, if not always flatteringly, as was the case with Fulke Greville.

On the other hand, and I had to give him this, he had at least been instrumental in organizing the supper with Ralegh. I now had plenty of new material to add to my notes (though not tonight! I added to myself, holding my head in my hands). What a pity none would be willing to speak up for Bruno in Rome. If only I could take some of them back with me, what a difference I imagined that would make. Not even one! Was the whole world against him?

We reached Shoe Lane as first light began to show in the east. As we approached Florio's house, we saw several men, soldiers, loitering on the steps. When they spotted us, they came to their feet and stood at attention, their pikes at the ready. An officer stepped forward.

"Which one of you is John Florio?" he asked.

"I am," answered Florio.

"Step aside, sir. Our business is with him," the officer said, pointing to me. "Pietro Guidotti, in the queen's name you are under arrest. You will come with me," he said in faltering Italian.

"On what charges?" demanded Florio.

"Espionage," the officer responded, and without another word he wheeled and walked away, followed by two of the soldiers with me between them, and the third behind me. The soldiers did not look like much, but they were armed. There was little room for argument.

"Courage, Guidotti, I will get to the bottom of this!" Florio shouted after me.

With that *creatura debole* for my defender, I could count on rotting in prison before he gets to the bottom of anything, I thought. But I was not yet concerned. All I could think about was my aching head. I never even thought to ask where they were taking me.

Chapter 15

THE TWO SOLDIERS marching beside me were puny fellows. I half-considered taking them on, but a jab in my back from the third soldier's pike suggested otherwise. I would have to wait for a better time. Counting on Florio's help could not be part of my plan. I would be on my own as always, that much was plain.

They took me to a prison. Not to the Tower, this place was much too close to Shoe Lane for that, somewhere near Old Bailey. Newgate, I thought, but I could not be certain as there were no signs. None of them spoke to me along the route. I had such a throbbing head, I didn't care where they took me.

I was deposited in a large room with only a table and one chair in the middle of it and told to wait. There I sat for perhaps five hours. To hell with them. I put my head down on the table and went to sleep.

"On your feet, prisoner!"

The guard's roar awakened me. My mouth was like cotton, and I was dying of thirst. The headache had subsided to a dull throb that was at least tolerable. I stood uncertainly, curious to see what might come next.

Two guards entered the room backward, carrying between them a chair on which sat someone the top of whose head was barely visible above the back of the chair. Once inside the room, they turned to reveal a wizened old hunchbacked man sitting in the chair. He wore a great gold seal of office around his neck. His right foot, badly swollen and loosely bandaged, preceded him on a small footstool carried by yet a third guard. Two more guards with pikes, big men this time, as big as me, brought up the rear of this strange procession.

The man in the chair, disregarding this whole process, continued to read intently from a batch of notes on his lap. They were *my* notes, the ones I had carefully hidden away under the mattress in Florio's house!

The soldiers placed their charge at the table and stepped behind him. The other two, the big ones with pikes, settled themselves beside me, one on each side. They reminded me of the gang at Ripa.

"Sit down, please," the man said without looking up.

His Italian was good, but the accent made it difficult for me to understand at first. The guards on either side of me grabbed my arms, lifted me off my feet, and thrust me into the chair as though I had been a basket of feathers.

I cleared my throat.

"Could I have some water?"

He raised one finger; that's all, one finger, barely. One of the soldiers behind him silently left the room, returning with a cup of water, which I drank.

"*Grazie.*"

Not a word. He did not look up. We sat there, him reading, me waiting, the guards looking straight ahead without ever blinking their eyes. "Tell me, Guidotti, do you value your head?"

He still had not looked up.

"To tell you the truth, right now it hurts like hell and I wish I had another, but as it is the only one I have . . . yes, I value my head."

"Then I assume you wish to keep it?"

"Oh yes, I definitely would not wish to part with it. Kind of you to ask."

"*Buono.*"

He said nothing else for quite a while, just continued to read my notes, paging back and forth, occasionally knitting his brow as though trying to decipher my code. At last, he looked up.

"*Molto interessante,*" he said. His face appeared kindly enough. I smiled. "But what does all this mean?" Now his face took on a sterner look.

I shrugged, still smiling. "Just some personal notes I made," I responded innocently, "so as not to forget some things. It's really nothing very important, I assure you."

At this he scowled.

"Do you know who I am?" His voice had a hard edge.

"No, sir, I do not."

I was being very polite, I thought.

"My name is Burghley. Does that name mean anything to you?"

"Uh . . . the Lord Treasurer?"

"The same."

"I am pleased to meet you, my Lord. May I go now?"

I did not think the question discourteous. He thought otherwise.

The two guards at my side clamped their hands down on my shoulders like a pair of vices.

"I want you to consider very carefully what I am about to say to you."

"Yes, sir?"

"Your name is Pietro Guidotti. You are in the employ of Father Robert Bellarmine. You have entered my country as a spy for Pope Clement VIII. These are your coded notes. I wish to know what they say. You will be brought paper, pen, and ink. You will remain in this room at this table until these notes have been decoded in their entirety. Following this, you will be fed, escorted to Plymouth, and placed on a boat bound for France. From thence, you will be free to return to Rome, or anywhere else you may desire, so long as you never return to England. Should you ever seek to return to England, you will be executed. I will give you until tomorrow morning to complete your task."

"But what if I am not finished by then?" I asked.

"Should you fail, should you refuse or fall asleep or be too slow or make mistakes, you will be taken out and hanged. Your stomach will be sliced open, your entrails removed, your penis cut off and fed to my favorite falcon, your body drawn and quartered, your head displayed on a stake at Cripple Gate for a period of one week."

Burghley placed my notes on the table. He signaled his men with one finger, the same all-meaning finger as before — I suppose they had been with him long enough to interpret its specific commands — and heaved a great sigh.

I don't think he was feeling very well. By now, neither was I. They carried him and his gouted foot out, the earlier procedure reversed, so that I was able to observe him all the way through the door until it closed behind them. His eyes never left mine. I had the feeling he meant what he said.

I had no problem with his request, not with the alternative he had offered. He knew enough about me already; he needed no further excuse to hang me. There was little he could do with the information anyway. He could certainly do no harm to my master; and, if anything, Bruno was someone Burghley would help if he could, just to antagonize the pope. So when the guard returned with the writing materials, I began immediately.

But then I stopped. What if he didn't believe me? He thought I was a spy. He expected secrets. I did not have any. *Gesù Cristo! Madre Maria!* I was in big trouble.

I banged on the door.

"I have to talk to him again!" I pleaded when the officer of the guard came.

"Forget it, pal. You better do like he says, or say your Hail Marys."

I began again, but I had little hope. I am a good judge of character. Burghley wanted useable information, anything less he would not believe. Guidotti fornicating pals with Henri IV? I would not believe me if I were Burghley.

Big, big trouble.

I was not even halfway through when the guards returned with the officer.

"Listen, give me a little more time! Christ, is it morning already? I can finish this in maybe another hour or two. You wouldn't want to hang someone for the sake of a lousy couple hours! I am trying, honest to God, I am writing as fast as I can, but there's seven months' worth here! *Per carità, ho messo gindizio,* I've learned my lesson! "Save your breath, *compagno.* Let's go."

"Wait a minute! Where are you taking me?" I screamed, holding on to the table with all my strength. Five of them had hold of me, dragged me toward the door, table and all.

"Us to know, you to find out," the officer said with a laugh. I did not enjoy the humor. Lord Burghley's graphic account of my future rang in my ear.

Outside, they threw me into a closed carriage, bolted the metal doors from the outside, and the carriage took off for a wild ride through the London streets. I thought I must be headed for the Tower.

The carriage had no windows, only narrow slits in the doors to let air in. It was still dark outside. (So morning had not yet come?) There was a moon, but it was still low. It was not nearly so late as I had imagined when the guards had come for me. I could see the Thames. It was on our left, meaning we were heading *away* from the Tower. Thank God for that! But if that was the case, where were they taking me?

We passed Durham House. I could see the turret which was the site of last night's supper — no, *this* night's supper — outlined against the star-filled sky. It seemed so long ago, that supper. We passed Durham House and continued at gallop speed. Where was this carriage going? And why?

A while longer at this pace, and then we stopped. I heard voices, but I could not understand what they were saying. I heard "Lambeth" but did not understand the meaning. Was Lambeth a person? A place? The carriage moved again, slowly. The sound of the street beneath us was hollow. A bridge? No, we were moving but there was no vibration of the wheels. A ferry! We were crossing the Thames. I could see the moonlight kissing off the water now. I had no idea where they were taking me.

I gave up looking out the slits in the doors and went to sleep. Wherever we were headed, I would need my wits about me when we got there. If there was a way to escape, I would take it. If not, if they were going to do me in anyway, I would go down fighting, take a few of them with me. You don't learn to lie down and play dead growing up in Campo Marzio. I would show them a thing or two.

I was awakened by the sound of halloing off in the distance. A voice near the carriage responded. I recognized it as that of the Italian-speaking officer. My carriage apparently had an escort. Did they expect I might be able to pry myself free from this iron box?

The carriage moved cautiously forward until at last it came to a final halt. The bolt was slammed forward and the door of the carriage was opened.

"Fuori!"

I did as I was told, I got out. And looked around in amazement.

I saw it but I did not believe it. My wildest dreams had never revealed such a place! A castle. One such as could never have been constructed in a real world, and yet here it was before me, rising up out of the swirling country fog and continuing almost, it seemed, to the starry sky. All aglitter with gilt and white stucco, a pile of cupolas and towers, great sculptured beasts rising above the battlements, domed and turreted like the many facets of some great jewel. An enormous gleaming fountain stood splashing in the entranceway, a statue of nude Diana standing in its middle. Gardens and trees and fountains and marble animals in the bushes. The whole place was ablaze with torches that cast eerie shadows on the glistening walls. It was a dazzling place!

I thought I had surely gone mad. First Lord Burghley's grotesque threat that I would be hanged, drawn, quartered, and beheaded if I did not reveal secrets which I did not have. Then whisked away in a galloping iron carriage through the dark of night to God knows where. And now this make-believe castle in the fog. What next?

"Welcome to Nonesuch, Guidotti," proclaimed my escort.

"Who's place is this?" I asked him.

He just smiled knowingly.

"You'll see. Follow me."

✠

The interior of Nonesuch was even more ornate and bizarre than the outside. Understand, there is truly no other such place as this in all the world. Only a raving madman with a child's sense of humor could have conceived building it! I was led up a gilded circular staircase, suspended as if from the roof, though it disappeared high above into something resembling gossamer clouds of silk. Then down a long corridor carpeted, I swear it, with feathers, goose feathers, I think, each individually fastened somehow to a cloth mesh underlining, feeling underfoot as though walking on moss.

We reached a door, decorated with carved angels, the handle of which was a gold cupid, bow in hand. The officer knocked once. The door opened, and we entered a passageway leading to yet a similar door. Two men wearing elaborate uniforms of a type I had not seen before stood guard at this door. The officer reached between them and knocked once again.

A muffled "Come!" came from within.

The guards stepped aside and the door was opened by a lady-in-waiting. The officer pushed me in, the lady stepped out, and the door closed behind me.

The room was dark, lighted only by a few strategically placed candles. It appeared to be a bed chamber, what I could see of it, at least there was a bed in it to signify that it was, though it was a cavernous room, decorated elaborately and resembling no other bed chamber I had ever been in.

"Come closer, Guidotti."

I approached a seated figure near the middle of the room. It was a woman. She was at a desk. And on the desk were my notes. I wondered how she came to have them. I had last seen them on the table in the prison as I was dragged from that room. Someone had to have taken them after that and would have to have ridden like the wind in order to deliver them before we arrived. How strange that so much attention was being paid to my notes!

But no stranger than that was this lady herself. She was peculiarly attired, in a dress of silver gauze all decorated with pearls and rubies. She wore a great necklace of emeralds around her thin and scrawny neck. She was old, her face long and thin, white with powder, red with rouge I suppose that was intended to hide the wrinkles, though it merely called greater attention to them, as far as I could tell. Her teeth were yellow, a few of them black, many of them missing. But when she spoke, her Italian was flawless. I had difficulty understanding some words, those with s's and th's, because of the missing teeth.

On anyone else, it might have been humorous. On her, it merely added to her incredible dignity.

She wore a number of rings. Six, if I remember correctly, it could have been seven, and a reddish-colored wig, which was on not quite straight. Perched atop the wig, she wore a jeweled crown.

"Do not stare, Guidotti. Have you never seen a queen's bedchamber before? From the looks of you, I would wager you are no stranger to a lady's bed. God's wounds! Oh, come on, Guidotti..." (I was on my knees, not knowing whether to bow, prostrate myself, or what.) "...you have our permission to sit."

"Your Majesty, I,..."

"Sit, damn ye!"

I sat.

She poured a glass of wine and slid it across the desk to me.

"Salute!"

She toasted with an imaginary glass held high. Then she laughed. It was a deep, throaty laugh, like a man, not the high tinkling of a woman. And it was a sincere laugh, nothing feigned or threatening.

"I do not drink much, Guidotti, the doctors forbid it. But it pleasures me to see a man enjoy a good drink now and then," she said, her eyes twinkling merrily, as she studied me carefully. (This woman had a look to her that said go careful, Pietro, she is not to be diddled with.) "I can still sit a horse, did you know that?" she finished, almost challengingly.

I was still feeling awkward, this being my first ever queen, and an old one at that, but the wine was beginning to warm me up. There seemed no immediate threat. She was a woman, wasn't she? And did I not know about women?

"I have heard nothing but miraculous stories regarding Your Majesty's youthfulness since I arrived in England," I replied. It was the kind of flattery an older woman craves. "I hear that you ride and hunt and dance and drive the young men of your court to the brink of exhaustion. I hear that few are able to keep up with Your Majesty."

She laughed again. I liked the way she laughed. She used all of herself in it and held nothing back.

"Ralegh has been talking about me again, has he? I heard about your supper at Durham House. My 'Water' is not what he used to be, is my judgment. Aye, he is a desperate ache to me now, like this thumb...(She held up a swollen and bandaged thumb. Burghley's foot, Elizabeth's thumb, good God, the whole court was sick with gout!)...I am utterly at squares with this battle over my favor between Ralegh and Essex. God's blood, I will trust neither, they would both plot against me! One day they shall test my patience too far!"

Then she seemed to remember that I was present and that Ralegh and Essex were not the immediate concern. "Guidotti, you appear to have placed yourself in grave danger with these notes of yours. If 'Sir Spirit'... my Lord Burghley... has his way, you shall be separated into little pieces and spread over half of London town on the morrow, which in our opinion would be a sad waste of a splendid looking young man. I wager Burghley had something devilish raw planned for your privates too, did he? My Lord Burghley takes particular delight in the truth-revealing power of dire threats to a young man's private parts." She winked at me and chuckled mischievously.

"How old are you, Guidotti?"

The question was absently asked. Her mind seemed elsewhere.

"Thirty-eight, Your Grace."

"Thirty-eight," she repeated. "I am nearly twice your age. Old enough to be your mother."

This was a strange conversation, I thought, between a queen and her prisoner. Where was it taking us? She was looking right through me as though I were not there, her brows knit in deep concentration, but her fingers trailing up and down my arm, lightly, absently, the way she might play with a strand of pearls but be thinking about something far more important.

The idea popped into my mind that maybe the old girl was just looking for midnight thrills. After all, here I was in her bedchamber, wasn't I, and her discussing my "privates" and all? Listen, Guidotti, I said to myself, she may be a queen but she is a woman too, so maybe you should start treating her like one. If I knew anything about women, that was the kind of attention they craved. The older they were, the more they craved it.

Alzata d'ingegno! She read the thought on my face. The finger that had only a moment before been toying with my arm now jabbed at my chest like the point of a spear.

"God's wounds, sir, you flatter yourself! We've a mind to have you hanged and quartered here and now for what you are thinking. I am the queen of England, damn you!..."

She was a queen, all right. She let me know that plainly enough; and I was nobody. Yet, just as quickly as she had flared, her voice softened again and she smiled coquettishly.

"Still, I am not too old nor too spent to appreciate that look. Fear not, you shall come to no harm. It is not meet you should suffer the fate Lord Burghley has promised you. Nay, nor would that suit the purpose we have in mind for you. Now then, what exactly is at issue here?"

"Your Majesty, I am damned if I know. I was simply minding my own business, see, when these soldiers all of a sudden..."

"Don't bullshit me, Guidotti!" she screamed, stamping her foot in anger. She picked up my notes and shook them in my face. "We shall know what this gibberish signifies, or by God you will soon beg for a death so kindly as the one Burghley promised you, you whore's son!"

She threw the papers down in a fit of rage and began waving a great rusty sword in the air. This woman's temper was meteoric! And her language made the whores of Campo Marzio sound like nuns!

"Foul scorn if that heretic cleric in Rome thinks he can diddle with my kingdom! If ye be his spy, I will run you through myself, God's truth I will!"

But then she leaned the sword against her chair, point down, and lowered her voice once again.

"And yet, if ye be innocent of wrongdoing, as we so suspect, then shall ye have this prince's royal protection and a tired old woman's gratitude. We are no less desperate than this sore thumb of ours...(she held up her bandaged thumb, as if it were that of a child expecting to have it kissed and made well, a solitary tear rolling down her cheek)...and gravely concerned for the welfare of our realm in the face of seditious papist plots on all sides. Now speak, I pray thee, I must know it all."

I told her. No point in not. She would know everything soon enough anyway. I had come to realize that heads of state survived only by knowing, and that this one had survived so very long a time was sure indication she had the skills for finding out everything that I knew, one way or the other. If it was to be a question of serving a temperamental old queen or being returned to that cockcutting hunchback, well, that did not present me with a difficult choice. What I needed was a friend more powerful than Burghley, and Elizabeth was it. There had to be a reason she'd had me brought to Nonesuch right out from under the Lord Treasurer's nose in the middle of the night. Some mighty fancy politics were being played here, was my thought, and, though the game was way out of my league, as long as they needed me as their game ball I had some chance of getting out of England with all my parts intact, private and otherwise.

So I gave her the whole story and by the time I finished deciphering my notes for her, she was sounding like maybe I could breathe a little easier about Burghley.

"We always liked that little wop," she mused, referring to the Nolan. "A regular *'gallo della checca,'* as you Romans say. But nobody's fool, that much was plain. Sidney saw it, Greville, Ralegh, Gilbert and the rest, they all saw it. Small wonder they would burn him in Rome if they can. The ideas I read in those books of his are enough to bring the walls of their church crashing down around their heads. Serve them bloody damn right, too! Though between us, Guidotti, I should have to do the same in their place, were it come to that. "Our own bishops liked him not, demanded we send him away lest he corrupt our court...(her eyes flashed again)...We do not brook kindly demands upon our royal decree, least of all from the bishops of our own church. God's blood! We made them bishops and can as easily *un*-make them as well! We have said it many times before: We may have the body of a weak and feeble woman, but by God we have the heart and stomach of a king! Let them not treat with a king's patience, or they shall live — or die — to regret it!"

Her voice lowered and her tone became confidential.

"Clement yet conspires with Philip against our crown. Even now, he refinances the Spanish armada. We shall teach him that his ships are no match for ours. Ralegh and Essex will destroy them while they lay at anchor in their ports. Philip is old and near death, we are told. But his son may seek to carry on his evil work. Meanwhile, our cousin Henri of France continues to try to play both ends against the middle, as he always has. So long as that pot simmers, we remain threatened. But we do not intend that all of this shall continue much longer. We have plans..."

All of this as though I were not there, as though she were merely thinking aloud, but now she spoke directly to me: "Lord Burghley is our loyal and trusted servant. We rely on him still, despite his advanced age and his infirmities. But he shall not have you. We do not wish our enemies further encouraged in their plots by the death of another Catholic. Go, Guidotti, save your Nolan if you can; the world will thank you one day for it. In truth, we should not be disappointed to see the grand inquisitors foiled in one of their devious plots. You have a wise and gentle master — would he were ours and not Clement's, we would make him our archbishop, God's truth — perhaps he will see the wisdom of your arguments. If not, God have mercy on the Nolan; we have our own problems. But we do not wish your death to add to them.

"Captain Bothsly awaits outside our chamber. He serves his queen and has his instructions. We will handle Lord Burghley. Meanwhile, you shall have, as he promised, an escort to Plymouth and safe passage to Normandy. After that you are on your own and Godspeed. Goodbye, Guidotti."

She offered me her hand. I kissed it. The taste of lilac powder came away on my lips.

"Goodbye, Your Grace, and thank you for my life and my...uh... parts. I shall try to use them in good health."

She laughed.

As I reached the door, she added:

"And Guidotti..."

"Ma'am?"

"Take these bloody notes with you."

"Yes, Ma'am."

"One more thing, Guidotti."

"Ma'am?"

"Don't come back. Next time we may have to let Burghley cut it off."

I could still hear her laughing as I walked down the feather-carpeted hall with Captain Bothsly.

✖

I will not detail for you most of my return to Rome. Not because that trip was uneventful, far from it; there were many adventures along the way worthy of retelling, but because none of it, save for Venice, related to the Nolan. It is the Nolan's tale I am intent upon telling, not my own, though thus far it may have sometimes seemed otherwise.

I am anxious to get on with my account of the trial, wherein my master and the Nolan matched wits, and as far as I'm concerned both lost, although the Nolan, poor misunderstood man, lost the most. (Or did he?) Still, Venice must come first, at least briefly, before I get to the trial, for Venice held the secret that might save the Nolan's life, or so at least I thought once I stumbled upon it.

Venice, then. And then the trial.

Chapter 16

I WAS WELL ACCUSTOMED by this time to the art of traveling in foreign lands. Gentlemen like Monsieur Montaigne who travel the world with their servants and their fat purses, and then publish journals about their travels, describe the scenery well enough on fair days, and they love to write about the lavish banquets they are fed in the sumptuous homes of their foreign hosts, but when it comes to traveling alone on a modest budget, I could tell them a few things.

You learn little tricks of survival along the way, such as how to change your religion for a free room or a meal or a bath, about which I have already given example, how to tell if a mule is healthy if you are buying or how to sell one if it is sick, who to believe about what, especially when it comes to directions or which roads are safe, what the weather is going to do before it does it and where to make a dry camp that will stay dry and not wash away with the rains, that sort of thing.

There are those who make a living off inexperienced travelers who have not yet learned the way, travelers who do not know the language or understand the money changing, who believe whatever they are told and pay whatever is asked. If you travel for any length of time, you lose such innocence quickly. The hard way.

All right, I was seasoned, by which my traveling was made easier than if not. But after being on the road for ten months, the fun had gone out of it and my patience was wearing thin. By the time I reached Normandy, my only thought was to go home.

I reasoned thusly: With all the miles I had traveled, and after all the people I had interviewed, I knew this man almost as well as I knew myself, certainly well enough to give the master what he needed. When the Nolan left England with Mauvissière, he went back to Paris. I already had Cotin's account of that stay and did not dare risk returning to Paris myself. After Paris, Bruno went to Marburg, Wittenberg, and Prague. For me to follow that route could take a month or two. Odds were that I might learn nothing more than I already knew, except to see some new places, and I was in no mood for that. Seeing new places grows old fast.

Time was growing short, the weather was turning cold, and all I wanted to do was get back to Rome and stay in one place for a while. I was sick to death of riding mules and horses and living out of a pack.

I was cold and tired and homesick. If I never traveled again after this, it would be too soon. I am a Southerner. I hate cold weather. Just the thought of heading into northern Germany that time of year gave me the shivers.

Venice was a different story. First of all, it was south. And it was more or less Italian. I would not feel like such a foreigner. Plus, it would not be that far out of my way, not after the trip I had just made. The Nolan had nearly been freed at the end of his trial in Venice, according to my master's account. I was burning with curiosity about that. Therefore, I was willing to detour across the top of the boot to get to Venice, run the risk of another bout of seasickness on the boat ride from there to Ancona, and suffer the hardship of a winter mountain-crossing from Ancona to Rome, in order to find out if I could what happened to the Nolan in Venice.

The one name from Venice that stood out in my mind was that of the man who betrayed the Nolan to the Inquisition, the man whose testimony had been so damning to him before that tribunal and later before the one in Rome. It was a name the master mentioned to me with that peculiar inflection of voice he usually reserved for miscreants. I remember being curious about that because this man was supposed to be on *our* side.

The name of the man I went to see in Venice was Mocenigo...Sir Zuane Mocenigo.

✱

I stopped briefly in Padua to seek out the Jesuit agent there, who turned out to be an elderly and timid law professor at the university. By now I had learned to respect the Society's judgment in their selection of these agents. After Geneva, I was no longer misled by appearances. In any event, I needed money and information, and the professor supplied me with both.

As luck would have it, I found that the professor knew Mocenigo personally. Many in Padua did, as Mocenigo was a minor figure in Venetian government and came often to Padua. The professor provided me with a letter of introduction, which proved a real time-saver. We agreed that my best opportunity to obtain an interview — I did not reveal my reasons for this interview and the professor was discreet enough not to ask — was to pose as an employee of the Vatican conducting a historical survey for the Curia. My name while in Venice — the name on my letter of introduction — would be Paolo Rogazzi.

The professor warned me that once I completed my interview with Mocenigo, I would be wise to depart Venice as quickly thereafter as possible. Mocenigo was still a functionary of the *Signori della notte* and was on speaking terms with the doge. He fancied himself a far more important personage than he actually was. People with such an inflated sense of self-importance, the professor cautioned, were weak and not to be trusted. After what I had already been through, I had to agree.

*C*hapter 17

20 ottobre 1597
Rio marin, Numero Due
Venezia

COMPARED TO THE GREAT *palazzi* along the Grand Canal, the *palazzo* on Rio marin was little more than a large house; but as houses go in Venice, it was of a style and size befitting a *Savio all'eresia del collegio.* I had already been there once this day, when earlier in the afternoon I had delivered up to Mocenigo's secretary the professor's letter and had requested a meeting with his master later in the day. Keeping in mind the professor's advice, I planned to see Mocenigo as soon as possible and then leave Venice immediately. I was delighted when the secretary returned to say that his master would see me at the sixteenth hour that evening. The cover of darkness would suit my purpose once the interview was completed.

I spent the afternoon pretending to pray at the abbey on the Isle of St. George the Great, just in case I had been followed, and I was now moving at a leisurely pace along the Grand Canal in the gondola I had hired at Fusina for the day — at a princely sum of two gold crowns, no questions asked. The gondolier, a skinny fellow with a patch over one eye and a rakish grin, seemed to know everyone on the water:

Eh, Giovanni! Che bon vento? Ha ha! Ciao, Carlo! Hai visto Luigi? Aha! Viva la faccia! Ciao, ciao!

Then, to me with another grin: *Uh...scusami, Signore* (he shrugged, gesturing toward the other boats), *mi amici.*

He returned to the monologue he had been giving of sinister murders on the Bridge of Sighs, of executions in the night at Canal Orfanello where the waters ran deep and fishermen were forbidden to cast their lines, lest they dredge up the bodies of dead prisoners garrotted at the prison they call the "Vulcano" with its low dungeons and the windowless stone cell known as *l'orba,* and of masked assassins and robbers who plied the Canal de la Paille.

In between, he pointed out the sights. The Ducal Palace and St. Mark's, now behind us, the Fondaco dei Tedeschi with its frescoes by Titian and Tintoretto, the fish market. We passed the many palaces along the Grand: Palace Dario, Palace Venier, Contarini Palace, Foscani Palace, Pisani Palace, Balbi Palace, Mocenigo Palace — not my target, his brother. Though a senator, Zuane was a lightweight in a heavyweight family. He never made it to a palace on the Grand Canal — Palace della Cà d'Oro, Barbarigo Palace, and so forth.

Just then, the bark of the doge, the *buzino d'oro* with its forty oarsmen, came barreling around the bend heading fast in the direction of the Palace and bearing right down on us! The bark was so wide it took up most of the waterway. There seemed no way to escape its path! Only quick action by my gondolier saved us from being swamped. He skillfully maneuvered us out of the way at the last possible moment, hurling obscenities all the while and shouting gondoliers' epithets: *Your saint is too dumb to make decent miracles!* and *The Madonna of thy landing is a streetwalker not worth two candles!* Incongruous perhaps, considering the status of the target, but that did not seem to bother him. He simply laughed and shrugged it off, then went right on with his commentary as though nothing had happened.

A cool customer in a crisis, I decided. I might have need of him later.

We completed the bend in the Grand and headed toward the Ponte Rialto. The *Caligo,* the mist from the sea, was already moving in, and it shrouded the bridge in so much fog that it was barely in view. We turned off the Canal just before we reached the bridge, at De San giovanni decola. Left again at Di canaregno to Rio marin.

"Remain here and wait for me," I instructed the gondolier when we arrived in front of Numero due. "Do not leave your gondola under any circumstance. If I am not out in two hours, come looking for me and do not let anybody stop you until you find me. There will be another gold crown for you when I emerge safely from that house, two more when you land me back at Fusina. *Capice?*"

"Ho capito l'antifona! For three more crowns I would swim you to Fusina on my back through a school of sharks! Signore Rogazzi, you need help in there, just holler. I'm your man!"

"Bene," I said.

My gondolier may have been skinny and with only one eye, but I had the feeling I could count on him if I had to.

✠

Mocenigo was as I expected. The professor had provided me with an accurate description, right down to the thin, sharp nose, drawn little mouth, and weak chin. I estimated him to be about my own age, but his was the kind of late thirties that was going on fifty. He already had an old man's ways about him.

His eyes were shifty, as though he was afraid to have you look into them for fear you might spot some inner failing that might give him away. When you did manage to lock eyes with him, his always looked away first. He was a bundle of nerves. Hand flutterings, finger drummings, and toe tappings, he could not sit still for a minute without having to shift his position or get up and pace around the room. And he had the most distracting habit of constantly stretching his neck and jutting out his jaw, as though either his collar was too tight or else he was determined to try to enlarge his undersized chin.

The picture I got was of a man with a problem. The shoes he wore were too big for him. An illustrious family name that he failed to live up to, no matter how hard he tried. Having a big brother who was greatly respected and had considerable power in the Senate did not improve matters. Zuane Mocenigo was weak. He knew it, and I suppose everybody who knew him knew it. At the moment, he was doing his best not to let me know it.

His greeting was cold and formal. He offered me a limp hand and with a condescending nod gestured toward the stiffest chair in his drawing room. It was a room of moderate size and modest decor. There were tapestries and paintings on the wall, carpets on the floor, and a number of pieces of furniture. My impression was that none was of first quality. Since I am a poor judge of such things, it could only be that my impression stemmed from an immediate distaste for the man.

"I understand from this letter from Doctor Spanato that you are employed by the Vatican, Signore Rogazzi?" he asked as soon as we were seated. Obviously, there was not going to be small talk.

"*Si, Senatore.*"

"I am naturally flattered that the august Roman Curia would seek out my assistance. However, I fail to understand how I may be of service. I am a Venetian. I have scant knowledge and even less interest in matters relating to Roman history. I should think you would do better at the University in Padua. But of course you would know better about that than I. Now then," he said in a condescending tone, gesturing toward the clutter on his writing table, "I have a very full schedule. I can give you fifteen minutes, no more. If you have some specific questions...?"

This weasel was trying to impress me with his importance! I could see right through him.

"*Senatore,* may I be frank?"

"Certainly." He was still confident that he had me figured.

I needed to cut through this act of his if I was ever going to get him to open up. Otherwise, I was in for more of the same for fifteen minutes and then goodbye Guidotti. So I ran a bluff.

"I should explain first that I do not know Professore Spanato. His letter is a fake."

Mocenigo's eyebrows shot up two notches. He stretched his neck.

"I am not employed by the Curia. Nor am I here on a survey of ancient Roman history. Like you, I could not care less about ancient Roman history. Actually, I represent a party who prefers that his identity not be revealed to you. He wishes this for your own safety and peace of mind. I am instructed, however, to assure you that you are under no suspicion at this time."

A nice touch, I thought.

His response was another nervous neck-stretching. He was about ready to erupt, but I gave him no time, not yet.

"My master has charged me to review with you, your best recollection of a certain event in which you participated some seven years ago. I am to assure you of his guarantee as to the absolute confidentiality of this interview, and to inform you that your cooperation shall not go unappreciated."

I paused for effect. I was enjoying this. A man in my station rarely gets to play at such roles, in this case to pose as an agent with secret powers. I could see where one might grow to enjoy being a spy. The trick was to use sincerity. To be believable, you had to believe yourself. That was the difference between Mocenigo and me. I really believed Paolo Rogazzi, I could even feel his power. But Mocenigo did not believe himself; and because he did not, he had to believe me. As a result, I was cool, calm, and confident. And Mocenigo was sweating.

"But I . . . I . . . don't understand . . . ?" he stammered apprehensively.

I held up my hand.

"Allow me to finish. The matter in question relates to your testimony before the Holy Office here in Venice pertaining to the Dominican friar, Giordano Bruno di Nola, now a prisoner in Castel Sant'Angelo and on trial in Rome these past five years for heresy."

Mocenigo fought to regain his composure.

"See here, you have no jurisdiction in Venice. Venice is an independent state. I am a *Savio all'eresia!* I am not required to respond to your impertinent questions. I shall complain to the father inquisitor about this!"

It was a weak and unconvincing threat. He was unsure of himself, uncertain of Rogazzi's power and authority. He was hooked, and I had no intention of letting him escape.

"That is true, *Senatore.* You are under no obligation whatsoever. And certainly you may, if you wish, lodge a formal complaint with the father inquisitor. I imagine that Fra Gabriele would then no doubt write to Cardinal Santa Severina. Cardinal Santa Severina would then appeal to His Holiness Pope Clement, who would then request Nuncio Taverna here in Venice to convey to the doge his eminence's disappointment at the refusal of a *Savio* to cooperate with an emissary of Rome. I should think the doge, not wishing to appear unresponsive to the pope's request and to thus reopen wounds that have only recently begun to heal, would then..."

I shrugged and left the thought hanging in mid-air.

I started to rise. "If that is your answer then, *Senatore,* I believe our business is concluded."

"No, no, wait! Please, Signore Rogazzi. We need not trouble Pope Clement or the doge over this trifling misunderstanding. Stay. Ask your questions. Take as long as you need. I certainly did not mean to convey to you an uncooperative spirit. It was only that I...uh...you understand...er...my position...I..."

I had him eating out of my hand!

People like Mocenigo do not mind ratting on their friends to the Inquisition if they can score some points, but let them think *they* might be on the receiving end and they die of fright. I knew his kind. A snake in the grass. Stab in the back in the dark and run. Never anything to your face. He would do it to me too, if he ever got the chance, just the way he did it to the Nolan. Right now he would be my pal, whatever it took to save his own skin. My bluff had worked like a charm!

I sat down again, in a more comfortable chair this time, and settled down to the interview.

✠

Q: How did you come to know Bruno?

A: I read two of his books, *De umbris idearum* and *Cantus Circaeus,* which I purchased from Giovanni Ciotti's bookshop. I have long been fascinated with mnemonic systems, the *ars memoriae,* but these books by Bruno proved most difficult. I wished to learn more about his system. Ciotti was acquainted with Bruno from meeting him in Frankfurt. He agreed to forward a letter for me, two letters, in fact, in which I invited the Nolan to Venice as my guest and offered to pay him to instruct me in his magic system of memory. He responded affirmatively and came to Venice...no, first to Padua for several months, then to Venice. He was a guest here in my house for about two months.

Q: Did you know when you invited him to Venice that he was wanted in Rome?

A: No, but after reading his books, I suspected that he might be a heresiarch. I decided that I would question him carefully, note down his beliefs, and if it developed that he was as I suspected, then I was prepared to do my duty.

Q: So you lured him here under false pretenses, knowing all the while you might turn him in? Some invitation! "Come into my parlor," said the spider to the fly.

A: It is unfair to say I "lured" the Nolan to Venice. My invitation was genuine. I voiced my suspicions to no one, not even to my loving wife. Not until he confirmed them. Even then, I went first to my confessor and asked what I should do. I am a good Catholic and a member of my government. I could not knowingly harbor a heretic.

Q: And yet you did invite him, knowing that he might be one, knowing also that to offer your hospitality would imply to him the protection of an important Venetian nobleman? Protection you, being a good Catholic, had no intention of granting him. Why else would he accept your invitation, when he knew there could be trouble for him in Rome? I do not suggest you were wrong to lure him, but lure him you did.

A: The Nolan was homesick. He wanted badly to return to Italy. But he believed he would be rewarded, not punished, he said so often. He spoke of dedicating his latest work to the Pope and presenting it to him personally. He said the Catholic religion pleased him more than any other but that there was a great deal wrong with it that he wished to discuss with the Pope, philosophically. He told me he expected to be rewarded because this Pope favored philosophers, as witness the chair in philosophy at the university which was given to Patrizi following the printing of his book, which Patrizi had dedicated to the pope...Pope Gregory in that case. Therefore, I believe the Nolan saw my invitation as a way to begin redeeming himself with Rome. You might almost say he was using me, rather than the other way around as you seem to be indicating.

Q: Did you like him?

A: He was brilliant.

Q: But did you like him?

A: I did not find him a good teacher. Nor was he an appreciative guest. He used my house as if it was an *albergo*, an inn, to eat and sleep in only. He ordered the servants around as though he were the master of the house. He ensconced himself in my private study to work on his book, spread his papers about everywhere! As for teaching me his memory system — for which he had been hired in the first place and for which he was paid a handsome sum! — he gave away more secrets in his talks to my friends for nothing than I ever got from him in our private sessions...

✠

Giordano was packing.

Mocenigo burst into the room without knocking. He was highly agitated. Giordano was hardly surprised. Though Giordano had been hinting for days about leaving, his host had chosen to ignore the hints. Mocenigo had made it clear to Giordano that he expected him to stay until the job for which he had been hired was completed.

Completed? As if that could ever be! Mocenigo was *capo scarico*, empty-headed. Even little six-year-old Katherine Marie Mauvissière had been a more apt pupil! Mocenigo would never learn the Nolan's system; it would be beyond the poor man's grasp no matter how long Giordano might stay! Two months was all the time he could afford to waste. The book was done and must now be printed. Giordano was leaving. If his host was unhappy, too bad.

"The servants told me you were packing. I did not believe them! Just where do you think you are going? Your job is not finished! You cannot leave until you teach me the magic!"

He kept circling Giordano, jabbing his finger in the air as he ranted. Giordano continued to pack without looking up.

"I keep telling you, Giovanni," he said calmly, in an even voice, "there is no magic. I have taught you all there is, and now you must simply practice. My work here is finished. I must go to Frankfurt now, to have my book printed so that I can take it to Pope Clement in Rome."

Although he had not yet looked up, Giordano knew that Mocenigo was even at that moment doing that thing with his neck, stretching it the way he did when he was nervous or up-set. The thought made him smile, because it always reminded Giordano of an ostrich.

But Zuane misinterpreted his smile.

"Don't you dare laugh at me!" he shouted, flying into a rage at this latest insult. "I will not be trifled with! You shall see! I will go to the Inquisition about you. I will, I swear it! You have secrets of magic which you have kept from me. I have paid you well, and you have not taught me everything you know. I must have it all! Everything! Or I promise you, you will live to regret it. You will not leave! I will have you arrested and thrown into prison first!"

Giordano stopped packing and looked up quizzically.

"For not teaching you magic?"

"Never mind. You know what I mean. There is plenty I can tell them about you. I have notes," he threatened vaguely.

"Why is it that you always threaten me with the Inquisition? What have I ever done to you? You invited me to Venice to teach you my memory system. I have done so. I never prom-ised you magic. You keep asking for secrets and magic. There is none. Giovanni, why do you wish to cause me harm? Have I not enough trouble already? If I have sometimes spoken to you from my inner doubts and fears, it was in confidence, as a friend, be-cause I trusted you even though I was aware of your connection with the Signori della Notte. These were private conversations, philosophical conversations, discussed in confidence with you be-cause I thought you to be a kind and honorable gentleman. These doubts could never be twisted into heresy, but to expose them would surely be troublesome for me to explain. I cannot believe you would so betray our friendship."

"Don't try to hand me that crap! You know you have been hold-ing out on me! I have overlooked a great many things since you came into my house, but only because you promised I would have your secrets. I have given you everything . . . everything! Half of Padua knows more from you than I do. You lecture at Ciotti's for free, you speak at Morasini's for free, anybody can have your se-crets for the asking, yet you withhold them from me and I am the one who pays you! You have made me out to be a fool. I give you

fair warning: *do not attempt to leave this house!* I can make more
trouble for you than you can even imagine possible!"

"Giovanni, I leave tomorrow for Frankfurt. Nothing is going
to change my mind. My work comes first."

Giordano resumed packing.

"You'll pay for this," screamed Mocenigo. He turned and
stormed out of the room, slamming the door behind him.

✠

Later that evening, there was a knock on Giordano's door.
It was Zuane. His voice was subdued. Although he was in better control of himself, he seemed even more nervous than usual.
He asked Giordano whether he still intended to leave for Frankfurt in the morning. Giordano answered that he had not changed
his mind.

"I am sorry, Giovanni, but I really must have this book printed.
So much depends on it. When the pope reads my book, he will
understand the true nature of my philosophy. I will be rewarded.
My ideas will be taught for generations. You'll see. A New Age is
coming, Giovanni, an age of peace and of scientific exploration.
Catholicism will have thousands of converts, millions! People will
flock to the church. They will be converted with preaching and
with the example of the good life. Not by force but by love, that
was the way the Apostles did it. Soon the world will see great
reform! Do you understand now why it is important for me to go
to Frankfurt?"

"Yes, of course I do, and I apologize for threatening you earlier," he said, surprisingly. "You are a great man, and I am but a
stupid, selfish, and ungrateful student. Forgive me."

Giordano was greatly relieved. Empty-headed or not, Mocenigo
had influence in Venice. He could cause Giordano trouble if
he wished to. It was better this way, to have Mocenigo on his
side again.

"Look," he said, responding to Mocenigo's sudden change of
heart, "maybe after the book is printed in Frankfurt, I could
come back for a couple of weeks before I go to Rome. Would you
like that? You could practice the Thirty Seals and so forth, and
then when I come back I could review it all with you once more."

"Yes, certainly. I would be most grateful for that opportunity. Giordano, I am sorry to trouble you, but there is something I want show you. As you will be leaving early tomorrow morning, I may not have another opportunity. Would you mind coming with me for a minute?"

"What is it?"

"I would rather show it to you. It is very special. You will see. Come."

Zuane was acting strangely indeed. First the apology and now this. But Giordano was not yet suspicious. Why should he be? In the past fifteen years, the Nolan had met a great many Zuane Mocenigos. Narrow, cynical, closed-minded men who felt themselves threatened by the Nolan's revolutionary new ideas. (All of that would change once Clement read this new book. The Nolan's star would be in the ascendency then. A chair in the university, wealth, perhaps personal advisor to the pope. Why not? It was all part of the plan, was it not? Then King Navarre would come to Rome to meet with the pope and the Nolan, and the New Age would unfold for all the world to see!) Like the others, Mocenigo was a weak and envious man, and not to be trusted, but he would never have the courage to do Giordano harm. None of them ever had. They had merely sent him away because they feared his ideas, because they were too lacking in vision and imagination to see that where he was headed was not only the right direction, it was the *only* direction!

Giordano went with Mocenigo. He followed him up the dark stairway to the third floor and waited patiently while Mocenigo fiddled with the key to the door.

"What is it you wish to show me up here? I hope it won't take too long. I must get some sleep if I am to leave early in the morning. You know, I don't think I have ever been on this floor, I...wha...?"

Someone grabbed Giordano from behind, pinning his arms to his sides. Mocenigo had the door open and stepped out of the way. Whoever had hold of Giordano now thrust him forcefully into the dark room. The door was slammed shut and locked!

"What's going on? Giovanni, what are you up to? Who is that with you? Let me out of here!"

Giordano pounded on the door with his fists.

"It will do you no good. The door is too thick to break down, Giordano. I have with me Captain Mattheo de Avantio, who is in the service of the Council of Ten. The Captain and I are old friends. You have twenty-four hours to think this over. If you fail to reconsider, the Captain will return tomorrow evening with his men. You will be arrested and taken to prison. It is your decision, Giordano."

"How do I know the man with you is a Captain and not a rogue?"

"Because, Signore," said a deep, gruff voice on the other side of the door, "if you do not do as the *Senatore* requests, tomorrow night when I return and my men escort you to the jail of the Holy Office, you will have the opportunity to see for yourself."

The Captain laughed at his joke. There were a few words exchanged with Mocenigo, and then footsteps withdrawing down the stairs. Giordano looked around, but the room was pitch dark and he could see nothing, not even the size of the room or whether there might be a chair or a bed in it. He sighed and sat down on the floor, leaning his back against the door. As he had been in bed when Mocenigo had knocked, he was dressed only in a thin wool nightshirt. He shivered.

There was a sound on the other side of the door.

"Giovanni, is that you?"

"Yes."

"What are you doing?"

"I am sitting on the floor with my back to the door."

"No. I mean what are you doing to me? Why have you done this?"

"I warned you. I told you I would turn you in. You wouldn't listen to me."

"Giovanni, don't do this to me! You don't know what you are doing. The world depends on me! This is no exaggeration. This may be the most important event since the first coming of Christ! Do you understand, this is the dawning of a New Age! You cannot do this! Do not betray me. Think of your soul!"

"Never mind about my soul. If you want to get out of there, all you need do is promise you will teach me the secret behind your memory system, the secret of your geometry, the magic which you have denied me. I know what you are going to Frankfurt for, you are going there to reveal your magic! I don't want anyone else to have it, only me! Teach it to me and you shall go free, I promise. Deny me and the Inquisition shall have you, all tied up in a neat little package. I warned you I could be dangerous. You think you are so high and mighty!"

"You are talking nonsense! There is no secret. There is no magic. There is only hard work, and you have been unwilling to do it. Don't you understand?"

"I understand that I am out here with the key, while you are locked in there. You were wrong to take me for a fool, Giordano. It is Mocenigo who is the smart one now!"

"Let me out of here!"

"Not until you promise."

"I will not. I cannot. Zuane, be reasonable."

"Captain de Avantio will return tomorrow night. If you have not changed your mind before that, let it be on your head. I have given you your chance."

"Giovanni...Zuane! Let me out!"

"On your head, Giordano! Remember that when you are in the dungeon! Think about it, Giordano: the magic or the dungeon. It is your decision."

Mocenigo went back downstairs.

It was all a bluff, Giordano decided. Mocenigo would keep him locked here until morning and then let him out. He would never turn the Nolan in. After all, what could he accuse him of? There was no evidence.

✠

Q: What did you accuse the Nolan of in your testimony?
A: That he said he would be known as a great man, and that he hoped the affairs of the king of Navarre would succeed well in France, and that Navarre would come into Italy and then it would be possible to live and think freely. I testified that he often denied the Trinity and believed in the Arian doctrine; that he mistrusted the sacraments; that he did not believe Christ to be the Son; that he professed the universe to be infinite and that there were an infinity of worlds, all of them

peopled; that he had composed books in which he praised the queen of England and other heretical persons. There was more. I kept very detailed notes of his heretical statements.

Q: Where are these notes now?

A: I destroyed them.

Q: How very convenient. So it was your word against his?

A: No, it was the word of an honest Catholic against that of an avowed unbeliever.

Q: How did he come to be extradited to Rome?

A: Ciotti and Bretano both testified that they knew nothing of his heresies. Forgacz and Andrea Morasini also testified that he had lectured to them and to their friends — can you imagine! I was feeding him and paying him a salary, and there he was lecturing to these gentlemen for nothing the whole time he was under my roof! — and that he had never given them cause to believe he held opinions contrary to the faith. So the only real testimony they had, aside from his books — which should have been more than sufficient to prove his guilt! — was mine.

But then, toward the end, he confessed. He renounced his errors, stated that he detested and abhorred them, and claimed that he repented. They were all set to let him off, the idiots! It was then that Cardinal Santa Severina requested the transfer to Rome. The matter came before the Collegio dei Savii in which I sat, and still do. The Senate thought it would set a bad precedent, and instructed Ambassador Donato to refuse. Next, the nuncio appeared before the Collegio, arguing that since the Nolan was a Neapolitan, not a Venetian, no precedent would be set in consigning him to Rome as we had done so with other Neapolitans in the past.

By this time I had succeeded in enlisting my brother's support in the Senate. Together, we swung a majority of the Collegio to our way of thinking. With a majority against them, most of the holdouts finally agreed. So the Collegio summoned Procurator Contarini and announced our findings. Contarini advised the doge that it would be wisest to satisfy the desire of His Holiness in the matter. Bruno himself approved; he was that positive the pope would listen to him!

So the Senate and the Doge's Council passed a Resolution — 142 affirmative, 10 negative, 20 abstentions — and it was then read to the Collegio. The Nolan was consigned to Rome and everybody was happy. Even Bruno, the stupid fool.

Q: What did you say?

A: Nothing.

Q: Everybody was happy. You most of all? As a good Catholic, of course?

A: I did my duty, that's all.

✳

Something lingered in the back of my mind, some small doubt perhaps, or this growing feeling I had of identification with the Nolan. I have said before that in many ways we were alike. I was beginning to really understand him by now. There had also been a particular inflection in Mocenigo's voice when he mentioned his wife. His "loving" wife was the way he had referred to her. Why "loving"? Why not just "wife"?

There was a wedding portrait of Mocenigo and his wife in the drawing room. He had pointed it out to me earlier with considerable pride, and yet as he looked at that portrait his lips had drawn tight and his face had taken on a yearning sadness. Trouble? She was much younger than Mocenigo, that much was obvious from the portrait. Young, vivacious, with raven black hair, large, mysterious dark eyes, and a sensuous mouth. The contrast in looks between the two people in the portrait was hardly flattering to the husband. A man like Mocenigo, I imagined, would have great difficulty holding onto the reins, let alone sitting tall in the saddle, with a comely young wife like her.

✳

Q: During the time the Nolan was in your house, your wife was here also?

A: My wife?

Q: Yes, your wife.

A: (defensively) What has my wife to do with this interview?

Q: I was wondering how they got along, your wife and the Nolan?

A: (angrily) You leave my wife out of this. You have no right to ask questions about her! She had nothing to do with that lecher! (voice rising) I saw the way he looked at her, the evil in his eyes, the lust. I told him to stay away from Anna. She is young and high spirited, easily swayed by sophistication, about which she knows nothing. Worldly men fascinate her, because they have traveled and been in the royal courts of Europe. One could easily misunderstand her fascination,

- 210 -

misinterpret it as infatuation. She is so pure and innocent! She is a gem that must be protected! The Nolan was a lustful creature, a sinful little man, a heretic! (screaming now, stretching his neck so far that I feared his head might fall off) I warned him! I warned him to leave her alone, to stay away from my Anna or...!"

End,
Book One

BOOK TWO

THE TRIAL

You speak of reasons, ah, be still,
With reasons I can all yours reasons kill.

Chapter 18

dicembre 1597
Casa Penitenzieria
Roma

IT WAS THE FIRST WEEK in December. I had been away almost a year, traveling alone, without friends, always the foreigner, the stranger just passing through. And most of the time homesick for Rome. Now that I was back, Rome seemed less like home. The feeling of being the stranger lingered within me.

I suppose I imagined while I was away that everything would simply remain exactly as it was when I left, a frozen tableau awaiting my return. At the very least, I expected to see some sign that I had been missed. Who wants to think of himself as expendable, after all? Had not Rome always revolved around me at the center, was I not the hub of my own experience? One does not expect the wheel to continue rotating without its hub!

"You won't find things to be the same as when you left, Guidotti. I am majordomo around here now." Things might have changed, but Vignanesi was still the same. A weasel.

"Is that so? And where is your employer, *Signore majordomo?*"

There would be time to deal with Vignanesi later. First things first.

"Father Bellarmine has been in Ferrara this past month with the Holy Father," he answered. Wary still, but feeling more sure of himself by the minute. If you expect a storm and none comes, you think maybe it will not rain after all.

"Why Ferrara?"

"As that concerns official church business, you will have to take it up with Father Bellarmine."

"But you know, eh?"

He said nothing.

"Did Cervini go with him?"

"Yes."

"When do they return?"

"I expect them back sometime next week. Now, if it's all the same to you, Guidotti, I am rather busy at the moment..."

(Take more rope to hang yourself, *donnola,* you are helping me to feel at home again.)

"Certainly. You go ahead," I said. "I am tired from the road anyway. I'll just go up to my room and grab some sleep. We can talk later."

There was a glint in Vignanesi's eye. He had been waiting for this.

"You don't have a room here anymore, Guidotti. As a matter of fact, the one you used to have is mine now. We stored your things in the basement. If you need a bed, I can provide you one in the dormitory. There isn't a private room available in the whole house. We are full up, Guidotti. Too bad no one told us to expect you."

"But I sent a letter as soon as I arrived in Venice, saying when I would get home!"

"I know nothing about that. Look, nothing personal, you understand, but Father Bellarmine is rector of the house now, and he left me in charge. A bed in the dormitory is the best I can do. Maybe when he gets back we can see about making other arrangements."

Take it or leave it, he was saying.

"The dormitory will do fine, *grazie*," I said softly.

You could almost hear Vignanesi's sigh of relief. I suppose he was the hub of his experience, too. Eleven months with no cat around, a mouse can imagine himself an elephant.

✠

I slept. I took a bath. I went out and had the meal I had been dreaming about for months: fresh Roman pasta al dente with virgin olive oil and minced garlic, served with Italian bread still warm from the oven and a bottle of red wine dry enough to make your mouth pucker, ahhh, it was the best food I had tasted since leaving Rome. Now I was ready to deal with the weasel.

I found him at his desk in a corner of the common room. It was shortly before Vespers and many of the brothers had gathered in the room. Not a familiar face among them. Vignanesi had been right about that at least, the house had changed. By the end of '97, the Society had a membership of almost thirteen thousand. There were 372 colleges in thirty-two provinces. Headquarters was shifting brothers around like soldiers, and there was a steady stream of Jesuits moving in and out of Rome. Penitenzieria House more resembled a country inn than a convent.

"I want to talk to you," I said quietly.

He looked up, surprised. But he made a pass at maintaining control.

"Not now, Guidotti. Can't you see I am busy? Come back later."

"Now," I said, taking his arm and helping him up from the chair. "Come with me."

He pulled himself free of my grasp, but went with me. He was not anxious for a scene in front of the brothers. I led him down the hall toward the rector's office. Realizing my intention, he raced ahead and barred the door with his arms spread wide.

"You can't go in! This is father's private office!"

"Step aside."

"I tell you, you can't...!"

"Step aside," I repeated.

Some flicker of recognition at my tone of voice, a familiar gleam in my eye, whatever it was, Vignanesi surmised right then that it was all over. A sad look crept onto his face. He was not afraid, nor even surprised, only disappointed to have lost power so soon after having thought he had won it. He dropped his arms and stepped aside.

I went in and sat down. He followed without a word.

"Shut the door, Giuseppe, and sit down."

He sat in a chair facing me and waited.

"Giuseppe, I will come straight to the point. We have never been friends, we are never going to be friends. But you and I are both working for the same man, and there are a few things we need to get straight between us, *capito?*"

If Vignanesi had been surprised by my calm yesterday, he was even more so now. This was not the way he remembered me when I had grabbed him by the throat and threatened his life eleven months ago. That Guidotti no longer existed, but of course I could hardly explain that to him. I was only just beginning to discover it myself.

He nodded glumly.

"The man we work for is *molto importante*. Soon he will become even more so, when he is named to the purple. For us it is an honor to serve him, and a very great responsibility. We must allow nothing to distract him from his work, nor must anything be allowed to cast the slightest shadow on his household. Therefore, there will be no more squabbles, *capito?* None. You will remain majordomo. That is now your job — Vignanesi's eyebrows shot up. (Did that mean he wasn't going to have to relinquish his position?) — and you will do it well, or you will answer to me. As for me, you will show me respect. I am no longer "Guidotti" to you, I am *Signore* Guidotti. You don't give me orders, I give them to you, and you don't tell me what I can or cannot do...not ever."

I said all this quietly, in measured tone, and then I stood and extended my hand.

"Now that we have that straight, we shake hands and go back to work for our master."

Vignanesi took my hand limply and pumped it once, without spirit. He might still be majordomo, but his heart was no longer in it. When he got to the door, I stopped him.

"A moment, Giuseppe..."

He waited, his head downcast, his hand poised on the knob.

"Tonight I sleep in my old room, with all of my things returned to their proper place... or you get to spend all the rest of your nights at the bottom of the Tiber."

Vignanesi's back straightened. His shoulders squared. His head snapped erect.

"Now *that*," he said over his shoulder in a voice greatly relieved, "is the Guidotti I used to know. Signore Guidotti, we have a deal!"

I never cared for that weasel and I never trusted him, but from then on there was no more trouble between us.

✠

The business with Vignanesi did little to raise my spirits, however. What good to teach him his place, if I was no longer certain of my own?

I went out again and roamed the streets of Campo Marzio looking for a woman. I was not particular. When I found one, I got drunk and took her to bed. Even that did not help. I was like a soldier who goes off to war and the whole time he is away all he can think about is coming home to his wife, and then he finally comes home and she's not there to greet him. Eleven months on the road ferreting out information about Bruno for my master — oh, yes, I enjoyed the fringe benefits — who would not? — but mostly what I kept thinking was wait until the master hears this or wait until I tell the master that! All the way down from Venice, I could hardly wait to surprise him with what I had discovered about the Nolan and Mocenigo's wife!

But when I get back, what do I find? He has given my room to that turd Vignanesi and gone off to Ferrara without so much as a message left for me. I felt let down.

In my gloom I wandered around his office, picking up some object of his and sniffing at it like a dog lonely for his master, then putting it down again, his familiar smell lingering in my nostrils. Even now, if I close my eyes I can conjure that smell, a musty mixture of soap, wool, and old manuscripts, that reminds me of the inside of a little church in Campo Marzio where I used to go with my father as a boy.

Being there, feeling his presence all around me, helped me to find myself again. I began to inspect the room more carefully, as though seeing it for the first time. The rector's office was easily five times the size of the *cameretta molto piccolo* the master had previously occupied, and yet he had added so many more books that it seemed almost as tiny and had exactly the same disordered appearance. I knew better, of course.

Bellarmine had the habit of grouping his books according to projects he was working on at the time, a pile here, a pile there, each pile a work station consisting of numerous books and manuscripts with little pieces of string dangling out of them, marking passages to which he might later refer. His notes would be spread out, waiting to be completed. These, in his usual scribblings in Italian, his *"zampe di gallina,"* later to be dictated in Latin to Father Marcello Cervini, who would then transcribe the final draft in his neat hand.

No less than seven of these work stations were scattered around the office. As usual, there was no shortage of problems. Easy for the pope to say, "Look into this for me, Father," or, "Give us your opinion on that, Father," but for the master it might mean weeks or even months of hard work and long hours of research, of reading and writing and rewriting until a project was completed. Not one of the others in the Curia took their work so seriously as Bellarmine.

"God's work is never done, Pietro," he used to say to me.

"Then He ought to pay you more for doing it," I would complain.

He would simply smile and tell me he was rich in God's glory. Try paying bills with God's glory, but you couldn't tell him that.

The biggest pile was on the table nearest his desk. Several books had been left open, a thick stack of notes, two or three volumes of the *Summa*, other volumes with titles I could barely read, much less understand, and one volume, heavy with strings, that bore the title *Concordia liberi arbitrii cum gratiae donis*. Beneath the title, the name of the author: Luis Molina. (So that battle was still on, was it?)

The top sheet of the notes was part of a long letter from the master to the pope:

> It does not seem that the present dissensions can be healed by a decision on the theories in dispute, for the matter with which they deal is a most serious and important one that would require many years and protracted investigations for its elucidation, es-

pecially as both parties have dealt with it in book after book. Besides, it is not possible easily to convict either party of manifest error since both admit the authority of the Councils of Orange and Trent, and each alleges on its own behalf at least apparent testimonies from St. Augustine and St. Thomas.

Further, it is difficult to believe that the Holy See could be induced to fix a charge of error in doctrine on a whole religious order and on entire universities. Now, according to my information, the University of Salamanca favors the Dominicans to a certain extent, while the University of Alcalá is almost certainly on the side of the Jesuits. Therefore it is vain to hope for an end of the controversy by a definite decision on the points in dispute. It seems to me, then, with deference to better judgments, that the dissensions and scandals could be stopped, that both parties could be satisfied, the security of doctrine maintained, and the Holy See relieved of great trouble and uneasiness, if the pope would deign to issue an edict to the following effect:

First, he would seriously and paternally exhort the contending parties to be mindful of brotherly charity in their mutual relations, to avoid dangerous teaching, and to turn their literary weapons against the enemies of the church alone. Second, he might forbid each order in virtue of holy obedience, or if it be thought well under pain of excommunication, to qualify the teaching of the other as temerarious or erroneous, much less heretical, in lectures, disputations, sermons, or even in public or private conversation. Each party, however, would be permitted to refute the opinions of which it did not approve, by solid arguments. In this manner all opportunity for unseemly quarrelling would be removed...

Fat chance. It was obvious the master did not expect the pope to follow his advice or this would not still be an active work station in his office. The argument between Bañez and Molina was just one more excuse for the Dominicans to attack the Jesuits, if you ask me. They had been after the master's crowd since '42 when the Jesuits first became an order. Clement knew no better how to handle the problem than did his predecessors. So what does he do? He stalls, what else? Let the next guy worry about it. Meanwhile, he gives the dirty work to the master. Who, from the size of the pile, was still up to his armpits in efficacious grace.

There was a short stack of books by the window, consisting of

Plato and Aristotle. Not a very high priority, I judged, since there were only a few sheets of notes. Probably the master was studying up on ideas to apply to other problems, since the church usually sided with Aristotle and the heretics with Plato. Or was it the other way around? I was never altogether certain about that. Three other piles, one English, one French, one German. No notes. Reading stations only, I surmised. At another it appeared the master was embarked on the writing of a new book, children's catechisms this time. (The younger the faith, the more enduring the tithe, I suppose.)

God's work may never be done, but neither was that of His hardest working servant.

I was drawn eventually to the seventh pile. It was situated in a far corner of the room, well removed from the others. There were several small volumes, a substantial sheaf of notes, and a separate stack of papers tied together with a red ribbon of cloth. A film of dust had settled over everything, thick enough to indicate that this was a station which had not been worked at in some time.

I blew the dust off the stack of papers and carefully undid the ribbon. They bore a handwriting I had not seen before, and yet I knew it immediately. The Nolan.

Strangely, the hand resembled the master's. The way the words seemed to rush at the paper from all angles, as though racing to keep up with the thoughts of the writer. And tiny, so as to cram as much as possible onto each page. Yet, it was different as well, with far more tension in the letters, less roundness in the loops, sharper at the points. Unlike the master's neat notes, these had many words and phrases scratched out, as though the writer had struggled for just the right way to say certain things. Since the master always knew that he would be able to make changes when he dictated the final version to Cervini, that was a problem he never had to face. Of course, he never had to face the Sant'Offizio either.

It took me several hours to read through the whole stack. There were statements from the Nolan to the Holy Office in Venice, seven in total, all dated 1592. There were others written from Castel Sant' Angelo here in Rome, variously dated over the past few years. Each was numbered. The early ones were taken up mostly with a relating of personal history, beginning with his boyhood and including details from his later travels. The more recent statements dealt with his writings and with his beliefs concerning such religious matters as the Trinity, the Sacraments, Mass, the Transmigration of Souls, and so forth. Also, about the nature of the universe.

Much of Bruno's writing was philosophical and obscure, difficult for me to follow, but there was one in particular that greatly
moved me. I copied it down and saved it. It was his final statement
from Venice, the shortest of the writings in the packet, dated 30th
July 1592:

> I have confessed and I confess now my errors, and I am in the
> hands of the Holy See to receive remedy. Having to do with
> my repentance and my misdeeds, I cannot express it as well as I
> would like in my soul. Lastly, I ask the pardon of God and of
> the Holy See for all the errors that I have committed, and I am
> here ready to follow their prudence that will be deliberated and
> that will be judged expedient to my soul. Moreover, I ask that
> they give me a hard and difficult punishment which will serve
> to demonstrate to the public the dishonor to the religion that
> I have brought; and that by the mercy of God and the Holy
> Office my life should be spared. I promise to reform my life.
> I will compensate for the scandal that I have given with great
> edifications.

What more could they have wanted from him? The man was obviously frightened out of his wits and pleading for his life. This was
hardly the Bruno I had heard about all across Europe, the brash know-
it-all breathing fire and telling everybody to agree with him or piss off.
This was a Nolan on his knees. Punish me, but spare my life! Did the
Venetian inquisitors have any idea what it would take for somebody
of Bruno's conceit to admit to error, to beg forgiveness? It must have
nearly killed him to write such a statement.

It had almost worked. The Inquisition in Venice had been ready
to let him off. But for some reason somebody had it in for him
down here. And what Rome wants, Rome gets. Well, all was not yet
lost. When I had a chance to explain to the master how that snake
Mocenigo had lied, then we would see some action. Bellarmine was
a fair man.

Who in Rome had been in such a sweat to get Bruno extradited
from Venice, I wondered. Santa Severina? It was he who had made the
official demand of extradition on the part of the Holy See in a letter
to Fra Giovan Gabriele se Saluzzo, the father inquisitor of Venice. Or
was it somebody else on the tribunal, perhaps pope Clement himself?
And why? There was much about this I still did not understand, but
I resolved to find out.

Meanwhile, I would use the time remaining before the master's return to write down my notes from the trip, leaving out the more personal exploits, naturally. When he read what I had learned, I was certain my master would feel as I did, that Giordano Bruno might not be very loveable but he was at least harmless, and that five and a half years in prison — considering he had been falsely accused of heresy by the jealous husband of a beautiful young wife — was punishment enough for a loudmouth.

Chapter 19

"*Scusami se ci metto bocca, ma*... I don't get it, Boss. You send me off for almost a year, I come back, and you don't even ask what I found out. If you aren't interested, why did you send me in the first place?"

It was a little game he was playing. Bellarmine had returned from Ferrara two days before, yet, except for five minutes of conversation about how pleased he was to see me, he had been closeted here in his office the whole time. He had us back to the old routine as though I had never been gone. And not a word about the Nolan. As often as I tried to bring it up, that's how many times the Boss changed the subject.

The game was this: like me with Vignanesi, only more subtly, the master was reminding me of my place. The saying goes: *Lega l'asino dove vuole il padrone:* An ass must be tied where his master will have him. This was Bellarmine's way of telling me he had plenty going on in his life besides Bruno; that he, not I, would decide priorities; and that meanwhile, he had his duties and I had mine and we had both better get on with them.

My part in the game was to pretend I did not know it was a game, even though variations of it had been played between us for years and would continue right up to his death. This particular variation was called "teaching Guidotti humility."

"Certainly I am interested," he said, feigning surprise. "I am truly anxious to read your report...(he gestured toward the neat stack of my deciphered notes that had been sitting on the edge of his desk for two days, untouched)...and to hear your personal observations. But, my dear impatient Pietro, you must understand that I, too, have been away. As you can see...(he waved around the room)...my work has been piling up. It is already Wednesday, and I am as yet unprepared for my weekly appointment with His Holiness in the morning."

"You two were just together for a whole month. You mean you still have to attend the Thursday meeting? You would think he would give you off this week!" I grumbled. (See? Already he has me off my subject and onto his!)

"There are no holidays from God's work," he chided, softening his tone with a rueful smile, though almost immediately frowning again as he continued to voice his private thoughts aloud: "In Ferrara last week the Holy Father again broached the possibility of establishing a chair in Platonic philosophy at the Sapienza. He has suggested this idea many times, but now he requests a formal opinion. There are many who would welcome such a chair at the university, none more so than Valiero, but this would be a dangerous move. We must avoid the mistake of Origenes Adamantius. The church must remain firm in the view that Holy Scripture is incompatible with pagan philosophy."

He tapped the pile of books and notes on his desk. For the first time I noticed that the voluminous correspondence which had occupied that surface had been replaced by an eighth work station.

"It is here in Origen's *Contra Celsum*. Had Justinian handled the matter correctly, there would never have resulted the terrible schism within the church of his time. We dare not make the same mistake in ours. I shall do my utmost to dissuade the Holy Father from appearing to embrace the teachings of the Platonists... Ah, forgive me, Pietro," he said, suddenly reminded of my presence, "but you can see why I will have to review your report later. Let us postpone discussion on the priest from Nola until Friday morning, shall we?"

E fatto così, That's the way it is. He was the boss. Friday it would have to be.

✠

And Friday it was, bright and early. Bellarmine was in a relaxed mood for a change. Clement's gout was better, praise God, he said, though thanks also to the pills sent by the master's cugino, Mgr. Herennius Cervini (the whole Cervini clan was in the priesthood!), and in gratitude the pope had decided to favor Bellarmine's recommendation against a chair in Platonic philosophy at the university. *Non bella forza,* no big deal, but a win all the same.

Old Cardinal Valiero's feathers would be a little ruffled, himself such a lover of Plato, though fortunately an even greater lover of Bellarmine — whom he referred to as *"del maggiore piccolo che sia al mondo,"* the greatest little man in the world — so he would get over it and no harm done. All in all, the master was well pleased and said as much, that they should all be so easily solved, meaning his problems, of which I wanted to remind him the Nolan was one.

But we had not gotten to that yet. We were discussing Vignanesi.

"Did that *donnola* come whining to you?"

"Not at all, Peter. As a matter of fact, he paid you a compliment. He said you have changed, and he even said it with *ammirazione.* You have earned new respect from him, my friend. (He paused, removing his glasses.) Giuseppe is right, you know. You *have* changed. There seems a new air of restraint about you, of self-control and maturity, one might even say of humility."

"Humility? Don't get carried away, Boss. I admit I have changed. You would expect that, wouldn't you, from a man who has just traveled the world for eleven months? I have been a few places, seen a few things."

"So I notice," he interjected with a smile, indicating my report with his glasses. "He who travels far knows much."

"But he who lives always at home sees nothing but home," I said, completing the saying, "True, but I have no humility where that weasel is concerned. I do not trust him."

"I ask only that you live with him in peace. Nonetheless, I am pleased at the way you have managed to resume your position without hurting the poor man's feelings. That is at least one welcome change in you. God willing, we may discover others as well. But now," he said in a more serious tone, "let us discuss Giordano Bruno. I find your report extremely interesting. To be truthful, it is far more complete and discerning than I had anticipated. I am heartened that my confidence in your ability to carry out this mission has been confirmed. There is no one else in all of Rome I could have entrusted to accomplish for me what you have. You have my gratitude, Pietro. *Che Dio ti benedica!*"

He paused and leaned forward earnestly.

"But this is a report containing no conclusions. Tell me, how do you see this man? What is he really like? Describe him to me."

"This could take a while," I warned.

He glanced at his little alarm clock.

"Sext is not for two hours yet," he said, leaning back and closing his eyes to rest them. Friday was a day of serious prayer and fasting for my master, even more so than the other days of the week. Not that he ever seemed to mind. Me? When I pray is usually when I need something, and even then I feel embarrassed and uncomfortable doing it. Not so the master. To watch him pray, you would think he was having a quiet conversation with his best friend. In Latin of course. Except, he never asked for anything for himself. Only forgiveness for his sins and the strength to serve Christ.

I envied him. With such faith, you never have to worry about protecting your back. I don't mean to say Bellarmine was without problems, but they were always church problems. He never had to worry about personal problems; they were all taken care of by his faith. Whereas, even my doubts had doubts. And when you start having doubts, you open the door to confusion.

It had not always been so. Before all this Bruno business, I had learned to accept what the church prescribes for all good Catholics. After all, why make life more complicated than it already is? The trial drove a wedge into that. Life was never the same for me afterward.

The church has its own ax to grind. It does not invite questions concerning faith. It knows that if you once start asking such questions, you will quickly discover that the church has few satisfactory answers. Which is why it calls you a heretic if you persist in asking. *Non c'è peggior sordo de chi non vuol sentire:* There is no one as deaf as he who will not listen. The church's response to questions of faith is very simple: *Guanto di velluto o mano di ferro?* Which do you choose, heaven or purgatory?

✠

"Have you seen him?" I asked.

"Not yet. But others of the congregation have visited him in Castel Sant'Angelo."

"In some ways I think he must resemble you, Boss. He is short and dark, like you. A loner, like you. And a hard worker. He is also very smart. Some think he is a genius, though you would know more about that than I would, having read his books."

"But you have not met him either. How can you be so certain we are alike?"

"I said he was like you in *some* ways. But in other ways he is very different. He does not have your gentleness, for one thing, and for another there is no love in him. Yet, when he believes he is right, he can get just as stubborn as you. The difference is he *always* thinks he is right. That gets him into trouble. You would say that he lacks humility. He has no tact either. He says what he thinks, and he does not care what anyone else thinks, so he always ends up with his foot in his mouth.

"You ask how I can be so sure, since I have never met him. This will probably sound crazy, Boss, but I know Bruno as I know myself. Sometimes, when somebody would be telling me about some incident involving him, I would feel like I was there, actually there taking part in the incident. I could see it as if it were really happening. Don't ask me how, I cannot explain it, but sometimes I could *feel* him, I could feel his presence. Yet, how could that be, with him stuck in a cell in Castel Sant'Angelo and me half the world away? I cannot say. Magic, maybe. He is supposed to know of such things, about the ways of the ancient Hebrews and Egyptians and such.

"All I know is I *know* Bruno, I really know him. *Non è uno stinco disanto neppure lui,* he is no angel, God knows. But he is no more a heretic than I am, of that I am certain."

Bellarmine had been quiet through all this. Too quiet. I knew what he was thinking, that Guidotti had gone over the edge.

"What convinces you he is not a heretic?" he finally asked in a low voice, still with his eyes closed.

Now, this was no easy thing for me to explain to my master. As I have said before, he did not live in the real world. When you work for the church in Rome, you are surrounded by others who work for the church in Rome. Everybody believes alike. So you get to thinking that save for an occasional soul lost to the Fallen Angel, the whole world must have the same values. It is very reassuring, to have your whole life spelled out for you that way, with faith as the fuel for a fire that lights your way and keeps you warm. You don't spend much time trying to imagine what it must be like to be cold, let alone why anyone would choose to be warmed by a different fire. The church is not the real world. Sometimes it gets into trouble thinking it is.

"Boss, how free am I to talk?"

You would have thought I had just slapped him across his face, such a look of pain and consternation came over it as his eyes blinked open.

"Che ti gira? How can you even think to ask such a question? Are we not friends? What have I done to incur such distrust? I am shamed beyond words, that you could think so poorly of me!"

"Don't take it personally. Maybe I have seen too much betrayal on my trip, people saying one thing and doing another to each other. It could be that friendship goes only so far. No offense, Boss, but you are about to join the Sant'Offizio. I just wouldn't want to say something that could get me into hot water, that's all."

"Have I not already indicated this matter rests strictly between us? What you have written in your report and what you say to me privately in this room shall remain confidential, as secret as..."

"As the confessional? Will it be as secret as the confessional?" I interrupted, pointedly.

"You have my word," he said solemnly.

"Not even to Aquaviva or Clement?"

He sighed.

"My lips are sealed."

"Then let me ask you this: what is a Catholic?"

It was like asking a marathon runner to describe the act of walking. What is a Catholic is not the sort of question one of the world's foremost Catholic scholars and the pope's very own religious advisor is typically called upon to answer. At the master's level, you tend to take what is a Catholic as a given.

He seemed on the verge of dismissing my question as impertinent when I hastily added that if he was serious about wanting to know my reasons for thinking the Nolan was not a heretic, he would have to allow me to proceed in my own way. That caught him up short. He pondered the question for some time before replying.

At last he began, intoning: "*I believe in God the Father Almighty: Maker of heaven and earth, and in Jesus Christ, His only Son, our Lord, Who was conceived by the Holy Ghost, born of the Virgin Mary, suffered under Pontius Pilate, was crucified, died, and was buried: He descended into Hell: the third day He rose again from the dead. He ascended into heaven. And sitteth on the right hand of God the Father Almighty: and from thence He shall come to judge the quick and the dead. I believe in the Holy Ghost, the Holy Catholic Church: the Communion of Saints, the forgiveness of sins: the resurrection of the body and the life everlasting.'*

"That is the Apostles' Creed, and it could easily serve as a principal guideline for all Catholics," he concluded.

"What about the sacraments?" I asked.

"Yes, surely. The sacraments constitute an additional and appropriate guideline. The Council of Trent declared these to be the seven sacraments instituted by our Lord Jesus Christ: Baptism, Confirmation, Holy Eucharist, Penance, Extreme Unction, Holy Orders, and Matrimony. Indeed, it is the sacraments which impart grace, *ex opere operato.*"

He was being patient with me, hearing me out, but he was uneasy about where this was all heading. I sensed his growing annoyance. Still, I persisted.

"And to do all that, you have to go to church, right? I mean, to attend Mass and so forth?"

"The Fourth Lateran Council decreed that there is no salvation outside the church. To be saved, one must assist at Mass on Sundays and on holy days of obligation, fast and abstain on the days appointed, confess one's sins at least once a year, receive Holy Communion, contribute to the support of the church, and observe the laws of the church concerning marriage. But, Pietro, I do not see...?"

"Do you suppose every Catholic believes all that, what you just said?"

He smiled, as though he were explaining the catechism to a child.

"Faith is a process, Pietro, not a product," he answered. "It is natural for a Catholic to have some doubts, if that is what you mean. We all do. That is what we pray so hard for God to help us to overcome. The church has a wide and sympathetic understanding of human frailty."

"Now, there I think you are wrong, Boss," I said. "Most Catholics have no doubts at all. They can't afford to. I am talking about Catholics like me, not like you, the ones who sit in the back pews, not the ones up front or in the pulpit. They believe whatever the church tells them to believe, and they believe it because they are afraid not to. You said it yourself: we can only be saved if we are *within* the church. In, we go to heaven; out, we go to hell.

"Do you think most Catholics know anything about Trent or the Fourth Lateran Council? Or that they even care? They know their parish priest and their nuns, they know that if they do what they are told and say their Ave Marias and don't eat meat on Fridays and put a little something in the Poor Box on Sundays, they're in. And if not, they're out. So *that* is what they believe."

"*Stai attento*, Pietro!" he warned. "You go too far!"

"You agreed I might speak my mind!"

"I gave you no license to blaspheme."

"But this is not blasphemy; that is exactly my point," I protested. "I am trying to explain the way it is in the real world, Boss. Not everyone thinks the way you do. Most people do not even think on this subject. They can't afford to. Why do you imagine people go to Mass every Sunday anyway, when they do not understand a word of Latin? Get down on their knees and make the sign of the Cross and say the Rosary? Because they are afraid not to, that's why! The church has the power of life and death over every Catholic. And the power of life *after* death. It…"

"Enough!" he bellowed, slamming his palm on the desk. I never saw the Boss that angry. All the color was drained from his face and the finger he pointed at me was shaking like a thin reed in the wind. "You are speaking heresy against the Holy Catholic Church, and I will not have it!"

It was true. I surprised even myself! This was a subject I always kept my mouth shut about — the less said the better. All of a sudden I was sounding off, and Bellarmine did not like it one little bit. He was furious! I admit it was a risky thing for me to have attempted. But it worked.

"*Ma questo, scusa…* do you see what has just happened? You told me I was free to speak, as free as in the confessional. 'Are we not

friends?' you said. 'The church has wide and sympathetic understanding,' you said. So I tell you what is on my mind, and you accuse me of
heresy. I am no heretic. I am a Catholic like most other Catholics. I go
to Mass, I pray to God, and if I keep my mouth shut about the rest,
no problem. But if I say something critical, suddenly I am a heretic.
What is a heretic, anyway? Around the Vatican I hear everybody call
the Lutherans and the Calvinists 'heretics.' I hear the Church of England called 'heretical.' But do you know over there what they call
us in Rome? Heretics! I am a simple man, Boss. I find that a little
confusing.

"Look, I think of myself as a Catholic, right? I was baptized and
confirmed. I have been a Catholic all my life. But for eleven months
I didn't go to Mass, I didn't go to confession, and I didn't receive
Holy Communion. I didn't fast, and sometimes I even ate meat on
Fridays. Well, I didn't stop being a Catholic, did I? I'll bet the Nolan
still thinks of himself as a Catholic. Everybody I talked to thought of
him as a Catholic. They even thought of him as a priest, even though
he quit. He never took their sacraments, not in Geneva or Toulouse
or Paris or London. He wanted no part of their religion because he
was a Catholic! Do you know what I think? I think maybe he had
some doubts, that maybe he was not cut out to be a priest, that maybe
there were too many things he did not agree with the church on. That
may not make him a very good Catholic, but I say it does not make
him a heretic. No more than it makes me one."

He saw it now. He didn't like it, but he saw my point. He started
to calm down. The color slowly returned to his face. From the tone
of his voice, I knew he was still very upset with me, but — it was just
like him to do this, too — now he assumed blame for my indiscretion.

"Non pusi dare un giudizio," he said softly. "I see now that your
feelings for this man have blinded your judgment. I should have
understood. We shall speak no more of this. I ask your forgiveness
for having raised my voice to you in accusation. At Sext I shall do
proper penance."

"Che cosa? It is I who should beg *perdono,* not you," I said, shamed.
"Please, Boss, I apologize. I was only trying to get you to understand.
Poveraccio! Do you know how he got into this trouble in the first
place? In Venice this man Mocenigo — it is in my report...one of
the *Savii* — he sent for Bruno to tutor him, and then when he would
not give him secrets, he turned him in to the Inquisition!"

"Yes, I know about Mocenigo."

"But, Boss, what you do not know is that he lied about the Nolan!"

He looked at me calmly, without expression. I thought he did not understand what I was saying.

"Don't you see? He made it all up, all those things he accused the Nolan of saying! This is the part I did not put into the report: Mocenigo was jealous. He as much as told me so. He was an older guy with a beautiful young wife, and he thought Bruno was fooling around with her! That whole trial came about because of a jealous husband! The Nolan would not be in Castel Sant'Angelo right now if it had not been for Mocenigo's lies!"

The master was unmoved.

"God's will be done," he murmured, his voice tinged with fatigue. "I am afraid there is other evidence against him as well, Pietro."

"But...?"

"Canon law requires that there be an accuser other than the church," he explained, his patience only partially returned. "Zuane Mocenigo was Bruno's accuser. Having served that function, he is no longer relevant. The process once begun must proceed based upon all the evidence of the internal attitude, externally manifested, of one who pertinaciously denies or doubts any one of the truths which must be believed *de fide divina et catholica*."

"You mean you don't even care about Mocenigo, that he lied when he accused the Nolan of heresy, that he was just jealous of his wife? *Per carità, non capisco!*"

"I would not expect you to understand, Pietro. This is a complicated issue of canon law, and an extremely delicate case politically as well, as I have explained. There is still a great deal I must study before making my report to Cardinal Santa Severina. Now then, you have served me well in this regard, and I fully understand your exuberance, but your assignment has been completed. You need trouble yourself no further in the matter of Giordano Bruno. There is much else of importance for you, now that you are returned.

"But, Boss...?"

"The issue is closed, Guidotti."

Chapter 20

gennaio 1599
Casa Penitenzieria
Roma

THROBBING WITH ANTICIPATION one minute, impotent the next.

The frustration of that next year returns to me now like the memory of a lost erection. Had I not been the *amico intimo* of a famous duke? Had I not wenched with a king, supped with a knight, flirted with a queen? Me, the bone-setter's son from Campo Marzio! And in addition, had I not returned to Rome armed with the secret of Mocenigo's treachery, a secret which I personally had unearthed, the knowledge of which would enable my master to end the nightmare of injustice that had been twice thrust upon the Nolan, first by the Venetian tribunal and now by the Sant'Offizio in Rome?

Yet, in response to my accomplishments — to my loyal and dedicated service, if I might add — what? *Niente.* Business as usual. The dossier I had prepared, my notes, the complete report on my journey, all of my findings, the ground had opened up and swallowed it all. Not another word passed between us concerning the prisoner in Castel Sant'Angelo.

Instead, I spent another year doing my master's errands. Wrestling with meager budgets and haggling with greedy pawnbrokers. Trading gossip with the *maestri di casi* of other Curia households. The eternal packing and unpacking, other dull and boring chores too numerous to mention, too banal, certainly, for a world traveler, an equal among men of birth and high standing, now painfully relegated to the duties of the servant of a servant of the Lord.

And yet, I returned to that life without objection, without even an awareness that it was happening. Routine is insidious. So caught up in my master's worldly affairs and my own occasional weekend carousings in Campo Marzio was I that soon I hardly thought about the Nolan at all. The sense of urgency and of personal mission with which I had returned to Rome as Giordano Bruno's champion faded. In fact, the whole adventure — Naples, Geneva, Paris, London, Venice — was like a mighty wave dashed into fragments on the shore, gradually receding into the vast sea of my memory until, little by little, it disappeared into the past altogether. Such was the thoughtlessness with which I let that year slip away without lifting a finger for him.

How painfully this realization comes to me now. I returned to Rome believing I held the key to his freedom — never mind that I did not, that I know better now, I *believed* that I held the key. And yet I did nothing about it. I cannot forgive myself for that. I let the Nolan rot in his cell, alone, forgotten, misunderstood, while I went about doing the business of the very same church I knew to have wrongfully imprisoned him in the first place. Yes, and within days of my return I was doing it without so much as giving him a second thought.

I would like to report that I finally saw my error and atoned, but I cannot. Instead, I have Cervini's ague to thank for putting to an end my shameful neglect of the Nolan's cause and affording me the opportunity once again to be of help.

✖

The master was playing the lute. Which meant he was thinking. He played the violin for love of God's music, he used to say, but he strummed his lute because it soothed him and helped him to think.

We were in the office, he playing his lute and I playing his accounts. Doing my best to juggle things around so maybe we could make it through January, us broke already with almost the entire month still ahead of us. His music would not improve the state of our finances.

December had been ruinous. Pope Clement, Cardinal Baronius, and my master had traveled to Ferrara for Princess Margaret's marriage by proxy to King Philip III of Spain (Philip II having died in September), and we returned on the fifteenth to find half of Rome under water from the worst floods in the history of the Tiber. The Arenula and Campo Marzio were the worst, flooded more than four meters in depth and filled with stinking mud.

Naturally, the Boss felt obliged to give away all of December's budget to aid the flood victims. We spent a week trudging around — wading, more like it — to every hospital in the city, to S. Giacomo degli Incurabili, to the pilgrims at Trinità dei Pellegrini, to Convertite della Maddalena to bless the prostitutes, and to Santa Maria in Aquiro to bless the poor orphans. A wonder the man did not wear out his arm making the sign of the cross!

Christmas wiped out our reserves, every last *scuda* I had managed to ferret away behind his back for the past six months. And for what? Handouts to bums. I swear, each year every *borsaiuolo*, *ladro*, and *mendico* in the city moved into our parish the day before Christmas and moved out again the day after. And he knew it. And it made no difference to him.

We end up freezing with no heat in January and nothing but potatoes for a month, so those *ladra*, those thieves, can drink his health for the New Year with free vino bought with my household allowance: *Alla salute, il Padre de' Poveri!* "Pietro, how are we for favors in the house of Cardinal Cinzio?"

His lute was on his lap, and he was regarding me with a thoughtful frown.

"Thin, Boss, very thin," I answered, meeting frown with frown. "Truth is, we are thin all over town. We owe everybody."

"I would like to borrow his scribe for the meeting of the Holy Office on the fourteenth," he said, ignoring my response.

"Not a chance! Cardinal Pietro attempted to borrow him last week when his own scribe broke his wrist in a fall. Cardinal Cinzio said he could not be spared. If now he loaned him to you, he would be insulting Pietro. They may be cousins, but Cardinal Pietro is still too powerful for him to insult that way, even if he wanted to. Sometimes I think if the pope were not their uncle, those two would never survive in the same town, much less under the same roof in the Vatican. But why would you need a scribe on the fourteenth? What's wrong with Cervini?"

"I must send Father Cervini south to take the warm air. The physicians have warned me that without the benefits of a long rest, his ague will be the death of him before spring. Naturally, he protests to the contrary, but it is easy to see by looking at him that the physicians are correct in their prognosis. He leaves tomorrow, and with the grace of God, for which I shall pray daily, we will see him well before summer.

"Meanwhile...," Bellarmine's voice turned cold and officious, "...we have a most important meeting of the tribunal on the fourteenth regarding the Bruno affair, and I shall be without Father Cervini's services for the taking of notes."

I was startled to hear the name, there having been no mention of Bruno in over a year.

"Let me do it!"

I knew it was a mistake the minute I blurted it out. His first reaction was one of surprise. Guidotti a scribe? His second, of disbelief. Guidotti a scribe? He dismissed the idea with one word:

"Macche!" Not a chance!

He went back to his music.

The idea took hold of me and would not let go. Cervini gone for a few months and a chance to sit in on the Bruno trial? I would stand on my head naked in St. Peter's Square at high noon for such an opportunity! But letting on how bad I wanted it was a sure way not to get it. There was a better way. Guidotti could play the game, too.

"Just kidding, Boss. Let's see, who could we get for you?" I mused aloud. "What about Finali's new kid?"

"Impertinent," he snorted.

"You're right. He would not do. Ridolfi?"

He shook his head emphatically. The master did not care much for Cardinal Ridolfi, he was not about to ask him a favor. Which I knew, of course.

"Cardinal da Carpi?"

He rolled his eyes.

"Um, I see what you mean. There must be somebody. What about the old man who scribed for Cardinal Toledo toward the end? You know the one. They say he was the best...oh, I just remembered, he died last year."

At mention of Toledo, the master stopped playing long enough to cross himself.

"I have it," I said. "I know just the one! He's perfect. Giacomo Borletto, Cardinal Madruzzo's scribe. I know him personally, and he owes me."

His face brightened momentarily, then clouded as he remembered what I already knew, that Madruzzo was on the tribunal himself.

"*Scuzza,* I forgot about that," I said. "*Dio,* this is going to be tough."

I waited. I waited some more.

"You know, Boss, I wasn't serious before when I said let me do it, but it might not be a bad idea. I know about the case. I know everybody on the tribunal, so I would know who was saying what. And I would know exactly the sort of things you would want noted. Plenty of times I helped Father Cervini out when he wasn't sure what you wanted. Who knows you as I do? You said yourself that my notes from my trip were the best you had ever seen."

I stopped there. Let it sink in. Don't push him too fast.

"True, true," he said, strumming.

"It is not as though I would be the only layman there, even in the private sessions. Pinelli's scribe is a layman, and Boccafurco's is only a subdeacon."

"Cardinal Boccafurco no longer serves the Holy Office," he said patiently.

"Well, Cardinal Pinelli, anyway."

He seemed to be thinking it over.

"What about your duties?"

I had him hooked. Now was the time to reel him in.

"Vignanesi could handle the little things. I can easily cover the rest. It would only be for a short while, just until Father Cervini recovers his strength. I can do it, Boss, no problem. *Ma solta agli occhi*, it's as plain as the nose on your face. You need somebody you can trust, somebody you can rely on. What's the problem, you think I can't do it? You don't trust me? *Bene. Sono affari tui.* Find somebody else then."

I let him have this last with a hurt tone, as though here I had been willing to do him a great favor, and he was rejecting me. I stuck my head back in the books. It was a good act. If that didn't work, nothing else would.

Twenty minutes of the lute before he said anything. Then...

"Pietro?"

"*Si?*"

"It would be extremely helpful to me if you would serve as my *segretario* when the Holy Office convenes on the fourteenth."

"*Certamente*, Boss. I will do a very good job for you."

"That is exactly the conclusion I came to last night, Pietro."

He was smiling at his little joke. The fish had hooked the fisherman.

Chapter 21

12 gennaio 1599
Palazzo della Santori
Roma

THERE WERE CARDINALS in the Curia with more money, and there were those who had more influence with the Holy Father, but few were as powerful and none was more feared than Giluio Antonio Santori — the Cardinal Santa Severina — secretary, grand penitentiary, and ranking member of the Sant'Offizio, the *Sacra Congregatio Romanae et Universalis Inquisitionis seu Sancti Officii*...the Inquisition.

Whether it was the man or the office that turned strong men's marrow to jelly, I don't know, but I do know that whenever I was in Santori's presence it was all I could do to fight down the sensation that the cold bony finger of Death was about to tap me on the shoulder. It was enough to make even an innocent man tremble, and nobody ever accused Guidotti of innocence.

From the moment I entered the salon trailing behind the master, I could feel his piercing gray eyes boring into me, even after I sat down and went about setting up my lap desk in preparation for notetaking. I was tempted to return the stare, but thought better of it. Unwise to risk antagonizing this particular cardinal. Let the master handle it. I kept my eyes lowered and waited.

Today was Tuesday the twelfth. On Tuesdays the "Red Hat Gang," as I secretly thought of them, met at Palazzo della Santori on Via del Governo Vecchio. Though the pope was officially the prefect of the Holy Office, he rarely attended these Tuesday sessions, as that was his day for meeting with the Segnatura di Grazie.

Thursdays were the days Pope Clement presided over the tribunal, and those sessions took place at the Vatican. In two days, on the fourteenth, the master was scheduled to present at long last his case against the Nolan, the "favor" Santa Severina had requested two years earlier. Today would serve as a trial run, before he wrote his final brief. It was an opportunity, he said, to size up the latest views of the cardinals and compare them with his own arguments. Not that their opinions much mattered. The master was the type to make up his mind independently, even if his opinions were the opposite of those of everyone else. Knowing him, his mind was already made up. I just wished I knew which way.

As I looked around the room, still avoiding Cardinal Santa Severina's imperious gaze, I thought how much like its owner this room was. I had been to the *palazzo* many times, of course, though never in this particular salon. It was, like the rest of the place, austere and foreboding. Tasteful, yet without warmth or elegance. No mean feat in this neighborhood, since each palace on Via del Governo Vecchio was more sumptuous than the next.

The floor was marble, although not the best. The rugs and tapestries were expensive but gloomy. The walls boasted no Raphael or Botticelli cherubs and angels, only a collection of stern portraits of churchmen in reds, purples, and blacks, a forbidding-looking gallery of keepers of the faith that was the only effort at aesthetic adornment in this cheerless place.

I sneaked a sideways glance at the grand penitentiary himself. Plainly, he was irked by my presence. His portrait belonged up there with the rest, I thought to myself, his long, gaunt, unsmiling face with dark, deepset eyes would be a fit companion to the others. It was a face that was enough to give you nightmares, were you prone to having them.

My master's clearing of his throat brought me back to the moment.

"Your Eminence," he said quietly, rising to address Santa Severina, who sat all the way at the other end of the long table. Everyone turned to hear what he would say.

Arigone, Saxus, Pinelli, and Deza had arrived ahead of us and were already seated at the table, their aides in chairs immediately behind them, as was I in a chair behind my master. Cardinal Asculano had sent word that he was indisposed and would be unable to attend. The remaining two cardinals of the tribunal, Madruzzo and Borghese — the heavyweights — were late. It was their arrival we now awaited before the session could begin.

"Your Eminence," Bellarmine repeated, "Father Cervini, who customarily assists me, has been taken with the ague and will unfortunately be confined to bed for some time. I have brought in his stead Pietro Guidotti, who has served me and the church for many years and whom you already know. He shall be attending these sessions as my scribe until such time as Father Cervini is well enough to return to his duties."

He sat down.

I felt the cardinal's icy appraisal.

"It will be necessary for him to take the *iuramentum de fidelitate et silentio*," he said coldly. The oath of silence and fidelity.

Half rising, Bellarmine responded: "He has already done so, Eminence."

"Have you discussed this with Aquaviva?"

The master rose yet again: "I did not think that necessary or appropriate, Eminence."

Which it was not, of course. The reference was a dig. Every chance the Dominicans got to stick it to a Jesuit, they did. In this case, the idea that the master might need his general's permission for so petty a matter as who should scribe was Santa Severina's little bit of sarcasm, meant primarily for the benefit of the others. His expression, however, was deliberately bland and showed no trace of sarcasm. The master played it straight. Santa Severina, after all, was actually an admirer of Bellarmine, and everybody knew that, so the barb had little sting. Oh, the games these people played!

"Guidotti."

"Your Eminence?" I answered, standing.

For the first time, I met his steady gaze head on. Jesus, he was truly sinister! Was he that way even as a young man, I wondered to myself? Most likely. People rarely change as they grow old; their eccentricities merely grow more exaggerated.

"You understand that in taking the oath to truth and silence, you are bound to the strictest secrecy, to the *secretum S. Officii?*"

"Yes, Your Eminence, I..."

"What Guidotti understands is that if he opens his mouth, he's going to find your foot in it, that's what he understands!" boomed a laughing voice from the entrance to the salon.

A barely perceptible frown scurried across Santa Severina's face, gone as quickly as it had appeared. I turned to see Cardinal Madruzzo and Cardinal Borghese heading for their places at the table. They seemed in no particular hurry.

It was Borghese who had made the joke. His irreverence, combined with Santa Severina's fleeting sign of displeasure, served to confirm what I already knew: there was no love lost between these two.

Camillo Cardinal Borghese was a stocky man with a round jovial countenance, a double chin, and a thick bull neck. His large nose and quick-flashing grin managed to soften what might otherwise have conveyed a more pugnacious aspect. Borghese was an enormously wealthy and influential cardinal, who in only six more years was destined to become Pope Paul V. At forty-nine, he was at this point in time the youngest member of the tribunal.

A good eighteen years Borghese's senior, his friend and mentor Ludovico Cardinal Madruzzo was by contrast short and reed-thin. He gave the appearance of a white-haired, mild mannered old man, which was about as far from the truth of him as you could get. He was one of the illustrious Madruzzos from Trent, and he had been the most powerful papal legate in all of Europe under Gregory XIII. Shrewd as well as experienced, Cardinal Madruzzo was one of the kingmakers in the Curia, those who traded votes like backroom politicians when it came time to hole up in the Consistory to elect a new pope, which was exactly the job for which he was grooming Borghese.

Borghese was no slouch of a protégé. His jocular charm and well-fed bulk notwithstanding, this was nobody you wanted to trust your back to. Borghese was a tough infighter, and I had long ago decided to stay on his good side at all times. Only one of the current contenders among several factions, he still had his work cut out for him if he expected to sit on the throne of St. Peter.

The gossip among the *maestri di casi* — I could gain no insight from my master on this sort of thing, he avoided Vatican politics like the plague — had it that Cardinal Borghese was a four-to-one favorite for the job. There was speculation concerning the possibility of an interim pope, a token gesture to Clement's old cronies after he would be gone — which, as it turned out, was exactly what transpired when they elected Leo XI as a compromise, sick from the day he was chosen and dead little more than three weeks later — but, so it was said over Saturday night vino at the Boar's Head, if Borghese played his hand right with Madruzzo, he as much as owned the tiara already.

Though there were places closer to Santa Severina, the two cardinals took seats across from the master at the far end of the table instead. They both nodded deferentially to Bellarmine, for indeed there was real respect for my master among even the most powerful of cardinals, all of whom acknowledged this nephew of Marcellus II as a formidable theologian and a political neutral whom most credited for more of the pope's ear than he actually had. Then, their two heads turning as though connected, they nodded to Santa Severina, as if to say, now that they were here, he was free to proceed.

As far as I could tell, the three — Santa Severina, Madruzzo, and Borghese — ran the show. As to which wielded the most power on the tribunal, I would say it was definitely Santa Severina. The remaining cardinals either kept their mouths shut, or used them to say yes when one of these three took a position. Asculano never showed up until the final sentencing, for which he was carried in and out on a litter looking like death warmed over. (Being close to God offers little certainty of either long life or good health.)

The session began. It continued all afternoon.

�֍

The grand penitentiary started things off with a brief supplication: would God please bless this humble and righteous assemblage of His faithful and so forth in performing their difficult but necessary duties on His behalf to restore the True Faith to unbelievers and heretics and so forth... *in nomine Patris et Filii et Spiritus Sancti, Amen.*

The master and I went round and round on this one over the years, and while I suppose "humble and righteous" applied to a few inquisitors — certainly it applied to Bellarmine when he became a cardinal and was appointed to this tribunal — it was a very, very few. As far as I could tell, membership on the tribunal was just another power play for the rest of them, of the worst kind. Too many innocent lives were wrecked, and taken *in nomine Patris*, in the name of the Father. My master's problem was that he wanted to believe his fellow clerics were as humble and righteous as he was. So he did, but they weren't.

Next came the reading of the proceedings from the last session of the tribunal. Flaminio Adriano, a Dominican from Lombardy, was in second place among the consultors. He was known as the "Commissarius S. Officii," whose job it was to conduct a process up to the final sentence. Adriano was one of those colorless bureaucrats who could read out the death sentence of his own mother without so much as moderating his intonation from that of reading sentence on an unremitting rapist or murderer.

Adriano was barely into it, though, when he was interrupted by Borghese. "I propose that the Commissarius dispense with the reading of the minutes from our last session. With the secretary's concurrence, of course," he added, perfunctorily. "Our business today is to hear from our Qualificatore, Father Bellarmine, the results of his investigation and his recommendations regarding the little friar in our prison, this Bruno from Nola who seems to have our Spanish friend Philip in a lather of sweat. Now, it happens that Cardinal Madruzzo and I expect to meet later with de Guzmán — informally, of course — and it would be nice to be able to tell him where we stand. Could be we may be able to make a little trade of favors for His Holiness."

I entered all that in my notes, but I was puzzled by the reference to de Guzmán. I recognized the name. Enrique de Guzmán, Count of Olivares, was Spanish ambassador to Rome. Or at least he had been ambassador, I was not certain whether he was still, now that Philip III was king. For sure, de Guzmán was influential, but what "trade of favors" there might be between Spain and the pope was a mystery.

There was ill feeling between Pope Clement and the Spanish throne. At the conclave to elect a new pope after Pope Innocent's death back in '91, King Philip II had let it be known among the cardinals that he favored Cardinal Santorio, since Santorio was known to oppose Navarre. Though he had won out over Santorio, I think Clement was probably still fuming. His family and Spain had never been on good terms.

Then there was the controversy over Luis Molina, the Spanish Jesuit who their Inquisition had already denounced but who the pope and my master were still "studying." Clement was a cautious pope. He always said that important matters could not be satisfactorily solved in a hurry; they had to be well weighed. This one was being weighed for nine years already, and the Spaniards were getting itchy.

They were also still smarting over Clement's absolution of Henri Navarre and his recognition of Henri as "Most Christian king of France and Navarre." The pope had taken his time about that one, too. He had actually polled every cardinal, one on one, as to what each would do as pope. This was in the summer of '95. Then he announced in Consistory that since more than two-thirds of the cardinals had told him they were in favor, he had decided to grant absolution. And once he made up his mind, he staged a huge ceremony that September in St. Peter's, followed by trumpets and bells and fireworks the likes of which Rome had not seen in years! Relations with Spain had been bad ever since. Word was that Philip II never forgave him, and now it appeared his son had picked up the grudge. So what were Borghese and Madruzzo up to, I wondered? And what had Philip of Spain to do with the Nolano?

"I concur with Cardinal Borghese," Madruzzo said smoothly, addressing Santa Severina. "This is a diplomatic matter which we are conducting quite unofficially at the request of His Holiness, a matter with which we need not bother our colleagues here... (This last he seemed to address more to his protégé.)... but I do think it would be helpful to hear what Cardinal... uh... Padre Bellarmine has to say regarding canon law in this matter."

Everybody knew, despite my master's attempts to alter the situation, that the pope intended to make him a cardinal at the next creation, scheduled for March. Lately, they were all making little intentional tongue-slips, like Madruzzo, calling the master "Cardinal" Bellarmine and then correcting themselves with a grin. For the moment, however, it was still Father Bellarmine, and he was still only a consultant to the tribunal, albeit an important one, a Qualificatore whose job it was to examine and to qualify the theological tenets and opinions of the accused as *opinio haeretica, erronea, temeraria, falsa, iniuriosa, calumniosa, scandalosa,* or *piis auribus offensiva.*

They all turned to see what the secretary would say. A diplomatic mission for the pope, that was serious politics. Madruzzo had clout. On the other hand, so did Santa Severina. The pope was prefect, but he presided only over solemn assemblies. The rest of the time, it was Santa Severina who headed the powerful Inquisition. Was this a test of strength between the two cardinals? Or was Borghese trying to draw them into such a test? I would not put it past him. Or was this something Borghese and Madruzzo had hatched up beforehand? Were they working together on this? Was this an attempt by them to take control of the Bruno trial and turn it somehow to Borghese's advantage? Anything was possible.

But Santa Severina was too shrewd to be drawn into the trap, if it was one. He looked up without expression and said in a dispassionate coldness of tone that masked any feeling he might have had, "We will hear now from Father Bellarmine."

All eyes turned to my master as he calmly spread out his notes. The cardinals eased into more comfortable positions, their scribes sat to attention with their quills poised and ready to write. This could take a while. The master began with a reading from a summary of Bruno's record.

"The accused, Giordano Bruno, is an ordained friar of the Dominican order. He was extradited from Venice on the twenty-seventh of February 1593, after his trial in Venice, and was transferred to Castel Sant'Angelo, where he has been kept ever since. Charges were read to the accused in December of 1593. On the twenty-second of December of 1593, he had visits and was heard and was given a cloak and a copy of the *Summa* of St. Thomas. He was visited and heard by cardinal members of the tribunal on 4th April 1594 and on 20th December 1594. From the 12th to the 19th January 1595, this tribunal heard the testimony of the Venetians Mocenigo, Ciotti, and several prisoners of the Venetian Holy Office.

"The accused was visited and heard again on 4th March 1595, on

1st April 1595, and on 4th April 1596. On 18th September 1596, the tribunal censured the propositions posed by the accused during trial. On 16th December 1596, the accused was visited and heard upon the causes and what he said and about his works. On 24th March 1597 the accused was visited and heard, and he was admonished for his beliefs concerning the existence of many worlds. He was visited and heard again on 24th December 1597.

"During a visit and hearing by cardinals of the tribunal on 16th March 1598, the accused stated that he was being improperly heard and that only His Holiness could properly hear him. On 16th December 1598, the accused was visited and heard. He was at that time given paper and provided with the breviary of the Preaching Fathers... (the master looked up from the summary)... His Holiness had requested that on Thursday next, I present our propositions to the congregation."

This was the master's way of saying that push had come to shove. Three years in Venice, eight so far in Rome, Bruno's "trial" had been going on long enough. It was time to make some decisions. So, it looked like they were coming after the Nolan from two points: one, political, whatever that was all about, and the other religious. I still did not know how bad that might be.

"And what are the propositions you suggest, Father Bellarmine?" asked Santa Severina.

"Eminence, I am respectful of your time and that of the tribunal, especially in light of the appointment mentioned by Cardinal Borghese. There is a great deal of material, both published and spoken by the accused, and much of it is complex and intellectually convoluted. To cover all of it would take nearly as long as I have had to take in studying it, much too long even for the tribunal's deservedly acknowledged patience. However, and with apologies to all of your eminences, it will be necessary to review some of the material in question..."

"Go ahead, Father," Borghese interrupted with a laugh. "We'll get up and scratch if we find our posteriors getting too itchy."

Arigone, Saxus, Deza, and Pinelli laughed. Santa Severina frowned. Madruzzo's expression never changed. His was the bland expression of one who wields power but has no need to show it. Cardinal Madruzzo had obviously decided long ago to overlook the raw edges of his protégé. Though the two cardinals were different from each other in stature and personality, they thought much alike, and that, apparently, was sufficient for Madruzzo.

The master was not unaware of the undercurrent of tension

between Santa Severina and the Borghese-Madruzzo coalition. Power struggles within the upper echelons of the congregation were commonplace these days. With eleven popes in less than fifty years, and Pope Clement not the hardiest of them by any means — each time he was laid up in bed with gout, the astrologers waxed gloomier in their predictions — at least a dozen cardinals had their eye on the tiara, and two of them were seated right at this table . . . Borghese and Santa Severina.

Still, the master had the respect of both. He was their expert, after all, their Qualificatore. He was politically neutral and they knew it. He was also, as the master had already pointed out to me, the only Jesuit among them. Thus, they needed him and not the other way around. To his credit, none of these factors, nor even Borghese's constant needling of Santa Severina, deflected my master from his assigned task. He continued, calmly and deliberately.

"The indictment for heresy and apostasy prepared by the Commissarius . . . (he cast an approving glance in Adriano's direction) . . . was based upon the testimony of several co-prisoners of the accused in Venice; the depositions of the booksellers Ciotti and Bretano; three letters addressed to the Holy Office by Zuane Mocenigo, a *savio all'eresia* of the Venetian Holy Office and, in this action against the accused, the secular accuser required by canon law; on seven statements made by the accused while imprisoned in Venice and, to date, eight statements made by him before the Holy See in Rome. Altogether, the indictment contains thirty-four charges.

"I will summarize these charges briefly: That the accused harbored evil feelings against the Catholic faith and its ministers, about the Trinity, divinity, and incarnation, about our Lord Jesus Christ, about transubstantiation and the Holy Mass. That the accused has written and taught that the earth moves, that the world is eternal, that the universe is infinite, that there are many peopled worlds. That the accused is against Moses, the laws of the church, invocation of the saints, holy relics, and sacred images. That the accused has blasphemed concerning the virginity of the Blessed Virgin, the divinity of our Lord Jesus Christ, and the sacrament of penance. That the accused has read forbidden books, has sought after other things while in his holy office, that he has eaten meat on days when it was prohibited, that he was in England and Geneva and other territories held by heretics. And that the accused has spoken out about sins of the flesh, about soothsaying and magic, about the souls of humans and animals, and about the leadership of the pope."

This was the first time I had actually heard the specific charges against the Nolan. *Per carità!* If he had done half the things on the list that the master had just read off, he was as good as cooked! It was written all over their faces... thumbs down for Bruno, no question.

Still, these were just charges. They had to have proof, didn't they? Surely they were not going to condemn the man based on Mocenigo's jealous rantings and the testimony of a bunch of prisoners who would have said anything to lighten their own loads. I was certain my master would be fair. And yet, somehow I could not shake the memory of how quick he had been to accuse even me of blasphemy, of speaking heresy against the Holy Catholic Church. The recollection of our conversation in his office that day caused me to feel vaguely uneasy as the master continued.

"These charges have been most well prepared and drafted... (this was a great compliment from one whose own work was so widely admired and respected, Adriano was beaming!)... However, much of the material on which the indictment is based relies on the recollection of others, which, as this Sacred Congregation has often noted, is subject to distortion... (*Bravissimo!* I knew my master would be fair!)... I have reviewed as well the statements of the accused in his own defense, both those from Venice and those in Rome. These statements are sometimes contradictory, occasionally confusing, often disingenuous, and consistently self-serving, as we would expect them to be, coming from a contumacious apostate who has yet to demonstrate true penance and a sincere desire to recant.

"One of his statements to the Venetian Holy Office, for example, reads as follows:

Humbly beseeching pardon from the Lord God and Your Most Illustrious Lordships for all the sins I have committed, I am here ready to perform whatever shall be decided by your wisdom, and shall be adjudged expedient for my soul.

And furthermore I pray that you will give me a punishment severe to excess, if so be I might avoid a public exhibition which might bring disgrace on the sacred habit of the order, which I have worn; and if by the mercy of God and Your Most Illustrious Lordships my life shall be spared, I vow so notably to reform my life that the edification of my new estate may purge the scandal which I have occasioned.

Here we discern how the accused contrives to speak in generalities of his 'sins' yet offers no assurance that he intends to rejoin the religious house, nor does he make assurance that he will show no longer the obstinate disregard for church authority that he has so egregiously demonstrated in the past. We see in particular that he abjures none of the specific opinions that he has held and taught. It is on this last that I suggest we concentrate our attention."

"I do not understand," Cardinal Pinelli interjected. The others looked at him in surprise. Pinelli rarely spoke at these meetings. "If we have so much damning testimony against him, that should be sufficient. I fail to see why this investigation must be further prolonged. When I interrogated him, I found him arrogant and condescending, as though he believed me incapable of understanding his explanations. This monk who has forsaken his order is a heretic; let us have done with him!"

If the Nolan had so evaluated Cardinal Pinelli, he would not have been far wrong, I think. Pinelli was not the brightest in the congregation. But he had apparently voiced a silent concern of at least some of the others on the tribunal. Dega, Arigone, and Saxus were nodding their heads in agreement. The others seemed to reserve judgment, awaiting the master's response.

"St. Thomas has said that through the instruction of God's law and the assistance of His grace, we are helped to do right," he began, patiently. "His three conditions for a judgment to be an act of justice are: first, that it must proceed from the inclination of justice; second, that it must come from one who is in authority; and third, that it must be pronounced according to the right ruling of prudence, not formed from suspicions... (he glanced briefly toward Cardinal Pinelli)... that doubts should be interpreted in favor of the accused. Further, St. Thomas has instructed that the accuser must be on guard against false accusations out of malice and collusion.

"This Supreme Sacred Congregation of the Holy Office is charged with deciding the admissibility or inadmissibility of theological doctrine and opinion. The accused has challenged established doctrine of the Holy Catholic Church in a number of significant categories, substituting views that are both calumnious and heretical. Some of these views are particularly dangerous.

"Be aware, this is not some simple provincial monk with a few erroneous ideas. This is a clever and devious man who has developed a broad system of belief. He has traveled extensively throughout Europe and has consorted with known heretics, with Calvinists and with Lutherans, and with many who were and still are of considerable influence in the court of the heretical English queen. Most importantly, he has written a number of books which have been widely circulated and discussed in these places, books that attack the teachings of the church fathers, and which, if allowed to go unanswered, have the potential of doing incalculable harm to the authority of the Holy See.

"These books and the messages they contain were largely ignored by the Venetian tribunal, which, as you know, is a secular authority and is perhaps not as well schooled in theological doctrine as this Holy Congregation. Many of the heretical concepts contained in these works may have escaped the notice and understanding of the Venetian tribunal because they are concealed within a most subtle system of allegorical allusion.

"I have concentrated my investigation, therefore, on several of these books, and on the statements by the accused in their defense, and not at all on the letters, statements, and depositions of the others to whose testimony I have already alluded. As a result of my study of these works, I have narrowed the numerous charges of the indictment to these eight propositions, which I intend, with Your Eminences' concurrence, to put to the accused for explanation in response ... (Madruzzo, Borghese, and Santa Severina all nodded their heads in concurrence) ...

1. The distinction of persons in God.

2. The Incarnation of the Word.

3. The nature of the Holy Spirit.

4. The Divinity of Christ.

5. The necessity of Nature.

6. The eternity of Nature.

7. The infinity of Nature. And

8. The Transmigration of Souls.

"I have numerous excerpts from the works of the accused ... *Lo spaccio della bestia trionfante* in particular, but also from *De la causa, principio et uno; De l'infinito universo e mondi;* and *La cabala del cavallo Pegaseo;* plus numerous statements made by the accused in the Latin poems *De Minimo, De Immenso,* and *De Monadi;* and in the One Hundred and Twenty Articles on Nature and the World against the Peripatetics ... it is with regard to these excerpts that the accused will be required to respond to the eight propositions.

"I regard the most dangerously heretical statement of the accused to be his belief — which he has stated in terms of fact — in the existence of infinite worlds and in the motion of the earth revolving around the sun. This belief is contrary to Holy Scripture; it upsets the whole basis of our theology and threatens to undermine the authority of the Holy See. Scripture forms the essence of Catholicism. St. Augustine, in his Commentary on the Book of Genesis, said: 'Nothing is to be accepted save on the authority of Scripture, since greater is that authority than all the powers of the human mind.' Your Eminences, this belief, and the teaching of this belief, must be unequivocally recanted. It may not...it dare not...go unchallenged.

"At this point, I am, of course, prepared to address any questions you may have and to review these excerpts with Your Eminences. Yet, I am conscious of constraints on your time and would not wish to abuse your patience...(this last was addressed to Madruzzo and Borghese)...What is your desire?"

The cardinals were deep in thought. The only sound in the room was that of quills scratching, as the scribes struggled to catch up in their notes. My master's presentation appeared to bring home to the tribunal the importance of this particular prisoner. He was obviously suggesting that of the thirty-six or so prisoners in Castel Sant'Angelo awaiting trial or sentence, none was so important as Giordano Bruno, nor, indeed, so great a threat to the power of the church. I was at a loss to reconcile my own impression of the Nolan with that of my master. Pinelli's seemed a better fit. Arrogant and condescending, Bruno was certainly that. But getting from there to being a dangerous threat to Catholicism was a leap greater than I could follow.

What difference did it make whether the sun went around the earth or the earth went around the sun? Or whether the universe was infinite? Everyone looks at the night sky and wonders, right? But nobody has the answer; so who can say which guess is right or wrong? What good Catholics worry about is putting bread on the table in this world, not in some other. It seemed to me that if these cardinals had the same worries as the rest of us Catholics, they would have less time to spend tormenting prisoners like the Nolan, who probably did nothing more serious than to step on the wrong toes once too often.

It was not as though he had done something truly bad. For instance, there was an Englishman four years before who attacked a priest with a dagger during a procession that was leaving the Church of St. Agata a Monte Magnanapoli. The priest was forced to drop the Blessed Sacrament to the ground, and oh, that deeply grieved the pope! Not so much as it grieved the Englishman, though; he was burned at the stake for it.

That was not the only execution, either. Clement had decreed more humane treatment for prisoners in March of '95, but he did not ease up on heretics. Thirteen were condemned before the Englishman burned and five more after him, all in one year. There were seven the next year, and one more in '97. Things had been quiet the last year or so, but it definitely looked like they were fixing to add the Nolan to the list. It just did not seem right to me, not that I would have anything to say about it, I was just a substitute scribe, after all, barely a cog in this wheel. I was worried by the direction this was taking.

"Father Bellarmine," said one of the major spokes in the wheel. It was Santa Severina, attempting to assume the lead again. "Regarding your seventh proposition, in his third statement before the Venetian tribunal, the accused said with respect to this issue: 'In my books you can see my intention... (Severina was reading from the statement)... that I believe in an infinite universe which is the effect of an infinite Divine Power because I consider it unworthy of the Divine Goodness and Power that, being able to produce infinite worlds, He produced a finite world. Along with Pythagoras, I believe the world to be a star similar to the moon and to the planets and to the other stars, that are infinite, and that all these bodies are inhabited worlds and they constitute a universality in infinite space. In this universe I put a universal Providence for which each thing lives, and it moves in its own perfection in the same way a soul would be in a body. This is what I call Nature, a shadow and a vestige of divinity. I believe also in an ineffable way in which God in His essence and power is in everything and above everything, not as a part, not as a soul, but in an inexplicable way.'

"Now, I take it, *Padre*," Severina continued, narrowing his eyes as he addressed the master, "that the essence of the argument put forth by the accused in this statement was that only an infinite God would be capable of producing an infinite universe, and that it would be unworthy of an infinite God to produce only one world in a finite universe. According to our records, the Venetian tribunal was unable or unwilling to treat such an argument. How do you propose that this tribunal respond to what you have informed us is the most dangerous of all the heretical contentions of the accused?"

The master had a ready answer.

"God is not an object in the realm of finite knowledge, as Archbishop Anselm posited and St. Thomas refuted. Since we cannot comprehend all the ways in which something was done, it makes no sense to say that God did some particular thing in some particular way or in even in all possible ways. In setting forth consistency in the universe, we must not necessitate God. Therefore, we may not suggest that God *had* to do something in a particular way; even less, that it would have been unworthy of God to do something in a different way. The argument of the accused is as philosophically fallacious as it is theologically heterodox."

Bruno was going to have his hands full with my master, that much was certain. Clement and Santa Severina had made a wise choice when they brought Bellarmine into the picture. There was no doubt in my mind that the pope had been behind the choice of my master as Qualificatore. I was beginning to see why the pope had decided to appoint him to the college of cardinals.

Cardinal Borghese saw it too. He stood, stroked his goatee and pinched his double chins, applauded lightly and said, "Excellent, *Padre,* excellent," as though it were he who had posed the question to the master, instead of Severina. "I commend you on your thoroughness. I am confident that you will conduct the rest of this investigation with the same degree of thoroughness, and will await your final recommendation to the tribunal. Lodovico . . . (amazing! to use such informality in addressing Cardinal Madruzzo in front of others would have been unheard of coming from anyone else but Borghese!) . . . ought we not to be going?"

Madruzzo nodded. "If Your Eminence will forgive us," he said to Santa Severina, "we must leave to keep our appointment. Your question of Father Bellarmine was well put. As prefect, I want you to know how much I admire the way you continue to conduct this tribunal. It is an honor to serve with you. Your Eminences, Father Bellarmine, Consultor Adriano, I apologize that we must leave. God be with you."

Masterful. As brusque as Borghese's style was, that's how shrewdly polite and diplomatic Madruzzo's was. In that little speech he had reminded Santa Severina that he, Madruzzo, was prefect of the tribunal, and that he and Borghese were on a mission for His Holiness. And yet, he had also managed to pay homage to Santa Severina, who was then left in no position to object to their abrupt departure. Had he not, after all, just been paid a sweet compliment by the king-maker himself? Besides, it was too late to do anything about it. Madruzzo and Borghese were already gone. The meeting had in effect been adjourned.

Chapter 22

15 settembre 1599
Stanza del Paradiso, The Vatican
Roma

MARCH WAS A BUSY MONTH, starting off with Pope Clement nominating us for cardinal on the third, and the red hat ceremony on the very same day.

I have always looked with suspicion on these pontifical nominations. Popes nominate their close family members, friends, distant relatives; and they make political nominations, sometimes to appease foreign royalty, sometimes to subvert it. Once, not long after Cardinal Gian Angelo de' Medici from Milan became pope Pius IV, even two boys of eighteen and eleven were nominated!

But this was one time I agreed with Pope Clement's choice. "We elect this man," he said of my master in his announcement, "because he has not his equal for learning in the church of God." Of course, the cynic in me would have to add that Robert Bellarmine was also nephew to Pope Marcellus II, who had befriended Pope Clement's father, Sylvester Aldobrandini, on his banishment from Florence fifty years earlier. *Cane non mangia cane,* Dogs don't eat dogs. Powerful people don't hurt each other.

With what the master later referred to in a letter to his brother Tommaso as "the burden of the purple that was imposed" on him came a move to the Vatican and the sudden addition of thirty-five more retainers to the household. The master's dear friend, Father John Baptist Carminata, Jesuit provincial of Sicily, was shocked. The master had to explain that Cardinal Borromeo, who everybody knew despised worldly pomp, had forty-five retainers, that other cardinals who were considered modest in their establishments had sixty or seventy, that more powerful cardinals like Madruzzo and Borghese had as many as one hundred or more, and that even Cardinal Sandoval, who received his biretta at the same ceremony as my master, had a total of eighty-three retainers. (Of course, Sandoval was nephew to the duke of Lerma and a favorite of King Philip III of Spain, so he had an image to keep up.)

Imagine having to apologize for having a paltry thirty-five retainers! That's my cardinal! Well, thirty-five more in the household just about tripled my expenses, and with Cardinal Bellarmine still giving away most of his income to the poor, thirty-five was all the addition I could handle anyway. I couldn't complain about our new quarters, though. Stanze del Paradiso was a welcome improvement on Penitenzieria House. The apartments overlooked a beautiful colonnaded courtyard with nice shade trees and a pleasant fountain. It was far more private quarters than many of the other twenty-five or thirty resident cardinals had for their "families."

Vatican Palace is an awesome place in which to live. The wealth of it is beyond most peoples' imaginations. The collection of art alone is unrivaled. Paintings and tapestries by Botticelli, Ghirlandaio, Rosselli, Raffaello Sanzio of Urbino known as Raphael, Titian, Carpaccio, Correggio, Caravaggio, Fra Angelico. The Borgia Rooms are lavish, as are the newer rooms on the upper level to the Stanze, decorated by Raphael, the Sala di Costantino and the Sala dei Palafrenieri, especially. And there are the state rooms of the southwest part of the palace, the ones that were renovated by Pope Paul III, especially the Sala Regia and the Sala Ducali. The frescoes in the Cappella Paolina are beautiful, and the four that were done by Raphael in the Stanza d'Eliodoro are magnificent. And, of course, the most dazzling of all...the Sistine Chapel...with its vaults by Michelangelo. It is beyond description. And this was my new "home."

Not that I had much time to enjoy it. Between running a much increased household, managing the affairs of an influential cardinal, and acting as scribe to the most sought after clergyman in Rome — Father Cervini was still recuperating in the South — I had my hands full. This or that committee one day, this or that council the next, plus he was still Pope Clement's theological adviser, and now he sat on Santa Severina's tribunal as a grand inquisitor of the Sant'Offizio instead of as a consultant. I was working for a man who could never say no to a new assignment. Nor dared I complain, or I would have risked losing my inside track on the Nolan's trial.

Something else had changed for me. I had made up my mind to somehow help the prisoner in Castel Sant'Angelo. I could see which way the wind was blowing with my master, and I had not succeeded in convincing him otherwise. Bruno was inching closer and closer to condemnation.

On 14th January, my master formally presented his Eight Heretical Propositions before the congregation. On the 18th, Bruno was given six days to abjure, but on the 25th, he insisted on his right to defend his views. On 4th February, His Holiness himself gave him forty days to abjure. The Nolan was not doing much to help himself. Twice in Venice and once already during his imprisonment in Castel Sant'Angelo, he admitted he had made errors and begged forgiveness for his sins. But then, within days, he changed his position and defended the very same errors and sins. Insisting that he was being misunderstood, he constantly ran off at the mouth with long-winded explanations.

The tribunal was losing patience. Borghese and Madruzzo seemed especially anxious to speed my master to a final recommendation. Even Clement was starting to ask questions. Not that the master was anyone to be pushed. He would decide when he would decide and not a moment sooner, pope or no pope. Still, I could tell the pressure was on and that he was beginning to feel it. I decided I would put the squeeze on Borletto, Cardinal Borghese's scribe, to see if I couldn't find out why the rush with Bruno.

Meanwhile, how to help the man was my big problem. And it was a knotty one. The only way to help the Nolan was to save him. But how? Not only did I have no idea how to accomplish that; saving him might mean going up against the Sant'Offizio. That was very dangerous... *my life* kind of dangerous. Moreover, were I to go against the Sant'Offizio, I would also be opposing my own master, whom I dearly loved and had no wish to disappoint, let alone to antagonize, let alone to place in a compromising position with the other cardinals because of my actions. Oh, these were deep waters!

And if you asked me, Why this great urge to save the Nolan, Guidotti? I could not have answered. Something deep inside me seemed to agree with him that he was misunderstood, that this eight-year persecution for heresy was unjust, that a man should not be condemned for having wrong ideas and an oversized mouth. Laugh at him, scoff at him, drum him out of town, don't hire him, or fire him if you do, but burn him? take his life? No! That did not seem right!

I understood him; that was the strange thing. Not his ideas, certainly most of them were beyond me... but *him*, Bruno the man. This feisty little ex-monk actually believed himself, believed that he was right and everybody else was wrong, that if only he could bring them to understand, they would call him a genius and proclaim that he alone had changed the world and made it a better place. And yet, instead, they had stuck him in a cell of one kind or another for eight years, insisting that he abjure and beg forgiveness... left him sit there stewing in his own juices month in and month out with nary a word on which way it was going. No wonder he was up and down like a yo-

yo, blowing hot and cold, pleading for mercy one minute, demanding his rights the next.

Isolation does strange things to a man. He gets to living inside his head. Especially in the dungeons of Castel Sant'Angelo. They tell bad stories of the place. Of cold, damp cells, of terrible shrieks in the night and torturings with the *strappado, "la corda,"* where a prisoner's hands are tied behind his back and he is hauled high above the ground by a rope tied to his wrists, and then suddenly dropped to just short of the ground so that his shoulders are dislocated. Of never seeing the light of day or the evening stars or the moon. Of poor food and too little water, nothing to read, nothing to do, no company but your own thoughts and your own bad odors, no women . . . no women! . . . and never knowing if this will ever change, if you will someday be free again or will die tomorrow.

I try to imagine what that would be like, and I shudder. Eight years of that? I think I would agree to go to Mass every day and twice on Sundays, confess to any sins, make any abjurations, teach the catechism to the deaf and dumb if that were the tribunal's wish, anything to avoid that.

And yet here I was, about to risk my own freedom to attempt saving a man who was meanwhile digging himself a deeper hole with the Inquisition every time he opened his mouth or put his quill to paper. And I did not even know why. Crazy Guidotti . . . *É matto da legare* . . . he is mad!

✠

"Pietro, would it be convenient for you to sit with me a short while and to write as I dictate? I fear that I am for the moment unable to use this right arm that has suffered so much and been so roughly used by the doctors."

"Certamente, Boss. Rough time again last night? Maybe you should let me send for your physician."

Last few years, the master was beginning to age. For a long time, he seemed to be growing younger instead of older. At fifty-four, you would have taken him for forty. Not a gray hair was in sight. But now, at fifty-seven, his head had gone almost completely white, though at least his beard was still red.

This business of his right arm seemed to be getting worse. Some nights he was in such pain he could not sleep a wink, and there were days when it was so bad he could not get out of bed. His personal physician kept telling him it was nerves and overwork. If too much work was what did in right arms, mine would be in a sling! It had to be more than just overwork. I don't think he knows what he is talking about. Physicians! My father used to say: *piscia chiaro e fa le fiche al medico,* piss clear and thumb your nose at the doctor.

"There is no need to send for the physician. He has already removed so much blood from my arms, feet, and shoulders, I doubt I have sufficient left to affect a cure. God will see to my needs," he said with a sigh.

"Well, if He needs any help, let me know."

"*Vergogna!* Shame on you, Peter of little faith, to speak of God with sarcasm."

It was only a gentle chide. The master knew me well enough to know that I meant only to raise his humor, not criticize his faith. Surely no one's faith was greater than his.

"He has no need of your assistance, but I do," he continued in a gentler tone. "Please, sit here on my right side by my good ear. You can use the table to write upon. I would like to dictate some notes so that I may keep a record of my sleepless musings of last evening."

So, just as I thought, he had not slept. But of course he would take no time to nap. Too much work to do. His schedule had to be kept. Who knows, maybe the doctor had something after all.

"Boss, *scusa,* before you begin, I have some news."

"Oh?"

I had been waiting all day to tell him. The master was death on politics. My guess was he would not enjoy being used as a pawn, especially by Spain. And I hoped that might somehow tip the scales a little for the Nolan.

"You know Giacomo Borletto, Cardinal Borghese's scribe?" (The one whose arm I had to twist with the promise of a free night in bed with the finest *donna allegra* in all of Campo Marzio.)

"Yes, I know of him...?"

"Well, I think I know why Cardinal Borghese and Cardinal Madruzzo are in such a lather about Giordano Bruno."

"Are we about to trade in gossip, Pietro, because if we are, you know how much I...," he said, frowning and leaving the rest unsaid.

"Your Lordship, *me* gossip?" I said, feigning shock. "*Nemmeno per sogno!* I would not dream of it! This is news, plain and simple, and I thought you ought to know, that's all."

"Very well, then what is your 'news'?"

"I think the pope has made a deal with King Philip of Spain. Madruzzo and Borghese have held several meetings with Philip's emissary, Count de Guzmán. Remember at the meeting of the tribunal back in early February, right before you got your biretta, when they mentioned they had an appointment with de Guzmán? That was probably the first time, but there have been other times as well. Anyway, King Philip has it in for Bruno because for some reason he seems to think Bruno was out to unite King Henry and Queen Elizabeth against Spain. So Philip has offered to return some high-born adulterous couple . . . Borletto didn't know their names . . . who eloped from Rome to Spain and who I guess Pope Clement has excommunicated or something, if His Holiness will agree to extradite Bruno to Spain or at least insure his speedy dispatch to the Netherworld. Now . . ."

"Enough, Pietro, enough," interrupted my master, in an ominous tone of voice that said: One more word, Guidotti, will be the one too many. "This 'news' of yours, you say it comes from Cardinal Borghese's scribe?"

I knew where this was heading.

"Boss, you once made me a promise that we could speak frankly between us, and that it would stay there. From time to time I hear things. I pass it on to you if I think it might be something you should know about. You don't need to listen to it, you don't need to believe it, and you don't need to do anything about it. But you do need to keep what I say *a quattr'occhi*, private between us. Otherwise, I am of no use to you in the real world. So, do you stick to that promise, or do you break it now?"

"Very well," he said with a frustrated sigh. *"Teniamocelo per noi,* we shall keep it to ourselves. But I wish to hear no more. And I forbid you to have further discussion with Borletto. He has breached his confidential duties and one day he shall have to answer for it. Meanwhile, your news alters nothing in the Bruno affair. His Holiness has already apprised me of the communications between the Holy See and King Philip of Spain. He has assured me that it is to have no effect on my investigation or on our deliberations, and it will not. The trial is drawing to a close. I will meet with the accused myself within the coming months, and then I will prepare my recommendation. It has been a troubling chapter in the history of the Holy Church, not the first such and probably not the last, but no less troubling for that, and I shall be grateful when it is concluded."

So much for that idea. I knew I was on shaky ground, revealing what I had learned, but I thought it might help Bruno. I was wrong. Lucky for me, and luckier for Borletto, the master was in an understanding mood. Probably, if his arm were not paining him so much and sapping his energy, the outcome would have been less favorable for both of us.

"Boss, there is something I do not understand."

"The issue is closed, Pietro."

"No, no, it's not about that. This is a . . . a theological question."

Theology was a sure subject-changer to use on my master. He could never pass up a chance to imbue his Peter-of-little-faith with a little more faith.

"A theological question?"

"What possible difference can it make if the sun moves around the earth or the earth moves around the sun? Whichever way it is, God makes it so, right? So isn't God still Supreme either way? And how can anybody prove the size of the heavens when nobody can go up there and check? One man says the void is endless and another says the opposite. Who can say for sure which is right? If science speculates about such things, why is that heretical? This puzzles me."

I thought I knew the answer, that it was all nonsense and double-talk, a power struggle instead, and the church was not about to let some little monk from Nola make waves. But I could not tell him that. In truth, I was trying to draw him out on this, see if I could find what he had in mind for the Nolan. What I got turned out to be a rehearsal of the reasoning the master would soon use against the Nolan. He did not so much answer my questions as use me as a substitute audience. I might as well not have been there, but I listened intently to what he had to say. Perhaps there would be something I could use to help the Nolan.

"The Council of Trent," he began slowly, rubbing his eyes with his fists in that way that seemed to help him think, "forbids the interpretation of the Scriptures in any way contrary to the common opinion of the holy fathers and of the modern commentators on Genesis, the Psalms, Ecclesiastes, and Joshua. All agree to interpreting them literally.

"In Joshua 10:12-14, we find for example: *'Then spake Joshua to the LORD in the day when the LORD delivered up the Amorites before the children of Israel, and He said in the sight of Israel, Sun, stand thou still upon Gibeon; and thou, Moon, in the valley of Ajalon. And the sun stood still, and the moon stayed, until the people had avenged themselves upon their enemies. Is not this written in the book of Jasher? So the sun stood still in the midst of heaven, and hasted not to go down about a whole day.'*

"In Psalm 103:11: *'For as the heaven is high above the earth, so great is His mercy toward them that fear Him.'*

"In Ecclesiastes 1:4: *'One generation passeth away, and another generation cometh; but the earth standeth fast forever.'* And again in Ecclesiastes 1:5–6: *'The sun also ariseth, and the sun goeth down, and hasteth to his place where he arose. The wind goeth toward the south, and turneth about unto the north; it whirleth about continually, and the wind returneth again according to his circuits.'* And so on. There are many similar scriptural examples.

"The man who wrote that the sun rises and sets and returns to its place was Solomon, who not only spoke from divine inspiration but was wise and learned above all others in human sciences and in the knowledge of created things. The doctrine of the double motion of the earth about its axis and about the sun is contrary to Holy Scripture, and to gainsay the absolute and specific declarations of Holy Scripture, which prove that the sun and heavenly bodies revolve about the earth, is to dispute revelation and is heretical.

"The accused Friar Bruno has, among other heretical disputations, espoused the Copernican heresy, that the sun is the center of the world and is immovable from its place, that the earth is not the center of the world and is not immovable, but moves, and also with a diurnal motion. To support such a position in theory as a mathematician, as a scientist or a philosopher, may be defensible. But to affirm as fact that the sun, in truth, is at the center of the universe and does not go from east to west, and that the earth revolves swiftly around the sun, is an extremely dangerous attitude.

"The accused has, in addition, espoused the doctrine that the universe is infinite, that there are many populated worlds within the universe. Such a doctrine is expressly contrary to Scripture. It upsets the whole basis of theology, for if the earth were only one of many planets, then it could not be that such great things have been done for it as Christian doctrine teaches. Since God creates nothing in vain, if there were other planets they would have to be inhabited. But if that were the case, how could they have descended from Adam? How could they trace their origin to Noah's ark? How could they be redeemed by the Savior?

"The holy fathers concur that Scripture teaches that the sun is in the heavens and revolves around the earth with immense speed, that the earth is very distant from the heavens and is at the center of the universe and motionless. If there were any real proof to indicate a contrary interpretation, to do more than merely offer a better explanation of celestial appearances, then we would have to proceed with great circumspection in explaining these passages from Scripture. However, the church is not yet ready to subject the Copernican heresy to such an examination. The day may come when that will become necessary. That day has not yet arrived. Your friend, Giordano Bruno, constitutes a grave threat to the church if he persists in holding to his heretical positions.

"And now, Pietro, I think that I am in need of some rest. I am afraid we will have to postpone to another time the dictation I had in mind. If you would be so kind as to close the door behind you as you leave?"

Inquisitor Robert Cardinal Bellarmine had made up his mind. Unless the prisoner in Castel Sant'Angelo recanted, abjured, cursed, and detested his sins and heretical errors, relinquished his opinions and admitted that he was wrong — which, knowing the Nolan as I thought I did, was doubtful at best — or unless I could figure some way to help him out of this mess, Bruno's *resa dei conti*, his day of reckoning, was fast approaching. If I was going to be of help to him, time was running out for both of us.

Moreover, the master's seemingly casual reference to Bruno as my "friend," sounded a little alarm in the back of my mind. I knew him well enough to know that he was not given to making casual remarks. We had a saying on the docks in Ripa: *Non c'é peggior sordo di chi non vuol sentire...* there's no one as deaf as he who won't listen. I had heard my master plain enough. He was putting me on notice: *stai attento*, Guidotti, I know of your sentiments for this man.

I would have to be very, very careful from now on.

C*hapter 23*

12 ottobre 1599
Campo Marzio
Roma

THE WRITING ON THE NOTE was large and plain, without flourish:

If you care about the prisoner in Sant'Angelo, be at the Inn of Three Coins near Ponte Fabricio on Via Portuense at ten o'clock tomorrow night.

There was no signature. It had been left by someone on my table at the Boar's Head the night before, I did not see who. Probably I was too drunk to notice.

Lately, I had been drinking more than my usual ration on my Friday and Saturday carousings in Campo Marzio. I had grown bitter and frustrated and confused. All I could think about was saving the Nolan; yet I still had no plan. Cervini was back, and my temporary job as scribe had come to an end. Worse still, my master had grown very close-mouthed with me on the whole subject of Bruno. When I would try to ask him something about how his investigation was proceeding or how the trial was going, he would just say that everything was under control or it was in God's hands, and then quickly change the subject, sending me off on some errand or other. It was as though a door had been slammed in my face. With me on the outside.

Cervini was my only hope, but I had to move cautiously. I went out of my way to brief him on all that had transpired during his absence, but I asked him nothing about the work now that he had returned. Had I pumped him, I had no doubt the master would find out somehow. A careless word here or there from Cervini, and I might lose my best potential source of information. I let Cervini know, however, that whenever he needed help transcribing his notes, I was available. His gratitude was a good sign.

This note had me worried. Was it a trap? That was my first thought. Santa Severina had eyes and ears everywhere, even in Campo Marzio. One slip and I could find myself in a cell next to Bruno. Still, I had expressed my thoughts to no one. Why should Santa Severina suspect me? Or could he be trying to get at my lord cardinal through me? But that seemed unlikely, didn't it, since Santa Severina was widely known to have great admiration for the master? I doubted there was anyone in the entire college of cardinals, actually, who would think evil of Robert Bellarmine or try to harm him. Well, then, could someone be trying to lay a trap for me so as to get at Santa Severina by embarrassing one of his tribunal? Circles within circles? No, surely that was too far fetched!

Who could have sent the note? Bellarmine himself? Not his style. He would confront me head-on had he suspicions. I had given him no reason. Vignanesi? He would give his eye teeth to embarrass me if he could steal my job, but he had neither the brains nor the courage. Besides, he knew that if I so much as suspected treachery from his quarter, he would find himself belly up in the Tiber with bottom fish feeding from the slit I would put in his neck. No, not Vignanesi either.

Who then? Who could possibly suspect what was still only in my mind? Maybe a better question was who might profit from knowing? Wait. The note was ambiguous. *If you care about the prisoner...* no name mentioned. I had taken that to mean Bruno, but there were many others imprisoned in Castel Sant'Angelo. Did the note refer to someone else? It was no secret in Campo Marzio who I worked for. I was *maestro di casa* of an important cardinal who was advisor to the pope and a member of the Inquisition. Could be a trap or could be someone wanting to use me to get to my cardinal on behalf of some prisoner stuck in Sant'Angelo. On the other hand, what if it was someone with a way to help Bruno? If that was a possibility and I ignored the offer, I would never forgive myself.

What was I so worried about anyway? I was no stranger in Campo Marzio. Plenty of people knew me, knew that I could be found in one inn or another on any Friday or Saturday night. Nothing suspicious if I happened to be at the Inn of Three Coins on Saturday night at 10 o'clock. Besides, had I not had been well schooled by one of the best, by Nicco Baroniti, master spy of Geneva? Had I not survived Montmorency in Paris and Burghley in London? Guidotti is no fool. I would drink a little less and watch a lot more, keep my mouth shut, and see what developed.

✠

I often wonder what life would have been like had I not traded insults with a jealous Corsican in Ripa, had I not then wandered into Bellarmine's classroom to elude the rain and the Corsican. Would I have married, settled down in a cottage in the *campagna* somewhere, had five or six bambinos? Stayed in Campo Marzio and become a bonesetter like my father? Become a sailor and gone to sea, maybe lived with some bare-breasted native girl on an exotic island?

You come to a crossroad, turn right instead of left, you think it's just another turn in the road at the time. You have no idea that turn will change the entire course of your life. Pretty soon, the road you take has made so many additional turns there is no way to get back to that first crossroad to see where the left turn would have taken you. So...no wife. No bambinos. No bare-breasted native girl.

Not that I didn't enjoy my life. I had a good job and a great boss. The work was most of the time interesting. I got to travel, I had adventures, I met many important people. I had friends. I had women. I had money in my pocket, food on my plate, a roof over my head. What more should life be about?

You are here because your mother and father had nothing better to do one night. You are born, you live, you die. If you are lucky, you have more pleasure than pain; if you are not, you have more pain than pleasure. *Cosi va il mondo*, so it goes. My luck, I have had my share of pleasure. I don't miss a wife and children.

I was thinking about that as I sat by myself at a table in the Inn of Three Coins, nursing my second wine and watching the crowd. Watching and waiting.

It was still early for Campo Marzio on a Saturday night, but the crowd was already loud and raucous. The air was thick with smoke, with the smells of garlic, spilled wine, human sweat, and freshly baked bread, and the sounds of laughter and singing and curses, all mixed together. Two burly Slavs were arm wrestling at a table near the fireplace, their tattooed arms quivering and straining side by side, their hands locked together in a grip that would have choked a horse, sweat rolling down their faces, neither man giving an inch, both focused intently on winning over the other. A small crowd surrounded them, shouting encouragement. Bets were being laid on who would win. This was my kind of place.

I had been here before, though it was not one of my usual haunts. I saw familiar faces, a few nodded to me in recognition, but so far no one had approached me. It was after ten. Perhaps whoever had sent me the note had gotten cold feet. Or perhaps it was not a trap but a joke, somebody out for a laugh at Guidotti's expense. Or...that fellow looking in my direction, was he watching me? Was he one of Santa Severina's spies, waiting to see what I was going to do? *Dio*, I was acting like a nervous hen!

What would Nicco Baroniti say? Sit here and wait. You have done nothing wrong. Sip your wine, observe the scene, act natural. Well, not exactly what he would say. More likely he would curse me for a fool. But I had the feeling it was what he would do, were he in my place tonight. I sipped my wine and observed the scene.

The arm wrestlers near the fire were tiring. Both arms wavered, though there was not yet a clear winner. The cheering, meanwhile, had turned to curses, as the crowd grew restless and impatient. If the match did not end soon, a fight would break out. One might break out anyway. There would be many fights before the night was over; it was a way to release steam after a long week of hard work and aggravation. There was another way, of course, if one had a little money in his pocket. And there was no lack of women willing to help. It was Saturday night, after all, and there were empty rooms waiting upstairs for just such a purpose. The thought had crossed my own mind.

The match ended with a great shout, followed by the expected fight, and I was about to go looking for a companion for the night when one sat down at my table.

"Some fight, eh?" she said, flashing a quick smile and indicating with her head the crowd by the fire. "Buy a thirsty girl a drink? I'll have what you're having." The smile spread to a grin, and she winked.

She was pleasant looking, in a rough sort of way, dark haired and buxom. Hard to tell her age. Was she old young or young old? I could not decide which. There was something both lively and at the same time reserved about her. Her manner said what you see is what you get, but her eyes spoke differently. They were dark and intense, and they gave you the feeling that as deep as you might see into them you would never see what was behind them. Everyone has secrets. I wondered what hers were.

I bought her wine but told her I was expecting someone who was late. She laughed. Is she prettier than me? she wanted to know. What makes you think it is a she? I asked. Why else would you sit alone on a Saturday night? she replied. We continued that way, bantering, circling, getting to know each other, at least know each other well enough to strike a bargain. I was about to ask her price, when she stopped smiling and grew serious.

"Signor Guidotti, they tell me you are one of *il popolino*, one of the common people...one of us." She emphasized the "us." "You work for an influential cardinal, but you are from Campo Marzio, like me. Your family was from Campo Marzio, like mine. Are you *Vaticanarsi* or *popolarsi*? Can I trust you?"

By now, her eyes were boring into mine so hard I could feel the heat.

"Trust me to what?" I said, covering my surprise with a snort. "If we make a deal to sleep together, will I pay you what we agree upon? Of course! What do you take me for?"

She ignored the remark.

"I am Maria Riotti. I am the one who left you the note."

"And I am Pietro Guidotti, as you already seem to know. What note?"

If this was a trap, it was slick. She was good.

"I understand your suspicion," she said, nodding. "But you must understand this: I am taking a big chance talking to you. Your cardinal is an inquisitor. One word from you to him, and I could be in serious trouble with the Sant'Offizio. It is very dangerous for me to talk to you this way. I have to know if it is safe for me to do so, and yet all I can have is your word. I must at least have that, or I can speak no further. Signor Guidotti, I am desperate. Have I your word that I may speak to you in confidence?"

She had moved closer to me, put her arm around my neck as though we were already lovers for the night and spoke this last into my ear, so that no one could overhear. Every nerve of me was on edge. Was it a trap or was it the truth? I felt that she was telling me the truth, but there was no way to be sure. What she was saying was that we would have to trust each other or it could be our life, but I considered my life worth more to me than hers was worth to me, so from my perspective I had more to lose. Still, where was the harm if I just listened? Make no commitment to do anything, just listen?

"Look...Maria, is it?...look, Maria, I don't know anything about a note and I don't know what you are talking about, but I am willing to listen. Maybe I will help you, maybe I won't. Depends on what you have in mind. I make no promises. But you have my word that I will keep your confidence."

She hesitated only briefly, then appeared to make up her mind. All right, she said, but not there. She instructed me to hand some money across the table to her, as though we had struck our deal, then to follow her upstairs to one of the rooms where we would talk. We got up from the table together and made our way upstairs, arm in arm, her head on my shoulder, the two of us laughing conspiratorily as though in anticipation of a rowdy event.

As soon as we entered the room, she began talking almost immediately, quietly, intently. There was no fencing around, no mincing of words. It was as though once she had made her decision downstairs, it was for all or nothing, and if she died for it, why then, she died for it. Once she began, there was no going back. And once I heard what she had to tell me, there was no going back for me either. If this was a trap, I would surely lose my head for what I was about to agree to do.

I will say this for Maria Riotti, she was a brave woman. She did everything she set out to do, and if we did not succeed, it would not be because she faltered. Not once did she hesitate to do anything I asked of her, no matter how difficult or how dangerous to her own safety. She was strong and she was courageous, and, frankly, I think she deserved better than the Nolan, but who am I to say? Love is not subject to reason.

This is *una storia, ti assicuro, de far piangere i sassi...* a story, I tell you, to make the stones weep. It will break your heart.

Before I met Maria, I thought we are none of us on this earth for any special purpose other than to serve as one more little ant in a long line of ants connecting the past with the future. If there is a purpose after all, it is on too grand a scale for a mere mortal like me to discern. I think differently now. I think now that I have survived plagues and floods and Corsicans' knives, kept my skull intact through countless drunken brawls in my youth, managed to stay out of the clutches of anti-papist spies in half the courts of Europe, that I have lived this long for the sole purpose of telling you this story. And Maria played a big part in its ending.

✠

She was Maria Riotti, daughter of Lucco and Annamaria Riotti of Campo Marzio. She was thirty-four years old and a widow. Her husband, a soldier, had died twelve years before, having been ingloriously kicked in the head by a mule he was in the act of shoeing. They had been married less than a year; there were no children.

Lucco Riotti was *tenente* Riotti, a lieutenant in the *guardia* and a shift supervisor at Castel Sant'Angelo. Giordano Bruno was his prisoner. To my surprise, I learned from Maria that the Nolan was not being held in a dark dungeon cell like the other prisoners, but lived in a clean, warm, dry, comfortable room. He had all the writing materials he requested, and a change of towels, bed, and personal linen twice a week. He was also allowed out of papal funds a pension of four crowns a month... forty *giullii*... which enabled him to order whatever food he liked. Not even the master had told me about this!

The pay in the *guardia* was low, even that of a *tenente*. Four crowns a month was a lot of money. Annamaria Riotti was a superb cook and so was her widow daughter who lived with them. For fifteen *giullii*, the two of them could easily prepare the Nolan's favorite dishes. Maria could bring the food to him each day. And the Riotti family income would be supplemented by twenty-five *giullii*. Bruno was agreeable, and thus the deal was made. It was not even technically against regulations, Lucco decided, so where was the harm?

Well, I guess you know what's coming. Maria is a good-looking widow without a man for twelve years. The Nolan, imprisoned for almost nine years, has been without worldly distractions other than to figure out how to save his life with his mouth and his pen. As Bruno later told my master in response to a question concerning carnal knowledge — Cervini was present taking notes at the time — he had never had the desire to become a eunuch, and if, as regards the number of women, he had not rivaled King Solomon, at least, Bruno said, he had done his best.

So, there they were, voluptuous Maria and, as she described him, this thin little fifty-one-year-old man with a pointed beard, flashing eyes, and a glib tongue, meeting almost every day while the Nolan partook of the sensual pleasure of his evening meal. They never discussed his work, she said, which did not surprise me; she would never have understood what he was talking about. And Maria fell in love. She made no bones about it. Nor did she hesitate to tell me that they had shared dessert in his bed. If anything, she was fiercely proud of it.

But Papa Lucco was not to know any of this love business, for that would require his turning his head a bit too far in the other direction. Friendship, okay. You bring the food, wait until he finishes it, bring the plate back. You talk while he eats, that's all right, I don't need to know what you talk about. But that's all you do, *capisci?* And then you go straight home. Forty *giullii* was forty *giullii*. She could not afford to arouse Papa's suspicion, especially with what she was beginning to hatch in her head.

She said nothing to anyone, but she began to ask around. My name kept coming up. Maybe it was all the money I spread around for my master. Or maybe she talked to a few of my ladies of the Campo. Whatever the case, she determined that she would enlist my help. How pleased she was to learn, eventually, that I was just as eager to enlist hers.

But not just yet. There was still a need to be cautious. I arranged to meet her again in two weeks. That would give me time to make a few inquiries of my own. If it was a trap, I should be able to sniff it out by then. Meanwhile, I said I would think about it, without acknowledging that I knew what "it" was.

I told her that I would leave the room first and she should follow soon after, just in case we were being watched. As I walked through the crowded inn and out the door, I saw nothing suspicious, and, so far as I knew, no one followed me. Time would tell.

✠

Two weeks later we met again, this time at the Boar's Head. We followed the same procedure as before, exchanging money at the table and taking a pleasure room upstairs to consummate our transaction.

In the two weeks since we had met, I found myself looking over my shoulder often, but I detected nothing out of the ordinary. Nor did anyone appear unduly curious as to my activities.

Father Cervini had twice taken me up on my offer to assist him with the transcription of his notes. The notes I transcribed held only one reference to the Nolan. The master was scheduled to examine him on the tenth day of November. Otherwise, the entries were routine. The French ambassador had complained to Cardinal Santa Severina about the burnings at Campo di Fiori in front of his house; Pope Clement requested he be diplomatic in his response. There was a brief reference to the Cenci case. Beatrice Cenci had murdered her father with the help of her lover and her stepmother, and she had been beheaded in front of Castel Sant'Angelo. The trial had created a big sensation in Rome. Though it was all over now, some members of the tribunal thought she should have been tried for heresy, not tried by the secular authorities for murder. I couldn't see the difference, since her head would have been parted from her body either way. While that was all I gleaned from helping Cervini, the most important thing was he had used my help in the first place. That meant I could count on Cervini to keep me posted on Bruno without him knowing he was doing it, which would keep me in the clear with the master.

The other good news was that Maria's story checked out. I asked around, discreetly, of course. The Riotti family was well known. Campo Marzio is a small region, not like the Ponte or the Borgo. Maybe it is the constant flooding and the stinking mud that brings the people of Campo Marzio together, but everyone seems to either know everyone else or know about everyone else. The fruitsellers and the bakers knew Maria, the butchers in the Scortecchiara knew her mother, a couple of barbers knew the *tenente*. I was beginning to feel a little more secure about Maria, enough at least to take the next step.

This time, I did most of the talking.

"All right, Maria. Maybe I trust you and maybe I don't, so we do this in stages," I told her. "The first thing is, I want to know everything about Castel Sant'Angelo. How many guards on the night shift? What are their names? Where do they live? Are they married? Do they have girlfriends? Do they gamble? Do they owe money? How much and to whom? What is their schedule? When do they come on. What time do they take breaks? When are they finished? Do they rotate with the day shift? If so, how often and when.

"I want a diagram of the prison. Where are the guard stations located? Where is your father's station located? Where is the Nolan's room? What else is nearby? What is the most direct route from the room where the Nolan is held to the front entrance? Are there other ways to exit? Are there any secret exits? What is the procedure for receiving visitors? Where do they come in, who checks their credentials, how long do they usually stay, what happens when they leave?

"What is the Nolan's schedule? When does he rise, when does he bathe and where, how are his linens changed and who changes them and when? When does he eat, when does he sleep, and so forth. Is every day the same or are there certain days that he does certain things. What is your procedure for taking in his food? When do you arrive, how long do you stay in his room, when and how to you leave? Is your schedule the same every day or different, and if different, in what ways? Do the guards all know you? Are any of them sweet on you, do you have any special relationship with one or more of them?

"I want to know everything you can find out about that place and the people who live and work in it. But of course we don't want anyone to know that you are gathering this information, so be very careful how you go about getting it," I concluded.

It was a lot to ask and a lot for her to remember, but I didn't dare trust it to a list.

"And *il tempo stringe,* time is short," I added. "Can you do it?"

"I'll do it," she replied, her lips tightly set. "How soon do you need all this information?"

"Yesterday," I answered. "And Maria...nothing to Bruno about this. The less he knows until the time is right, the better."

"I understand. Meet me at Three Coins in two weeks."

"No. I will meet you a week from next Wednesday on the left bank side of Ponte Fabricio after the bells strike nine in the evening. If anything changes, I will get word to you."

Nothing would change, but I wanted her to know that it could and that I knew where she lived and that I would call the shots, not she. I was beginning to conceive a plan, and the less she knew, the safer I would feel. Right now I was not feeling particularly safe.

I have done some dangerous things in my life, and I was no stranger to risk; but I was getting pretty far out on the edge here, and I did not welcome letting someone I did not know very well get close enough to push me off the cliff. My master had already given me fair warning. If I got in trouble, I was not going to be able to yell to him for help. There is a saying: *Raglio d'asino non giunge in cielo*...The voice of a fool does not carry very far.

*C*hapter 24

11 novembre 1599
Stanza del Paradiso, The Vatican
Roma

FATHER CERVINI WAS SICK. I hate to say it, but that was my good luck.

The poor cleric was coughing and wheezing, runny nose, bloodshot eyes, weak as a kitten, and unable to get up from his bed. He was beside himself with worry. How was he ever going to manage transcribing his notes for his eminence on the interview yesterday with Giordano Bruno at Castel Sant'Angelo?

Guidotti to the rescue.

I propped him up with some pillows, fed him some broth, handed him his notes, pulled a chair and table up next to his bed, and sat down with pen and paper. Anyone else that sick, I would have given him wide berth. No one knows how sickness spreads, and I would just as soon not find out the hard way. I figure the safest bet is to surround yourself with healthy people and avoid the sick ones when you can. But Cervini was not just any sick person. He was my link, perhaps my only link, to what was happening with Bruno's trial. I couldn't afford to do otherwise.

"*Padre, nessuno problema.* Read me from your notes and recollections. I'll write it all out for you, just the way you would. You get tired, take a rest. You want to nap, take a nap. You get thirsty or something, let me know and I'll get what you want. I will stay with you until we get this finished. And when we are done, I will see that his eminence gets the transcription. I'll give it to him myself."

"Ah, Pietro, you are a such a good friend. So helpful. So caring. I will say a prayer for you..."

He was interrupted by a fit of coughing. Then he blew his nose loudly, put on his glasses and picked up his notes, and we began. I could only hope that I did not catch his sickness before we finished.

"*Padre,* before we begin," I told him, "it would help me if you could describe the room and perhaps give me your impressions of the prisoner."

It would not really help me one way or the other. We both knew that. Cervini would assume my request was prompted by idle curiosity. I, on the other hand, had a need to know as much as I could.

He tipped his glasses up on his bald head, closed his eyes, and tried to recall the scene.

"Small man. Thin. Beard, pointed (he demonstrated by stroking an imaginary beard between his thumb and forefinger). Dark eyes, very intense. There was not a lot of light in the room, no windows, just candles. But his eyes seemed to reflect an inner light. Not at first. At first he was not very animated. He looked tired, wan. He mentioned his Lordship's name several times, as though he could not believe his good fortune. Said he knew who he was and had great regard for his work and his intellect. But later, as the discussion became more heated, he seemed to come to life. He started to wave his arms and to gesture excitedly with his hands. Toward the end he grew quite wild. But he was very respectful of his Lordship."

"And his eminence? What was his demeanor? How did he treat the prisoner?"

"Kindly, gently, with respect. But firm, very firm. I'm sorry, Pietro, that is all I can really say. It was not my place to be an observer. I simply sat in the corner and made notes on their conversation. I seldom looked up. The content of their discussion, if you could call it that, was often beyond my comprehension. And there were such feats of memory from both of them as I could hardly believe. I did my best, though I understood very little. It was all I could do just to record these notes. Now, if we could begin . . . ?"

"Of course, *Padre*."

I would have liked to learn more about the room than that it was dark and had no windows — where it was located in Castel Sant' Angelo, the route they took coming and going — but to press Cervini for such details would no longer seem idle curiosity on my part. So we began. Father Cervini dictating from his notes and recollections, in fits and starts, pausing often to cough, blow his nose, rest, several times to nap briefly, to relieve himself with my help, twice to take more broth, once or twice to wait for my return as I too relieved myself, and me transcribing. Occasionally, I asked questions. Several times, the master stopped by to inquire of Father Cervini's health. He of course knew what we were doing, and though he said it was not critical that he have the transcriptions so quickly as to inconvenience Father Cervini in his present state of health, he thanked us both for working on them now. He was most solicitous.

✠

"Friar, I am a representative of the Holy Office. My name is Robert Bellarmine. I have come to discuss your case."

"Your Eminence, I am most gratified that you have come. Robert Cardinal Bellarmine! Oh yes, I have heard such great things of you! I am familiar with your work; it is most schol- arly, most scholarly. And your intellect . . . your intellect . . . I have heard that the intellect of Robert Cardinal Bellarmine is unsur- passed in the entire Consistory. Pope Clement's spiritual advisor! I cannot believe you are actually here at last! I heard your name spoken with reverence throughout Europe, even among the heretics of London and Geneva! Please, Eminence, sit down, sit down. Alas, I have nothing more comfortable on which to sit than this wooden chair, but you are most welcome to my humble chamber."

(He was nervous. Understandably. Of all his interrogators, this one was perhaps the most important. And the one most likely to understand his theories.)

"Are you being well treated, *Padre?*"

"Eminence, I would rather not be here. Given that I am, I would say I am fairly treated."

"Have you sufficient paper and ink, books that you require?"

"Yes, Eminence. Some time ago I requested a cloak, and, as you can see, I was given a warm one. And I have the breviary of the Preaching Fathers, which I also requested."

"And which you use often, I am told. As befits a religious. 'Prayer heals the errant soul.'"

"Christ is my Savior. I believe that we have been on good terms and that He forgives me my sins and transgressions . . . as I pray you do, Eminence."

"*Padre*, it is not to me that you must pray for forgiveness. We are all sinners for whom divine forgiveness awaits. But we must repent our sins. It appears that you are not of one mind on this, however. On numerous occasions you have professed to us your repentance, only to retract each time. You did the same in Venice. Does your faith so waiver?"

"I have tried to be a good and orthodox Christian, Eminence, in my life and in my work. In all that I have sinned according to the faith, I have told the Holy Office. By myself, spontaneously, without anyone's influence."

"Then I beg you to pray, to offer supplication, to bare your conscience and to tell the truth to the tribunal that it may be helpful to your soul. Allow the Holy Office to bring piety and Christian clarity into your life that may otherwise remain in darkness and outside the path of eternal life."

"I respect your advice, Eminence, as I know it to be heartfelt and sincere. But I assure you that I have already answered truthfully all of the questions put to me and in everything I have remembered. In my work many things can be found that may be contrary to the Catholic faith. Likewise, in my reasonings I may have said things that could be said to be scandalous. Christ will pardon me. I never said or wrote these things to impugn the Catholic faith, but rather in fear of the rigor of the Holy Office and for a love of liberty. I hold firm that I have not disparaged the Catholic religion. In some of my works, Eminence, perhaps my tongue was looser than it should have been."

"It is upon some of your works that I have come to question you, *Padre.*"

"Then please understand that my work is that of a philosopher, not a theologian. And that often I have drawn from the works of the great minds who came before me. As it has been said: 'There is no child that of itself has understanding.'"

"A quote from Ptahhotep, I believe. I see that you still admire the work of the ancient Egyptians. But was it not also Ptahhotep who said: 'Be not arrogant because of thy knowledge, and have no confidence in that thou are a learned man. Take counsel with the ignorant as with the wise, for the limits of artistry cannot be reached and no artist fully possesses his skill. A good discourse is more hidden than the precious green stone, yet it is found with slave girls over the millstones. If thou ploughest and there is growth in the field, God causes it to be much in thy hand. Do not boast about this among thy kindred. Great is the respect that the silent one calls forth.'"

(I knew it! Bellarmine's is a mind! An intellect capable of discourse. At last, someone who will understand!) "Your Eminence is indeed well read. I am greatly impressed. Tell me, please, what questions has Your Lordship of my work? Have you brought neither notes nor annotations? Your mnemonic powers must indeed be prodigious!"

"Foremost, I remember not the Egyptians but the teachings of the church fathers and the proscriptions of canon law."

"Speaking of law, Anaximander wrote: 'The beginning of that which is, is boundless; but whence that which is arises, thither must it return again of necessity; for the things give satisfaction and reparation to one another for their injustice, as is appointed to the ordering of time.' I interpret that to mean that the essence of the law, as St. Thomas also said, is 'nothing else than an ordinance of reason for the common good, made by him who has care of the community and promulgated.'"

"And yet, as Cicero wrote: 'There is in fact a true law, right reason, agreeing with nature, diffused among all men, unchanging and eternal; it summons to duty by its commands and deters from wrong by its prohibitions. Its commands and prohibitions are not laid upon good men in vain, but are without effect on the bad. It is a sin to try to alter this law, nor is it allowable to repeal any part of it, and to annul it wholly is impossible.... One law, eternal and unchangeable, binding at all times upon all peoples. There will be one common master and ruler of men, namely, God, who is the author of this law, its interpreter and its sponsor.'"

"True, true, but there is more to the quotation, Eminence, there is more! Cicero went on then to say that the man who will not obey natural law will abandon his better self '...and in denying the true nature of man will thereby suffer the severest of penalties, although he has escaped all the other consequences which men call punishment.' *That* is the basis for all of my work! I have been misunderstood, Eminence! God's law is interpreted in all of us. '*Equitas est correctio legis generatim latae qua parte defecit.*' Thus does even Aristotle say that equity is the correction of the law in those particulars wherein, by reason of its generality, it is deficient."

"St. Augustine's response may be found in his Commentary on the Book of Genesis: '*Major est Scripturae auctoritas quam omnis humani ingenii capacitas*... Nothing is to be accepted save on the authority of Scripture, since greater is that authority than all the powers of the human mind.' God's law may be interpreted in all of us, as you suggest, but not *by* all of us. The church fathers were quite explicit on this."

"But, Your Eminence, I always defined my terms philosophically, according to natural principles and natural understanding, being in no way concerned with that which principally must be maintained according to faith. If, speaking according to natural reason, I pronounced impious judgments, it was not to impugn religion but rather to extol philosophy!"

"So you said in Venice. I have in fact carefully studied all of the statements that you prepared for the Venetian tribunal, and it is not my purpose to review them with you now. Rome is not Venice. I would remind you, *Padre,* that you are a religious under vows. It is disingenuous of you to attempt to defend your work as purely philosophical, for all of theology is indeed philosophy. You are no simple philosopher; you were ordained in the robes of a Dominican. When you write and when you teach and when you discourse, you do so as a theologian, as a member of your order, as a Regular in the Catholic faith . . . not as a philosopher. I would advise you not to persist in that argument; it is not, I can tell you, well regarded by this Holy Office."

"With deference, Your Eminence, I was and am more aptly suited to the profession of philosopher than theologian. The same was true, you may recall, of Nicholas de Cusa, whose philosophical works were honored by Pope Eugenius IV, and of Cusa's student, Widmanstadt, who was similarly honored by Pope Clement VII. Cusa would easily have equalled Pythagoras had his genius not been stifled under priestly garments. I had hoped to return to Rome that His Holiness might so honor me. Instead, I find myself his prisoner. 'We would wish this law to be vigorously observed, that reason is as true as it is necessary, and the authority of no men, however true and excellent persons they may be, is admissible as an argument.' So I have written. 'But God knows and is acquainted with the infallible truth that just as that type of men is foolish, perverse, and wicked, so I, in my thoughts, words, and deeds, do not know, do not have, do not pretend anything else but sincerity, simplicity, and truth.' "

" 'Thus fear, piety, and our religion, honor, respect, and love leave, after which depart strength, providence, virtue, dignity, majesty, and beauty, which fly from us otherwise than the shadow together with the body. Only Truth, with Absolute Virtue, is immutable and immortal.' Did you not also write that?"

"Yes, Eminence, but...?"

"And did you not write that Egypt is the image of heaven, the colony of all things that are governed and practiced in heaven?"

"Yes, Eminence, but I also wrote that I do not abolish the mysteries of the Pythagoreans, I do not belittle the faith of the Platonists and do not despise the ratiocinations of the Peripatetics insofar as these ratiocinations find a real foundation."

"Then let us pursue the 'real foundation' and 'truth' of your work. What is the real foundation and truth of your belief in the Holy Trinity, Padre, as you discussed it in your book *Spaccio de la bestia trionfante?* For example, regarding the character Orion, whom we take to represent allegorically the life on earth of our Lord Jesus Christ, you write: 'Now what do we wish to do with this man inserted into a beast, or this beast imprisoned in a man, in which one person is made of two natures and two substances concur in one hypostatic union? Here two things come into union to make a third entity; and of this there is no doubt whatsoever. But the difficulty lies in this, namely, in deciding whether such a third entity produces something better than the one and the other, or better than one of the two parts, or truly something baser.' What you imply with this is a refutation of Catholicism, perhaps of Christianity itself. Is that not so?"

"Eminence! Eminence! It is not so that I refuted Catholicism, I swear my oath it is not so! I doubted, yes, I have said so, I doubted. It is an opinion I have held since I was eighteen years old up until now. But it is not something I denied, or taught, or wrote, just something I doubted. Let me try to explain, as I did in Venice and have done again in my statements to the Holy Office since coming to Rome as your guest.

"I understand three attributes: power, knowledge, and goodness ...or really, the intellect and love with which things have to be first reasoned in the mind, then the intellect. Thirdly, there must be harmony and symmetry because of love. No thing can be without this essence. Just as nothing can be beautiful without present beauty, so in divine presence nothing can be immune, and so by way of reason and not by way of substantial truth, I intend the distinction in the Divinity.

"Insofar as it pertains to faith — I am not speaking philosophically — we come to, on an individual basis having to do with divine persons, a knowledge that son or offspring of the Mind, called by the philosophers 'The Intellect' and by theologians 'The Word,' which it is to be believed became flesh. I, having the terms of a philosopher, did not intend that but doubted that, and with inconstant faith held that.

"Therefore, as far as the Divine Spirit, the Third Person, I cannot believe according to the way I am supposed to believe, but according to a Pythagorean way, it conforms to the way shown by Solomon. . . . 'Spiritus Domini replevit orbem terrarum, et hoc quod continet omnia . . . The Spirit of the Lord filled the earth and all that it contains.' Also, in the sixth book of the Aeneid, Virgil writes: 'In the beginning the spirit sustains from within the heaven and the earth and the waters, the shining orb of the moon and the titanic stars; and a soul infused through the members sways the massive structure.

"So, accordingly, the Divine Spirit is the Soul of the Universe and gives life to it. So speaking Christianly, I in effect doubted the name of the Son and the Holy Spirit, and I did not intend these two to be distinct from the Father. Assigning intellect that the Father gave the Son and the love for the Holy Spirit without knowing the name of this person was grasped by St. Augustine, and declared not an old name but a new one.

"Now, I held everything that every faithful Christian was to believe having to do with the First Person. As far as the Second Person is concerned, I held that it is in essence one with the First and the Third, because all the attributes that converge on the Father converge on the Son and the Holy Spirit. But I doubted how the Second Person could be incarnate, and how he had suffered, but I have never denied, or taught, or said anything of the Second Person. I referred to opinions of others like Ario and Sabelio. As far as my own beliefs, I doubted within myself how the Word can become flesh.

"So, Your Eminence, I hold firm that I believe in one God, distinct in the Father and the Word and the love that is the Divine Spirit... and all three are God in essence... but I doubted that these can have the name of persons because it does not seem that these names come together in divinity. And St. Augustine comforts me in this. I see that the divinity of the Word assists the humanity of Christ individually, but I could not believe that there was a union that has similarity of soul and body. Still, it could be said that this man was God and that this God was man, the reason being that between the infinite and divine substance and the finite and human, there is no equation, as between the soul and the body. That is why St. Augustine feared that name of the person... I don't remember in what place St. Augustine said it.

"I have said before that I doubted the divine incarnation, but I have been misunderstood. I will try again. To be a divinity is to be naturally infinite. Humanity is finite. It did not seem proportionate to me that humanity could be joined to divinity. It seems, as Abbott Girachino said, unworthy to link up a finite thing with an infinite thing. I have been told that it follows from this explanation that Christ was a human personality. I know that. I did not offer this explanation in order to defend it, but only to explain myself and to confess my error. I may have erred in principles but not in conclusions.

"As to the way divine nature and human nature were in union, I was ignorant and doubtful. The doubt came that there were three persons in the Holy Trinity, and that these three persons were eternal. Humanity is temporal. God became man in a way that is incomprehensible."

"Padre, that you have had difficulty comprehending the mystery of the Trinity is understandable, for this glorious union is indeed unfathomable to the human mind. But it was a grave sin for a religious under vows to teach that what is incomprehensible is unbelievable. The existence of the Trinity is a revealed truth in Christ and is, as St. Augustine has demonstrated, the source of great insight into the true nature of man.

"I am unfamiliar with any doubt by St. Augustine regarding this union of divine substance and human. His faith, indeed, was inspired and unchangeable. Your reference to St. Augustine's reluctance to name the person comes, I believe, from The Epistle, but you have mistaken his veneration for fear: 'There is One invisible, from whom as the Creator and prime cause all things seen by us derive their being; and He is supreme, eternal, immutable, and comprehensible by none save Himself alone. There is One by whom the supreme Majesty reveals and proclaims Himself, namely, the Word, not inferior to Him by whom it is begotten and revealed. There is One who is Holiness, the sanctifier of all that becomes holy, who is the inseparable and undivided communion between this immutable Word through whom that Prime Cause is revealed and that Prime Cause which reveals Himself by the Word which is His equal. But who is able with perfectly calm and pure mind to contemplate this whole essence — whom I have attempted to describe without naming, instead of naming without describing — and to draw blessedness from that contemplation, and losing himself in such contemplation to become, as it were, oblivious of self, and to press on to that of which the sight is beyond our perception, in other words, to be clothed with immortality and obtain eternal salvation?'

"To doubt may be understandable, but not to disbelieve and to teach disbelief. The Trinity is the foundation of the Catholic faith. Unless a man believe it faithfully, he cannot be saved. You are aware of that, I am sure, from your studies of the Creed of St. Athanasius: 'He therefore that will be saved must think of the Trinity. Furthermore, it is necessary to everlasting salvation that he also believe rightly in the Incarnation of our Lord Jesus Christ. For the right faith is, that we believe and confess, that our Lord Jesus Christ, the Son of God, is God and Man: God, of the Substance of the Father, begotten before the worlds: and Man, of the Substance of His mother, born in the world: Perfect God and perfect Man: of a reasonable soul and human flesh subsisting: equal to the Father, as touching His Godhead, and inferior to the Father, as touching His Manhood. Who although he be God and Man, yet He is not two, but one Christ: One, not by conversion of the Godhead into flesh, but by taking of the Manhood into God. One altogether is Jesus Christ, not by confusion of Substance, but by unity of Person. For as the reasonable soul and flesh is one man, so God and Man is one Christ.'"

(To battle rhetoric with reason is fruitless. There can be only one winner here...the church. Concede! Concede! Lose a battle, win a war.) "Your Eminence, I have already confessed my error in doubting the Trinity. I do so again: I confess that I had doubts concerning the union of divinity and humanity, and I humbly beg forgiveness. But I make an oath that I never doubted the divinity of Christ, nor wavered in upholding the Catholic faith to the best of my ability."

"Confession heals a troubled soul. You are right to confess this error. Let us examine other of your beliefs and teachings in an effort to clarify your errors that you may avail yourself of God's understanding forgiveness and set yourself again on the path to eternal life.

"In the Fifth Dialogue of your book, *De l'infinito universo e mondi,* you write: 'It is then necessary to investigate whether there is beyond the heaven Space, Void, or Time. For there is a single general space, a single vast immensity which we may freely call Void; in it are innumerable globes like this on which we live and grow. This space we declare to be infinite; since neither reason, convenience, possibility, sense-perception nor nature assign to it a limit. In it are an infinity of worlds of the same kind as our own. For there is no reason nor defect of nature's gifts, either of active or of passive power, to hinder the existence of other worlds throughout space, which is identical in natural character with our own space.' On what do you base this hypothesis?"

"Your Eminence, I have been indebted to the work of Ptolemy, of Copernicus, and other diligent mathematicians who from time to time have added light on the subject with their principles and have finally brought me to this insight."

"We have already reminded you of St. Augustine's admonition that nothing is to be accepted save on the authority of Scripture. The Scripture is unequivocal: only God is infinite."

"But, Eminence, there are different forms of infiniteness. In the *Summa* St. Thomas says: 'There is no obstacle to the infinite intervening in God's handiwork, but it will always be a relative infinite; the infinite in an absolute sense is impossible.' Though I have said the universe is infinite, I have also said that God is infinite because He excludes all limit from Himself and because everything that can be attributed to Him is one and infinite. Indeed, God is totally infinite, for He is everywhere in the whole universe and in each of its parts, infinitely and totally.

"In this way I presuppose an infinite universe that is the work of an infinite Divine Power, because I consider it unworthy of the Divine Power and Goodness to produce only this world when it could have created infinitely many worlds similar to our earth, under which I understand, along with Pythagoras, a celestial body similar to the moon and other planets and stars. All these bodies are inhabited worlds, the immeasurable number of which, in the infinite space, forms an endless universe."

"And these are your thoughts, Padre?"

"These are my thoughts, Eminence."

"Aristotle has said that thought is only an accident on which one cannot base certainty. 'We can imagine a man of colossal size, but that is not a reason for his existence.'"

"I ask you, Eminence, why should the power of imagination not mirror reality? Because otherwise, imagination, which is natural, could exceed nature, which would not be possible. We put our faith too exclusively in tangible facts. Consider this, as Lucretius himself pondered: if the universe is finite, what lies beyond? Even Cusa believed that if the universe had in itself its beginning and its end, it would be bounded with respect to something else. Despite that we cannot perceive infinity with our senses, how can the universe be anything else but infinite? If the matter be well considered, sense establishes the infinite, since we see that an object is always contained by another object, whereas it never happens that we see or imagine an object that is not contained in another."

"You have told me, Padre, that in your efforts on this subject, you have drawn from the work not only of Ptolemy and other mathematicians, but also of Doctor Copernicus — whose heretical ideas, incidentally, were declared by no less than his publisher, Osiander of Nuremberg, to have been postulated by the author of *Revolutions of the Celestial Orbs* not as fact but merely as a hypothesis. In your books, you not only posit an infinite universe, but, in keeping with the Copernican heresy, you also subscribe to the belief that the earth is not the center of the world and is not immovable, and that the sun does not move.

And yet, it is well shown that were the earth to be in motion, a stone falling from a height would fall behind the point immediately below its starting point. Thus, the truth of Scripture and of the holy fathers is not to be denied: '...the world also is established, that it cannot be moved...' (Psalms 93:1); '...but the earth abideth forever...' (Ecclesiastes 1:4); '...The sun also ariseth, and the sun goeth down, and hasteth to his place where he arose...' (Ecclesiastes 1:5); '...And the sun stood still, and the moon stayed...' (Joshua 10:13); '...as the heaven is high above the earth...' (Psalm 103:11). These are but a few passages of Scripture that refute your ideas. What is your response?"

"Your Eminence is indeed a master of Scripture and of the teachings of the holy fathers. But with the greatest respect, Eminence, these teachings which would have the appearance of refutation may be interpreted otherwise. Didacus à Stunica in his *Commentary on Job* observed that there is scriptural authority to demonstrate the earth's motion. He refers, for example, to the following: '...Which shaketh the earth out of her place, and the pillars thereof tremble...' Job 9:6.

"But I would contend that rather than seek literal authority from Scripture, it would be better to view these scriptural references as allegorical. In the Ninth Article of Part One of the *Summa Theologica*, St. Thomas tells us that the use of metaphor in sacred doctrine is necessary and useful, for it is clear then that these references are not literal descriptions of divine truths. And in the Tenth Article of the *Summa*, St. Thomas explains that God is the author of Holy Scripture, and that he has the power to signify His meaning not only by words but also by things themselves.

"The movement of the earth and the immobility of the heaven, according to my reasoning and other authorities, do not prejudice the authority of Holy Scripture. I have shown in my work that the earth has motion, that it does not stand still for eternity, and that the sun does not rise and set. Eminence, the authorities of the church are saints and exemplary men, but they are not practical philosophers abreast of natural things." (Does he understand? Can I be more clear than that? Or can he not afford to understand? I simply must prevail!)

"*Padre,* the Holy Catholic Church has, since the days of the Apostles, built its foundation on Holy Scripture and the teachings of the church fathers. Indeed, that is the basis of Christian theology. For you to dismiss as metaphor the Word of God, and as ignorant the teachings of church authorities, is both contumacious and sacrilegious. But what you propose to offer in its place — infinite worlds, the transmigration of souls, distinction among the persons of God, doubting the humanity and divinity of Christ and the incarnation of the Word — is undeniably heretical."

"Eminence, you don't understand! You of all people I had hoped would understand my work, and you don't! Please, please, read my works . . . all of them . . . carefully and thoroughly, see that I have used allegory and satire merely as a means to arrive at the truth, know that I have not questioned the wisdom and the value of Holy Scripture and the teachings of the church fathers as the foundation of my own true Catholic faith, only that I have not taken Scripture literally, but rather have followed the teachings of St. Thomas. I have written as a philosopher, not as a theologian, but I have always believed and still believe all the teaching of Mother Church concerning the First Person. I am a good Christian and an errant Catholic, but mine has been the pursuit of truth, for truth is the path to Truth, and I have offered not substitutes for the teachings of Mother Church but merely alternative perceptions! Some aspire toward Truth by wandering, others by parabling, others by inquiring, others by opining, others by judging and determining, others by sufficing of natural magic, others by superstitious divination, others by means of negation, others by means of affirmation; others by way of composition, others by way of division; others by way of definition, others by way of demonstration; others by means of acquired principles, others by means of divine principles. Meanwhile, Truth cries out to them, nowhere present, nowhere absent, proposing to them before the eyes of sentiment, by means of writing, all natural things and effects, and intones in the ear of their inner mind, by means of conceived species of visible and invisible things. And so I have attempted to do, simply and sincerely. I have done my best to explain this to Your Eminence in a way that is understandable. If I have failed, blame not my faith but my ignorance." (I give up!)

"Padre, in the name of His Holiness the pope, and the whole Congregation of the Holy Office, I ask you now to relinquish altogether these opinions which we have stipulated, to not henceforth hold, teach, write about, or defend in any way whatsoever, verbally or in writing, these same opinions, and to confess your sins and recant your errors, to abjure and to mend your ways." (He has not listened to a word I have said! Never, never will I give in to these sanctimonious Vatican pedants! Let them do as they will!)

"Eminence, I have nothing to abjure. Hence, I have no reason to mend my ways."

"Then I will pray for your soul, Father, and I will pray to Holy God that He help you to find reason before it is too late."

✠

Father Cervini put down his notes with a sigh.

"The man is doomed," he said with great sadness. "I will never understand how a man can be so stubborn as to not see the eternal damnation to which he has consigned his soul. For what? For the satisfaction of defying Mother Church, when all it seeks is to extend its love to him, to clarify its truth, to *save* his soul for eternity? I too shall pray for him, as our master does, but frankly, Pietro, I think Satan may already have won him over. I know that my order teaches forgiveness, but sometimes I think some souls are beyond redemption."

I was not about to debate with Cervini, to tell him that maybe, just maybe, there are some things worth dying for, that maybe the freedom to think and to write as you please and not as the church pleases might be worth trading one's life for. Father Cervini was tired from his illness and exhausted from spending the better part of the day with me on these notes. It would hardly serve either of us to prolong a discussion. Better he should rest and I should work on a plan for saving the Nolan; for I still had no plan, and now more than ever, one was going to be needed. If Bruno held to the position he had taken with my master, that he had nothing to abjure and refused to recant, then Bruno's fate was sealed.

Timing is everything. The Nolan was in the right place at the wrong time, and he was going to burn for it...unless I could save him.

Chapter 25

15 novembre 1599
Campo Marzio
Roma

ROME IS A CITY of bell towers. In addition to those of the titular churches of the cardinals, great basilicas such as St. Peter's and St. John Lateran, there are 130 parish churches, 200 other churches, hospitals, and asylums, plus numerous monasteries and nunneries, all with bells to toll the hour. One hundred thousand Romans, or at least those of us who can count, have no problem knowing what hour it is. The bells of Rome never let you forget. It is a wonder more of us don't go deaf.

On the last stroke of nine, I approached the near side of Fabricio Bridge on the left bank of the Tiber. Maria was there already, waiting for me. No one else around that I could see. As far as I could tell, no one had followed me, though I had taken no special pains to evade anyone who might have. This was the same route I always took from the Vatican Palace in Leonine City to my favorite haunts in Campo Marzio. Nothing unusual in that. Still, it would seem peculiar to anyone observing us had we remained there for long on a dark and chilly night, so, arm in arm like lovers, we walked to the Boar's Head after all, talking quietly together along the way.

Maria had managed to learn almost everything I had requested. Based on the plan I had conceived, most of the information was now useless, but she didn't need to know that yet. Who gambled, who owed money, who cheated on his wife or slept with little boys, who we might be able to bribe or blackmail, none of that would be of much use. I had decided we could trust no one. The Inquisition looks cross-eyed at a man, he will betray his own mother; for those who won't, there are tortures enough to persuade a man to tell the tribunal anything they want to hear, even if it is untrue. The schedule, however, was more important, how many and where they were stationed, and Maria had that information as well.

Better yet, she slipped into my hand a crude sketch she had managed to make of the section of Castel Sant'Angelo in which the Nolan was held, with all of the entrances and exits marked and where each guard was stationed. The *guardia* was not part of the Swiss Guard stationed at the Vatican, but neither were they a part of the secular authority of Rome. They worked for the Vatican, and their job was to watch over the prisoners of Castel Sant'Angelo until they were released, or until they were convicted, sentenced, and turned over to the secular authority that would carry out the sentence. It was a boring and routine job.

Castel Sant'Angelo, originally built as the mausoleum of Hadrian, was connected to the pope's residence by a walled passage, and it contained vaults, rooms, dungeons, courtyards, ramparts, bastions, and fortifications. Whether these last were intended to keep Hadrian in or evildoers out, I don't know. But since 1569 when it began to be used by the Sant'Offizio to house heretics, no prisoner had escaped. With a record like that, the *guardia* would either be on its toes to make sure no one became the first to succeed, or it would be lulled into a false sense of security thinking no one would even dare try. My plan relied heavily on the latter condition.

We reached the Boar's Head and went inside. It was more crowded and noisy than usual. Lots of new faces. As the Great Jubilee of 1600 approached, all of Rome was getting more crowded and noisy; not just inns like Boar's Head and Three Coins, but the wine shops and taverns and dossing houses as well. Tourists and pilgrims were beginning to arrive in droves, clogging the streets, buying out the *pizzacaroli* and *botteghe,* the millers and the fruitsellers and the street vendors. Goods were getting scarce. The merchants loved it and the locals hated it, except there was more money around for everybody, so, despite the inconvenience, even the locals were in a joyful mood. Tonight was no exception.

We sat at a small table against the wall in the back and ordered some wine. Fearful of being overheard, we spoke guardedly. Maria kept an eye on one side of the room and I on the other. Two men came in soon after we sat down; one was small and skinny, eyes close together like a weasel; the other was almost as big as I am but fat in the belly. They found a table some distance from ours and sat with their heads together in deep conversation.

"Pietro," Maria whispered to me, "those two men over there...I've seen them before. They were at the Scortecchiara this morning when I was buying meat from a butcher."

"Could be a coincidence, could be not. I saw no one following us here. Besides, we are doing nothing out of the ordinary. We finish our wine and go upstairs, same as before. Don't stare at them. Keep your eyes on me," I told her.

But I was less confident than I let on. I was not so naive as to suppose that a meeting between the *maestro di casa* of an important cardinal inquisitor and the daughter of a lieutenant in the *guardia* at Castel Sant'Angelo could be above suspicion. On the other hand, I had been careful to speak of the Nolan to no one, and I trusted Maria enough now to believe that she had been no less careful than I. Santa Severina might have eyes and ears everywhere, but for me to be in Campo Marzio, where it was well known that I spent almost all of my free time, was neither unusual nor suspicious. If I wanted to bed with the daughter of a *tenente*, that was my business. Even if it was Santa Severina's business as well, I had done nothing wrong...yet, and he would have to wait until I did. Or, so I hoped. I was prepared to take the risk.

Upstairs and in our room, we continued our conversation in hushed tones. I questioned Maria regarding Bruno's daily routine...when did he eat, when did he sleep? And about Bruno himself...how tall was he, how did he look, what was his attitude and how were his spirits? She answered all of my questions, but plainly Maria was worried.

The Nolan had related to her something of his visit from my master, especially the part at the end where he refused to recant his ideas. What worried her was that he did not seem depressed about it. Instead, he appeared to be the opposite, elated, cheerful, as though some great weight had been removed from his shoulders. She said that when she pleaded with him to abjure, to throw himself on the mercy of the Holy Office, he had sneered at her, told her he was unafraid and that anyway his fate was none of her business.

As she was relating this to me, she glanced at the door and froze. She pointed to the door handle. It was turning slowly. The door was bolted, but it was a flimsy affair and would hold no one out who wanted in.

"Quick!" she whispered. "Take your clothes off and get into bed! Hurry!"

In an instant, she was out of her clothing and standing by the bed naked, a look of sheer panic on her face. Her breasts were magnificent! I could hardly take my eyes off them. Full as ripe melons, with great brown areolas, each with a beautifully formed nipple at the center. I stared, bewitched, even as I too hurried out of my clothes.

"Quickly!" she hissed. "Into the bed!"

We barely managed to cover ourselves with the blanket when the door burst open. It was the two men from downstairs. The larger of the two had put his shoulder to the door and easily forced it open, bolt and all.

I bellowed like an enraged bull and leapt out of bed.

"*Bastardo! Figlio di una cagna!*" I cursed, bellowing, rushing the two of them. I hit the big one hard in the gut, and he went down like a sack of flour. I picked the weasel up by his coat, held his face close to mine and screamed: "Who the hell are you and what are you doing in my room!"

"*Per carità!* Please, put me down!" he pleaded, his eyes wide with fear. "My friend here, he is *ubriaco fradicio*... dead drunk. I told him this was not our room! He wouldn't listen, the drunken fool. *Scusi, scusi!* I beg your pardon, Signore! Christ, I think you may have killed him."

"*Altro é parlar di morte, altro é morire*...it's one thing to speak of death and another to die," I growled, putting him down. "The next time I see either of you anywhere near me or her (I gestured to Maria with my head), it won't be my fist in your gut, it'll be my knife. Now, get this drunken tub of lard on his feet, and the two of you get out of my sight before I decide to do you in here and now."

"*Grazi, grazi,*" the Weasel murmured, looking down at his oversized companion who by now was beginning to come around. "How many times have I said you drink too much, you fool? Come on," he said to his friend, "let's get out of here. I told you this wasn't our room."

The two staggered out of the room, the big one still reeling from the blow to his fat gut and the Weasel nearly collapsing under the weight of his companion leaning on his shoulder. I slammed the door shut and turned with a grin, thinking *ecco,* as long as we have our clothes off, we may as well...

But Maria was already dressed again. Her face was still white as a ghost, but her eyes were fixed on my groin. Wrong time, wrong place, wrong circumstances, and yet, it's nice to look and nice to think about what might have been. No harm in that. A man does it often. I am uncertain, though, whether that is a shared experience. Is it just the man who lusts after the woman's body or does it work the other way around as well? Maria's look confirmed that at least that time it was mutual.

"I wouldn't want to be on the wrong side of you," she said, finally.

"I wouldn't mind being on the right side of you," I replied. But my mind was no longer on sex. I was not fooled by the act of the Weasel and his fat friend. They were spies, all right, probably for the Sant'Offizio. Well, they had learned two things. One, whether Maria and I were up to no good was still uncertain, but for sure we were lovers. They had seen us in bed together with no clothes on. And two, Guidotti was no one to cross. Next time they would be more wary of getting too close, I had made sure of that. As for me, I had learned what I already knew ... that saving the Nolan was very dangerous business.

This time, we left the room together. I promised Maria I would contact her again soon, and that the next time we met I would reveal my plan.

Chapter 26

23 dicembre 1599
Inn of Three Coins, Campo Marzio
Roma

TIME WAS GROWING SHORT. Not by most standards, of course, still the same number of hours and minutes to the day, days to the week, but by Holy Office standards the Bruno trial was speeding up.

The Nolan was first arrested in Venice on 22nd May 1592, he had been extradited to Rome and imprisoned in Castel Sant'Angelo on 27th February 1593...almost eight years...and in all that time, he probably was not seen by the authorities more than half a dozen times. All of a sudden, three times in one month.

Two days ago he had been visited at Castel Sant'Angelo by my master and other inquisitors, at which meeting the Nolan declared that he neither should nor would retract, that indeed there was nothing for him to retract. And right after that he was brought to the Hall of the Congregation, where he insisted that he had been misunderstood and proceeded to try to explain to them why the earth moves and why the universe is infinite, and how the stars are angels, animated rational bodies that praise God and the power and greatness of Him, and that he did not preach or write against transubstantiation but only had doubted that bread and wine actually turned into the flesh and blood of Christ, and that he never doubted the divinity of Christ, and that he had never preached or written that souls migrated from body to body, but only had said he thought it possible, and that he said all these things as a philosopher and not as a theologian...same things he had been saying all along. I heard all this from Father Cervini.

Bruno had gone on to announce to the members of the congregation that he had nothing to abjure and that from now on he would no longer debate the issues with them, but would address his defense directly to Pope Clement whose judgment he would accept. And with that he was removed from the hall.

"Ho l'impressione che gli manchi un venerdi!" was the way Cervini described his impression that the Nolan was a little on the nutty side. More than a little nutty, I would have said; that, or he had finally

made up his mind to defy the system and was now daring them to execute him.

After the Nolan was removed from the hall, the congregation decreed that the Reverend Father Hippolytus Maria, the general, and the Vicar Reverend Father Paul, of the Order of Preaching Fathers, to which Bruno belonged, should visit "Brother Jordanus" and show him the propositions to be abjured... (as if he didn't already know them by heart!) ... "that he might acknowledge his errors, reform, and dispose himself to recantation," and that they should prevail over him so that he could be liberated.

Father Cervini saw the decree as a further sign of the congregation's boundless compassion. I saw it as just another way for them to be able to sleep nights. It wasn't the Nolan they wanted to "liberate," it was themselves. We see things the way we want to see them.

The decree from the congregation was of particular interest to me, though, because it fit in neatly with my plan. Vicar Paul was my ticket to freeing the Nolan... you would have to see him to know why... he was exactly of my height and build.

✠

Ever since the night we met up with the Weasel and his fat friend, any lingering doubts I might have had about Maria were gone. I trusted her completely. It is not easy to explain, but something happened between us that night. I think we both felt it, though we never discussed it afterward. The brief stirring in my loins on seeing her naked body was a feeling I had had many times before with other women. Purely physical. Perhaps she had shared it, perhaps not. But what I felt toward her now was like nothing I had ever felt for a woman before. She was like a sister... no, like a friend, a close friend.

I never had a woman friend before, nor since. With Maria I felt neither lustful nor protective. I just felt that I could share with her whatever was on my mind, that she would understand and that I could count on her never to reveal to anyone what I had said. And I knew that I would do the same for her.

Had we actually been together as man and woman that night, had we used the room for its intended purpose, I do not think we would have ended up feeling the same way. I would have had doubts and she would have had guilt, and I don't think we would have trusted each other as we did now. We might have still used each other, but there would not have been the same trust. And what I was about to ask Maria to do would require all the trust each of us could muster.

What an unlikely triangle we made! Bruno and Maria, daughter of a lieutenant of the guards become the prison lover of her father's prisoner, an accused heretic. Maria and Guidotti, *maestro di casa* of a cardinal inquisitor, friend and conspirator with the lover of the very same heretic whom his master is prosecuting. And Guidotti and Bruno, the unlikeliest pairing of all, two complete strangers who had never even met, somehow drawn together by Fate to share the same woman in a plan for which each of us might yet die if we were caught. Who knows why our paths crossed. We are pawns in a chess game of the Furies.

✠

Maria was on time. She always was. We had our wine and went upstairs, as usual. Anyone watching would know our pattern by now, since we made no effort to hide it or to change it. They would know from the Weasel that we were lovers. They would also know to approach with caution. Best, then, for us to be open and obvious when we were together and could be observed, to act the part. On the other hand, now that we knew that they knew, we had to be that much more diligent not to be overheard, not to put anything in writing, not to confide in anyone other than each other, to remain above suspicion.

I revealed my plan to Maria at last. Her mouth tight with determination, she nodded her head from time to time but never questioned the plan in any way. If she was frightened — and she must have been, for hers was the most dangerous part — she never showed it. Just as the Nolan had made his decision, come what may, so apparently had Maria made hers. She never wavered.

"The pope has scheduled a convocation of the congregation for the 20th day of January, at which he will preside. It looks like this is the day Bruno will be brought before the whole congregation. From what Father Cervini has told me and you have confirmed, Bruno's mind is made up and he will not abjure. Probably wouldn't make any difference to the outcome even if he did. I think the pope has made his deal with Philip. They will pass sentence, set a date to turn Bruno over to the secular authorities, and he will be transferred to Nona Tower to await execution. That's the way it usually works when they decide to do it in public, and I am pretty sure that is what has been decided with the Nolan. Whatever we do has to happen before he is transferred to Nona Tower."

Maria was fighting back her tears. I paused, but she waved me on.

"Here is my plan," I continued, lowering my voice to a whisper.

"Reverend Father Paul is the Vicar of Giordano's Order of Preaching Fathers. He and the general of the order have been charged by the congregation with the task of getting the Nolan to recant, so they will be paying him regular visits at Castel Sant'Angelo. Father Paul is my height and build. The Nolan, on the other hand, is about your size, skinnier than you but we can fix that. You and I go in, with me dressed as Father Paul. Bruno and I come out, with him dressed in your clothes.

"We leave you tied up and gagged in his room. They won't discover you until the next morning. You will say you thought I was Father Paul, that by chance you encountered me when you entered the prison with Bruno's dinner as you do every evening — I had introduced myself to you once before, I'll come to that in a minute — that once in the room, we overpowered you, took your shoes and outer clothes, and made our escape. You did not get a good look at me, it was dark, you don't think you could recognize me if you saw me again. If anyone suggests that it was me, Guidotti, you say don't be ridiculous, we are lovers and you would have known me in an instant. They will have to believe you. I am not the only big man in Rome. Maybe they will even be so glad to have Bruno off their hands, they will just let it go without a fuss."

I am not sure I even believed that myself. I would have to figure a way to be above suspicion somehow. Maybe work with Cervini until he fell asleep, then do the deed, return, wake him up so he could see that I was still with him, make him believe he had only dozed off briefly. I had not worked that out yet, but I would. Bruno's escape route from Rome was something else I had not worked out. I figured he would know, since he had managed it once before. I would have a boat and provisions ready if he wanted to use the Tiber, a horse if he wanted to escape overland. More than that I could not do without leaving Rome forever, and I had already decided I was unwilling to do that.

"Couple of question marks. I need to have a sense of how long this will all take. And I want to make sure it can work. So I think we need to make a dry run. That's what I meant when I said you had met the Vicar once before, this would be the time. We will meet at the entrance to Castel Sant'Angelo just after dark tomorrow night, as though by accident. That's an hour before the day shift is relieved. It's a slow time. It is also Christmas Eve. They will be tired and thinking of festivities and, I hope, more lax than usual. With any luck, we will have no trouble. Wear a cloak with a hood, do you have one?"

She nodded.

"Look, Maria, this dry run could be even more dangerous for you than the actual escape, because you will be going in and out with me instead of being left tied up. If we are caught, it means big trouble. But we can say that I begged you to get me in so I could meet the Nolan, and you agreed to help. I think your father would believe you and stand behind you, and I am certain my master would believe that I would take such a risk to at last meet the man he had me travel all over Europe to find out about. He would be angry with me, certainly, but I doubt he would let them do anything big to me. It is a chance we have to take. Plus, I think it is better the Nolan knows what is coming, so he can be ready. If you want out of this, now is the time to tell me."

She shook her head. "I am prepared to do anything for him, Pietro, even to lose him. I could not bear to see him burned at the stake."

"Then pray for us all," I said, standing up, "and I will see you at the front gate of Castel Sant'Angelo tomorrow night."

✠

It was a foolish plan, full of hidden traps and what-ifs. I realized that afterward. Too many things could go wrong, both during and after. But at the time, it was all I could think of, and both Maria and I were driven by the same uncontrollable desire to see the Nolan free of the awful cloud he had lived under for almost eight years' of prison. He may have been offensive and rude and disagreeable, he may have had a big mouth and stepped on too many toes, but the only person he had actually harmed was himself and he did not deserve to die for it.

Bruno would die someday, we all do, but ... *La Morte ci ha da trovar vivi* ... Death must find us alive. With Maria's help, I would get Giordano Bruno out of at least this particular trouble alive. After that, he would be on his own.

Chapter 27

24 dicembre 1599
Castel Sant'Angelo
Roma

ROME LOVES A PARTY. Why not? Life for most people is one long hard struggle, to earn a living, to survive sickness and disease, to stay fed and warm and dry, just to exist. One relishes every opportunity to escape from the struggle, if only for a little while. Church is one way. It offers a chance to enjoy beauty and magnificence and pageantry, to forget for an hour or two the ugliness of reality. Except, *mano di ferro in guanto di velluto*... the church has an iron hand in a velvet glove. As payment for the privilege of enjoying all that splendor, you have to confess your sins and earn forgiveness, so there are guilt and tithe and Hail Marys to suffer in exchange. Parties exact nothing in return.

Rome was full of parties this night. Christmas Eve and a Great Jubilee combined. Great feasts, dances, theatrical entertainments. The streets were jammed with celebrants, all headed somewhere on foot, on horse, and in coaches. Party-goers mixed with the swelling population of tourists and pilgrims. Churches would be overflowing for Christmas Eve mass. The spirit of Christ was in the air.

It would be this way all week. People actually looked happy for a change, joyful, greeted each other with smiles and slapped each other on the back as they passed, as though they really did love their fellow man after all. I was counting on that spirit to reach the guards at Castel Sant'Angelo. I wanted them good and relaxed for my visit as "Father Paul" of the Order of Preaching Fathers.

I left the Vatican dressed as Guidotti, circling around the Pantheon, past Sta. Maria sopra Minerva and Palazzo Venezia so that I could approach Sant'Angelo from a different direction than Maria, who would be approaching from the south from Campo Marzio. Along the way, I ducked into the hiding place where I had left clothing to wear as Father Paul, slipped into the habit that included an outer hooded cloak that I hoped would conceal most of my face, hid my own clothes, and proceeded back toward Sant'Angelo, praying that I would not come across someone who knew me... either one of me.

As I drew closer to the main gate of the prison, I could see Maria approaching from the other direction. We timed our approach so as to arrive together, pretending to bump into each other as we reached the front of the gate. Pausing, I introduced myself to her and she to me. Then we turned toward the guard at the Gate.

"Hello, Marco, Merry Christmas!" Maria said to the guard.

"'Evening, Maria, same to you. Who's this?" he asked, his eyes on me.

"We've just met, as a matter of fact. This is the Reverend Father Paul, vicar of the Nolano's Order of Preaching Fathers, here to see the prisoner. Oh, by the way, Marco, is my father inside?" she asked in an attempt to distract the guard's attention away from me.

"Ah, yes, Father Paul. You were here day before yesterday, weren't you? Well, Merry Christmas, *Padre*. What's that, Maria? Oh, yes, your father... no, Tenente Riotti has not arrived yet. Shall I tell him when he gets here that you want to see him? I can..."

"No, no need, Marco, thank you. I will see him later on my way out. You'll be gone by then, I suppose, out celebrating, if I know you? Don't forget to go to church tonight!" she threw over her shoulder as the two of us passed inside.

"Before or after?" he called to Maria, laughing loudly, the laugh trailing off abruptly as he realized that maybe it was not the best idea to joke about church on Christmas Eve with a Vicar of the Preaching Fathers nearby.

Good. I had said nothing to the guard, merely nodded. No voice for him to recognize later. He would remember a big friar entering with Maria, same as we would do the next time, and he could describe witnessing our accidental meeting in front of the Gate.

Inside, all was quiet, gloomy, and foreboding. Our footsteps echoed as we proceeded through the dark and empty halls. The lighting was poor. I was surprised to see so few guards, only two so far in addition to the one at the main gate. We did not pass either of these, since we turned down a hall before reaching the one and descended a stairway to the next lower level before passing the other, though Maria called out a hello to each and they waved back. The way was familiar, since I had memorized Maria's sketch. So far, no surprises.

I have to admit, prison gave me a queasy feeling. I had never been inside one before, much less inside a prison of the dreaded Inquisition. With any luck, most of us go through life without ever having to be at the wrong end of the authorities, our largely insignificant misdeeds undetected. But cross them, however innocently, and it's a different story. The thought of being confined in a prison, locked away in a cell for years, perhaps being tortured or dying there, is enough to make one's skin crawl. I made a solemn vow then and there...to whoever might be listening to my thoughts...that if I got out of this risky venture in one piece, I would never do anything again that could land me in prison.

On the other hand, I have to also admit that even though my skin was crawling at the idea of being in this place, my heart was pumping with excitement. I had not had such adventure since my trip to Europe and England! Not that I had forgotten having been caught and having come close on at least one occasion to torture and death; but to be honest, one remembers more clearly the exhilaration of the chase than the pain of capture. I was not unaware of the consequences were we to be discovered in this plot, but the thrill of doing it overshadowed reason.

It was, of course, the thrill of an amateur. A professional like Nicco Baroniti would have spotted the holes in my plan in a minute and would have had no part of it. I realize that now, with hindsight. I didn't at the time. Maria and I were wandering into the lion's den as though I knew what we were doing. But Guidotti the experienced spy was in actuality a lucky amateur. In this business, you could not afford to trust in luck. I should have learned that from Nicco.

"This is his room," Maria whispered to me as she stopped in front of a closed door. She glanced quickly down the hall. There was a guard slumped in a chair at the end of the hall, dozing. Probably he had been there for ten or eleven hours. Besides, down here how would you know whether it was day or night?

"Do you know him?" I asked, indicating the guard.

"His name is Paolo."

"Yell to him. Wish him Merry Christmas. Let him see us entering the Nolan's room. Better he sees us for the first time going in than going out."

"Merry Christmas, Paolo!" Maria shouted down the hall.

The guard's head came up with a jerk. Then he recognized her and waved.

"Who's that with you?" he asked.

"Father Paul from the Preaching Fathers, here to see the prisoner while I give him his dinner," she answered casually.

We held our breath.

"*Bene.* Merry Christmas, *Padre.* Did you bring me anything to eat, Maria? I'm starved."

"Next time, Paolo. I promise."

"Only kidding, Maria. The wife will have a big meal ready when

I get home tonight. Wouldn't want to spoil my appetite, or she'd hit me over the head with a pot." He laughed and settled back down for the last hour of his shift.

Maria opened the door and we entered the room. No key. That surprised me. This place seemed more lax than I had expected. Oh well, the better for us.

✠

He did not notice us at first. He was at the far side of the room, working at a table cluttered with books and papers.

There was a candle on the table to light his work, two more in wall sconces that barely gave light to the rest of the room. No windows. Scant furnishings. A cot against one wall with a small table next to it. Two hard wooden chairs. And a wooden box on the floor at the foot of the bed, which I took to hold extra clothing and whatever personal belongings he was permitted to have. That was all, save a small crucifix on the wall just inside the door. Considering who owned the place, I imagine there was one inside every door, and woe betide him who would attempt to remove it. The room was small but ample. I think I would have gone crazy in it within a week.

He looked up and caught sight of Maria first. He rose slowly from his chair.

"Maria!" he said with a tired smile. "Is it that time already?" He started to approach. Then he paused, straining to see me, the smile replaced by an expression that was impossible to read. "Father Paul, are you here again? . . . No . . . you are not Father Paul. Who this time? I said that I would speak with no one further on these matters, only with His Holiness."

He had stopped in the middle of the room, hands on his hips. The expression on his face changing again, this time to reflect the annoyance that was in his voice. For the moment, he ignored Maria standing next to me with his food. His eyes bore steadily into mine. Where they had been dull before, now they had fire in them.

He was a small man, my master's height but thinner. His hair was unkempt, wild, his beard untrimmed, his habit shabby, his sandals worn. His fingernails and toenails were long, and I remember thinking that so many of the little things we take for granted on the outside must be difficult to manage in prison. Almost eight years in this room. *Poveraccio!*

I had never seen the Nolan before, nor had I ever seen his likeness, and yet when I saw him there in that room, he was as familiar to me as a member of my own family. I knew so much about him that I knew *him*. I think I would have been able to pick him out in a crowd. I, on the other hand, was a total stranger to him.

"Who are you and what do you want?" he repeated, raising his voice. He was clearly growing agitated.

Maria interceded.

"Mi amore, this is Pietro. He is a friend. He has come to help you."

"I need no help," he said, abruptly.

It was an awkward moment. The three of us stood there in the middle of this dark prison room, the Nolan glaring at me with his hands on his hips, Maria with a huge basket of food in the hands and love written on her face, me towering over the two of them and wondering what to say to this man who had been so much of my life for the past three years without his even knowing it. Finally, I remembered where we were and what we were about. This was no time for social niceties. I walked to the two chairs, sat down in one and gestured him to the other.

"Sit down, Giordano. I have a lot to say and not much time to say it. My life is on the line here and so is Maria's. If you want to get out of this place in one piece, I will do the talking and you will do the listening. Sit down *now,* Giordano."

Maria put her basket down on the floor, and, taking the Nolan by the elbow, she steered him to the chair and gently pushed him down. Then she took up a position next to the door, listening, in case the guard should take it upon himself to investigate. For the next twenty minutes, in a low voice, our faces nearly touching, I told Bruno everything. Who I was, where my master had sent me and who I had spoken with, what I knew about the disposition of his case and its almost certain outcome, how Maria and I had met the first time and the many times after that, and finally, I told him my plan for his escape.

At first he was overwhelmed. It was indeed *una storia fantastica...* an unbelievable story. His old friend Father Anselmi at San Dominico Maggiore, Silvia Gandini, Professor Antoine de la Faye, duc d'Épernon, Guillaume Cotin the librarian of the Abbey St. Victor, John Florio... John Florio!... Ralegh, Gwinne, Gilbert, Gentili, Dee, Fulke Greville, even Elizabeth Regina!... and the name that Bruno despised as he had despised no one in his life... Zuane Mocenigo (he actually hissed at the mention of the name). It was as though his life were being recounted to him by his own shadow! No wonder he was overwhelmed.

But more amazing still to the Nolan was who was recounting all this to him. The *maestro di casa* of Robert Bellarmine, the most renowned Catholic scholar of our time, a cardinal, a grand inquisitor, the very same cardinal whom he now knew to be his mortal enemy charged, in all but name only, with deciding the fate of the Nolano...a *servant* of Robert Cardinal Bellarmine, here to lead his escape from Castel Sant'Angelo, the Inquisition, and Rome forever? This was too much to digest!

But digest it he must. I emphasized that all of our lives were in danger here, not just his. There was not much time, and he must be ready. I reviewed the plan once again. Maria was putting up a brave front. I knew what his escape would mean for her, not only the risk of discovery as a conspirator but the loss of her beloved, probably forever. That she was ready to make this sacrifice to save him no doubt eluded the Nolan, for I was certain his feelings for her were far different than hers for him. Maria was probably the last thing he was thinking about at this moment.

"I need to think," he said quietly. He rose and began to pace the floor.

"There is no time, *mi amore*," Maria whispered pleadingly from her position at the door. "Please, Giordano, you must let us help you escape."

He flashed her an annoyed look.

"I do my own thinking," was his impatient response. Eight years of prison had apparently had little effect on his disposition. He was still as loveable as ever.

He turned to me.

"My decision is no," he said flatly.

"No? What do you mean, no?"

"No means no. No means not yes. To escape would be to capitulate to these pedants, to admit that they are in control. They are not in control of the Nolano's mind; *he* is in control!

"You and Maria have been very brave, but, I must tell you, you and your plan are unnecessary. Even now I am drafting a memorial to His Holiness Pope Clement, in which I summarize my work and explain all of my theories. He will understand, only he, how the Nolano has been misunderstood. You will see. Soon the Nolano will be released from this hell hole. His Holiness himself will appoint the Nolano as his chief philosopher and scientific advisor. Do you understand the significance of such an appointment?

"Francesco Patrizi was brought back to Rome and given a chair in philosophy at the university by His Holiness shortly after he became pope. If Patrizi, a philosopher who believed absolutely nothing save an infinite universe and who once urged Pope Gregory to have the Hermetic philosophy taught in schools rather than relying on ecclesiastical censures and force of arms...if 'il Patritio' was understood by His Holiness, then surely the Nolano will be. And he will be even more greatly honored. So you see, all of your efforts have been unnecessary."

The man was cracked. Crazy in his head. So many years in this one room had destroyed his sense of reality. The pope would honor him with an appointment as chief philosopher and scientific advisor? Complete madness! He had not listened to a word I had said about the deal between the pope and King Philip, about the 'favor' Santa Severina and the pope had asked of my master, about Clement's hardness toward heretics.

"Suppose you are wrong, Giordano? Suppose His Holiness fails to understand your memorial, or more likely does not even read it? What then? Have you considered what they will do to you? They will cut off your head with an ax, or, worse yet, they will tie you to a stake and burn you alive. Think about that and tell me we are unnecessary!"

I thought to shake him, to force some sense into him. He was too much like my own master, living in a world of his imagination, a world as he wanted it, not the real world.

"Do you take me for an absolute fool?" he said softly. "I have had almost eight years to think about it. I pleaded with them, begged them, apologized, tried to make them understand that I am no heretic ...they do not listen. This has been going on now for a long time, a very long time...(he sighed deeply)...and I am tired, tired of their narrowness and their pedantry. You were in England. You were in France. You were in Geneva. You must have seen it. It is the same everywhere. I had thought that Henri Navarre might find a way to unify them, bring them out of their darkness. No use. They are not ready. They are blinded by their intractable beliefs and by their desperate need to cling to their power. Where there is fear of change, fear of losing power, fear of new ideas...there can be no justice.

"I am through groveling. My ideas are sound, my motives are pure, and I am right! Lord God knows this and understands. He will forgive me for my errors and reward me for my work. Someday all the world will know and understand. If the church is not ready yet...I am. What more can they do? Take my life? They already have."

Maria looked first at him, then at me. Her eyes pleaded with me to convince him. But I could see there was no point. I had seen that same look on the face of the man I had served for most of my adult life. Though one was a Dominican and the other a Jesuit, one was a powerless friar and the other a powerful cardinal, they were almost mirror images of each other. Brilliant, obstinate, pigheaded stubborn. Once their minds were made up, there was no changing them. I shrugged to Maria. It was useless to argue further with the Nolan.

"You must leave and never return...either of you," he warned, as if reading my mind. "I have much to do before I finish my memorial to His Holiness. I can ill afford the added distraction of your endangerment. I would not have attempted escape in any event. They will not have the satisfaction of thinking they were right all along. Someone must stand up to them, must insist on the freedom to explore new ideas, new ways of thinking. Whatever happens, they must be forced to make the decision as to what happens to me and to live with it in history. Maria, you have been a good friend. I am sorry it ends this way, but it could have ended no other way. We both knew that from the start. Be content that we had what we had. Now leave. The Nolano has work to do."

He turned and walked back to his table, sat down, and began writing almost immediately. No goodbyes. No kiss for Maria. No thank yous. Not even a backward glance. Looking at Bruno now, hunched over his work at the table, papers strewn everywhere, a stack of books nearby, little pieces of paper sticking out to mark important passages, I could almost imagine that it was my master sitting there.

A man with such limited time must decide for himself how to spend it. We were in his way. There was nothing left for us to do but leave.

✠

Our exit from Castel Sant'Angelo was, thankfully, uneventful. We walked away, side by side, until we came to where the road forked. We looked at each other long and hard. Tears streamed down Maria's face. To tell the truth, my own eyes were moist. But there was nothing either of us could say. We stood silently for a moment or two, and then parted. I never saw Maria Riotti again.

✠

Numbly, I retraced my earlier steps, changed back into my own clothes, and once again hid those I had worn as Father Paul. I felt somehow...empty. The load I had been carrying for so long, for three years, since my master had sent me abroad on a mission to learn all I could about the Nolan, a load, I grant you, that was self-imposed, was gone. Much had happened to me in those three years, yet the load had never left me for one minute. If anything, it had grown even heavier. It had been as constant in my life as the day and the night. And now it was gone, and I was empty.

Part of me was vastly relieved, of course. Deep down, I suppose I had known all along how foolhardy my plan to free Bruno had been. Now, instead of freeing him, Bruno had freed me. I would no longer have to endure the risk of being caught, the dishonor of betraying my master, perhaps my own imprisonment or death.

But another part of me was already beginning to experience that awful feeling of dread that creeps in like a lengthening shadow with the certain knowledge of doom. To know an ending before it arrives, and to know that it is a bad ending coming, somehow that only serves to increase the tension rather than to relieve it. The taste of metal in the mouth, the sense of evil lurking just behind you, night sweats from bad dreams. I would have preferred the load.

Only much later did I begin to understand the full glory of the decision the Nolan had made this night.

*C*hapter 28

17 febbraio 1600
Campo di Fiori
Roma

SOME SAY THAT WHAT HAPPENS in the end was intended all along; others, that each of us has the ability to make changes and so there are many possible endings. The church says that both exist, predetermination and free will, but that even though we may exercise our free will to change what was predetermined...that, too, is predetermined.

My own belief is that there is neither predetermination nor free will. Everything happens at random. We are as leaves blown in the wind, merely deluding ourselves that we have the power to set our own direction. It is the events that shape us and not we them. Afterward we contrive reasons and explanations, but only afterward. That provides us the illusion of purpose. "God's will be done" sustains the illusion. I have a hard time believing God gives a damn.

How otherwise to explain what happened nearly twenty-two years ago at Campo di Fiori, the Field of Flowers? What purpose was served? What good was accomplished? What lesson was learned that was not already known? What example was shown? If life is sacred, how can the taking of life be anything but sacrilegious? And how can the taking of life in God's name not be the worst sacrilege of all?

Oh, the horror.

Not for the dead. The dead die and the pain passes. A minute, an hour, a day, a week, a month...an eye blink...and it's over. Not for the living, either. Because it is too easy for the living to find the right words. No, for all humanity. To have been given the opportunity and to have thrown it away. To repeat the same mistake and never to learn. That is the horror.

On 20th January, the Nolan's memorial to Pope Clement was opened but not read. Reverend Father Hippolytus Maria and Reverend Father Paul reported to the Sant'Offizio that Bruno would not recant, that regarding his teachings or writings he would not abide by the decision of theologians but only by the decision of the pope. At that point, Pope Clement decreed that the cause should be carried to "extreme measures, *servatus severandis,* sentence should be pronounced, and the said Brother Jordanus de Nola be committed to the secular court."

On 8th February, Bruno was summoned again before the Inquisition, and the indictment was read:

... On 4th February 1599, a year ago, it was determined that the eight heretical propositions should once more be presented to thee, and this was done on the 15th; that, shouldst thou recognize them as heretical and abjure them, then thou wouldst be received for penitence; but, if not, then shouldst thou be condemned on the fortieth day from then for repentance; and thou didst declare thyself ready to recognize these eight propositions as heretical and to detest and abjure them in such place and time as might please the Holy Office, and not only these eight propositions, but thou didst declare thyself ready to make thine obedience concerning the others which were shown to thee. But then, since thou didst present further writings to the Holy Office addressed to His Holiness and to Us, whereby it was manifest that thou didst pertinaciously adhere to thine aforesaid errors; and information having been received that at the Holy Office of Vercelli thou hadst been denounced because in England thou wast esteemed an atheist and didst compose a work about a Triumphant Beast, therefore on the 10th September, 1599, thou wast given forty days in which to repent, and it was determined that at the end of these days, proceedings should be taken against thee as is ordained and commanded by the holy Canon law; and since thou didst nevertheless remain obstinate and impenitent in thine aforesaid errors and heresies, there were sent unto thee the Reverend Father Hippolytus Maria Beccaria, General of thine Order, and Father Paul Isaresio della Mirandola, Procurator of the Order, that they might admonish and persuade thee to recognize thy most grave errors and heresies. But thou hast ever persisted with obstinate pertinacity in these thine erroneous and heretical opinions. Wherefore, the accusation brought against thee has been examined and considered with the confessions of thy pertinacious and obstinate errors and heresies, even while thou didst deny them to be such, and all else was observed and considered; thy case was brought before our general congregation held in the presence of His Holiness on 20th January last, and after voting and resolution decided on the following sentence.

Having invoked the name of Our Lord Jesus Christ and of his most Glorious Mother Mary ever Virgin in the cause and afore-

said causes brought before this Holy Office between on the one hand
the Reverend Giulio Monterenzii, doctor of laws, Procurator Fiscal
of the said Holy Office, and on the other hand thyself, the afore-
said Giordano Bruno, the accused, examined, brought to trial and
found guilty, impenitent, obstinate, and pertinacious; in this our final
sentence determined by the counsel and opinion of our advisers the
reverend fathers, masters in sacred theology and doctors in both laws,
our advisers: We hereby, in these documents, publish, announce, pro-
nounce, sentence, and declare thee, the aforesaid Giordano Bruno, to
be an impenitent and pertinacious heretic, and therefore to have in-
curred all the ecclesiastical censures and pains of the Holy Canon, the
laws and the constitutions, both general and particular, imposed on
such confessed impenitent pertinacious and obstinate heretics. Where-
fore as such we verbally degrade thee and declare that thou must
be degraded, and we hereby ordain and command that thou shalt
be actually degraded from all thine ecclesiastical orders both major
and minor in which thou hast been ordained, according to the sa-
cred canon law; and that thou must be driven forth, and we do
drive thee forth from our ecclesiastical forum and from our holy and
immaculate church of whose mercy thou art become unworthy. And
we ordain and command that thou must be delivered to the secular
court — wherefore we hereby deliver thee to the court of the gover-
nor of Rome here present — that thou mayest be punished with the
punishment deserved, though we earnestly pray that he will mitigate
the rigor of the laws concerning the pains to thy person, that thou
mayest not be in danger of death or of mutilation of thy members.
Furthermore, we condemn, we reprobate, and we prohibit all thine
aforesaid and thy other books and writings as heretical and erro-
neous, containing many heresies and errors, and we ordain that all
of them which have come or may in future come into the hands of
the Holy Office shall be publicly destroyed and burned in the square
of St. Peter before the steps and that they shall be placed upon the
Index of Forbidden Books, and as we have commanded, so shall it be
done. And thus we say, pronounce, sentence, declare, degrade, com-
mand and ordain, we chase forth and we deliver and we pray in this
and in every other better method and form that we reasonably can
and should.

Thus pronounce we, the undermentioned Cardinal General In-
quisitors:

Ludovicus Cardinalis Madrutius
Jul. Ant. Cardinalis Santa Severina
P. Cardinalis Deza
D. Cardinalis Pinellus
F. Hieronymus Cardinalis Asculanus
L. Cardinalis Saxus
C. Cardinalis Burghesius
P. Cardinalis Arigonius
Rob. Cardinalis Bellarminus

The above sentence made and given by the aforesaid most Illustrious and Reverend Lord Cardinals, General Inquisitors, sitting in Rome as a tribunal in the General Congregation of the Holy Roman and Universal Inquisition in the presence of the aforesaid Illustrious and Reverend Cardinal Madrutius in the Church of St. Agnes in Agony, in the year of the Nativity of our Lord Jesus Christ 1600, on the 8th day of February, having been recited yesterday to the aforementioned Giordano Bruno, who was brought by one of the police of His Holiness our Lord the Pope in order to hear the aforementioned sentence.

On the day after it had been signed, the aforesaid brother Jordanus having been summoned by the aforesaid most Illustrious and Reverend Lord Cardinals of the General Inquisition and having been brought forth from the said prisons of the Holy Inquisition and removed to the palace which is the usual residence of the aforesaid most Illustrious and Reverend Cardinal Madrutius and having been brought into the hall of the aforesaid Congregation into the presence of the said most Illustrious and Reverend Cardinals, then in his presence and while he did listen, the said sentence was by their order promulgated and read by me the notary hereaftermentioned, in a loud and clear voice, the doors of the hall of the said Congregation being open, there being present the most Reverend Father Benedictus Manninus, Bishop of Caserta, the most Reverend Father Petras Millinus of Rome I.U.D. and Referendario of each of the Signatures of His Holiness Our Lord the Pope and the Reverend Father Franciscus Petrasancta de Ripalta of the Order of the Preaching Fathers, prelates and counsellors of the said Holy Inquisition, several other persons being present as witnesses.

Flaminio Adriano, Notary
Sacred Roman and Universal Inquisition

Father Cervini said that Bruno was on his knees before the tribunal for the entire reading of the sentence. At the finish, he was defrocked, his habit ripped from his body. But, far from what one might expect after hearing so fearsome a sentence passed upon him, the Nolan was unbowed. He rose to his feet, looked straight at the tribunal, and said in a low but resolute voice: *"Maiori forsan cum timore sententiam in me fertis, quam ego accipiam...* Perhaps your fear in passing this sentence upon me is greater than mine in accepting it."

Bravo, Nolano!

They turned him over to Msgr. Martino Cappelletti da Rieti, the governor of Rome...and washed their hands of him. Their request of the secular authority: *"...seculari Magistratui eum tradiderunt puniendum rogantes, ut quam clementissime et sine sanguinis effusione puniretur...,"* that Bruno be punished as mercifully as possible and without the shedding of blood, was just another way of saying: burn him. The Nolan was transferred to Tor di Nona, the senatorial prison on the left bank of the Tiber near Sisto Bridge.

The sentence was set for 12th February, but for some reason it was postponed. In the hope that given more time he might still repent, I suppose. They never like to give up.

At two o'clock in the morning on 16th February, word was sent to the Company of St. John the Beheaded, the "Company of Mercy and Pity" as they are known. At six, they went to Nona Tower to be with the Nolan. They were accompanied by two holy fathers from the Dominicans, two from the Jesuits, two from the new church, and one from St. Jerome. It must have been quite a scene, all those priests packed into the Nolan's cell, doing their best right down to the last minute to get this one little defrocked priest to abjure and beg for mercy. I don't know which must have been worse for the Nolan, that day or the next.

Finally the day came.

My God, how I hate to recount this. Even now, almost twenty-two years later, I am so ashamed that such a thing was done, ashamed but also still deeply incensed. The anger has lived inside me like a clenched fist. I want to strike out at someone, I wanted to even then, but at whom? The church that sentenced him? The State that carried out the execution? My fellow Romans who came to enjoy the entertainment? Everyone was guilty, as everyone always has been, and I was as guilty for doing nothing as they for doing something, and that is the reason for my shame. My shame is for the whole human race.

His Holiness did not attend. Nor did the Cardinals. Nor did anyone at all from the Vatican. I myself wanted badly to stay away...but I couldn't. I thought I could not bear to witness the death of one so close, one to whom I was so strangely connected. I was wrong about that. His dying gave me strength.

They brought him to Campo di Fiori, in front of Pompey's Theatre. *Nudo come un verme*, without a stitch of clothing on, hands tied behind his back, his tongue spiked so that he would be unable to utter wicked words. The square was mobbed with a Jubilee crowd. They had been disappointed at last Saturday's postponement. Now they were intent on making up for their lost amusement.

Accompanied by a number of police and by the Company of Mercy and Pity chanting their litanies and prayers with great solemnity, the Nolan led the procession toward the stairs, head high, looking straight ahead, ignoring everyone...police, chanting priests, tourists, pilgrims, drunken Romans, mothers holding babies, children playing tag, street vendors selling their wares, pickpockets, prostitutes, and beggars.

He mounted the stairs, calmly turned his back to the stake, and stood motionless as they bound him to it. His eyes turned skyward. He appeared to be looking straight into the morning sun.

A priest stepped up and held a crucifix before his face. The Nolan turned away. The priest shook his head sadly, made the sign of the cross, and stepped back. The Nolan turned his eyes back to the sun.

The pyre was ignited. Orange flames leapt up immediately and quickly engulfed him. The dry tinder crackled and snapped as the fire grew and dark smoke rose high above the square. A low moan was heard, and the crowd let out a loud roar of approval as the "Lutheran" burned. Romans think of all heretics as Lutherans. In Europe Lutherans and Calvinists think of all heretics as Catholics.

The air was filled with a faintly sweet and pungent odor.

After about twenty minutes the fire began to die down. In less than an hour it was out completely, save for a few smoldering embers. Where the Nolan had stood...there was nothing. The police prevented the crowd from surging forward for souvenirs. Gradually, they dispersed in search of other diversion. Other than the police, the square was empty.

Later, his ashes were scattered to the wind.

THE END

Epilogue

19 aprile 1611
Via del Seminario
Roma

POPE CLEMENT IS DEAD. So is Pope Leo XI who died three weeks later. Cardinal Madruzzo is dead. Santa Severina is dead. Cardinal Borghese is now Pope Paul V. *Morto un Papa sene fa un altro...* no one is irreplaceable.

We have moved again. After Clement and Leo died, my master had a yen to live elsewhere. The Vatican was too fancy for his taste. We moved to a house near Sta. Maria in Trastevere, which I liked because it was closer to Campo Marzio. Then we moved to the Piazza Colonna, because it was closer to his own church, Sta. Maria in Via. The master wanted to walk to church and his legs were not what they used to be. Now we have moved again, this time to a house near the Obelisk of St. Malo, a poor one for a cardinal but it suits him because he would prefer to be poor and also because it is close to the Roman College where all his friends are, especially Father Clavius.

The master has slowed down in many ways. He is ill even more frequently than he used to be, plagued with violent headaches and terrible pains down his right arm. I do as much as I can for him. This morning, I have been taking his dictation.

"Pietro, write this letter, if you would be so kind, to Father Clavius and..."

"Boss, maybe you should take a break for a little while. I could get you something to eat, and we could pick up again this afternoon. You have nothing on your calendar until your three o'clock meeting with His Holiness. Do you good to rest."

"Write, Guidotti. There will be time for me to rest in the grave. 'Very Reverend Fathers...'"

Very Reverend Fathers,

I know that your Reverences have heard of these new astronomical discoveries which an eminent mathematician has made by means of an instrument called a cannone or ocular tube. I myself by means of the same instrument have seen some very wonderful things concerning the moon and Venus, and I would be grateful if you would favor me with your honest opinion on the following matters:

1. *Whether you confirm the report that there are multitudes of fixed stars invisible to the naked eye, and especially whether the Milky Way and nebulae are to be regarded as collections of very small stars.*

2. *Whether it is true that Saturn is not a simple star but three stars joined together.*

3. *Whether it is a fact that Venus changes its shape, increasing and diminishing like the moon.*

4. *Whether the moon really has a rough and unequal surface.*

5. *Whether it is true that four moveable stars revolve round Jupiter, each with a different movement from that of the others, but all the movements being exceedingly swift.*

I am anxious to have some definite information about these matters, because I hear conflicting opinions expressed with regard to them. As your Reverences are skilled in the science of mathematics, you will easily be able to tell me whether these new discoveries are well-founded, or whether they may not be a mere illusion.

If you like, you can write your answer on this same sheet.

Your Reverences' brother in Christ,
Robert Cardinal Bellarmine

"Just one question, Boss."

"Yes, Pietro?"

"If the reverend fathers tell you it's true, does that mean Scripture is wrong?"

He sighed.

"I think I will take that rest after all, Pietro."

Giordano Bruno, 1548–1600
Selected Excerpts

Whatever cruel fate awaits me yet,
far back in my boyhood the struggle began,
and, God my witness, I follow the truth unvanquished,
and death itself cannot bring me the smallest terror
and I do not shrink at the powers of any man....
I have fought. It is much....
In Fate's hand, Victory lies. Then let that be,
however it will; whosoever proves the victor,
future times will not deny I owed no dread of death,
was beaten into constancy by none,
and preferred a spirited death to a craven life.

— from *De monade*

. . .

Let him who will, think my fate cruel because it kills in hope and revives in desire. I am nourished by my high enterprise; and although the soul does not attain the end desired and is consumed by so much zeal, it is enough that it burns in so noble a fire; it is enough that I have been raised to the sky and delivered from the ignoble number.

— from *De gli eroici furori*

. . .

Behold now, standing before you, the man who has pierced the air and penetrated the sky, wended his way amongst the stars and overpassed the margins of the world, who has broken down those imaginary divisions between spheres — the first, the eighth, the ninth, the tenth, or what you will — which are described in the false mathematics of blind and popular philosophy. By the light of sense and reason, with the key of most diligent enquiry, he has thrown wide those doors of truth which it is within our power to open and stripped the veils and coverings from the face of nature. He has given eyes to blind moles, and illuminated those who could not see their own image in the innumerable mirrors of reality which surround them on every side; he has loosened the mute tongues which cared little for intricate discussion; he has strengthened the crippled limbs which were too weak to make that journey of the spirit of which base matter is incapable.

— from *La cena de le ceneri*

• • •

If, most illustrious gentlemen, I worked a plough, pastured a flock, cultivated an orchard, and tailored a garment, no one would look at me, few would observe me, by very few would I be reprehended, and I could easily be pleasing to everybody. But since I am a delineator of the fields of nature, solicitous concerning the pasture of the soul, enamored of the cultivation of the mind, and a Daedalus as regards the habits of the intellect, behold one who, having cast his glance upon me, threatens me, one who, having observed me, assails me, another who, having attained me, bites me, and another who, having apprehended me, devours me. It is not one person, it is not a few, it is many, it is almost all.

— from *De l'infinito universo e mondi*

• • •

The fools of the world have been those who have established religions, ceremonies, laws, faith, rule of life. The greatest asses of the world are those who, lacking all understanding and instruction and void of all civil life and custom, rot in perpetual pedantry; those who by the grace of heaven would reform obscure and corrupted faith, salve the cruelties of perverted religion, and remove abuse of superstitions, mending the rents of their vesture.

It is not they who indulge impious curiosity or who are ever seeking the secrets of nature and reckoning the courses of the stars. Observe whether they have been busy with the secret causes of things, or if they have condoned the destruction of kingdoms, the dispersion of peoples, fires, blood, ruin, or extermination; whether they seek the destruction of the whole world that it may belong to them; in order that the poor soul may be saved, that an edifice may be raised in heaven, that treasure may be laid up in that blessed land, caring naught for fame, profit, or glory in this frail and uncertain life, but only for that other most certain and eternal life.

— from *Cabala del cavallo Pegaseo*

• • •

When the sun of clear concepts disturbs those used to vulgar thinking, the defect is not in the light, but in the sight: insofar as the sun in itself is more beautiful and more excellent, to that extent will it be of odious and disagreeable benefit to the eyes of the nocturnal screech-owl.

— from *De la causa, principio et uno*

• • •

Who does not see that there is a single principle for corruption and generation? Is not the end-point of corruption the principle of the generated? Do we not say in the same breath: That was taken, this brought in — that was, this is? Certainly, if we estimate well, we see corruption to be none other than a generation, and generation none other than a corruption; love is hate, hate is love, in the last resort. Hate of the contrary is love of the similar; love of one thing is hate of another. In substance and root, then, love and hate, amity and discord, are one and the same thing.

Where does the physician seek the antidote more profitably than in the poison? Who offers a better theriac than the viper? In the worst venoms are the best medicines. Is not one potency common to two contrary objects? Now, where do you believe this comes from if not from the fact that, as the principle of being is one, so is the principle of conceiving the two contrary objects — and that, as the contraries are relative to a single substratum, so are they apprehended by one and the same sense? I leave aside the point that the orbicular rests on the plane surface, the concave sinks down and settles into the convex, the irascible lives together with the patient, the humble most fully pleases the most arrogant, the prodigal the miser.

In conclusion, he who wants to know the greatest secrets of nature should regard and contemplate the minima and maxima of contraries and opposites.

— from *De la causa*

• • •

I shall place you in the body of the moon; your senses, through proper adaptation, will enable you to use your faculty of reason and see these things... From this side I shall show you the face of the earth shining in the opposite region, in the light of the radiant sun diffused into the surface of the ocean. Do you see the vast machine seems contracted into a small mass?... Notice how Britain is condensed to a small point and the very narrow Italy is condensed into a thin and short hair.... Seize the road, rolling through the threshold of the great sun; mother nature discloses the route.

— from *De immenso et innumerabilibus*

• • •

Elpino. How is it possible that the universe can be infinite?

Philotheo. How is it possible that the universe can be finite?

Elpino. Do you claim that you can demonstrate this infinitude?

Philotheo. Do you claim that you can demonstrate this finitude?

Elpino. What is this spreading forth?

Philotheo. What is this limit?

—from *De l'infinito*

· · ·

Death does not destroy the substance of the body, and still less the soul.... We are what we are only by virtue of the indivisible spiritual substance around which atoms are gathered and clustered as around a center. Through birth and development the creative spirit expands into the mass of which we consist by diffusing itself from the heart to which its intermingled threads return like arrows. In this fashion the spirit returns by the same road down which it came and exits through the same door through which it entered.

—from *De triplici minimo et mensura*

· · ·

You see then...how treacherous time subdues us, how we are all subject to mutation. And that which most afflicts us among so many things is that we have neither certainty nor any hope of at all reassuming that same being in which we once found ourselves. We depart, and do not return the same; and since we have no recollection of what we were before we were in this being, so we cannot have a sample of that which we shall be afterward.

Thus fear, piety, and our religion, honor, respect, and love leave, after which depart strength, providence, virtue, dignity, majesty, and beauty, which fly from us not otherwise than the shadow together with the body. Only Truth, with Absolute Virtue, is immutable and immortal. And if she sometimes falls and is submerged, she, necessarily, in her time rises again, the same, her servant Sophia extending her arm to her.

Let us beware, then, of offending the divinity of Fate by wronging this twin god, so greatly entrusted to it and so favored by it. Let us think of our future state, and not, as if we were little concerned with the universal deity, fail to raise our hearts and affects to that lavisher of all good and distributor of all other fates. Let us beseech it that during our transfusion, or passage, or metempsychosis, it grant us happy spirits; since, although it is inexorable, we must indeed await it with prayers, in order either to be preserved in our present state or to enter another, better, or similar, or little worse.

I say that to be well affected toward the highest deity is like a sign of future favorable effects from it. Just as for him who is prescribed to be a man, it is necessary and ordinary that destiny guide him as he passes through his mother's womb, so, for the spirit predestined to incorporate itself into a fish, it is necessary that it first plunge into the waters; likewise for him who is about to be favored by the gods, it is necessary that he submit himself to prayers and good works.

—from *Lo spaccio de la bestia trionfante*

• • •

He is blind who does not see the sun, foolish who does not recognize it, ungrateful who is not thankful unto it.

—from *Lo spaccio*

• • •

Hilaris in tristitia, tristis in hilaritate. (Laughter in tears, in sadness, joy.)

—from the title page of *Il candelaio*

Acknowledgments

Even a stubborn Aries such as me could not have undertaken a project like this without help. I am deeply indebted to all of the authors whose works are listed below, but special thanks are also due the following for their help and interest in this project: Maurizio Marmorstein, my Italian translator; Professors Ed Gosselin and Larry Lerner of California State University, Long Beach; Professor Luigi Firpo, Fondazione Luigi Einaudi, Torino; Professor William Wallace, the Catholic University of America, Washington D.C.; Professor J. Dietze, Martin Luther Universität, Halle-Wittenberg; Professor Paolo Galuzzi, Istituto e Museo di Storia della Scienza, Florence; Rev. Juan Casanovas, S.J., Castel Gandolfo, Specola Vaticana; Dr. George Coyne, Steward Observatory, the University of Arizona, Tucson; Professor Owen Gingerich, Harvard-Smithsonian Center for Astrophysics, Harvard University, Cambridge; Wynne Segall, Esq., for his efforts in my behalf at Oxford University; and the Reverend Father Smith, S.J., St. Patrick's Seminary, Menlo Park, California, for his many insights into the life of a Jesuit priest and cardinal.

A partial list of sources:

Atanasijenic, Ksenija. *The Metaphysical and Geometrical Doctrine of Bruno, As Given in His Work De Triplici Minimo.* Trans. George Vid Tomashevich. St. Louis, Warren H. Green, 1972.

Besant, Annie. "Giordano Bruno, Theosophy's Apostle in the Sixteenth Century," a lecture delivered in the Sorbonne at Paris on June 15, 1911, and *The Story of Giordano Bruno.* Madras, The Theosophist Office, 1913.

Boulting, William. *Giordano Bruno: His Life, Thought and Martyrdom.* New York, E. P. Dutton, 1914, reprinted by Books for Libraries Press, 1972.

Brodrick, James. *The Life and Work of Blessed Robert Francis Cardinal Bellarmine, S.J.* 2 vols. London, 1928.

Bruno, Giordano. *The Ash Wednesday Supper (La cena de le ceneri).* Trans. with an Introduction and Notes by Stanley L. Jaki. Paris: Mouton & Co., 1975.

———. *The Ash Wednesday Supper (La Cena de le cenari).* Ed. and trans. Edward A. Gosselin and Lawrence S. Lerner. Hamden: Archon Books, 1977; Toronto: University of Toronto Press, 1996.

———. *Cause, Principle and Unity (De la causa, principio et uno).* Trans. with an Introduction by Jack Lindsay. Essex: Daimon Press Ltd., 1962.

———. *The Expulsion of the Triumphant Beast (Lo spaccio de la bestia trionfante).* Trans. and ed. Arthur D. Imerti, with an Introduction and Notes. New Brunswick, N.J.: Rutgers University Press, 1964.

———. *The Heroic Frenzies [Enthusiasts] (De gli eroici furori)*. Trans. with Introduction and Notes by Paul Eugene Memmo, Jr. Chapel Hill: University of North Carolina Press, 1964.

———. *The Heroic Enthusiasts [Frenzies] (De gli eroici furori)*. Trans. L. Williams. London: George Reway, 1887.

———. (Philippus Brunus Nolanus; Iordanus Brunus Nolanus, il Nolano), *Dizionario Biografico degli Italiani*. Pp. 654–65. Instituto della Enciclopedia Italiana, Fondata da Giovanni Treccani, Rome.

Butler, Albin. *Butler's Lives of the Saints*. Concise Edition. Ed. Michael Walsh. San Francisco: Harper & Row, 1985.

Gosselin, Edward A. and Lawrence S. Lerner. "Galileo and the Long Shadow of Bruno," *Académie Internationale d'Histoire des Sciences* 25 (December 1975): 223–46.

Hardon, J. *A Comparative Study of Bellarmine's Doctrine on the Relation of Sincere Non-Catholics to the Catholic Church*. Rome, 1951.

Horowitz, Irving Louis. *The Renaissance Philosophy of Giordano Bruno*. New York: Coleman-Ross Co., 1952.

Limentani, Ludovico. "La Lettera di Giordano Bruno al Vicecancelliere dell'Università di Oxford," *Sophia* 1 (1933): 317–54.

Martin, Eva. *Giordano Bruno: Mystic and Martyr*. London: William Rider & Son, 1921.

McIntyre, J. Lewis. *Giordano Bruno*. London: Macmillan, 1903.

Mercati, Angelo Cardinal. *Il Sommario del processo di Giordano Bruno, con appendice di documenti sull'eresia e l'inquisizione a Modena nel secolo XVI*. Città del Vaticano: Biblioteca Apostolica Vaticana, 1942.

Michel, Paul-Henri. *The Cosmology of Giordano Bruno*. Trans. R. E. W. Maddison. Ithaca, N.Y.: Cornell University Press, 1973.

Paterson, Antoinette Ann. *The Infinite Worlds of Giordano Bruno*. Springfield, Ill.: Charles C. Thomas, 1970.

Plumptre, C. E. *Giordano Bruno: A Tale of the Sixteenth Century*. 2 vols. London: Chapman & Hall, 1884.

Ryan, Edward Anthony, ed. *The Historical Scholarship of Roberto Francesco Romolo Bellarmino (St. Bellarmine)*. New York, 1936.

Salvestrini, Virgilio. *Bibliografia di Giordano Bruno (1582–1950)*. Seconda edizione postuma a cura di Luigi Firpo. Florence. Sansoni Antiquariato, 1958

Singer, Dorothea Waley. *Giordano Bruno: His Life and Thought; With Annotated Translation of His Work: On the Infinite Universe and Worlds (De l'infinito universo e mondi)*. New York: Greenwood Press reprint, 1968.

Spampanato, Vincenzo. *Documenti della Vita di Giordano Bruno*. Florence: Leo S. Olschki, 1933.

———. *Vita di Giordano Bruno con Documenti editi e inediti*. Messina: Casa Editrice Giuseppe Principato, 1921.

White, Andrew D. *A History of the Warfare of Science with Theology in Christendom*. 2 vols. New York: George Braziller, 1955.

Yates, Frances A. *Giordano Bruno and the Hermetic Tradition*. Chicago: University of Chicago Press, 1964.

———. *John Florio: The Life of an Italian in Shakespeare's England*. Cambridge, 1934.

————. "Giordano Bruno: Some New Documents," *Revue Internationale de Philosophie* 16 (1951): 174–99.

Special thanks also to the Warburg Institute of the University of London. For the most complete reference available, see Catalog of The Warburg Institute Library: Giordano Bruno, Collected Works (1967 ed., vol. 5, pp. 286ff and pp. 313ff; plus First Supplement, 1971, pp. 274–75, 278–80).

ABOUT THE AUTHOR

For many years, Morton Yanow (known simply as *my* to his read-
ers) published his one-man journal of social commentary *Observations
from the Treadmill*, portions of which appeared in collected form in
the 1973 book of the same name. His other books include *What
Do We Use for Lifeboats When the Ship Goes Down?* (1976), *The
Door in the Wall: An Experiment in Autohypnosis* (1978), *Lazar: The
Autobiography of My Father* (1980), and *Cook Fast, Eat Slow* (1997).
An attorney mediator, legislative consultant, and board member of
ACLU-Washington, he lives in Seattle, Washington, with his partner,
Nadia Aronson, and their Cairn terrier, Laird Amicus MacIntosh. He
is currently at work on a novel of survival in the Yukon wilderness.

OTHER CROSSROAD NOVELS
YOU MIGHT ENJOY

Joan Ohanneson
SCARLET MUSIC
Hildegard of Bingen: A Novel

"Ohanneson has dramatized the life of twelfth-century
Hildegard of Bingen in this fascinating novel.
Highly recommended."
— *Library Journal*

"Like an episode of Masterpiece Theater
at its most arresting and enlightening."
— Eugene Kennedy

0-8245-1646-X; $14.95

Asta Scheib
CHILDREN OF DISOBEDIENCE
The Love Story of Martin Luther and Katharina of Bora

A sweeping historical novel that traces the unconventional friendship
of two unusual and unforgettable people. The marriage of Martin Luther
to the nun Katherine of Bora took place in a period that rocked
the church and the world. Well researched and poetically written,
this novel gives a sensitive account of their relationship and a
vivid sense of the tumultuous time in which they lived.

0-8245-1695-8; $14.95

Please support your local bookstore, or call 1-800-395-0690.
For a free catalog, please write us at
THE CROSSROAD PUBLISHING COMPANY
370 LEXINGTON AVENUE, NEW YORK, NY 10017

We hope you enjoyed The Nolan. *Thank you for reading it.*

crossroad